3 0132 023

D1180840

GODDESS

Josephine Angelini is a Massachusetts native and the youngest of eight siblings. A real live farmer's daughter, Josie graduated from New York University's Tisch School of the Arts in Theatre, with a focus on the classics. She now lives in Los Angeles with her screenwriter husband . . . and she can still drive a tractor.

Books by Josephine Angelini

Starcrossed

Dreamless

Goddess

Chat to Josephine Angelini and find out
about her other books here:

facebook.com/josephineangelini

twitter.com/josieangelini

mykindabook.com/josephineangelini

GODDESS

JOSEPHINE ANGELINI

MACMILLAN

First published 2013 by Macmillan Children's Books
a division of Macmillan Publishers Limited
20 New Wharf Road, London N1 9RR
Basingstoke and Oxford
Associated companies throughout the world
www.panmacmillan.com

ISBN 978-0-330-52976-1

Copyright © Josephine Angelini 2013

The right of Josephine Angelini to be identified as the
author of this work has been asserted by her in accordance with the
Copyright, Designs and Patents Act 1988.

All rights reserved. No part of this publication may be
reproduced, stored in or introduced into a retrieval system, or
transmitted, in any form or by any means (electronic, mechanical,
photocopying, recording or otherwise), without the prior written
permission of the publisher. Any person who does any unauthorized
act in relation to this publication may be liable to criminal
prosecution and civil claims for damages.

3 5 7 9 8 6 4 2

A CIP catalogue record for this book is available from
the British Library.

Printed and bound by CPI Group (UK) Ltd, Croydon CR0 4YY

This book is sold subject to the condition that it shall not,
by way of trade or otherwise, be lent, resold, hired out,
or otherwise circulated without the publisher's prior consent
in any form of binding or cover other than that in which
it is published and without a similar condition including this
condition being imposed on the subsequent purchaser.

For my husband, Albert. This was all your fault.

CHAPTER ONE

Helen could see what she guessed was the River Styx just off to her left. It was a roaring torrent, riddled with icebergs. No sane person would dare swim across it. Feeling stranded, she limped around in a tight circle. A quick scan of the horizon showed that there was no one else on the barren plain.

'Damn it,' she swore to herself, her voice breaking. Her vocal cords were not completely healed. Less than an hour ago, Ares had slit her throat, and although it still hurt when she spoke, cussing made her feel better. 'So typical.'

She'd just made a promise to her friend Zach. He was dying in her arms, and she'd sworn that she would make sure that he drank from the River of Joy in the afterlife. Zach had sacrificed himself to help her, and in his final moments he'd given her the clue that had allowed her to kill Automedon and save Lucas and Orion.

Helen intended to keep her promise to Zach even if she had to carry him to the Elysian Fields and right up to the banks of the River of Joy herself – broken ribs, wonky leg and all. But for some reason, her usual way of navigating in the Underworld wasn't working. Normally, all she had to do was say out loud what she wanted and it just happened.

She was the Descender, which meant that she was one of the exceedingly few Scions who could go down to the Underworld in her living body and not just as a spirit. She could even control the landscape to a certain extent, but of course just when she needed that talent the most it found a way to go on the fritz. It was just so *Greek*. One of the things Helen resented the most about being a Scion was that it meant that there was an appalling amount of irony in her life.

Helen pinched her bruised lips together in frustration and raised her hoarse voice to the empty sky. 'I *said* – I want to appear by Zach's spirit!'

'I have that one's soul, niece.'

Helen spun round and saw Hades, lord of the Underworld, standing several paces behind her. Tall and poised, he was wreathed in shadows that dissipated like fingers of fog relaxing their grip. The Helm of Darkness and the extra yards of fabric from the black toga he wore obscured most of his face, but she could just make out his lush mouth and square chin. The rest of his toga was draped over his body like a decorative afterthought. Half of his smooth chest and his powerful arms and legs were bare. Helen swallowed and concentrated on focusing her swollen eyes.

'Sit, please. Before you fall,' he said softly. Two simple, padded folding chairs appeared, and Helen eased her abused body into one while Hades took the other. 'You are still wounded. Why did you come here when you should be healing?'

'I have to guide my friend to paradise. Where he belongs.' Helen's voice trembled with fear, although Hades had never hurt her. Unlike Ares, the god who had just tortured her, Hades had always been relatively kind. But he was still the lord of the dead, and the shadows around him were filled with the whispers of ghosts.

'What makes you think that you know where Zach's soul belongs?' he asked.

'He was a hero . . . Maybe not at the beginning when he was still being a jackass, but at the end, and that's the bit that counts, right? And heroes go to the Elysian Fields.'

'I wasn't questioning Zach's valour,' Hades reminded her gently. 'What I asked was: what makes *you* fit to judge his soul?'

'I . . . huh?' Helen blurted out, confused. She'd taken one too many knocks to the head that night, and she wasn't up to a lesson in semantics. 'Look, I didn't come here to judge anyone. I made a promise, and I just want to keep it.'

'And yet I'm the one who makes the decisions here. Not you.'

Helen had no argument for that. This was his world. All she could do was stare at him pleadingly.

Hades's soft mouth curved into a distant smile, and he seemed to consider what Helen had said. 'The way you handled the freeing of the Furies proved that you are compassionate. A good start – but I'm afraid compassion is not enough, Helen. You lack understanding.'

'Was that a test then? The Furies?' An accusing note crept into her voice as Helen recalled what she and Orion had gone through on her last mission in the Underworld. She got even angrier when she considered what the Furies themselves went through. If those three girls were tormented for thousands of years just to prove that Helen was a compassionate person, then there was something terribly wrong with the universe.

'Test.' Hades's lovely mouth twisted bitterly round the word, as if he could read Helen's thoughts and agreed with her. 'If life is a test, then who do you think grades it?'

'You?' she guessed.

'You still don't understand.' He sighed. 'You don't even understand what this is.' He gestured to the land around him, indicating the Underworld. 'Or what you are. They call you the Descender because you can come here at will, but the ability to enter the Underworld is the smallest manifestation of your power. You do not understand what *you* are enough to judge others yet.'

'Help me then.' He seemed so sad, so beat down by

his lot in life. She suddenly wanted to see his eyes very badly and leaned closer to Hades, trying to dip her head down to see under the fabric obscuring his face. 'I want to understand.'

The shadows spun out again, hiding him and murmuring the regrets of the dead. Helen's insides chilled. The words from the tyrant prophecy came to her mind – *born to bitterness*. She sat back.

'Shadowmasters,' Helen whispered. 'Do they get their power from you?'

'A long time ago, a woman known as Morgan La Fey from the House of Thebes had the same talent you have – the one that allows you to come to the Underworld. She bore me a son named Mordred, and since then my burden has haunted the House of Thebes.' His voice trailed off regretfully before he stood and held out a hand to her. She slipped her hand into his and allowed him to help her stand. 'You must go back now. Come to me as often as you like, niece, and I will try my best to bring you to understanding.' Hades tilted his head to the side and laughed quietly to himself. His lips parted, revealing diamond-shaped incisors. 'That's why I've allowed you, and those with the same talent before you, to enter my realm – to learn about yourselves. But right now you are too badly injured to be here.'

The world shifted, and Helen felt his mile-wide hand lifting her out of the Underworld and placing her gently back in her bed.

'Wait! What about Zach?' she asked. As Hades released her, Helen heard him whisper in her ear.

'Zach drinks from the River of Joy, I swear it. Rest now, niece.'

Helen reached out to move the shadows away from his face, but Hades had already left her. She fell into a deep slumber, her broken body greedily sucking up sleep as it tried to heal itself.

After Ares was sealed away in Tartarus and the rift in the ground closed, Daphne had carefully collected her daughter's broken body as Castor carried Lucas and Hector carried Orion back to the Delos compound. Daphne had only been running for a few moments when her daughter fell asleep in her arms. For a moment, Daphne was worried. Helen's injuries had been horrible – some of the worst Daphne had ever seen – but when she listened for the sound of Helen's heart, she heard it beating slowly but steadily.

It wasn't much past dawn by the time they made it back to Nantucket from the caves on the Massachusetts mainland. In the early morning light, Daphne carried Helen up the Delos staircase and down the hallway to the first room she could find that seemed to belong to a girl. She looked regretfully at the pretty silk comforter that her filthy, blood-soaked daughter was about to ruin. Not that it mattered. The House of Thebes had a large enough fortune to replace it. A fortune that had, in part, once belonged to Daphne and Helen's House – the House of Atreus.

Tantalus could scream 'holy war' and rant about how it was the 'Scions' turn' to rule as much as he wanted, but he'd never fooled the Heads of the other Houses. The Purge some twenty years ago was just as much a grab for the other Houses' wealth as it was a grab for immortality.

The prophecy that had started the Purge said that when the Four Houses were made into One House by the shedding of blood, then Atlantis would rise again. The exact wording that Daphne had memorized stated that in the new Atlantis, the Scions could find immortality. The prophecy didn't actually say that the Scions would *become* immortal – it just said they could *find* immortality there. Daphne wasn't optimistic enough to think immortality was a sure thing. But Tantalus was, and he'd used this prophecy to rally the Hundred Cousins of Thebes around him to kill off all the other Houses.

The whole thing was a sham, as far as Daphne was concerned, sanctified by a lot of mumbo jumbo from the last Oracle – who they all knew had gone crazy after making her first prophecy. But it worked.

Lots of Scions left their vast properties behind to be plundered by the House of Thebes in order to play dead and avoid the slaughter – like Daedalus and Leda, Orion's parents. Like Daphne herself. But Daphne had never cared for money. Then again, she'd never had any moral qualms about taking money when she needed it. Other

Scions, like Orion and his parents, did have qualms about theft, and they'd struggled for the last two decades while the House of Thebes lived in luxury. Remembering this, Daphne placed Helen on the bed and destroyed the lovely comforter with a little smile.

Before Daphne could turn to get water and gauze to clean her daughter's rapidly healing wounds, Helen disappeared and life-draining cold took her place. Daphne assumed that Helen had descended. Time ticked by. Daphne waited, her anxiety growing with each moment. She had thought that trips to the Underworld were instantaneous – that time didn't pass. So much time went by that Daphne began to wonder if she should wake up the rest of the house, but before she made a move Helen reappeared. Her body smelt like the barren air of the Underworld.

Daphne's teeth chattered, not from the cold, but from the fearful memories the smell of that air awoke in her. She had nearly died so many times now that she could guess what part of the Underworld Helen had visited. The smell was not baked enough to be the dry lands, and there was a touch of damp mud clinging to Helen's feet. Daphne guessed that meant she must have gone to the banks of the River Styx itself.

'Helen?' Daphne cooed. She smoothed her daughter's hair and peered into her chilled face.

Helen had been terribly injured in her battle with Ares, but if she were going to die Daphne knew she would be dead already. Helen must have used her ability to descend to the Underworld on purpose, probably to look for her newly dead friend – the envious one who'd unfortunately got himself enslaved by Automedon.

More than once, Daphne had gone on similar journeys looking for Ajax, but she did not have her daughter's ability to come and go in the Underworld at will. She'd had to all but die to get there. After Ajax had been murdered, she had no will to live, but she knew that killing herself wouldn't reunite her with her lost husband. Daphne had to die in battle like Ajax had, or she would never end up in the same part of the Underworld. Heroes went to the Elysian Fields. Suicides went – who knows where? She had thrown herself into every honourable fight she could find. She sought out the other Scions in hiding and recklessly defended the weak and the young – just as she'd done for Orion when he was a little boy. Many times, Daphne had been nearly killed in battle and made the journey down to the Underworld, always seeking her husband by the banks of the River Styx.

But all she had found was Hades. Unrelenting, enigmatic Hades, who would not restore her husband to life and take her instead no matter how much she begged or bargained. The lord of the dead did not make deals. She hoped Helen hadn't descended in the hopes that she could raise her friend back to life. It was a fool's errand – for now, anyway. But Daphne had been working for nearly two decades to change that.

'Can't see you,' Helen murmured, and her fingers flexed, like she was trying to grab something. Daphne immediately understood. She too had wanted desperately to see Hades and had tried to pull the Helm of Darkness off his head. Eventually, after Daphne half died enough times to pay off all her blood debts and rid herself of the Furies, Hades had finally shown her his face.

It was recognizing Hades that had set her plan in motion. The plan that had broken her only daughter's heart by separating her from the one she loved.

'Oh. Sorry,' Matt said from the doorway, startling Daphne out of her spiralling thoughts. She wiped her damp face and turned to see that Matt had Ariadne draped limply across his arms. She was a ghastly shade of grey and barely conscious, having exhausted herself trying to heal Jerry. 'She wanted to sleep in her own room.'

'I'm sure they'll both fit,' she said, gesturing to the wide bed. 'I didn't know where else to take Helen.'

'Seems like there's an injured person on every piece of furniture in the house,' Matt said. He carried Ariadne over and laid her down gently next to Helen.

Strong boy, Daphne thought, staring at Helen's friend.

'It'll be easier to watch over them together, anyway,' Daphne said, still surveying Matt.

He'd shaped up and put on a lot of muscle since last she'd seen him, but even so. Ariadne was a buxom girl, not a willowy thing like Helen, and Matt wasn't even breathing hard after carrying her down the long hallway.

Ariadne mumbled something unintelligible to Matt before he pulled away, her face crinkled in protest at his departure. He stopped to smooth her hair. Daphne could nearly smell the love wafting off him and filling the room, like something sweet and delicious baking in an oven.

'I'll be back soon,' he whispered. Ariadne's eyes fluttered and then stilled as she fell into a deep sleep. He ran his lips across her cheek, stealing the smallest of kisses. He turned to Daphne and looked down at Helen. 'You need anything?'

'I can handle it. Go. Do what you need to do.' He gave her a grateful look, and she watched him stride out of the room – back straight and shoulders squared in the new light of morning.

Like a warrior.

Helen saw herself running down a beach towards the biggest lighthouse she'd ever seen.

It was strange at first. How in the world could she be watching herself like she was watching a movie? It didn't feel like a dream. No dream had ever felt so real or been so logical. Still not understanding what was going on, she quickly got wrapped up in the drama and just went with it.

Dream Helen was wearing a long, diaphanous white

dress, held together by a richly embroidered girdle. Her sheer veil had come loose from the pins in her hair, and streamed behind her as she ran. She looked frightened. As the giant lighthouse loomed closer, Helen saw her dream-self recognize a figure standing at one of the points of the octagonal base. She saw a flash of bronze as the figure undid the buckles at his neck and waist, and allowed his breastplate to fall into the sand. She saw herself cry out with happiness and pick up speed.

After shedding half his armour, the tall, dark young man turned at the sound of her voice and ran towards her, meeting her halfway. The two lovers crashed together. He caught her up against his chest and kissed her. Helen watched herself throw her arms round his neck and kiss him back, then pull away so she could kiss his face over and over in a dozen different places – as if she wanted to cover every bit of him. Helen's mind drifted closer to the entwined pair, already knowing who the other Helen was kissing.

Lucas. He was strangely dressed and wearing a sword round his waist. He had sandals on his feet, and his hands were wrapped with worn leather straps and covered with bronze gauntlets, but it was really him. Even the laugh he gave as the other Helen smothered him with kisses was the same.

'I've missed you!' the other Helen cried.

'A week is far too long,' he agreed softly.

The words were not English, but Helen understood

them just the same. The meaning echoed in her head, just as the relief of being reunited with her love echoed through her – as if it were her body pressed against his. Suddenly, Helen knew that it was her body, or had been, once. She had spoken this language, and she had felt this kiss before. This wasn't a dream. It felt more like a memory.

'So you're coming with me?' he said urgently, catching her face in his hands and forcing her to look at him. His eyes glowed with hope. 'You'll do it?'

The other Helen's face fell. 'Why, always, do you talk of tomorrow? Can't we just enjoy right now?'

'My ship leaves tomorrow.' He let her go and pulled away, hurt.

'Paris . . .'

'You are my wife!' he shouted, pacing in a circle and tugging his hand through his hair exactly like Lucas did when he was frustrated. 'I gave Aphrodite the golden apple. I chose love – I chose *you* over everything that was offered to me. And you said you wanted me too.'

'I did. I still do. But my sister has no head for politics. Aphrodite didn't think it was important to mention that, while you may have been tending sheep that day, you were not a shepherd boy as I believed, but a prince of Troy.' The other Helen spared an exasperated sigh for her sister and then shook her head, giving up. 'Golden apples and stolen afternoons don't matter. I cannot go with you to Troy.'

She reached for him again. For a moment, he looked like he wanted to resist, but he didn't. He took her hand and pulled her to him as if he couldn't bring himself to reject her, even when he was angry.

'Then let's run away. Leave everything behind. We'll stop being royalty and become shepherds.'

'There's nothing I want more,' she said longingly. 'But no matter where we go, I would still be a daughter of Zeus and you a son of Apollo.'

'And if we had children, they would have the blood of two Olympians,' he said, impatience making his voice harsh. Apparently, he'd heard this argument many times already. 'Do you really believe that's enough to create the Tyrant? The prophecy says something about mixing the blood of four houses that are descended from the gods. Whatever that means.'

'I don't understand any of the prophecies, but the people fear any mixing of the blood of the gods,' she said. Her voice dropped suddenly. 'They'd chase us to the ends of the Earth.'

He ran his hands over her belly, cupping it possessively. 'You could be pregnant already, you know.'

She stopped his hands. Her face was sad and – for just a moment – desperate. 'That's the worst thing that could happen to us.'

'Or the best.'

'Paris, stop,' Helen said firmly. 'It hurts me to even think about it.'

Paris nodded and touched his forehead to hers. 'And what if your foster father, the King of Sparta, tries to marry you to one of those Greek barbarians like Menelaus? How many kings are asking for your hand now? Is it ten or twenty?'

'I don't care. I'll refuse them all,' the other Helen said. Then she cracked a smile. 'It's not like anyone can force me.'

Paris laughed and stared into her eyes. 'No. Although, I'd like to see one or two of them try. I wonder if Greeks smell better after they've been struck by lightning. They certainly couldn't smell worse.'

'I wouldn't kill anyone with my lightning,' she chuckled, twining her arms round his neck and moulding her body closer to his. 'Maybe just singe them a bit.'

'Oh, then please don't! Singed Greek sounds like it would smell far worse than fully cooked,' Paris said, his voice growing heavy as he smiled at her. Suddenly, the humour ran out of their shared gaze and sorrow replaced it. 'How am I going to sail away without you in the morning?'

The other Helen had no answer. His lips found hers, and he threaded his fingers through her hair, tilting her head back and taking her weight as she gave herself up to him. Just like Lucas did.

Helen missed him so much she ached – even in her sleep. It hurt so much she woke up and rolled over, groaning as she accidentally put too much pressure on her healing bones.

'Helen?' Daphne asked softly, her voice inches away from Helen in the darkness. 'Do you need anything?'

'No,' Helen replied, and let her swollen eyes drift shut again. The dream that greeted her made her wish she'd stayed awake, despite her injuries.

A terrified woman was struggling against a massive claw that was wrapped round her waist. Enormous wings, fringed with feathers each larger than a person, beat the air as the giant bird hauled her into the night sky. The skyline of New York City flashed past as the woman struggled.

Helen saw the bird tilt its beaked head to look down at the woman in its talons. For the briefest of moments, the menacing eye of the eagle rounded until it was shaped like a man's. He had amber eyes. Blue lightning flashed in the black middle of his pupils. The eagle screamed, freezing Helen's blood and sending shivers through her sleeping body.

The Empire State Building rose up in front of them, and then Helen saw no more.

Orion was screaming his brains out.

Helen shot up at the sound, shoved her mother aside, and started running. She charged down the dark hallway and halfway across the room, Lucas a blur at her side, before the two of them suddenly processed the situation and froze.

'What the hell?' Hector roared from the foldout bed that was set up next to Orion's. He flipped on a light.

Orion was standing on his mattress, wearing a pair of brief shorts, pointing at a tiny, dark figure crouched in the narrow gap between the two beds. It was Cassandra, huddled on the hardwood floor with only a pillow and a thin blanket to sleep on.

'What are you doing down there?' several voices clamoured at Cassandra. Castor, Pallas and Daphne had come up behind Helen and Lucas in the doorway.

'You bit me!' Orion howled, still dancing on the bed, freaking out. Noel, Kate and Claire, running at a human pace, arrived shortly and filled the room.

'I'm sorry!' Cassandra wailed. 'But you stepped on me!'

'I thought you were a cat until I . . . I nearly took your head off! I could have killed you!' Orion raged back at her, oblivious to the large audience. 'Don't *ever* sneak up on me!'

Orion suddenly clutched his chest and bent double with pain. Hector jumped up to grab him before he fell down – but not before everyone saw. Orion had two fresh wounds on his chest and stomach from his fight with Automedon. They were an angry red, but healing fast and in a few days they would disappear completely and leave him unmarked. But what caught everyone's attention wasn't the new wounds, it was the long scars that marred his otherwise perfect physique.

One cut across his chest, and another was on his left thigh. As he slumped against Hector, his strength spent, they all saw the worst one on his back. Helen stared at the ghastly bone-white seam that ran parallel to his spine. It looked like someone had tried to hack him in two from the top down. She felt Lucas take her hand and she clung to it, squeezing back.

'Everyone out!' Hector barked when he noticed the shocked silence and the stares. Tilting his shoulders, he tried to hide Orion with his body. 'You too, little pest,' he said softly to Cassandra, still crouched on the floor.

'No,' she protested. The thick, black braid that snaked down her back was coming undone in wild ruffles, and her face was a stubborn mask of alabaster skin, dark eyes, and bright red lips. 'I'm staying here. He might need me.'

Hector nodded, giving Cassandra his reluctant assent, and folded Orion's fainting body back into bed. 'Get out,' he said over his shoulder to the rest of them, quietly this time. Everyone turned at once.

Passing through the doorway, Helen and Lucas leaned towards each other, both of them feeling their injuries again and needing support now that the adrenaline rush had passed. But instead of letting the two of them help each other, Pallas caught Lucas, and Daphne propped up Helen, pulling them apart.

'Did you know about those?' Lucas asked before they were led away in opposite directions.

'No. I've never seen him without his clothes on,' she answered, too shocked to be anything but blunt. She had seen Morpheus *as* Orion half naked, she reminded herself, but not Orion himself. Lucas nodded, his face shadowed with concern.

'Back to bed, Helen,' her mother said sternly, and urged her to turn.

Helen let her mother lay her down next to Ariadne's slack form. As she shut her eyes and tried to fall back asleep, she heard Noel and Castor speaking to each other in the next room. For a moment, Helen tried to block it out and give them some privacy, but the urgency of their voices wouldn't allow even a mortal with normal hearing to ignore them.

'How did he get those scars, Caz?' Noel asked, her voice trembling. 'I've never seen anything like it. And I've seen plenty.'

'The only way for a Scion to scar like that is for it to happen before he or she comes of age,' Castor said, trying to keep his voice down.

'But our boys fought all the time when they were little. Remember Jason's javelin pinning Lucas to the *ceiling* that time? They don't have one scar between the three of them,' Noel snapped, too upset to take Castor's cue to be quiet.

'Our boys always had plenty of food and a clean place to heal after they beat each other up.'

'And Orion didn't? Is that what you're saying?' Noel's voice broke.

'No. He probably didn't.'

Helen heard the sound of rustling fabric, followed by deep sighs, like Castor was pulling Noel close against his chest.

'Those scars mean that Orion was very young when that was done to him. And afterwards, he must have starved through his heal without anything to eat or drink or anyone to care for him. You've never seen those scars on a Scion before because most wouldn't survive what it takes to get them.'

Helen gritted her teeth and turned her face into her pillow, knowing everyone on the top floor had heard the exchange between Noel and Castor. Her face got hot as she thought about how they were all probably judging Orion – pitying the abused and abandoned little boy that he once was.

He deserved better than that. He deserved love, not pity. Helen also knew that her mother was watching her while she tried, and failed, not to weep with pity for that little boy herself. She pulled the covers over her head.

Daphne let her cry herself back into a deep sleep.

*

Helen saw her other self getting kicked down a dusty street by an angry mob.

The other Helen's dress was torn, covered in dirt and smeared with stains from the rotten food that had been thrown at her. Blood leaked from a huge gash on her head, from her mouth and from the heels of her hands where she had scuffed them on the ground as she fell repeatedly. The mob gathered around her, picking up stones from the side of the road as they closed in.

A blond man, twice her age and more than twice her size, ran forward to beat her with his fists – as if his anger needed a more immediate outlet than just hurling a stone. It seemed he had to use his own body to hurt her in order to feel satisfied.

'I loved you more than anyone! Your foster father gave you to me!' he screamed, half out of his mind as he hit her. His eyes bulged and spittle flew from his mouth in a white spray. 'I will beat the child out of you and love you still!'

Helen could hear the mob murmuring, 'Kill her, Menelaus!' and, 'She may carry the Tyrant! You must not try to spare her!'

The other Helen did not fight back or use her lightning to defend herself against Menelaus. Helen watched her other self get knocked down so many times she lost count, but each time the other Helen got back to her feet again. Helen could hear the thumping of his fists against her back and hear the man grunting with exertion, but the other Helen did not cry out or plead for him to stop. She made no sound at all, except for the huffing of her breath as it was knocked out of her lungs by the blows he dealt.

Helen knew what those fists felt like, she even knew what Menelaus smelt like as he beat her. She remembered it.

Finally, Menelaus fell to his knees, unable to beat her any longer. The other Helen was simply too strong to die by his hand, though it was clear to Helen that dying was what the other Helen had intended to do all along.

When the first stone struck her, she did not cower or try to cover herself. More stones followed, battering her from all sides, until the mob ran out of stones to throw. But still the other Helen did not die. Frightened now, the mob began to back away.

A sickened hush fell over the crowd as they watched the gruesome spectacle they had created. Still alive, the other Helen twitched and flailed amid the piled-up stones, her skin pulpy and ragged over her broken bones. She started humming softly to herself – a groaning tune sung in desperation to keep her mind off the unbearable pain she was in. She rocked back and forth, unsteady as a drunk. She was unable to find relief in any position, but she swayed as she hummed to comfort herself as best she could. Helen remembered the pain. She wished she didn't.

The crowd began to whisper, 'Behead her. It's the only way. She won't die unless we behead her.'

'Yes, get a sword,' the other Helen called out weakly, the words garbled in her ruined mouth. 'I beg you.'

'Someone have mercy and kill her!' a woman shouted desperately, and the mob took up the cry. 'A sword! We need a sword!'

A young man, hardly more than a boy, strode out of the crowd, tears streaming down his pale face at the sight of the other Helen. He unsheathed his sword, swung it high over his head and brought it down on the gory mess at his feet.

A slender arm knocked the blade out of the way before it could strike.

A woman appeared, bathed in golden light, her shape changing repeatedly. She was young and old, fat and thin, dark-skinned and fair. In an instant, she was every woman in the world, and all of them were beautiful. By choice, it seemed, her shape settled on one that looked very similar to Helen's.

'My sister!' she screamed pathetically, scooping the injured girl up out of the rubble. Sobbing, Aphrodite cradled the other Helen in her arms, wiping blood from her face with her shimmering veil.

The crowd shrank back as the goddess wept, their emotions captured by her magic. Helen could see their faces turning into masks of sorrow as their hearts broke along with Aphrodite's.

'Let me go,' the other Helen begged the goddess.

'Never,' Aphrodite vowed. 'I would rather see a city burn to the ground than lose you.' The other Helen tried to argue, but Aphrodite quieted her and stood up, cradling her close, as she would a baby.

The goddess of love faced the mob, glaring at them. Her eyes and mouth glowed as she cursed them all in a thunderous voice:

'I abandon this place. No man shall feel desire, and no woman shall bear fruit. You will all die unloved and childless.'

Helen heard the pleas of the crowd beneath her as she felt herself soaring up into the air along with the goddess. They were tentative, confused at first. Soon the pleas turned into wailing as the crowd understood how dark their futures had become with a few words from an angry goddess. Aphrodite flew out over the water with her beloved sister in her arms, leaving the cursed place behind.

Far out on the horizon was the mast of a great ship – a Trojan ship, Helen remembered. The goddess flew straight to it, carrying both of the Helens with her.

Matt looked out at the dark horizon. The wind off the water was cold, and the sky was so full of stars that it looked like a city dangling upside down in mid-air. He'd just survived the longest two days of his life, but Matt wasn't tired. Not physically, anyway. His muscles didn't ache, and his legs didn't drag. In fact, he'd never felt better in his life.

Matt looked down at the ancient dagger in his hand. It was made of bronze, and even though it was mind-bogglingly old, it was still razor sharp and balanced perfectly from tang to hilt. Matt held the pretty thing across his palm and watched it settle into the muscles of his hand like one was made for the other. *But which for which*, he thought bitterly.

Zach's blood had been washed off the edges, but Matt still imagined he could see it. Someone Matt had known his whole life had died with this dagger in his heart before bequeathing it to Matt. But long ago it had belonged to another, much more famous master.

The Greeks believed that a hero's soul was in his armour. The *Iliad* and the *Odyssey* told of warriors who had fought to the death over armour. Some had even dishonoured themselves to get their hands on the swords and breastplates of the greatest heroes in order to absorb that hero's soul and skill. Ajax the Greater, one of the most revered fighters on the Greek side of the Trojan War, had gone on a rampage to possess Hector's armour. When Ajax woke from his madness, he was so horrified with how he'd tarnished his good name that he fell on his own sword and killed himself. Matt had always puzzled over that part in the *Iliad*. He would never have fought over armour, not even if it meant he could become the

25

greatest warrior the world had ever known. He wasn't interested in glory.

Matt tossed the dagger as far out into the churning water as he could. It flew, end over end, for a very long time. He watched it moving away from him, impossibly far and fast. Many seconds later, Matt could hear the faint splashing noise the dagger made when it hit the water, despite the roar of the surf.

It was humanly impossible to throw anything that far, and doubly so to hear it splash down. Matt had always relied on logic to solve his problems, and logic was telling him something so unbelievable that logic no longer applied.

He had secretly wished for this. But not *like* this. Not if this was the role he was meant to play. Matt didn't even understand. . . . Why him? He'd learned to fight because he wanted to help his friends, not because he wanted to hurt anyone. Matt had only ever wanted to protect people who couldn't protect themselves. He was not a killer. He was nothing like the first man to ever own the dagger.

A wave turned over at Matt's feet, leaving something bright and glittery behind on the sand. He didn't have to pick it up to know what it was. Three times he had tossed the dagger out into the ocean, and three times it had returned to him impossibly fast.

The Fates had their eyes on him now, and there was nowhere for Matt to hide.

*

The ship had square white sails. Above them, snapping in the wind from the tallest mast, was a red triangular pennant embossed with a golden sun. Row after row of oars stuck out from the sides of the ship. Even from the air, Helen could hear the rhythmic thumping of a kettledrum, sounding out the tempo of the strokes.

The water was not the brooding navy blue of the Atlantic but a clear, startling blue – the same jewel-blue as Lucas's eyes. *Azure*, Helen thought. Still clinging to consciousness, the other Helen moaned in Aphrodite's arms as the goddess brought her down to the ship's deck.

As Aphrodite landed, frightened voices cried out. From the place of command behind the tiller, a large man stepped forward. Helen knew him instantly.

Hector. He looked exactly the same, except for his hair and the style of dress. This Hector kept his hair longer than the one Helen knew in Nantucket, and he wore a brief linen garment tied round his waist with a leather belt. Leather straps were wrapped around his hands, and a thick, gold ornament encircled his neck. Even half naked he looked like royalty.

'Aeneas,' Hector called over his shoulder as he stared down disbelievingly at the bloody mess in Aphrodite's arms. A carbon copy of Orion, minus the disfiguring scar across his bare chest and back, stepped forward and stood at attention at Hector's right shoulder. 'Go below and wake my brothers.'

'Hurry, my son,' Aphrodite whispered to Aeneas. 'And bring honey.' He nodded respectfully to his mother and strode off, but his gaze stayed on the other Helen as he moved past. His face was drawn with sadness.

'Water!' Hector barked, and many feet marched off at once to obey him. Half a moment later, Paris ran up from belowdecks, with Jason one step behind. Like the other ancient versions of the men she knew, Jason looked exactly the same, apart from the clothes he wore.

A strange, choked-off cry burst out of Paris when he realized what he was looking at, and he ran to the other Helen on unsteady legs. His hands shook as he took her from Aphrodite, his face blanching under his deep tan.

'Troilus,' Hector said to Jason, indicating with his chin for his youngest brother to take the bucket of water that had just arrived. The other Helen pushed weakly at Paris's chest when he tried to bring water to her lips.

'What happened, Lady?' Troilus asked Aphrodite when it was clear that Paris wouldn't, or couldn't, speak.

'Menelaus and his city turned on her when they found out about the baby,' the goddess said simply.

Paris's head snapped up, his face frozen with disbelief. Hector and Aeneas shared a brief, desperate look and then both glanced down at Paris.

'Did you know, brother?' Hector asked gently.

'I hoped,' he admitted, his voice hushed with emotion. 'She lied to me.'

All the men but Paris nodded, like they could understand Helen's choice.

'The Tyrant.' Aeneas barely whispered the word, but it was obvious they were all thinking it. 'Mother. How did Menelaus find out that Helen was pregnant?'

Aphrodite tenderly brushed her fingertips across her half-sister's shoulder. 'Helen waited for your ship to clear the horizon and then she told Menelaus herself.'

Paris started shaking all over. 'Why?' he asked the other Helen, his voice high with the effort to hold back tears. The other Helen ran her bloody hand across Paris's chest, trying to soothe him.

'I'm sorry,' she whispered, and put her hand on her belly. 'I tried, but I couldn't do it. I couldn't kill us myself.'

Troilus leaned against his brother, propping him up as they all regarded Helen with a mixture of awe and dismay.

'Don't mourn, Paris. Your baby lives,' Aphrodite said. 'She will grow to look just like our beautiful Helen, and her daughter will grow to look just like her mother – and so on and so on for as long as the line lasts. I have seen to it, so that even after my half-mortal sister is gone I may always look upon the face that I love best in this world.'

The golden glow of the goddess brightened, and she regarded the men of Troy one at a time, her voice taking on the timbre of quiet thunder rolling in the distance.

'You must all swear to me that you will protect my

sister and her child. If Helen and her line of daughters die, there will be nothing on Earth for me to love,' she said, her eyes falling apologetically on her son, Aeneas, for a moment before they hardened against him. He dropped his head with a wounded look, and Aphrodite turned to Hector. 'As long as my sister and her line of daughters lasts, there will be love in the world. I swear it on the River Styx. But if you let my sister die, Hector of Troy, son of Apollo, I will leave this world and take *love itself* away with me.'

Hector's eyes closed for a moment as the enormity of the goddess's decree sank in. When he opened them again, the look he gave was one of defeat. What choice did they have? He glanced around at his brothers and at Aeneas, all of them silently agreeing that they could not say no, despite the consequences that were sure to follow.

'We swear it, Lady,' Hector said heavily.

'No, sister. Don't. Menelaus and Agamemnon have sworn a pact with the other Greek kings. They will come to Troy with all their armies,' the other Helen moaned urgently.

'Yes, they will. And we will fight them,' Paris said darkly, as if he were already facing the warships that would inevitably sail to their shores. He lifted her up, and she struggled lamely in his arms.

'Drop me over the side and let me drown,' she pleaded. 'Please. End this before it begins.'

Paris didn't answer her. Holding her up high in his arms to keep her close, he carried her belowdecks to his bunk. The other Helen finally lost consciousness, and Helen's visit to this terrible dream or vision or whatever it was ended abruptly as she fell back into a natural sleep.

CHAPTER TWO

Andy glared at the metronome on top of the organ she was playing and willed it to explode. It didn't. She took a deep breath, waited a measure and dived back into Bach. Ten swings of the metronome's pendulum later and she was growling through her gritted teeth and shaking her fists in the air rather than pounding them on the keys. Abusing instruments was an unforgivable offence in Andy's mind. But metronomes, on the other hand . . .

'You're lucky you're an antique,' she told it, just to let it know how close it had come to a splintery end. She emptied her mind and started again.

This time she let Bach do the work, and for several measures she found the art inside the complicated maths of the fugue.

Bliss. Right up until she was interrupted by the ding of an egg timer. Andy's fingers slid off the keys with the deafeningly loud blarting noise that only a giant, hundred-year-old organ could muster.

'Really?' Andy said to the heavenly glow of the Tiffany window that reached high above her head. Even the beauty of the patchwork colours, warming her face like a bright quilt made out of light, was not enough to calm her. Just when she was getting it, she had to stop.

She repressed the urge to swear in church and looked at her watch. It was 8:00 a.m. already. Drat. Her rehearsal time was over, and she had to hoof it in order to make it to her first class.

It was freezing cold. Outside, the sun was just starting to peek up over the far edge of campus. Andy hunkered down into the boxy layers of flannel and wool she used to conceal her stunning figure and made her way through the frost-stiffened scrub of her 'shortcut'. Truth be told, it was a long cut. What mattered was that it was off the path and furthest away from everyone else. Andy wasn't looking for friends at school. She liked her solitude. Actually, that wasn't quite true. She hated her solitude, but she trusted it more than she trusted people.

'I saw you playing,' said a young man with a musical voice.

Andy screamed and whirled round. She saw a tall, beautiful youth crowned with golden curls. The edges of him twinkled in the thin sunlight of the chilly November morning.

'What are you doing here?' Andy said calmly. She blinked her sun-dazzled eyes and glanced around for another person. Wellesley College was an all girls' school in the most blue-blooded, upper-crusty and thoroughly traditional area of Massachusetts. Unless this boy was a professor or a security guard, he was not allowed this deep into the campus without a visitor's badge.

'You're very talented,' he said, moving towards her.

'You said you saw me, huh?' Andy took a step back, not liking this situation. 'How could you see me in the chapel? I was alone.'

He laughed, his voice dancing around the notes like a wind chime. 'I wasn't in the chapel, of course. I saw you through that big window.'

'You saw me through a *stained-glass* window? How'd you pull that off?'

'I could find someone as beautiful as you no matter where you hide. You're so radiant, I bet you even glow in the dark.'

The way he said it didn't sound phony. He wasn't leering or rude in any way, but he was still moving towards her, even though she obviously didn't want him to. When he got closer, Andy saw something wrong in his eyes – something distinctly animal and not human at all. She remembered the sunlight hitting her face through the stained-glass window and figured out how he'd seen her. She knew who, or rather, what, she was dealing with now. Andy backed away quickly, her breath starting to rasp with real fear.

'Are you going to run from me?' the youth asked poignantly, like this had happened to him many times before.

'Would you chase me?' she asked, adding to her voice

the seductive, hypnotic edge that could drive mortal men to their death. She needed to stall for time, maybe get him to follow her back to the path. There was sure to be someone up there to help her.

'Of course I would,' he said, his eyes smouldering and his voice low. He was aroused, but not hypnotized – unfortunately for Andy. 'Only the ones who run are worth catching.'

Doesn't it figure? she thought with that desperate hilarity that only happens in the most hopeless circumstances. *I spend my whole life deathly afraid of tempting a boy, and I end up getting jumped by one at an all-girls' school.*

The light sparked off him again, catching his edges and making him look more real than real, like he existed in 4-D. Andy knew this was no trick of the rising autumn sun. She also knew this was no boy. Her mother had warned her of the possibility of something like this, but Andy had never thought it would come to pass.

'Hey, Andy!' called an intensely chipper girl Andy had met over a month ago at freshman orientation and avoided ever since. She eyed Andy and the boy uncertainly. The noisy cluster of girls behind her went silent when they saw that Andy was with a boy. 'Are you coming to class?'

'Hi . . . Susan!' Andy yelled back frantically, remembering the girl's name at the last moment. 'I want to go with you!'

The beautiful youth smiled sadly at Andy as the chattering knot of young women moved closer to collect her. Then he turned and ran off towards Lake Waban.

'Where did your friend go?' Susan asked, perplexed.

'He's not my friend,' Andy said, grasping at Susan's mitten-covered hand with relief. 'We need to go to campus security *right now*.'

'I can describe him!' squealed a girl in Susan's posse who had shiny black hair and cinnamon skin. She told the security guard, 'He must have been freezing because he was only wearing jeans and a tight T-shirt!'

'He had curly blond hair, and he was really tan. Like a Malibu surfer boy,' a chubby girl with stick-straight, blonde hair blurted out, like she couldn't contain her exuberance.

'He had really smooth skin too. Like a dolphin!' tittered the cinnamon girl back to the blonde girl, and the two of them fell in a fit of snickers, drooling over Andy's almost-rapist.

Andy dropped her face into her hand and rubbed her eyes while she listened to more of the same from the rest of the witnesses – or 'groupies' as she was beginning to think of them. She reminded herself that they couldn't help their response. They were only human.

After spending the next two hours with security, relating the entire experience, and walking the guards to the exact spot where she had been accosted, Andy had gratefully accepted a new fob for her key chain. She had an official stalker, one who had made it on to the campus, without a pass no less, and the guards were not about to let her wander around without taking a few precautions. The fob was a panic button that would bring them to her in an instant. If she even caught sight of the boy again, she was to summon them. Andy wondered if she would really press it and endanger them all, or if she would face him alone.

Although Susan and her gaggle had stepped up and corroborated Andy's story, they all did so with a touch of confusion. Andy had reported word for word what the boy had said to her, and any one of them would have given her eyeteeth to have the same things said to them by such a hottie.

Andy couldn't explain that this wasn't romance. Men had always said things like that to her, but it had nothing to do with love. She went to all-girl Catholic schools her entire life and had run away from every man who'd pursued her, but that didn't stop them from chasing. She'd run away from the girls who had pursued her too, and there had been plenty of those. After that horrendous experience in seventh grade when her best friend had tried to kiss her in front of Sister Mary Francis's history class, she'd never even allowed herself to have girl friends.

Andy stayed away from people as a rule. It was for

their own good. Her kind were too dangerous for mortals to be around.

Somehow, after several classes, she managed to get rid of Susan and her entourage. Susan had looked at her with a mixture of worry and longing when Andy made it quite clear that she was ditching them. Andy felt bad about it. Susan was pretty and popular and seemed like a genuinely good person. That was exactly why Andy had to nip this relationship in the bud. She didn't want to hurt someone as awesome as Susan just so she could have a friend. Susan deserved better than that.

It was after 9:00 p.m. when Andy's astronomy class ended, and she made her way past Paramecium Pond to her dorm. Her nose itched. She took her hand out of her pocket, letting go of the fob for just a moment, and felt thick, muscular arms grip across her chest from behind.

'Run,' he whispered in her ear. 'I love to chase.'

Helen dreamed of dolphins, but this was no happy little dream about visiting SeaWorld. The dolphin Helen saw did not do flips or tricks. The dolphin in the dream was hunting a girl about Helen's age. The girl tried to swim away from it, but the dolphin kept pushing her down beneath the surface, hitting her with its flippers and tail until she bled.

The girl swam for a buoy, bobbing out in the middle of nowhere, gasping and crying as she struggled through the waves. The dolphin attacked, but this time, instead of flippers, a man's arms wrapped round the girl and squeezed.

Helen's eyes snapped open and she gasped for air, feeling like a vice had clamped down on her chest. She awoke to darkness.

How many days had she been fading in and out? she wondered. She remembered her mother cleaning off the worst of the blood and dirt with a wet sponge, Kate spoon-feeding her soup and Claire dividing an orange between her and a puce-coloured Ariadne. She remembered Orion's scars, and her heart squeezed painfully for him all over again.

Helen remembered other things too – things that had never happened to her, like tying a toga (*Chiton*, she remembered. *The Greeks wore chitons, and the Romans wore togas*) and carding wool. Helen Hamilton was damn sure she'd never tied a chiton or carded wool in her entire life, but she *remembered* doing both.

Those 'visions' of Helen of Troy always felt like memories, and now that she was fully awake, Helen was pretty sure that's exactly what they were. But how could she remember someone else's memories? It was impossible. And, considering how horrible these borrowed memories were, what Helen really wanted to know was how she could make them stop.

'Lennie?' whispered Claire, somewhere by Helen's feet.

Helen looked down and saw Claire poking her head

up over the back of the fainting couch that Ariadne had at the foot of the bed. Usually, Ariadne just threw her clothes over it, so Helen thought of it more as a place to pile outfits than something to sit on.

'Are you awake for real or just visiting for a sec?' Claire asked. Even in the bleached predawn light coming through the window, Helen could see the worry in Claire's eyes.

'I'm awake, Gig.' Helen sat up painfully. 'How long have I been out?'

'About two days.'

That was it? To Helen, it felt like weeks. She looked over at Ariadne, still sleeping. 'Is she going to be OK?' Helen asked.

'Yeah,' Claire answered, sitting all the way up. 'She and Jason are going to be fine.'

'Orion? Lucas?'

'They're all right – beat up, but getting better.' Claire looked away, and her brow furrowed.

'My dad?'

'He's been awake a couple of times, but only for a few seconds. Ari and Jason are doing their best.'

That wasn't the response Helen had been hoping for. She nodded and swallowed the lump in her throat. Her father wasn't a Scion, and he'd come closer to death than any of them. It was going to take him a lot longer to recover. Helen pushed the thought that he might never fully recover out of her mind and looked at Claire.

'How are you?' Helen asked, seeing the sad look on her best friend's face.

'Wicked tired. You?'

'Starving.' Helen swung her legs out of bed, and Claire got up to help her. The two friends wobbled downstairs together to raid the refrigerator. Even though Helen knew she had to eat as much as she could shove down in order to help her body rebuild itself while she healed, she couldn't take her eyes off Claire.

'What is it, Gig?' Helen asked quietly after swallowing only a bite or two of chicken noodle soup. 'Is it Jason?'

'It's all of you. Everyone got hurt this time. And I know that this isn't the end of it,' Claire answered, still uncharacteristically sad. 'There's a war coming, isn't there?'

Helen put her spoon down. 'I don't know, but the gods are free to leave Olympus and come to Earth again. Because of me.'

'It's not your fault,' Claire began defensively. 'You got tricked.'

'So? Tricked or not, I failed,' Helen said in a matter-of-fact way. 'I let Ares corner me, even though I'd been warned that something was going to happen.'

She felt horrible, but she knew she couldn't allow herself to wallow in guilt, so she kept the self-pity out of her voice. The Underworld had taught her that indulging in negativity, no matter how justified, would never solve any of her problems. She filed that revelation away for some other conversation with Hades and got back on topic. 'Have the gods appeared anywhere yet? Have they done anything?'

The image of a big, beautiful stallion running down a beach flashed in Helen's head. There was blood on his forelegs. The image made her shudder with revulsion.

'We haven't heard anything,' Claire said with a shrug. 'At least, no wrath-of-the-gods stuff.'

'What has Cassandra foreseen?'

'Nothing. She hasn't made any prophecies at all since the three of you were brought back here.'

Helen pursed her lips together, lost in thought. Just when the Scions needed an Oracle the most, of course, she'd be silent. That's the way Greek drama worked. Still, it bothered Helen. Greek or not, there had to be a *reason* Cassandra couldn't see the future. 'Because it's ironic' just wasn't a good enough answer for Helen any more.

'Len?' Claire asked, her voice a frightened whisper. 'Can you stop the gods?'

'I don't know, Gig.' Helen looked over at her best friend. Claire was pale with fear and lack of sleep. 'But if any of them try to hurt any of us I'll fight them with everything I've got.'

Claire smiled, finally relaxing a little. 'Eat your soup,' she admonished suddenly, like it had just occurred to her.

Helen snickered and obeyed. She knew this was

Claire's way of reassuming her usual role as the boss, and she dutifully reached for her spoon while she thought about the gods. They might not be smiting any mountaintops just yet, but that didn't mean that they weren't out and about. After thousands of years in a prison, they had to be back on Earth, but where were they? The Scions were weak and scattered. If the gods wanted to fight them, now would be the time to strike. What were they waiting for? Helen took a few sips of soup before noticing Claire's wide eyes.

'What is it?' Helen asked around her food.

'You never picked up your spoon,' Claire responded, her eyes unblinking as she stared at Helen's hand. 'You held out your hand, and it just *flew* to you.'

Helen looked at the spoon and tried to remember picking it up. She remembered reaching for it, but that was it. She put the spoon down and held her hand over it. Nothing happened.

'I think you need to go back to bed, Gig,' Helen said with a dubious smile.

'Yeah. Maybe you're right,' Claire said, but she didn't look convinced.

When Helen had finished her large breakfast, Claire helped her back upstairs and into the shower. While Helen scrubbed away the last of the blood and dirt, Claire sat on top of the sink rubbing lotion absentmindedly on her legs and feet, keeping herself handy in case Helen got woozy.

'Are you sure you don't need help?' Claire asked for the tenth time.

'I'm sure,' Helen laughed as she towelled off. 'Honestly, I feel pretty good.'

'You really are the strongest, aren't you?'

Helen looked away. Although she and Claire had showered together after track meets a million times and were not the least bit shy around each other, Helen suddenly felt naked. She didn't like Claire thinking she was some kind of . . . well, demigod. They were more than best friends. They were sisters, really, and Helen hated to be reminded that there was anything unequal about them.

'What makes you say that?' she asked in a tense voice. Claire pursed her lips.

'You should see the guys as soon as you're done.'

'My dad first,' Helen said with a definitive nod.

Claire helped Helen dress and then let Helen lean on her as they made their way down the hallway. The door was open so she could see Jerry lying in bed, and Kate sitting up in a chair next to him. Both of them were fast asleep. Jerry was so thin and wan that Helen didn't want to believe it was her dad. She had to remind herself that she should be grateful, but it was difficult to feel anything but fear when he looked so ill.

They walked a few paces down to Hector's room. Helen could hear deep, male voices behind the door. It sounded like all the guys were in there. They knocked and went in to find that Hector had moved Jason and Lucas in with Orion.

Helen had another vision or memory, or whatever it was. All the men were bunking together in a tent at the middle of a large, dusty camp – the siege camp just beneath the great wall of Troy. She shook her head, and the vision cleared.

'Aren't you all a little old for a pyjama party?' Claire teased.

The guys laughed gingerly at Claire's joke.

'I got sick of running up and down the hall to check on them, so I just carried all the beds in here,' Hector admitted sheepishly.

Hector the Protector, Helen thought. *He could never bear to be away from any of his men when they were injured – whether they were indispensable generals like Aeneas, or simple foot soldiers. That's why every man in his army loved him and followed him to certain death.*

Helen shook her head and tried to blink away the unwanted memories. They weren't even *hers*.

'I can't believe you're walking,' Orion said to Helen. She could see that despite the adrenaline-fuelled burst of energy when Orion had woken them with his scream, he and Lucas were still bedridden. They were nowhere near as far along in their healing as she was, and Jason was completely wrung out from saving Jerry. The three of them could barely sit up without wincing in pain, let alone stand.

'Just trying to stick it to you guys. Make you look bad,' Helen joked, trying to hide how worried she was about them all.

Claire went to Jason, and Helen automatically went to sit on the edge of Lucas's bed. She realized what she was doing at the last minute and changed direction to join Orion. Lucas watched her, a tight expression on his face to hide his feelings. Helen swallowed and forced herself to avoid his eyes. In this life they were cousins, she reminded herself, regardless of what she'd seen in her dreams.

She took Orion's hand and felt better. He smiled tenderly at her, and her heart tingled. She *did* love Orion, she thought as she swelled with pleasant warmth. So what if it wasn't the dizzy rush that she felt around Lucas? Maybe 'dizzy' wasn't the best way to go through life, anyway.

'What are you all talking about?' Helen asked lightly, trying to tell herself that it would get easier some day to see Lucas wearing the blank look he adopted as he watched her hold Orion's hand. For a moment, Helen thought she saw a toxic, acid-green colour flashing underneath Lucas's skin. She blinked and looked away, hoping her eyesight wasn't totally messed up because of her damaged eye.

'We were talking strategy. The Scions need a plan, fast,' Hector replied, his face hardening. 'We're weak. Divided. This is the time to strike against us.'

Helen breathed a mirthless laugh. 'I was just thinking the same thing.' Hector looked at her approvingly, and Helen considered the possibility that he might have made a soldier out of her after all.

'But we haven't heard anything. As far as we know, the gods are still on Olympus,' Claire said, frowning with worry. Jason pulled her closer to him.

'Matt found some things. He's coming now to explain,' he told her. Jason looked at his brother. 'Where is he, anyway?'

'With Ariadne,' Hector replied, testily at first, and then his tone changed. 'He checks on her about a dozen times a day.'

'It's not a dozen times,' Matt protested as he came through the door, propping up Ariadne with one hand and carrying his iPad in the other. 'Ten. Tops.'

Helen nearly did a double take when she saw Matt. She'd watched her friend get stronger over the past few months. She'd even noticed that he was turning into quite the piece of man-candy, though the thought of Matt as a love interest was icky to her. But this was different. He looked electric.

'How're you feeling, little sis?' Hector asked Ariadne, but his eyes ticked up and down Matt, sizing him up. Whatever had changed, Hector saw it too, Helen was sure of that.

'Ugh,' she groaned comically as she plopped down next her big brother. 'Like cud.'

'Cud?' Orion asked like he must have heard her wrong.

'Chewed, swallowed, barfed and rechewed,' she told him with a grin.

'How are you?' Matt asked Helen while everyone laughed at Ariadne's gross analogy. And suddenly he was just Matt again, her old pal, and there was nothing strange about him at all.

'I'm all right,' she said, patting the hand that he laid on her arm.

'You sure?' he pressed, looking deeper into her damaged eye. Helen remembered that her confrontation with Ares had left a blue scar running down the iris of her right eye. She was told it looked like lightning, but she hadn't seen it yet. There had been more important things for her to do than look in a mirror.

'Yeah, I'm fine,' she said, and then she grinned. 'I'd be better if I could get Ari to stop kicking in her sleep.'

'Hey, at least I don't snore,' Ariadne joked back with Helen.

'You *both* snore,' Claire chimed in, grinning. 'It's like rooming with a couple of dudes.'

They all got a laugh in at Helen's and Ariadne's expense. Helen was struck by how happy they all were just to be together – safe and comfortable in each other's company as if they'd hung out like this a thousand times. But none of them could ignore why they were there for very long, and the easy feeling quickly dissipated.

'So what've you found out about the gods, Matt?' Orion asked, sensitive as always to the subtle shift in mood. 'Have you heard anything?'

'Yeah. There have been some . . . attacks,' Matt said reluctantly.

'What does that mean?' Claire asked.

Matt tapped his iPad and started flicking through newspaper headlines, and everyone crowded together.

'Two days ago, a woman in New York City was found on top of the Empire State Building gored to death by what looked like giant talons. And this morning, a girl's body was found trampled to death by a horse on a Cape Cod beach. Both women had been raped before they were killed.'

Hector took the iPad and looked at it. 'This is a tabloid headline,' he said dubiously. 'It says that the witnesses in New York claimed to have seen a woman getting carried off by a giant bird.'

'Eagle. It was an eagle,' Helen said softly, repressing a shiver. Everyone stared at her for a moment, expecting an explanation. 'It's just a hunch, but I've been having strange dreams and weird *flashes*, I guess you'd call them,' she admitted with a shrug, trying to downplay the full-blown memories she'd been experiencing until she understood them a bit better.

'When did they start?' Lucas asked, concerned. Helen scrunched up her face, trying to think back to the first time she'd seen him and the other guys in armour.

'Halloween,' she said, realizing it as she spoke. She looked at Orion. 'Remember how I forgot everything for a second there after touching the water from that river?' she asked. She avoided saying the name of the River Lethe almost superstitiously, just in case it made her forget everything all over again.

'Uh-huh,' Orion replied with a small smile. Helen smiled nervously back at him, remembering how they had jumped on each other as soon as they'd forgotten who they were. By the warm look he was giving her, Helen was sure he was remembering that as well. Then his face darkened. 'You couldn't even remember your own name for a bit. That was bad.'

'Well, when I did remember again, it was like there was too much in my head or something.' Helen sighed with frustration. 'I can't explain it yet, but now I'm getting all these weird images when I dream.'

'And one of them was of an eagle?' Matt asked.

'Yeah. Why? What are you thinking, Matt?' Helen asked, gesturing to his iPad and the articles about the murdered girls.

'I know this looks like tabloid nonsense, but Greek myths talk about women being carried off by gods disguised as animals all the time. I think the eagle is Zeus and the horse is Poseidon,' Matt said.

'Matt, I can turn into a horse,' Orion said with an apologetic look. 'Everyone in the House of Athens can.'

'Get the hell out,' Helen said, whirling on Orion with wide eyes.

'What? I can turn into a dolphin,' Jason said like he was telling them the time.

'Shut up!' Claire and Helen shrieked in unison. Jason laughed.

'Some Scions can shape-shift into their god's animal avatars,' Hector said, giving Helen a weird look. 'How can you not know this?'

'Nobody told me, and I've never been able to do it!' Helen shouted back. She rounded on Orion again. 'Why didn't you tell me?'

'It's not like it's useful or anything,' he said with a shrug. 'Think about it. How many horses do you see trotting around town these days?'

'Yeah,' Jason chuckled. 'And then when you change back you're buck naked. Try explaining that one. It's crazy fun to be an animal, don't get me wrong, but it's rarely practical.'

'Yeah, but . . .' Claire sputtered. 'Oh my god!'

'This is so unfair. I get all the miserable talents like descending and having freaky dreams, and you get to turn into a dolphin.' Helen pouted, throwing a pillow at Jason.

'OK, OK,' Matt interjected, holding up his hands to get everyone back on target. 'But how many Scions can turn into an eagle large enough to carry off a woman?'

'None.' Hector cocked his head to the side. 'OK, Matt. What do you think is going on?'

'I think the gods are doing exactly what they used to do before they were locked up on Olympus – running around and raping mortal women. But this time they aren't leaving their victims alive.'

'Huh.' Hector chuffed. 'They aren't taking any chances.'

'No. Not this time,' Matt replied.

'What do you mean?' Ariadne asked.

'In every single one of the stories about a god appearing to a woman as a bull or a swan or a shower of gold, nine months later a Scion was born,' Hector said, spreading his hands to indicate all of them. 'It's like they never miss.'

Lucas tactfully ignored Hector's off-colour comment and looked at Helen. 'What else have you seen in these flashes?'

'What other animals, you mean?' Helen said haltingly. She'd very nearly blurted out, 'I keep seeing *us*, and we're married!' but stopped herself just in time.

Lucas narrowed his eyes at her, sensing Helen's odd fumble, and opened his mouth to begin what she was sure would be an embarrassing interrogation.

'I've seen an eagle, a dolphin and a stallion,' she continued before he could start. Knowing Lucas the way she did, Helen was certain that she had only delayed his questions. He wouldn't forget, and since he was a

Falsefinder she had the choice of either telling the truth or staying silent. Lying to Lucas was not an option – which was a giant pain in the butt.

'And the dolphin is *Apollo*, right?' Claire asked sharply, looking up from the iPad.

'The dolphin, the wolf, the mouse and the crow were all Apollo's animal avatars,' Ariadne answered.

Claire showed them the article she'd been reading about a strange attack at Wellesley College. They all leaned their heads together to read. A girl, whose name was left out of the paper, had been terribly injured by a young blond man the previous night. She fought off his savage attack long enough for campus security to respond to the silent alarm she managed to activate. The young man got away under 'suspicious' circumstances. The Wellesley police were looking for leads from the public. They considered her attacker extremely dangerous.

Apparently, more than one eyewitness on the responding security team reported seeing the young man fly away when he realized he was surrounded. The girl was recovering from her injuries at a local hospital.

'And now for the real kicker.' Claire scrolled down to show a pencil drawing of someone who looked almost exactly like Hector.

'Oh. That's just great,' Hector deadpanned.

'What does this mean?' Ariadne asked, fear widening her eyes as she looked around at everyone. 'They're not going to come looking for Hector, are they?'

No one had an answer.

'I know a few places where you can lay low for a while,' Orion offered quietly. 'They're not exactly nice, but the people in them have a hard time remembering faces.'

Momentarily stunned, Helen studied Orion, wondering what kind of place he was talking about. All kinds of squalid images flashed through her head. For the life of her, Helen couldn't picture Orion in some seedy flophouse or den of thieves. But she had to admit to herself that he was much more familiar with that world than anyone she'd come in contact with before. Again, she wondered about Orion's awful childhood and whether he would ever tell her about it – and about how he got those scars.

'Thanks, bro. But I'm not leaving my family again,' Hector said, giving Orion a grateful look.

Orion nodded, but Ariadne started shaking her head vehemently. 'No, Hector. No,' she said, her voice getting panicky. 'We just got you back. I don't want someone coming here and dragging you off to jail.'

'It's all right,' he said, pulling his sister close and patting her shoulder with one of his thick hands. 'No one knows I'm on the island. They all think I'm still studying in Europe. I'll hide here in the house. It'll be fine.'

Believing him, Ariadne calmed down and squeezed her brother's chest in a fierce hug. Over her head Matt and Hector exchanged a look, Matt silently promising to look after Ariadne if anything happened to Hector. Somehow, Helen could see these emotions pass between the two young men as clearly as she could see colours painted on a canvas. She blinked her eyes furiously, hoping like crazy it stopped.

'What the . . .' Orion exclaimed suddenly, jerking up and breaking Helen's train of thought. He twisted round to reveal Cassandra, who had crept up behind him on the bed. He relaxed as soon as he recognized her.

'Were you here the whole time?' Claire asked, incredulous.

Cassandra shrugged in a noncommittal way, but she didn't say anything.

'She startles the hell out of me, like, five times a day. I swear, she makes no noise when she moves,' Orion said to Claire. He turned to Cassandra. 'Keep it up and I'll put a bell on you. Like a bad kitty,' he threatened with a stern look on his face, but he didn't push her away. Instead he scooped her up and placed her on top of his pillows, bringing her inside the circle of conversation.

'So, we all know that someone needs to find that girl and bring her back here as soon as possible,' Orion said, pointing to the article. All the guys nodded.

'Wait. Why?' Helen asked, surprised.

'She's not safe in the mortal world any more. Apollo didn't get her yet,' Jason answered, his voice trailing off at the end. Helen looked at Claire for an answer, but Claire shrugged, stumped.

'Apollo never let a girl get away,' Lucas said, like he hated admitting that he was the descendent of someone so loathsome. 'When he wanted a mortal, he chased her, even if she didn't want him back. Anywhere she ran, he followed. He wouldn't give up.'

'Unless she begged a goddess to turn her into a tree or a body of water or something that he couldn't violate,' Matt said testily. 'Haven't you ever wondered why the House of Thebes, the descendents of Apollo, have so many members?'

'*All* the gods were miserable, raping, warmongering bastards. Not just Apollo,' Hector said with a grimace. 'That's why we have to find a way to get rid of them. Again.'

Orion, Lucas and Helen shared a pained look, each of them keenly aware that this was their fault. The three of them had accidentally become blood brothers when they'd fought Ares, and that had joined the four Houses and unleashed the gods on the world again.

'Hang on. I wasn't blaming you three,' Hector began apologetically, but Orion smiled and put a hand on his friend's shoulder.

'We know you didn't mean it like that,' Orion said.

'But it was still our fault,' Helen reminded them all. 'The gods have always backed Scions into a corner and forced us to make a choice between bad and worse, but we're the ones who have always fallen for their traps. I won't let it happen again.'

Lucas gave Helen a worried look, but before he could lecture her on the dangers of hubris for the tenth time, she changed the subject. 'So who wants to come with me to get this girl?'

'You're not going,' Lucas and Orion said in unison.

'Yes I am,' Helen replied to both of them. 'You two are a mess, and Hector can't show his face in public. Who else is going to go?'

'I'll come with you, Len,' Claire said, cutting off Lucas and Orion before they could argue any further. 'Don't worry, guys. I'll watch her. If she keels over, she can land on me, OK?'

'And me,' Ariadne said.

'You're still way too drained,' Jason said, shaking his head at his twin.

'And that poor girl just got attacked by a god last night. She's probably too injured to be moved without a Healer. I'm also guessing that right now the last thing she wants is for a man to put his hands on her, so that counts you out,' Ariadne replied firmly to Jason.

'So, it's Larry, Moe and Curly to the rescue?' Hector said, rubbing his forehead like his brain hurt.

'Very funny,' Helen said, insulted.

He looked up at Helen, his eyes serious. 'How are your bolts?'

She held up a humming globe of power, cupped in the palm of her hand. It sizzled with compressed energy and threw heat out into the room in waves. 'Better than ever,' she replied with a cocked eyebrow. 'It feels almost effortless now. Like it isn't draining me at all.'

'Good,' Hector said, visibly relaxing now that he knew Helen could defend the three of them. 'Apollo is probably lurking around somewhere near the hospital, so keep your eyes open.'

'I will. But he's not likely to get too close to me after what I did to his half brother,' she said darkly.

Helen looked down at the ball of energy in her hand, remembering how she'd electrocuted Ares and imprisoned him in Tartarus after he'd tortured her. It felt good to know she'd defeated a god. When she looked up, everyone was staring at her.

She closed her hand and extinguished the bolt.

CHAPTER THREE

The streets didn't get bad until they got to the centre of town. Helen gazed out of the window of Ariadne's Mini with a lump in her throat as they drove past the vandalized storefronts. The damage done during the Halloween riots was localized around the high school and the News Store, but that included a large area of down-town.

Shop windows were broken, demolished cars were still sitting on the side of the road and some places were even showing the signs of fire damage. Houses that belonged to Helen's schoolmates and her neighbours – houses that were older than the country itself – had been torn up, covered with graffiti and scorched. She wondered how many people she cared about had been hurt or even killed. How many of her friends were still dreadfully injured like her dad?

'Claire? Did anyone we know . . . besides Zach?' Helen began, unsure of how to put it. She didn't have to spell it out. Claire knew what she meant and nodded.

'Hergie,' Claire said, her voice catching. 'Smoke

inhalation. He was trying to save books from the library fire at school.'

There was nothing to say. Mr Hergesheimer wasn't a relative or even a friend, but still Helen had loved that grouchy old man. Now that he was gone, it was like a door closing. Nantucket would never be same again.

She swallowed and refocused on what they needed to do. Right now she knew she needed to get angry, not hysterical. Eris and Terror, the small gods who had created the riots, were still out there somewhere. Helen clenched her fists and reminded herself to be patient. She'd get her chance at them soon enough.

During the long ride on the ferry from Nantucket to the mainland port at Hyannis the three girls took the opportunity to plan which hospitals they should try. Taking up a table by the concession stand at the centre of the ferry, they scrolled through Matt's iPad, checking out maps on the internet. By the time the ferry docked, Helen felt like they had a pretty solid list of possibilities.

The first two hospitals, although closest to Wellesley College, proved to be dead ends. By the time they got to the third, most of the day was spent. As they pulled into the parking structure, Claire pointed at a police car parked near the entrance.

'She's here,' Claire said with a firm nod. 'They're watching her to see if the stalker comes back.'

Ariadne parked and they went in, splitting up to save

time. Helen went right to the trauma ward. She saw a uniformed police officer guarding a door at the very end of the hallway, and texted Ariadne and Claire to meet her.

The officer was a man, and Helen needed him to let her into the room. She walked right up to him and smiled.

'Hi,' she said warmly, and watched the officer's face get hazy.

Helen had seen a lot of men look at her like that – like they were staring at a shiny brass ring that was too bright for them to look at directly and too high up for them to ever reach. She had always hated this look, even though she knew that it gave her a manipulative kind of power. She'd sworn that she would never use it, but now the game had changed. Helen needed all the power she could get her hands on to protect her family. She had to stop being squeamish, or the Scions didn't stand a chance against the gods.

'A boy attacked a friend of mine last night,' Helen said. 'I think she needs me. May I go in?'

'We're not supposed to let anyone in, young lady,' the officer said, shifting from foot to foot like he was really sorry to say no to her.

Helen could see he wanted to help as clearly as she could see the police badge on his chest. She could see his anger and compassion like a ball of vivid colours swirling around inside his ribs. Helen noticed he wore a wedding ring, sunk deep into the skin of his finger by time, and she just *knew*.

'It's OK, you know,' Helen crooned. She heard and felt Claire and Ariadne join her. They both hesitated, but Helen waved them forward until they were standing on either side of her. 'You can let all three of us in. We're going to take care of her. You have a daughter about our age, right?'

The policeman looked at Helen sharply, wondering how she could have guessed that, and then nodded slowly as he sank deeper into her gaze.

'Then you know that she really needs us. In your heart, you know it's the right thing to do.' Helen smiled her dazzling smile. The officer smiled back, nodding in a hazy way.

'It *is* the right thing to do,' he said with a definite nod of his head, and immediately opened the door for them.

'Thank you,' Helen said gently, pulling Claire and Ariadne in with her.

'How did you . . . ?' Claire began, but Helen cut her off with an impatient gesture and turned to the girl in the bed.

She was awake and staring at them. Her pretty face was cut up in a few places, her left arm was in a cast and her lip was swollen and purple. Helen read the chart on the end of her bed quickly and found her name. Andy Faiakes.

'Oh, crap,' Andy groaned, staring at Helen with a

fed up look on her battered face. 'So which goddess are you?'

'I'm not a . . . wait.' Helen stared at Andy through narrowed eyes. 'What *are* you?'

'You first,' Andy said in the most melodious voice Helen had ever heard. Helen opened her mouth to reply and had to forcibly stop herself from spilling her guts.

'That's some voice you got there,' Helen said, gritting her teeth against the temptation to answer the question.

'That's some face you got there,' Andy said back, her voice ringing inside Helen's head. *'What are you?'* she repeated, amping up the seductive quality of her voice.

'Scion,' Claire blurted out, and then slapped a hand over her mouth. Her eyes got wide, and she mumbled from behind her fingers. 'I'm so sorry, you guys. I don't know why I just said that.'

'Because you're completely human,' Andy said to Claire with a small smile. Then she looked at Helen and Ariadne in turn. 'But they're not.'

'And what are you?' Ariadne asked guardedly.

'Human,' Andy said. Even though she used her beautiful hypno-voice, the word jangled out of tune inside Helen's head.

'Liar,' Helen declared, shaking her head once. Andy stared at her for a moment before continuing.

'And half siren. Unfortunately,' she admitted reluctantly. It was obvious that Andy didn't like to think that half of her was a creature who sang people to their doom.

'So what are you three doing here?' Andy asked cautiously.

'You know who, or rather *what*, attacked you last night, right?' Ariadne asked bluntly. Andy's shoulders tensed with fear. She nodded. Ariadne softened her tone and went to stand by the side of Andy's bed, her big, hazel eyes filling with compassion. 'Then you know he'll be back for you. We came to take you home with us, to our family, so we can protect you.'

'You can't protect me,' Andy said, her lovely voice faltering as tears threatened to break through her tough-girl act. 'Not from a god. No Scion is strong enough to stop them.'

Helen could feel Andy's desperation, her absolute faith that eventually she was going to suffer and die at the hands of some supernatural brute. Just like Helen had been sure that Ares was going to kill her when he had her tied up in the cave. She remembered how Ares had abused her. How he'd revelled in her helplessness. Helen knew just by looking in her eyes that Andy had suffered something similar.

Furious, Helen got hot all over, and the tiny hairs on her arms stood on end. The room filled with the icy-blue glare of lightning as it coursed over her skin in a flowing web of sparks.

'Tell that to Ares. Oh, that's right, you can't. Because I

beat the crap out of him and sent him to Tartarus,' Helen said. The sparks fell from her fingertips, bounced and broke apart like glitter balls shattering silently as they skipped across the floor. She was aware that her voice had boomed a little bit when she spoke, but she couldn't seem to contain herself. All she could think about was Hergie dying in a fire to save his beloved books. And it was all the gods' fault.

'Um . . . Len?' Claire interjected in a tiny voice.

Helen noticed all three girls staring at her with open mouths, and snapped out of it. She shook the last of the sparks off her hands with a sheepish look on her face, cleared her throat and tried to speak again.

'Look, I'm going to be honest. We can't promise you'll be completely safe,' she said. 'But we can promise that if Apollo comes for you he's going to have to fight all of us to take you. Now. Isn't that better than lying here, waiting for him to bust in and carry you off like some helpless damsel in a Greek myth?'

'Uh. Yeah,' Andy said, her eyes wide.

Helen realized she was scaring the girl and forced a laugh. Glancing over at Claire, Helen caught a hint of fear in her best friend's expression before she looked away.

Once they managed to get Andy out of the hospital and through the parking garage, she was so wiped out that she fell asleep during the drive to Hyannis. Helen drove. Ariadne had worn herself out healing Andy's broken leg before they had left the hospital, and then had done a little more healing during the drive while they cruised down Route 495. Her effort left her as pale and sickly-looking as Andy by the time they boarded the ferry.

Helen couldn't help but think it was a good thing that neither Andy nor Ariadne had the strength to get out of the car. Even though it was night time and the darkness would have offered some cover, Andy's injuries were still far too obvious for her to be roaming around. Helen and Claire left the two of them sacked out in the back seat and went to scrounge up some food for them all.

'He really worked her over, didn't he?' Claire said in a crackly voice as they made their way to the concession stand. Helen could only nod, her lips pinched together. She looked at Claire's worried face and wished she could say something to comfort her, but came up with nothing.

She could feel Claire stealing little glances at her while they put coins in the vending machine, searching Helen's face for some kind of explanation. But Helen didn't have the words to explain what was going on.

'What?' Helen asked defensively when she couldn't take Claire's stares any more.

'Nothing,' Claire said, pursing her lips. A tense moment passed between them, and Helen's frustration grew.

'Just say it, Claire.'

'You're different.' Claire gathered their makeshift

meal out of the bottom of the machine and turned, but Helen reached out and stopped her.

'I'm different because I have to be,' Helen said, her voice harsh. 'The way I used to be wasn't enough. Not for this.'

'And how much more are you going to change?'

'As much as I have to in order to win.'

'Does that include manipulating cops?' Claire said hotly. 'What did you *do* to him, anyway?'

Helen felt guilty about the police officer, even though she didn't fully understand what she'd done. There was something wrong about being able to take away someone's will like that. Helen knew as much, but she wasn't about to admit that to Claire.

'I did what I had to do. Or do you think I should have killed him to get in the room?'

Claire opened her mouth to say something but quickly shut it again, edging away from her as they walked back to the car. Helen realized that Claire was genuinely afraid of her, not just afraid of a few sparks and a booming voice. Helen knew she should have said something to make her feel better. But she didn't. A big part of Helen was angry with Claire for not being more understanding. Even though it didn't make any sense, Helen resented her best friend for fearing her.

'I don't know if you've noticed this or not, but this isn't just about our friends and family any more,' Helen said bitterly. 'And I don't need to explain my actions to you. Or ask your permission to use my powers.'

'You're right,' Claire replied. 'You don't have to explain anything to me. Just make sure you can explain your actions to your conscience.'

They didn't talk much after that. Helen and Claire woke Ariadne up and made her eat a granola bar from the vending machine and drink a bottle of water before Helen drove them all back home. She dropped Claire at her parents' house with a few mumbled plans about meeting up first thing tomorrow, and then went on to the Delos place.

It was late when they pulled in, and Helen was so exhausted that she barely had the energy to carry the other two girls up to Ariadne's bed before she collapsed on the couch.

Helen sat opposite herself inside a covered, horse-drawn carriage. It was dark in the enclosed compartment. The only light came from between the slats of a tiny, shuttered window. Helen wondered how she would get in and out of the carriage, because she couldn't see a door. She guessed that the window might be large enough to let her squeeze through . . . if there weren't bars over it.

The other Helen who sat across from her was not the Spartan one from before. This one was wearing a gown made out of some kind of rough, homespun material. There were blue-dyed strings woven into her long, blonde hair and she sat on a pile of tanned skins and furs. The backs of her hands were painted with more blue dye in intricate curlicues that Helen vaguely recognized as Irish. The word *Celtic* bubbled up in her mind and she knew that description, while maybe not completely accurate, was closer to the true one.

At the other Helen's waist was a dagger. Her hand clutched it desperately at every sound she heard from outside the shuttered and barred window of her prison-like carriage. This other Helen looked like a savage and was being treated like a caged animal. Helen wondered if this 'other her' was dangerous.

'My lady Guinevere!' shouted a familiar voice outside the window.

Lucas's voice.

Guinevere opened the shutter over the window, and Helen immediately saw why this version of herself was so terrified. The Furies started weeping in the corner of the carriage as soon as Guinevere and the other Lucas made eye contact.

He was sitting on the huge, black horse that was trotting alongside the coach. He was wearing dark leather, a thick, black woollen cloak, and belted at his waist was a long broadsword. He looked big and fierce and beautiful.

'Do you need to relieve yourself?' he asked in a strange, lilting language that Helen understood although she'd never heard it before.

'My mother taught me to speak perfect Latin, as you well know,' Guinevere snarled back at him in a different language that Helen also understood without ever having heard it before. She assumed it was Latin. 'She wasn't a filthy Roman like you, but she was from the east.'

'I'm no Roman. Don't call me that,' the other Lucas said with a dangerous glint in his eye. 'Sir Lancelot will do just fine.'

Their baleful gazes met and held. The Furies wailed, causing both Guinevere and Lancelot to cringe as they tried to control themselves. Helen knew that if the bars in the window did not separate them they would have attacked each other.

Lancelot looked up and down the long line of warriors that accompanied them, as if reminding himself that there were witnesses who would keep him from doing anything stupid.

'Why don't you just kill me now?' Guinevere hissed at him quietly. Her low tone told Helen that Guinevere was also aware that there were other people watching – people who would not understand her irrational hatred for Lancelot or his hatred for her.

'That pleasure I leave to Arthur, my cousin and king,' Lancelot replied stiffly, almost reluctantly, like something about that bothered him. '*After* you marry him and ensure your clan's allegiance, of course. Then I'm sure he'll kill you with joy.'

'And you call us barbarians,' Guinevere snapped at him.

She slammed the window shut and threw herself back on the pile of furs. Helen knew – she *remembered* – that the furs were part of the large dowry from Guinevere's father. He was the head of her clan, and he had sent along many gifts with his daughter in this wedding train. All the rich goods were a peace offering to the undefeatable invaders from the east, and Guinevere was the ultimate spoil of war. The most beautiful girl on the island offered up as a gift to the big, golden-haired invader from a faraway land. And they desperately hoped he liked the gift – because, if he didn't, this King Arthur just might slaughter them all.

Guinevere knew her father loved her in his gruff way. He couldn't know that he was sending his favourite child to her death. He wasn't like these men from the east or like her late mother had been. Clan leader or not, her father was just a normal mortal, and he believed he was honouring his daughter above all others by giving her to the new, young, and, by all accounts, handsome High King. Guinevere had no defensible reason to object. Her father had every right to marry her off to whomever he chose, and unless she was ready to reveal her secret, and her late mother's secret, she had to go along with it.

Tears of rage and frustration brimmed in Guinevere's eyes. Helen remembered Guinevere's feeling of desperation in this impossible situation distinctly, because once it had been her own.

'You didn't answer my question,' Lancelot yelled stubbornly at the closed window. 'You've been shut up in there for over a day now. Do you need to relieve yourself, Princess?'

Guinevere proudly dashed the tears from her eyes, smoothed her mussed hair, and pulled open the window. 'No!' she howled, and slammed the window shut again.

Lancelot barked once with surprised laughter. A few moments of tense indecision passed. His black charger pranced anxiously outside Guinevere's barred window as if he were reluctant to leave her. Finally, he clucked his tongue at his Goliath of a mount and thundered away.

Guinevere dropped her head on to her folded arms and tried not to think of how much she needed to relieve herself.

Moments later, she lifted her head in alarm. Shouts were coming from the back of the wedding train – shouts and strange yelps. Someone screamed in agony. Guinevere leapt to her feet and pulled out her dagger, snarling like the heathen she was.

Her carriage lurched to a stop, and Helen could hear men shouting all around. Something jolted the side of the halted carriage, sending Guinevere sprawling against the wall of her cage. She steadied herself on her knees as another great shove knocked the carriage over on to its side – the window side facing down. The inside of the carriage went completely dark as the only escape was pushed into the earth.

'To the princess!' commanded Lancelot's voice from a distance. 'Surround the carriage!'

There was a great rustling of leaves, and the sound of many men moving into position around her. Guinevere listened to the clanging of metal on metal, and the pounding of feet running over her carriage. There were men grunting, shouting, screaming and dying in every direction. The dull thud of bodies hitting the carriage and the ground was coupled with the last rattling breaths of dying men.

Guinevere repeatedly slammed her shoulder into the side of the carriage, trying to tip it over and expose the window, but she did little more than rock the massive iron-and-oak enclosure back and forth. She let out a moan of frustration.

'Lady Guinevere! Are you injured?' Lancelot said in a strident voice from outside the wall of her knocked-over prison.

'No,' Guinevere said back firmly. 'Let me out so I can fight.'

Lancelot made a frustrated sound. 'They've taken to the trees.'

'Picts?' Guinevere guessed. There was no sound from Lancelot, probably because he didn't know who their attackers were and couldn't answer her. 'They'll be back with more warriors after dusk,' she promised him. 'Please believe me – you may have pushed them back for now, but they are *not gone*.'

'I know. I can't see them in the trees, but I can still smell them.'

'You must let me out of here!' Guinevere pleaded. 'They want *me*, not the riches we carry in this party.'

'How do you know that?' Lancelot asked, like he suspected she was telling the truth.

'The Picts are one of the oldest clans. They've handed down ancient stories about *our* kind – yours and mine, Sir Lancelot. They know better than to fight me, or you, head-on. Instead, they will try to lure you away, and they will leave me in this prison to starve. They'll wait until I'm too weak with hunger and thirst to stop them. They don't want to kill me. They want to . . .' She stopped here and struggled for a moment. 'They want children from me. To strengthen their clan.'

Lancelot uttered a foul curse. She could hear his elevated breathing as he fought with himself. 'But if I let you out . . . I don't know what *I'll* do to you. Are you sure that isn't worse?'

'I'd rather die in an honourable fight with you than be used as a brood mare. At least let me *fight*,' she said in a strangled voice. 'Don't leave me to face that.'

'If I set you free, you might try to kill me.'

'Please,' Guinevere choked out, desperately trying not to cry. 'Please don't leave me locked up in here. I know you hate me, but don't abandon me to such a terrible fate.'

Lancelot exhaled sharply. 'Stand back,' he ordered.

The walls of the carriage shuddered with massive blows as Lancelot hacked his way through the bottom of the metal-reinforced floor with a sword. When the first blade was ruined, he collected another from a fallen man and started hacking away again.

Three, four, five swords were broken to bits, but finally a large enough gash was opened for Guinevere to squeeze out. When she was freed, they stared at each other, both of them breathless with fear and anger and some other feeling they had no name for yet.

'You saved my life,' Guinevere whispered, overwhelmed by the chance he took by setting her free. 'Now I'll save yours.'

She looked around at the scores of bodies that littered the ground. Armoured men from the east were piled on top of the small, blue-painted Pictish people who wore only basic animal skins and carried stone weapons.

So many dead, or run off. Lancelot was the only man to stay behind to defend her, Helen noticed.

Guinevere took Lancelot's hand and led him away from the senseless waste of life and into the trees.

'A trap,' Lancelot growled, pulling away from her. 'You'll lead me right to them!'

'No. They won't come near you as long as you are with me,' she explained, trying to stay calm. 'Look.'

Guinevere held up her other hand. A globe of lightning spasmed inside her cupped palm. Lancelot jumped back momentarily and then moved closer, enchanted by the naked power he saw dancing on her fingertips.

'Why didn't you use that to get out of the carriage?' he asked, always inquisitive, just like Lucas.

'The metal soldered to the wood of the carriage surrounded me in arcs. My power would have died in the ground,' she said, and then shook her head. 'I'll explain someday, I promise. For now, I need to deal with *them*.'

Guinevere held her hand aloft and shouted up into the thick branches.

'Do you see this?' she said in a third strange language that Helen also seemed to understand, if only barely. 'If I see even one arrow loosed on my companion or me, I will burn your sacred forest to the ground. Do you hear? I will burn your mother goddess like dry tinder, and the sky gods will rule this island forever!'

The sounds of scraping bark and rustling branches added their whispery voices to the wind as the Picts dissolved into the misty distance. Lancelot cocked his head and held very still for a long time, listening and smelling and looking as carefully as he could.

'They're gone,' he said finally, exhaling with relief.

'Yes,' Guinevere breathed. 'They've *all* gone.'

'You saved my life.'

Lancelot and Guinevere stared at each other in amazement, both the Picts and Furies finally out of their way. In that instant, all the burning anger they felt toward each other was replaced by another kind of fire – a tender one that smouldered more than it consumed.

Leaves fell in the forest. The sun moved in the sky and tilted itself perfectly to light up Lancelot's sapphire eyes. The wind picked up pieces of Guinevere's long, golden hair and sent it wafting toward Lancelot like strands of sweetly scented silk. They took a step toward each other, both open and ready for the huge gift they saw offered in the other.

They stopped abruptly.

'Oh no,' Lancelot whispered, more afraid now than he had been in the heat of battle.

'Your king . . .' Guinevere said, her amber eyes darting around frantically as if looking for a way out. 'Hector . . . *Arthur*,' she said fumblingly, as her multilingual mouth tried to say both the traditional Latin name for the new High King from the east, and the Briton's approximation of that name.

'The clans will never accept his rule unless he takes a wife from among them. They need to know that his sons will be at least part Briton,' Lancelot said, shaking his head. 'They will never stop fighting unless you marry him. Many will die.'

They stared at each other. Guinevere was still wide-eyed with disbelief.

'I have a little sister – a half-sister of my father's. She's only ten now, but in a few years . . .'

GODDESS

'In a few years, thousands will already be dead,' Lancelot said quietly. He turned his head away, forcing himself not to look at her. 'You must marry Arthur, or there will be war.'

Chapter Four

Helen hit the ground with a loud thump.

'Wha-waz-that?' Ariadne gasped, bolting up in bed.

'Me,' Helen moaned from the floor, rubbing the bump on her forehead. 'I fell.'

'You fell off the couch?' Andy asked incredulously. 'I thought you demigoddesses were supposed to be graceful. Made out of dewdrops and rosebuds and crap.'

'No, that's fairies,' Ariadne said. 'Minus the crap, of course.' Then she snickered, and Andy snickered back. Helen peeked up over the edge of the jiggling mattress and saw the other two girls having a giggle fit.

'OK, OK. It wasn't *that* funny,' Helen groused as she stood up and trudged over to get Andy. 'I'm starving. Let's eat.'

Helen stood between Andy and Ariadne, propping the two girls up as they limped and shuffled their way toward the glorious smell of bacon and muffins coming from the kitchen.

'You're new,' Kate said cheerfully as soon as the three girls entered.

'Um . . . yeah,' Andy answered, dropping her eyes. 'They came to get me,' she mumbled, gesturing to Helen and Ariadne.

'This is the girl who got attacked,' Ariadne said. 'Her name is Andy.'

'Let me look at you,' Noel said kindly. She put down the tin of bran muffins she had just taken out of the oven and peered deeply at Andy. Her eyes softened with sadness, and she shook her head once. 'You're really banged up. But, even so, I'm good at recognizing the types, and I can't place your face.'

'She's not a Scion, Aunt Noel,' Ariadne said. 'She's half *siren*.'

Andy cringed slightly against Helen, her eyes darting around like she expected something terrible to happen.

'Uh-oh!' Noel said with mock horror and clutched her chest. 'Not one of those murdering sirens!' Then she laughed and turned back round to retrieve the muffins. 'Sit, girls. Before you all tip over.'

Helen could feel Andy stiffen with confusion. Helen helped her scoot on to the long wooden bench between her and Ariadne.

'Is this really OK?' Andy asked as Ariadne shovelled eggs on to her plate. 'I just sort of showed up. You don't have to feed me or anything.'

'Ha! Try *not* eating around here,' Helen said. Then she looked at Andy with wide, serious eyes and shook her head emphatically, silently mouthing the word 'Don't'.

Ariadne shook her head in agreement with Helen, and the three girls broke into quiet laughter.

'Helen. Your father woke up for a few seconds this morning,' Kate said as she took a sizzling pan of bacon off the range and brought it to the table.

Helen's mouth suddenly went dry. 'I checked on him before I left yesterday . . .'

'It's OK,' Kate interrupted soothingly. 'I wasn't accusing you of anything. I just wanted to let you know what's going on with him.'

'Has anyone told him anything yet?' Helen had no idea how to broach the subject. Did he know she was a Scion? Should she just come right out and ask if Jerry knew that he wasn't her father yet, or was Kate still in the dark about that point as well? 'Did Daphne . . . ?'

'They've spoken a few words back and forth. I don't know what about, though,' Kate said stiffly, whirling away from the table abruptly. 'He hasn't been awake long enough at any one time to have a full conversation, but he knows that *Beth* is back.'

Helen nodded. 'Beth' was the alias that Daphne had used when she conned Jerry, leaving Helen with him as a baby before she ran off. Helen wondered how her father had dealt with seeing her. 'Is Daphne around?' Helen asked. 'I'd like to talk to her.'

'No. She left a few minutes ago. Said she had some things to take care of,' Kate said through tight lips.

Helen could see about a dozen different shapes

swirling around inside Kate. Anger, sadness, worry and resentment – a blinding kaleidoscope of emotion that kept moving and changing until Helen had to squeeze her eyes shut and look away for a moment. This was not normal, and it was really freaking her out.

'Helen?' Noel's ever-watchful eyes regarded Helen sharply. 'Are you feeling OK?'

'Yeah,' Helen replied, shaking it off. When she looked at Kate again, the colours had dimmed and Helen found she could ignore them. 'Just woozy. What's up with those muffins?'

Noel finished transferring the sticky, molasses-and-raisin-laden treats into a basket and brought them to the table. 'Don't burn yourselves,' she warned uselessly as all three girls grabbed one.

Ariadne and Andy began juggling the scalding muffins from hand to hand until they both dropped their too-hot muffins on to their plates. Helen simply bit into hers and started chewing smugly. Andy stared at her, openmouthed.

'I'm fireproof,' Helen mumbled around her purposely over-full mouth, rubbing it in. 'I thought sirens had wings.'

'Some do,' Andy admitted sheepishly. 'My mom's kind don't, though. We're more the aquatic, singing type.'

'Can you breath underwater?' Kate asked excitedly. Andy blushed and nodded. 'Awesome.'

'And where is your mother, Andy?' Noel asked delicately.

'I'm not sure.' Andy looked down at her plate. An uncomfortable silence followed.

'So. Ever get the urge to drown anyone?' Ariadne asked.

'No!' Andy replied, horrified.

'She's just messing with you,' Helen assured her. Her face dropped. 'Seriously, though. What's your stance on strangling?'

'You mean apart from wanting to strangle both of you right now?' Andy asked, a smile tugging at her lips as she played along.

'You're going to fit in just fine around here, Andy,' Noel said as they all cracked up.

'Women laughing,' Hector drawled as he sauntered into the kitchen. 'My favourite sound.'

The reaction from Andy was immediate and frantic. She threw her fork at Hector's head with a startled gasp. Hector caught the fork easily and placed it back on the table with a shocked look on his face. Then he caught the muffin, the empty water glass and the napkin that immediately followed. Andy snatched anything and everything within reach and hurled it at him with all her might as she scrambled to get up from the table.

'What the hell?' Hector said, placing everything he had caught back on the table and then holding his hands up in a placating gesture as he came towards Andy.

Pinned by the bench, she slammed the backs of her legs against the wood, toppled over it and then scrabbled on hands and knees across the kitchen floor to get away from him. Hector reached out to try to help her up.

'No, no, no, oh please, no, not again!' she mumbled hysterically as she clawed her way across the floor.

'Hector, stop,' Helen said, spinning round on the bench and standing up between the two of them. Still confused, Hector kept moving towards Andy. Helen put her hands on his shoulders and shoved him back. 'She thinks you're Apollo, you big dummy!' Helen screamed in his face. 'You're scaring the life out of her!'

Hector suddenly seemed to register what Helen was saying, stiffened and stopped moving forward. Ariadne helped Andy off the ground and then struggled to keep her from bolting out the side door while Hector watched with a frozen look on his face.

'You have to calm down, Andy! You're still healing, and your body can't take this,' Ariadne said as she captured Andy's wrists to keep her from hurting her abused limbs any more.

Panting and wild-eyed, Andy finally stopped struggling and went still in Ariadne's arms.

'It's OK! That's not Apollo. It's just my brother, Hector. He's not going to hurt you,' Ariadne promised. Andy glared over Ariadne's shoulder at Hector, her sides still swelling with terrified breaths.

'I'm sorry,' Hector called gently across the room to Andy. 'I didn't mean to frighten you.'

A deep red throbbing inside Hector's chest captured Helen's gaze and she stared at it, dumbstruck, as a red-gold web of light illuminated Hector from the inside out. It was the most enchanting thing Helen had ever seen.

'Stay away from me, *Hector*,' Andy snarled, almost like she was mocking him. 'Got it?'

The brightness of Hector's light faltered. Helen looked up at Hector's face.

The Hector Helen knew – and usually wanted to punch in the kidney – would have said something hilarious as he left the room, grinning at Andy in a way that would make her unsure if she wanted to kick him or kiss him. But this new, glowing Hector only nodded at Andy's demand. He took one more moment to stare at the cuts and dark bruises on her battered face, his forehead pinching with sadness. He turned to leave the kitchen without another word.

As Hector got to the door, Orion and Lucas were just coming through it. Helen saw Orion's gaze immediately dart down to Hector's chest, then back up to Hector's face, his eyes wide with shock.

'We heard yelling,' Orion said, confused.

Hector pushed past Orion and Lucas. Searching the kitchen, Orion quickly found Andy, who was still glaring daggers at Hector's back. Andy's chest was a glowering nest of fear and anger. Helen saw Orion's expression fall, and she knew he understood the situation as clearly as she did.

'Hey, sunshine! What's the matter with you?' Lucas yelled at Hector's retreating figure. The only answer from his cousin was the slam of the front door. Lucas looked around at everyone else for an answer.

'I'll tell you later,' Orion said quietly to Lucas, his voice strained with worry. Helen knew Lucas was just about to say something impatient like, 'No, tell me now,' so she jumped in.

'Guys. This is Andy,' Helen said.

Lucas and Orion smiled at Andy and introduced themselves. Andy subtly looked back and forth between the two breathtaking young men – uncertain as to whom she wanted to stare at more. Helen laughed, sympathizing completely with Andy's predicament – Lucas's eyes or Orion's lips? She had trouble deciding that one herself. Helen clapped a hand over her mouth but not before she actually snorted. The odd outburst earned her a couple of wary looks.

It occurred to Helen that all the emotions she was so tuned in to were not apparent to anyone else – except Orion. Glancing over, she saw him studying her carefully, and her fear returned. She mouthed the words, 'We need to talk.' Orion nodded once in response.

'Breakfast is getting cold,' Noel said firmly.

'Maybe this is a bad idea,' Andy said, shaking her head. 'I shouldn't be here.'

'Can your family protect you?' Lucas asked directly.

Andy looked down at her feet. 'No,' she replied. 'I don't have family like you do. I've got a lawyer and a bank account. Sirens aren't exactly the nurturing type.'

'Then you're staying here with us. Now sit down and eat,' Noel said in the kind of tone that ends discussions.

Everyone scooted on to the bench or pulled up chairs and started passing around plates. Helen found herself between Orion and Lucas, but it wasn't awkward or embarrassing. It felt right, like they all belonged here at this table together.

Helen realized that the three of them were tied to each other by more than just mutual respect and attraction. She, Lucas and Orion were blood brothers now, and each of them felt the bond to the other as deeply as if it had been there from the day they were born.

Helen felt Lucas press his leg against hers under the table. She didn't dare look at him as she felt the heat of his thigh seep through her jeans and into her skin. She pressed back against his thigh and felt him inch a tiny bit closer to her as he ate.

Right or wrong, Helen knew she would always look for a way to touch Lucas under the table, or brush up against him as she passed him in the hall. She wasn't getting over him. In fact, she wanted Lucas even more now than she did weeks ago when she almost kissed him in his bed that first night after they fell.

Her brain filled with some other Helen's memories of

suffering because of their union. They were awful, but not even those borrowed memories of destruction and fire could bring Helen to break the contact between her leg and his.

More memories flashed inside her head, like a movie reel played on fast-forward. Helen and Lucas had been married for decades. They had only met two months ago. They were sharing their first kiss. He made her laugh. He made her cry. They talked tenderly. They argued bitterly. Over and over the images rolled behind Helen's eyes like giant waves. When they stopped, Helen could see everything clearly – like a beach wiped clean after a storm.

She and Lucas were woven from the same cloth, cut apart, and then stitched back together from one cycle to another. The circumstances changed, but they were always intertwined, no matter what.

The difference now was that in this life they were cousins. That had never been part of the deal before, and it didn't feel right to Helen. Lucas, or Paris, or Lancelot, or any one of the hundreds of names she'd called him over the centuries had *never* been her cousin before. They'd always shared a doomed, starcrossed love, but they had never been related. What had happened this time to throw everything so far out of whack?

I really don't care if he's my cousin any more.

As soon as Helen thought this, she remembered Aphrodite's curse. If Helen didn't have a daughter, love itself would be taken from the world. And Ariadne had once told Helen that close relatives like cousins almost always had insane children. Since Helen was quite sure that Aphrodite wouldn't forget her 3,300-year-old curse, and since Helen could never bear the thought of damning an innocent child to insanity, there were no options for her and Lucas. She jerked her leg away and tilted her knees to her other side, toward Orion. Sensing her uneasiness, Orion looked over at Helen with concerned eyes.

Setting aside her bias for Lucas, Helen had to admit that Orion was the most beautiful man she'd ever seen. She smiled at him, and he nudged her elbow playfully with his before they both returned to devouring their food.

Sometime later, Helen took her attention off her plate long enough to notice that Jason and Claire had joined them at the table. Claire had a newspaper with her.

'She found something,' Jason said seriously.

'It's not good,' Claire warned. She opened up the paper and showed them an article. 'Three volcanoes erupted last night in Europe.'

'That doesn't sound normal,' Kate said.

'It's not,' Jason replied. 'Especially since one of the volcanoes had been extinct for thousands of years.'

'Hephaestus?' Andy asked.

'We think so,' Claire said, looking at Jason.

'But why would he make volcanoes erupt? Just because he can?' Andy pressed.

'No. So he can forge weapons for Olympus,' Lucas replied. Several people started talking at once. In the commotion, Helen saw the opportunity to talk privately with Orion. She swung her legs round and straddled the bench, gesturing with her chin for him to follow her out into the hallway.

As she passed, she saw Lucas glance up at her. He looked at her like she was the big, blue sky, and he was watching it fall.

Something bright and pretty inside him seemed to burn up and turn to soot. Ashy-coloured hurt smeared around Lucas like a fog, darkening the air and stinging Helen's eyes.

Helen clenched her jaw and forced herself to keep going, heading blindly for the front door. She felt Orion hook his fingers round her arm. They were by the coats hanging in the front hall when he finally nudged her round to face him.

'What's going on with you?' he whispered. 'I could have sworn you just saw . . .'

'Parts of Lucas's insides *burn up* and come out of *his skin*? Or are you talking about Hector literally *glowing* when he fell madly in love with a girl who hates him? Because I just saw both of those things happen,' Helen said in a manic whisper. 'It's as if everything that everyone is feeling is splashed across their insides, and I can see it! I'm pretty sure I shouldn't be able to see inside people!'

Orion took a step back, momentarily thrown, and then nodded in acceptance. Helen looked up at him pleadingly.

'What the hell is going on with me?' she squeaked. 'I can see *love*, Orion, and it's making me totally hectic.'

'Yeah, love'll do that,' he said distractedly. Helen bounced on her toes, anxious for some kind of explanation or reassurance – anything, really. He put his hands on her shoulders and squeezed comfortingly. 'You're seeing emotions. It's perfectly normal. For members of the House of Rome, anyway.'

'News flash. I'm not from the House of Rome.'

'And that's the big problem, isn't it?'

'Lucas told me once that Scions are born with all their talents. Have you ever heard of this happening before?'

'What? A Scion taking such a huge beating they wake up with a new talent? No, I haven't.' He rubbed her upper arms with his palms a few times and then gathered her into a hug. 'There's got to be an explanation. We'll figure it out.'

'I don't want to figure it out,' Helen grumbled, her words muffled in his chest. 'I want it to go away.' She pulled back a bit so she could look up at him. 'How do you *stand* it? I usually have a hard enough time dealing with my own emotions. What the heck am I supposed to do with everybody else's?'

'You get used to it,' he replied with a little shrug. Helen gave him a dubious look and he chuckled. 'OK, you don't get used to it,' he admitted. 'But you do get better at blocking it out.'

'You know what? This *sucks*. I was just getting the hang of all the other things I can do,' she said, throwing up her hands. 'And it's like I woke up the other day with this whole new bunch of magic tricks to deal with, but no instructions for getting the blasted rabbit back in the hat.'

'What do you mean? What else is going on in there?' Orion asked, tapping Helen lightly on the tip of her nose with his pointer finger.

'I don't know,' Helen said with a frustrated sigh. 'Honestly? I'm so confused right now I don't know whether to spit or go sailing.'

Orion smiled and leaned back against the wall, letting his gaze drift down in thought. Helen stared at him for a few moments, just enjoying his company and the fact that he was there with her. No. Better than that. He was there *for* her.

Orion had saved her butt so many times now, listened to her whine when she couldn't figure something out. He'd followed her to hell and back, and he still didn't seem fed up with her. The gratitude she felt towards him, and towards whatever force put him in her life, was overwhelming. He sensed her flood of feeling and looked up, startled.

'There something I need to show you,' Orion said quietly.

'Sure,' Helen responded, concerned. The half-sad, half-afraid look on his face worried her.

Even more confusing than the look he gave her were the colours she saw boiling inside him. They twisted and changed before Helen could define them. He was hiding his feelings from her, she realized with a jolt.

She knew Orion had been through a lot in his life, and sometimes Helen had to run through the whole mess in her head just to keep it straight. Orion was a Rogue Scion. His parents were the Heads of two opposing Houses, the House of Rome and the House of Athens. He'd been claimed by the House of Athens when he was born, so the House of Rome hated him and wanted him dead, even though he had inherited the title of Head of the House of Rome. The House of Athens hated him as well, because he was born with the talent to cause earthquakes. Earthshakers were supposed to be left to die at birth, but Orion's father had gone against this rule.

When other members of the House of Athens found out that Orion was still alive, they had tried to kill him when he was still just a little boy. To defend his son, Orion's father – Daedalus – had killed one of his family members and became an Outcast, which meant that, for years before the Furies were finally dealt with, Orion couldn't be anywhere near Daedalus without feeling the Furies' influence and wanting to kill his own father. And his father wanting to kill him.

As if this weren't bad enough, everyone was terrified

Orion was going to turn into the über-bad guy, the Tyrant. The prophecy said that the Tyrant would come if the blood of the Houses mixed, and Orion was the son of two different Houses. The Tyrant was also supposed to be able to reduce all mortal cities to rubble. As an Earthshaker, Orion fitted that description too.

All the Scions had feared the Tyrant before the Trojan War. As Helen remembered it, the Trojan War had started, not because of an unfaithful wife with a pretty face who ran off with handsome prince, but because the rest of the world believed that Helen and Paris had created the Tyrant. The Scions would stop at nothing to kill the Tyrant, then and now. The only reason Orion was still alive was because they didn't know for sure that he really *was* the Tyrant.

And that's what bothered Helen the most. The Fates were cruel to Scions in general, but Orion had been hunted, neglected, shunned and feared since he was a small boy and he had never done anything to anyone. It was like the moment he was born he drew the short straw and the Fates had turned the whole world against him. That amount of adversity struck Helen as unnatural, even for a Scion. What did he ever do to deserve the torture he'd lived through? And Helen was pretty sure Orion had been literally tortured. She pictured the horrific scars on his otherwise gorgeous body, and her heart broke all over again.

Orion looked down at Helen's chest as tenderness for him welled up inside her. It was incredibly intimate and, Helen had to admit, a thrill to be that exposed to someone.

'Tonight,' he said in a gravelly voice, averting his eyes tactfully as if Helen were suddenly topless. In a way she was, and they both knew it. Helen crossed her arms shyly over her chest. He pushed himself off the wall and stood up straight until he was at his full height over her. It struck Helen again just how *big* Orion was. Maybe that was another reason everyone feared him. The guy was huge. 'I want to take you there tonight. Before I have to go back to school tomorrow.'

Helen nearly laughed, and then caught herself when she remembered that it was *her* school that had been demolished in the Halloween riots, not his. After everything, Orion still had to pretend he was a normal guy who went to prep school, did his homework, and gave a crap about what the other kids thought of him. It seemed so ludicrous, but no one could say for certain what was going to happen in the future. He was just covering all his bases.

After the big meeting of the Houses that was supposed to take place at some point over the next few days, Orion might have to go back into hiding again. Maybe Helen and Lucas would have to hide as well. The three of them were responsible for the breaking of the Truce, and there was a possibility they might have to run for their lives if the other Scions turned on them. Or they might have to face off with the gods.

'Where are you going?'

Orion and Helen both jumped at the unexpected sound. Cassandra appeared out of the shadows, slinking forward silently, her eyes unblinking as she glanced from Orion to Helen and then to the front door that they were standing before.

'Are you leaving?' she asked Orion gravely.

Cassandra's eyes were big and shiny in the dim hallway, like two still pools of deep water in a shady forest. Distracted by a strange shimmer, Helen glanced down at Cassandra's chest. A single silver orb captured Helen's eyes. Like a full moon in winter, it hung inside the midnight-dark of Cassandra's tiny rib cage and glowed a ghost-blue colour that danced across her pale cheeks.

As lonely as a rock in space, Helen thought, staring at the orb. *That's her heart.*

When Helen looked at Orion, expecting to see him fixated on the silver shimmer of Cassandra's core, she was shocked to see him smiling happily – as sunny and as bright as could be. It was as if the chill Helen saw inside Cassandra was invisible to Orion.

'Hey, Kitty,' Orion said, grinning down on Cassandra.

Cassandra didn't object to the nickname he'd given her. In fact, she seemed to *like* it, which was downright baffling. She smiled up at Orion, sending the silver light in her chest out in a wavelike dance across her face and down her arms and out to the tips of her braided hair.

'You said you were staying a while.' Cassandra's gaze was glued to Orion. 'You said you were going to make me a bell.'

Orion threw back his head and laughed, his bright teeth flashing in the dim entryway. 'I made it already. But I won't force you to wear it if you don't like it.'

He pulled a long, sparkly braid of silky purple twine from his pocket. It was studded with miniature jingle bells that were smaller than sunflower seeds. Cassandra eyes lit up.

'I like it,' she said enthusiastically.

'Never heard of a kitty that actually wanted to wear a bell before,' Orion said with a comical grimace. He motioned for Cassandra to hold out her wrist and, when she did, he began wrapping the long thread round and round, forming a multilayered, tinkling gauntlet as he did so.

'That's really beautiful,' Helen exclaimed as Orion began knotting the bracelet to Cassandra's wrist. The materials were simple, but the end result was surprisingly stylish. Helen wanted one herself. 'When did you get the chance to make that?'

'Oh, you know. Here and there,' he replied with a mysterious smile, his eyes on his task. 'Used to make jewellery for the tourists when I was kicking around India and Tibet. Just to make a buck. I got good at making little things like this fast.' He finished tying it off and released Cassandra's wrist.

'When were you in Tibet?' Helen asked, surprised and a bit envious. She'd always wanted to go there.

He locked eyes with her, his lips sealed. Helen glanced down at Orion's chest, but he was doing that thing where he snatched the colours away before Helen could really see them.

'We'll talk about that when we go out tonight,' he said finally.

'OK. But you gotta teach me how you do that cover-up swirly thing, or I'm not going anywhere with you,' she said, pointing first to his chest, then to hers. 'I'm at a serious disadvantage here.'

'So, you *are* leaving,' Cassandra said anxiously, turning to Orion. 'You two are going on a date?'

'Not exactly,' Orion said, staring at Helen with an enigmatic smile. Helen had no idea what he had in store, so she just shrugged.

'You're not going for long, are you?' Cassandra persisted, a desperate note creeping into her voice.

'No way,' Orion said. He took her hand up playfully and shook it, making the bells on her new bracelet ring for a moment. 'I'll be back before you know it.'

'Good,' Cassandra said, sighing the word with relief. She noticed Helen watching her carefully and squared her shoulders. 'Hector said w-we should all stick together. I-I think he's right.'

For the life of her, Helen couldn't remember Cassandra ever stammering before, and she wondered if Cassandra had foreseen something about her and Orion going out. Maybe it was too dangerous for them to leave the Delos compound at all? Then Helen remembered that Cassandra hadn't made a single prophecy in days. *Since Halloween*, Helen thought.

Before Helen could ask her if this was normal, Cassandra spun round and glided down the hallway.

'Speaking of Hector,' Orion said, completely unfazed by Cassandra's odd behaviour, 'I should probably go get him. He can't be wandering around right now when he's supposed to be lying low, no matter how lovesick he is.'

'Yeah,' Helen mumbled, still thinking about Cassandra. If Orion could see hearts, how could he not see how different she was around him? Helen decided that she had to be imagining it.

'Are you OK?' Orion asked, touching her arm gently. His concern for her only proved her point. If Orion didn't notice it, then there couldn't be anything going on inside Cassandra – she was just a strange girl, and Helen must have misinterpreted what she saw.

'Yeah. I guess.' She waved her hand, dismissing her thoughts and smiling at him. 'Go get Hector. Drag that numbskull back if you have to.'

'He's probably in the ocean. He likes to swim when he's upset. Shouldn't take me long,' he said, and then studied her closely. 'Are you sure you're going to be OK?'

'Yeah. Don't worry about me.'

The corners of Orion's mouth turned up in the faintest of smiles. 'Easier said than done.' He leaned across the few inches separating them and brushed his lips across hers. 'I'll be back soon,' he whispered, and turned to leave before Helen even had a chance to kiss him back.

Matt could feel his warriors getting closer. They were tied to each other by blood oaths and could sense one another, as if they were all different limbs of the same body.

Sometime over the next few days his troops would arrive on this beach in ships, echoing the journey they had made thousands of years before to claim Helen of Troy. Matt looked for their approaching mast from the beach. The remnants of this once-great army had begun their journey the moment the dagger had fallen into the chosen hand, but, scattered as they were to all parts of the globe, it would take time for them to reach this shore.

Finally, after so many millennia, they were to be reunited with their newly reborn master. And with the dagger on which they had all pledged their lives.

It was because of the dagger, the magical gift of silver-footed Thetis to her only son, that they were all fated to live until they died in battle for his honour and glory.

They had been unlucky.

Their nearly indestructible master had died before they had had the chance to die for him, but their oaths still bound them. They could not die of old age, or of sickness, or of broken hearts, no matter how horribly the world treated them. They could only die in battle, and most of them had. None but the strongest were left – those most committed to their master and their master's pledge to kill the Tyrant.

Just thirty-three in all.

But Matt knew that thirty-three 3,300-year-old Myrmidons were enough to set the world on fire.

CHAPTER FIVE

Helen stood over her father and watched him breathe. Every rise and fall of his chest was long and laboured. The twins assured her that he had no injuries left for them to heal – but for some reason Jerry just wasn't able to stay conscious. It was as if he were very tired. It might be that he only needed to rest, they said, but if that were the case it didn't make sense to Helen that her father wasn't physically able to stay awake for more than a few moments at a time.

Helen tried to pin down what she was feeling, but when she asked herself how she felt about the fact that her father was still in such bad shape, and that no one knew what to do about it, her mind started to wander.

Distracting thoughts kept popping up – like how Luis and his kids were doing after being hurt by Automedon, how the store had held up since the riot and whether or not anyone had checked on her father's house to make sure it wasn't vandalized. All of these thoughts were logical enough, but they were not the things she should be thinking when her father was barely clinging to life.

She sat down in the armchair that was pulled up to the side of her father's bed and wondered what was wrong with her. How could she be so distracted at a time like this? She noticed her leg was bouncing up and down and put a hand on her knee to keep it still, but it didn't work. About to jump out of her skin, Helen stood up and started pacing.

'A few more steps and you'll wear a hole in the floor,' Lucas said softly from the doorway. Helen spun and faced him, clenching her fists. She wasn't in the mood for an emotional encounter, and for once Helen wished Lucas would just go away.

Leaning against the frame, Lucas's eyes skipped over her. He gave her a half smile, gesturing over his shoulder with his head.

'Come on,' he said, his voice clipped.

'Where?' Helen challenged. She crossed her arms and glared at him.

'Down to the cage,' he fired back, not at all intimidated by the look she gave him. Lucas pushed himself off the door frame and crossed to Helen slowly. When he got to her, he took her wrists, unwound her tight arms, and parted them. He stepped closer, until he was nearly up against her. 'You need to hit something.'

Helen opened her mouth to argue and immediately shut it again. Lucas was right. Seeing her father so ill made her feel helpless and useless. She had got accustomed to being the one who had to fight all the tough fights, but she wasn't the one caught up in this battle. Her father was, and there was nothing she could do to help him.

She needed to pummel something or someone – anything to release the infuriating tension she felt sitting on the sidelines while her father struggled. And Lucas knew that because he knew her. Helen let her arms relax. Her hips swayed slightly toward him, like a challenge.

'Let's go,' she said, her voice humming deep in her chest.

A muscle in his jaw pumped as Lucas clenched his teeth. Heat rolled off his skin like his blood was boiling. Helen could smell him – baking bread and new snow, hot and cold, sunshine and darkness – all opposites that should cancel each other out, but that somehow managed to live next to each other inside Lucas. Helen shut her eyes and breathed him in shamelessly.

Lucas pulled away. He yanked hard on her arm and snapped her out of the spell. It really ticked her off when he bossed her around like that, and she had no doubt he knew it too. She wrenched her wrist out of his grip and shoved him towards the stairs. His back stiff in front of her, Helen stormed after Lucas as he led her through the house and down to the fight cage.

As soon as they reached the steps to the basement level, they started stripping off clothes. No shoes, no jewellery, no belts, no hard or sharp objects of any kind were allowed in the cage, but they couldn't be bothered to put on softer gear to replace what they shucked off so frantically. Every time Helen removed another article of clothing, all she could think about was how much she wanted to tear into him.

The jumble of 'other' Helens inside her head made it worse. In most of her memories, he'd been forbidden to her, dangling just out of her reach over and over again. She was so frustrated she didn't need the Furies to want to kill him any more. And she could tell by the sound of ripping fabric as he wrenched his shirt off, and the slap of leather as he yanked his belt from the loops on his jeans, that Lucas was just as fed up with their impossible situation as she was.

By the time they got to the ring, they were so worked up they'd barely shut the door of the cage before they began to whale on each other.

Helen started it. She threw her right and punched Lucas in the face. At the last second he deflected most of the blow and swept her legs out from under her, trying to bring the fight immediately to the floor, which was his speciality.

She rolled and leapt up before he could capture her under him, taking another swing at him as she did so. He brought his arms up to block, ate a few more shots as he pulled her into a clinch and then pushed Helen back against the chain-link fence. He leaned his shoulder into her sternum, pressing the air out of her lungs as he tied up her hands.

'What did you and Orion talk about in the hall after breakfast?' he hissed into her ear.

'Who said we were talking?' She said it on purpose to get to him, and it worked. A pained look crossed his face, and Helen took the opportunity to break one of her wrists from his hold and hit him in the gut.

Lucas grunted and lunged down to take her leg out. He slammed Helen into the mat and, wrenching her thighs apart, he took position between them. She pulled guard under him – wrapping her legs tightly round his waist and squeezing hard to cut off his air.

'I heard you *talking*,' he growled through gritted teeth. He was using all his strength to try to pin her arms down. 'And it's kinda hard to talk when your tongue's in someone else's mouth.'

She glared up at him, not answering his question.

'Tell me what you told him, Helen!' he yelled into her face.

If this were an MMA fight, the guy on top would start hammering on the guy under him in a move called 'ground and pound'. But Lucas didn't hit her. In fact, Helen realized that although his cheek was bruised, and he was bleeding from a cut over his eye, he hadn't taken one swing at her. He was doing this for her, so she could work out her frustration. He was trying to help her.

When she realized this, Helen's anger evaporated and she went still. She didn't need to be able to see through his chest to know how much he loved her. He was constantly proving it by how much of her crap he was willing to take.

'I can see emotions, like someone from the House of Rome can, and I have no idea why,' she admitted with an exasperated sigh. Lucas stared down at her with a startled look as she struggled to continue. 'And I didn't tell Orion this, but I think I can control other people's hearts too.'

'Keep going,' he said when she paused again.

'I made the police officer who was guarding Andy let us into her room – and he didn't even ask us our names. At first, I just thought it was the whole "face that launched a thousand ships" thing. It happens sometimes with men. But the more I think about it, the more I'm convinced that wasn't it. I did something to his heart. It feels wrong to do that to someone.'

'Huh.' Lucas released her slowly and sat back on his heels, frowning.

Helen sat up and rubbed her sore wrists, waiting for him to be ready to share what was going on in his head.

'Look at me,' he said suddenly, leaning close and locking eyes with her. 'You're the only girl I've ever kissed.'

'Liar,' Helen said so fast she practically cut him off. He flashed a grin at her and quickly dropped it again, gazing at her levelly.

'How do you know I'm lying?'

'Apart from the fact that I'm pretty sure you've done a heck of a lot more than just kiss other girls? Something was wrong in your voice, I guess. Also a feeling, like . . .'

'Like you'd lost something. And you needed to find it.' She nodded, agreeing with him. He stared at her for a moment, blank-faced. 'You're a Falsefinder, Helen. You can hear lies.'

'But how?'

'Our blood,' he said, nodding his head as if he could hear the truth in his own words. 'When you, Orion and I became blood brothers, you absorbed some of our talents through our blood. I haven't noticed any new talents in myself, and I don't think Orion has either or he'd have mentioned it while we were healing together. But apparently you got something from both of us. You took Orion's talent to control hearts, and my talent to recognize lies.' He cocked his head to the side. 'Maybe you took even more than that,' he whispered to himself, still mulling it over. Helen stared at him.

'Why? Why is this happening to me?' she asked fearfully. 'The last thing I need is more power.'

'I don't know yet. But I'll figure it out,' he promised.

'You figure out *everything*,' she murmured, adoring him.

'You figured out which river the Furies needed to drink from. Not me.'

'Yeah, but you helped. You always do.' Hating the inches of cold air between them, she slid closer to him, painfully aware that they were both in their underwear.

His bare shoulders curved toward her, and his chin

tilted down to come level with her mouth. With her new talent, Helen could see gold clouds spilling out of his skin in puffy gusts and a warm fire flickering low in his belly. Lucas reached out for her, his lips parting, eyes closing.

He stopped. The glorious golden haze that was enveloping them froze in mid-air, solidified and dropped to the ground in shards. Lucas's bright blue eyes darkened as the shadow slipped in and snuffed out his inner light.

'That's why you should come and talk to me when you're confused, Helen,' Lucas said heavily, and pulled back. 'No matter what happens between you and Orion, I'll always be here to help you work out your problems. Even if it means I have to get my ass kicked first.' He turned away, wiping blood out of his eye and flicking it on to the mat.

'Does that hurt?' Helen swallowed and stopped herself from reaching out and touching his wound – stopped herself from leaning forward and throwing her arms round him, really.

'No,' he replied, shaking his head. 'Not compared to the rest of it.'

Helen stayed in the ring long after Lucas left. She started to get cold sitting on the mat in nothing but her skivvies, and eventually forced herself to stand up and find her clothes. Jeans in one hand, she was hunting around for her shirt when she heard the door open.

'Why are you practically naked?' Hector yelled from the top of stairs.

Helen didn't even bother to jump or get embarrassed. It was only Hector, coming back at just the wrong moment to mess with her, as usual. She finally understood her contentious but still deeply caring relationship with Hector. It wasn't exactly like brother and sister, and it never had been.

She'd been *married* to the guy once, and from the snippets that Helen could vaguely recall, neither of them had been too happy about that fact even though they had tried their best to make it work. Sort of like being permanently handcuffed to someone that you love, but who also really annoys you.

'Lucas and I had a fight,' Helen said, figuring it was easier to just say it than make him wheedle it out of her. Hector came down the stairs while Helen yanked on her jeans.

'Uh-huh. And your clothes got so sick of all the bitching and moaning they jumped off your body and ran away?'

Helen had to laugh at that one. 'No. We finally decided to smack each other around physically instead of just emotionally for a change.' She motioned to the ring with her chin while she zipped.

'Funny, but you don't look beat up. *Tousled*, yeah. Beat up? No,' he said, raising an eyebrow and holding out her dark, V-neck sweater. She ignored his suggestive comment. Helen took her warm top and gladly pulled it on, and then looked at Hector carefully.

'How're you doing?' she asked pointedly.

Hector shrugged and turned away, heading towards one of the heavy bags. 'I'm fine. I don't know why you and Orion are all worked up about Andy.'

'You are so full of it,' Helen snipped, but not unkindly, as she followed him. She stood on the other side of the bag and held it steady so he could hit. 'You're hiding down here. Same as me.'

Hector started to jab the bag, giving it halfhearted whacks at best. He slowly amped up the intensity. Moving her feet as he worked his way through a few combinations, Helen watched Hector's face harden and take on the set of a real fighter.

No, more than that, she thought. *He's a warrior, right out of some legend.*

As soon as that thought crossed her mind, she saw his demeanor lose all its ferocity, and something vulnerable and sad moved in and stilled his restless body.

'She can't stand the sight of me, Helen. The one girl, the only girl who's ever really shook me up – and I horrify her.' He dropped his fists and leaned into the bag, facing Helen. 'I could take it if she thought I was an idiot or a pig. Eventually, I'd prove to her I wasn't. But fear?' He shook his head. 'I've got no chance. I can't chase her because that's what *he* did. The only thing I can do is stay away from her, like she told me to. The problem is . . . I don't know if I can do that.'

'Yeah, I know what you mean,' Helen said sadly, hugging the other side of the bag.

'Oh, the irony. Right?' he joked, and then frowned suddenly. 'But you've got other possibilities.'

'And you don't?' Helen laughed. 'Or is it just that you've already slept with every other hot girl in the world, and there's no one left?'

'I'm serious,' Hector said, no longer smiling. 'Do you feel anything for Orion, or is it like you and Matt? He's too much of a pal to you?'

'No, that's definitely not it.' She thought about what Morpheus had revealed to her – that in some ways she might want Orion even more than she wanted Lucas. 'I'm really attracted to Orion.'

'And do you care about him?'

'A lot.'

'Then commit yourself to him.' Hector regarded Helen with complete candour. 'They're both waiting for you to make a choice. And none of you are going to move on until you do. *You*, Helen. You have to make this choice.'

Helen wanted to shout 'Lucas,' but she pictured the disgusted look that she knew Hector would give her for preferring her cousin over Orion, and swallowed Lucas's name. 'I have,' she said with more conviction than she felt. 'I have,' she repeated.

Hector smirked at her. 'The first time you said, "I have" was pretty believable. The second? Not so much.'

'What am I going to do?' she groaned in response, hitting her forehead against the bag. 'I feel like a ping-pong ball.'

'I think we both need to get out of here and do something useful.' He caught her round the neck in a playful headlock and led her towards the stairs. 'Come on, Princess. Let's go see if your father's store is still standing.'

Hector and Helen loaded some spare lumber from the shed, a tool kit and a box of nails into the back of Hector's truck. After a brief argument about whether or not Hector should take the chance of being seen, it became apparent that if he didn't get out of the house that currently sheltered Andy he was going to run screaming through the streets anyway, so Helen reluctantly agreed. She put her foot down about who drove, though. Helen took the wheel for the trip past her house to make sure it was OK, and then on to the News Store while Hector hid in the back.

Hector stayed out of sight inside the store, sweeping up glass and debris left over from the riot, while Helen took the ladder from the storeroom out to the front and began nailing boards over the broken windows. It was depressing work. Every time she looked around, Helen was reminded that the store could be rebuilt, but it would never be the same again. Not really. As she climbed a ladder and started boarding up the smashed front windows, Helen realized that some things stay a little bit broken forever – even after they've been fixed.

Lost in her thoughts, Helen didn't notice that someone had come up behind her on the sidewalk.

'You know what? If that board was any more crooked, it'd come back round the other way and be straight as an arrow,' Orion said from the ground behind her, like he was in awe of how rotten a job she'd done. 'Are you drunk?'

Helen's shoulders started shaking with laughter. 'No! I've never done this before!'

'Apparently.' He grinned up at her and motioned for her to come down off the ladder. Laughing, she climbed down and stood next to him. 'Still got both your thumbs?' he asked, inspecting her hands. He took the hammer away from her like it might bite her. 'Better give this to the professional.'

'Professional, huh?' Helen didn't doubt it. She'd taken a peek at his driver's licence when she'd accidentally stolen his jacket and wallet, and she knew that he was cleared to operate heavy machinery.

'I've worked a couple of construction sites. Built some houses,' he said, a cagey smile on his face, like he'd done more than just that.

'Jewellery maker, carpenter . . . you're a real jack-of-all-trades,' she said, smiling up at him.

'Yeah. Of all trades that pay jack,' he added with a shy chuckle.

'Hey, you're a son of Aphrodite. You could have taken the easy way out. Puckered up those pretty lips for some rich woman and made her fall so madly in love with you she just *had* to give you a diamond mine or something.' Helen grinned up at him, loving how he always downplayed his talents – and not just the Scion ones. 'But you didn't. You work for your money.'

'All five dollars of it,' he said, rolling his eyes.

'An honest buck may not buy any more groceries than a dishonest one, but it'll always be worth more. Especially to me,' she replied seriously. He was a self-made man, just like her dad, and she respected that quality in him the most because his dignity was something he earned, not something he was born with.

'Hey, Orion? Put some pants on, toss her over your shoulder and carry her off like a man, for the love of Pete!' Hector hollered from inside. Orion cringed and shared a pained look with Helen.

'The caveman approach,' he whispered to Helen conspiratorially. 'Not really my style.'

'Ah, Hector. Our loveable lug,' Helen replied quietly. Their heads leaned close as they shared a muffled chuckle.

'Kiss. Kiss. Kiss,' Hector chanted, peeking at them between the misaligned slats over the broken window.

'Can I bring you on *all* of my dates?' Orion asked Hector, clapping his hands together in mock excitement.

'Sure, buddy! I'll walk you through the whole thing,' Hector replied with a wicked grin. 'First, you take the girl and grab her by the . . .'

'And this is exactly why I'm so glad testosterone isn't contagious,' Helen said loudly, cutting Hector off. She shoved Orion up the ladder to fix the mess she'd made, and went inside to help Hector finish cleaning up.

Somehow, between all the horsing around, they managed to get the whole store boarded up, swept and emptied of all the rotting perishables. Every now and again Helen would run across something personal amidst the smashed debris – an ill-shaped macaroni 'I LOVE MY DADDY' sculpture she'd made in elementary school, a butt-ugly, heavy-as-a-horseshoe pot she'd made for Kate when she was trying to learn how to throw clay freshman year and a bunch of second-place trophies from running track.

Worst of all were the photos. It killed her to see the broken frames and the smashed glass that nicked the pictures, ruining them. Some of the shots had been hanging in the store since she was a little girl. She'd seen them every day and, as she tossed most of them in the garbage, she was all-too aware that she'd never see them again.

Each time Helen came across one of these emotionally charged items, she noticed that either Hector or Orion would crack a joke or do something goofy to snap her out of it. She knew what they were up to, but that only made their lame attempts to cheer her up all the more touching.

They knew it wasn't really about losing a bunch of stuff. When Orion and Hector were goofing off to distract her, she couldn't think too much about what was really bothering her – that her father didn't seem to be getting better. Losing the pictures, the macaroni sculpture, and the hideous attempt at pottery were nothing compared to the fear she felt when she pictured her father lying unconscious in a bed. Why couldn't he wake up?

She wanted to say something to them both, to thank them for helping her get through this, but she knew enough about these two guys to keep her mouth shut. Hector would only tease her if she got all sincere on him, and Orion already knew how grateful she was because he could see right through her – literally. So Helen mentally filed away the hours they spent digging through her mugged childhood, knowing that she could never truly repay them for what they did for her.

'So . . . Hector's going to take the truck back,' Orion said, interrupting Helen's sad thoughts. 'By himself.'

'Huh?' Helen said blankly. 'No. Hector shouldn't drive. He can't be seen.'

'I won't be. It's too dark now. No one will be able to recognize me,' Hector said. 'And I can blur myself a bit if I hit oncoming lights – which I probably won't.'

Helen looked around and noticed that he was right. At some point when she wasn't paying attention, the sun had set. It was nighttime, and no one was on the streets to begin with. Not many people had ventured out of their houses since the riots. Nantucket Island had been like a ghost town for days now.

'OK, I guess you're right. Thanks for helping me out today,' Helen said to Hector, giving him a hug. She stopped herself before she got all mushy and said something he would find unforgivably sentimental.

'Have fun tonight, Princess.' Hector replied, his voice uncommonly soft as he released her. He looked at Orion and nodded once, and then turned to leave without one joke or snide remark.

Helen took Orion's hand shyly, knowing that Hector had just given them the chaperone's equivalent of a Hergie hall pass. No matter what the two of them did that night, they could be assured that Hector wouldn't put them in detention for it.

'So,' she said, looking up at Orion. Her throat was suddenly dry and she swallowed. 'You said you wanted to show me something?'

'Yeah,' he replied, biting his lower lip like he was regretting it. 'You've had a rough day, though. And what I want to show you isn't exactly uplifting.'

'Well, now you *have* to show me,' Helen said, throwing an arm out wide to include the whole store. 'I can't be the only one whose life is a total bummer.'

Orion laughed, flashing his bright, sharp teeth. He tugged Helen close, holding her against his chest. The laugh quickly disappeared and he kissed her temple, barely brushing her brow with his lower lip as his mood changed. A part of Helen was aware that he had pulled her close for two reasons. The first was that he sincerely wanted to hold her, but mostly he was dong it so she couldn't see what was going on inside his heart.

'Trust me. You aren't the only one whose life is a total bummer,' he whispered unevenly.

'So show me.' Helen pulled back and looked him in the eye. 'We've been to hell and back together, Orion. What could be harder to deal with than that?'

The corners of Orion's lovely mouth turned up in a wistful smile. 'Family,' he replied. Helen remembered how sad Orion got every time someone mentioned his father, Daedalus. She knew there was a deep, dark story there.

'Ah. Your father.'

'No,' he said, releasing her and looking away anxiously. 'Maybe this is a bad idea.'

'Hey, have you ever been flying?' she asked quickly. Orion gave her a puzzled look, like he was totally thrown, which was exactly Helen's intention. 'Not in a plane, I mean,' she clarified. 'Have you ever flown like I do?'

'No. Never.'

'Want to?'

'This is the craziest effing thing I've ever felt!' Orion giggled.

'Shhh,' Helen admonished, eyes closed. 'Quit moving

around. You're like, *three* of Claire.' She was trying not to smile at the sound of utter glee in Orion's voice, but he was making that almost impossible. He was adorable when he got excited. She needed to distract him so she could focus. 'Is anyone coming?'

Orion took a moment to look up and down the alley behind the News Store where they were standing with their arms around each other. 'We're good,' he said.

Helen felt his breath on her forehead as he returned his gaze to her down-tilted head and closed eyes. It was warm and sweet, and it skipped a bit as he let it out in excitement. She nearly had the full mass of him in her mind – the exact proportion of skin, blood and bone that was perpetually falling towards the centre of the Earth. She reached out with that other sense of hers, the thing that released gravity, and enlarged it until it slipped around Orion's big body.

'That tickles!' he gasped, his arms round her waist squeezing her tight.

'Shhh!' she repeated, concentrating hard. And then she felt it. His body suddenly clicked into place in her mind. 'Gotcha,' she whispered triumphantly.

Releasing his gravity was effortless once she had the shape and weight of him figured out. She opened her eyes so she could watch Orion's face as they soared up into the air and hovered among clouds that glowed white-violet with starlight. Orion had one of those faces that constantly surprised her. Just when she thought she was getting accustomed to how blindingly beautiful he was, she'd see a new expression on his face, and a huge part of her nervous system would seize up.

'So. Where are we going?' she asked him, her voice steadier than she thought it'd be. 'You said you wanted to show me something.'

He tore his eyes away from the view and regarded her, his face falling. 'Helen,' he started to say, dismayed.

'No, I'm serious, Orion,' she interrupted firmly. 'You agree to come fly with me even though you know I've only tried this with a passenger once before, but you won't tell me your big secret? So – you trust me with your life, but not your past?'

'That's not it,' he said, and then stopped to struggle with his thoughts.

'Like I'd think less of you because of what you've been through? How judgmental do you think I am?'

'No! It's not about what you'll think. Least, not entirely,' he said, the words half choking him. 'It hurts *me* to go back there.'

'And it will keep on hurting you as long as you keep it hidden,' Helen said in a softer tone. 'I know who you are, Orion. And maybe the process it took to make you wasn't the prettiest thing to watch, but trust me.' She ducked her head down, angling her face under his so he had to look at her. 'The result is spectacular.'

He chuckled quietly, blushing a bit, and then grew serious again as he thought it over.

'Besides,' she continued, grinning determinedly at him. 'You know I'll never let you back down on the ground until I get what I want.'

'OK, you win . . . as usual,' he groaned. 'Head north.'

'And where am I taking us?' Helen asked enthusiastically.

'Newfoundland. Where I was born.'

From the detached way Orion named his place of origin, Helen got the distinct feeling that he wasn't taking her to a place that he considered a home. She didn't try to distract him or make a joke, like she normally would when she saw him fall into one of his melancholic moods. Instead, she focused on flying as fast as she dared with a passenger.

After only a few minutes and a few course adjustments by Orion, they were hovering over a foamy, storm-bitten hunk of rock at the edge of the frigid Atlantic Ocean.

Clinging to the top of a high, spindly promontory crouched a tiny, nearly windowless cottage. It was a dark night. Fog rolled in off the ocean and blotted out the moonlight. Barely discernable, the cottage was lit from the inside by a single light.

Orion sighed heavily and nodded, like he was taking responsibility for an unfortunate act of vandalism. 'That's it. That's where my parents live.'

'Your parents?' Helen repeated, confused. 'But I thought your mother was dead. Did your dad remarry?'

'You'll see,' was all he'd say, shaking his head.

Orion directed her to land them just outside the circle of light cast around the one semi-large picture window on the ground floor.

Careful to remain in the shadows, Helen glanced inside. The first thing she saw was a big man sitting in an armchair, reading a book. He wore faded jeans, a tight black T-shirt, and he had black hair that was shot through with premature silver at the temples. He was older, maybe mid-forties, but still very handsome and incredibly fit. The sharp, aquiline angles of his face and the golden tan that warmed his olive skin reminded her of Lucas. Even the shape of his hand as it gripped the spine of the book was hauntingly familiar. It disturbed Helen to see this other, older man with Lucas's hands.

Helen had heard it mentioned several times by the family that Lucas looked like a son of Poseidon. Based on the striking resemblance, Helen knew she had to be looking at Daedalus, Head of the House of Athens, the direct descendent of Poseidon, and Orion's father.

The second thing Helen saw was her own mother, Daphne, fast asleep on the couch across from him.

CHAPTER SIX

Helen backed away from the window. There was a squeezing feeling in her throat, and her feet were bumbling over the uneven ground with shock. Orion reached out for her, but she threw his hands off blindly. Undeterred, Orion reached for her again and clamped a hand over her mouth when he'd captured her.

'Take it easy! It's not what you think,' he hissed in her ear.

He led them both away from the house, and as far back across the top of the promontory as he dared without shoving both of them off the cliff before he continued.

'Daphne helps my father handle my mother when she has one of her spells. She must have had one tonight, probably because my dad has to go to the meeting of the Houses. My mom hates all the Houses, even her own.' He paused in the middle of his rushed explanation, looking to see if Helen was keeping up. 'There was a Scion war before we were born,' he said.

Still muffled behind Orion's hand, Helen relaxed

her muscles and nodded, both in answer to his tacit question about the war and to let him know that she wasn't going to barge into the house or start yelling. He relaxed his grip on her mouth but kept her close to him. Helen had known that there had been some sort of final confrontation between the Scion Houses about twenty years ago, and that it had been a bloodbath – the End Times – or so it had seemed to them.

'My mom was Head of the House of Rome, and she killed a lot of people. The war really messed her up. And now my mother doesn't deal well with any mention of the Houses,' he tried to continue, but had to stop there, gritting his teeth to control his voice. 'She doesn't deal well with anything, actually. She's *sick*, Helen.'

Helen knew that Scions only get sick in one way. Orion was trying to tell her as gently as he could that his mother, Leda, was insane.

Based on the fact that Daedalus needed Daphne to help him control Leda, Helen knew Leda was not only strong, but that she had to be the kind of insane that was truly dangerous to be around. The house they lived in was miles away from anyone, as far away from civilization as they could get without tipping into the sea. Helen could only imagine the amount of screaming that must accompany the 'spells' as Orion had called them. She wondered what it was like for him to have grown up with all that as a small boy.

Orion released Helen gently and turned away from

her as he swiped the back of his hand across his face. Helen reached forward and took his other hand, cradling it close to her chest as he collected himself. She studied him carefully, waiting until he turned back to her and nodded, letting her know that he had it together again, and then he led her back toward the house.

'You said she was dead,' Helen whispered. Orion shook his head.

'You assumed she was dead when I told you I was the Head of the House of Rome, but death isn't the only way a House gets a new Head.' He looked away. 'I didn't know you well enough then. I was too ashamed to tell you . . .'

Helen nodded, stopping him. He didn't need to explain himself to her. 'It's OK,' she said quietly.

Another light switched on inside the house, and both Helen and Orion turned their heads sharply to look in the window.

Helen saw a frantic woman with long chestnut hair descend the stairs in a nightgown. Barefoot and mussed from sleep, her dishevelled state only added to her appeal. She was older, in her forties, but still shaped like a pin-up girl. Her light reddish-brown hair danced around her in a cloud of fat, silky curls that take most woman hours with a blow-dryer and a curling iron to achieve. They were Orion's curls, and the long, shapely arc of her muscled limbs had the same balance, the same perfect proportions as his did.

Half bursting out of her nightgown in all the right

ways even though she was obviously oblivious to this fact, Helen guessed that this woman would probably still look seductive even if she'd fallen ass over teakettle down the steps. She was a smaller female version of Orion, and as such she was the perfect temptation for the opposite sex. Everything about her screamed that this woman was Leda, a daughter of Aphrodite, and Orion's mother.

'He's here!' she rasped, running to the window. Orion pulled Helen away from the circle of light just as Daedalus jumped up from his seat and pulled Leda back before she could get a good look outside. Even from a distance, Helen could see the feral look on her face. Her eyes were opened so wide they were showing the whites, and they were rolling around like a spooked horse's. Helen shuddered involuntarily.

'There's no one here, love,' Daedalus said in a weary voice, taking Leda's shoulders and turning her away from the window.

'Adonis! I can *smell* you out there!' the hysterical woman shrieked, viciously fighting her husband to get away. 'I won't let you kill my baby!'

Daphne was up now and grabbing Daedalus by the shoulders so they formed a cage around Leda with their bodies. They pressed into her from opposite sides, using their weight to restrain her arms and keep her from tearing at her hair and face. Helen could tell by the gentle, but almost clinical way they went about this, that Daedalus and Daphne had done it many times before.

'I'll kill you if you try to hurt my baby!' Leda howled, sobbing now, her voice shredding with pure crazy. 'I'll kill you myself!'

'Adonis is dead, Leda! Your brother is dead!' Daphne shouted over Leda until the distraught woman stopped bucking and started to relax.

'My baby brother,' Leda said, calmed momentarily by her confusion. 'My baby. My baby brother. But which is which? I know I killed one of them. Who did I choose?'

Leda started rocking back and forth, quietly chanting the words, 'My baby. My baby brother,' over and over as Daedalus and Daphne tried to soothe her. Each time she repeated this pitiful mantra, her volume raised another notch until she was screaming.

'Get me out of here, Helen,' Orion said in a shaky whisper. Helen looked at him and saw tears streaming silently down his face.

She immediately wrapped her arms round him and they shot into the air, leaving behind the sound of Leda's inconsolable wailing. Orion buried his face in Helen's neck. She could feel his hot tears streaming across her skin and quickly turning cold in the thinning air as they gained altitude.

Shivering, they hovered high over the ocean, clinging to each other. Orion didn't make any noise. After what Helen guessed was years of practice, he'd got good at silencing the sound of his own crying until there was nothing – not even the flutter of his diaphragm – just the fast and deep throbbing of his heartbeat. Helen pulled him closer and flew him away from this nightmare, even though she knew she'd never get him far enough away to make it any better.

Heading south along the coast, she brought them to a pretty little beach somewhere around Cape Ann in Massachusetts and lowered them to the ground. They sat next to each other on the sand, him staring out at the water and her staring at his profile.

'They were close. Adonis and my mother,' he said finally. 'They loved each other very much – until she fell in love with my father. All the Houses, but especially the House of Rome, don't allow for Scions from different Houses to have children together out of fear that it will create the Tyrant.' Orion paused here and gestured to himself ruefully. 'When my mom got pregnant with me, Adonis came to kill me – and her, I guess, since she was still carrying me. But my mother killed him instead.'

Helen leaned against Orion's shoulder and looked out at the dark waves crashing on the beach. She'd figured it was something like that, but sensed there was more to the story. The dull colours crawling out of Orion's chest were heavy and leaden with guilt and regret.

'The worst part came later,' Orion continued in a strained voice. 'You know how the members in each House have certain physical characteristics? There's always some variation, like Lucas, Jason and Ariadne, who don't look like the other members of their House.

But, in general, Thebans are blond and look like Lucas's dad.' Helen nodded. 'Did you also know that every generation has a handful of *specific* characters who get repeated over and over? They are almost exact replicas of the main characters who fought at Troy. As soon as one of these main characters die, another is born to take his or her place.'

'No, I didn't know that.' Helen bit her lip, processing this. 'I don't think the Delos family knows this, either, or they would have explained it to me.'

'The House of Athens figured this out a long time ago, but the House of Thebes may not have. The Thebans have always had a lot of variation in their line, and probably haven't been able to spot the pattern yet. Your House, the House of Atreus is the only exception. You hand down the Helen archetype mother to daughter, but for the rest of us, an exact look-alike can only happen if a main character dies first.'

'Like the Fates have to recast the play with a baby when one of the lead characters dies,' Helen said musingly. 'You look exactly like Aeneas, you know.'

'Yeah, I remember Automedon calling me "General Aeneas" right after you electrocuted him,' he said, smiling a little at the memory. His face scrunched up momentarily. 'Wait. How could you know what Aeneas looked like?'

'Long story,' Helen said, waving a dismissive hand. 'Keep going with yours first.'

'Well, apart from Aeneas, there's someone else I look like exactly.'

'Your uncle Adonis.' Helen didn't even have to mull that one over. She knew how cruel the Fates were, and for some reason they seemed to be particularly cruel to Orion. Like they had it in for him.

As soon as she thought this, she made a guess at the reason why. Aeneas was one of the only male survivors of Troy. He'd *escaped* fate. Somehow, this one character had got away from his destiny. Helen wondered how in the world anyone could do that, but she put that thought on the back burner as Orion continued.

'It was fine while I was still a baby, but as soon as I got a little older my mother started confusing me with her brother.' He stopped and swallowed. 'She started to see me as an enemy. I haven't been able to go anywhere near her since I was eight. And my dad couldn't leave her alone for long. So he left me to fend for myself most of the time.'

Helen could hear the bitterness in his voice, even though he tried to tone it down. A thought occurred to her. She felt all the hairs on the back of her neck stand up and anger flushed hot under her skin. Her voice shook when she spoke. 'Did your mother give you those scars, Orion?'

'No,' he said sharply. 'My mother's cousin, Corvus. He didn't want me to succeed my mother when it became clear she was too far gone to lead any more. I was claimed by the House of Athens, and a lot of my cousins still don't think I should lead the House of Rome. Corvus came after me when I was eleven. He lost.'

Helen saw a dark fire burning inside Orion's chest. Black flames licked at his heart. *He killed his cousin*, she thought. Orion had only been eleven years old when he'd killed a man. Helen shook her head and decided to stick with a topic she could actually fathom at this point – his mother.

'Did your mom ever try to . . . you know . . . kill you?' Helen asked carefully. Orion only nodded, his eyes glued to the waves. Helen turned her head and looked back at the water with him.

'It was the scariest thing that's ever happened to me,' he admitted in a dead tone.

Helen wanted to ask him more about his scars and his cousin Corvus, but she knew from the numb look on his face that Orion had dug up enough painful memories for one night. Besides, she didn't know if she could bear to hear any more just then.

'You know what scares me?' she asked after a long silence. 'The ocean.'

Orion laughed softly. 'Not Tartarus?'

'Tartarus blows,' Helen agreed with a definite nod. 'But the ocean truly terrifies me.'

'And what about everything you just learned about me?' he asked quietly. 'Does that terrify you too?'

'No,' she replied. She thought about how Orion's father had left him to fend for himself. How this Corvus guy hunted him when he was just a kid, and how pretty much every second of his life he'd known that he would never get anything that resembled love from the people who were supposed to take care of him. 'It *really* pisses me off, though.'

They shared a comfortable silence, each of them thinking their own thoughts.

'Thank you,' Orion said after a long pause. He began untying his boots.

'What're you doing?' she asked, puzzled, as he kicked them off.

'First, I think it's pathetic that you grew up on an island and you're scared of the water,' he said, standing up and taking off his jacket. 'Second, I think it's time for both of us to stop being afraid.' He reached down to help her up off the sand. 'I'm going to teach you to swim.'

'Now? Wait,' she quibbled, tugging on his arm. 'I don't think I can do this.'

'Sure you can.' He grinned at her – back to his sweet, playful self again. 'Now take off your clothes.'

Helen laughed, but when he took off his shirt and she saw the scars on his chest, her laughter died away. After a brief moment she made up her mind and jumped to her feet. 'Why not?' she said, kicking off her shoes and pulling her shirt over her head. 'I killed a freaking Myrmidon. How bad can a shark be?'

'That's ma girl,' he said, shucking off his jeans. Helen did the same and immediately started shivering in the cold air.

'Am I going to die of hypothermia in there?'

'Not with me. That water will feel like a warm bath,' he promised, taking her hand. 'Ready?'

'I can't believe I'm doing this!' Helen screamed joyfully, and they ran towards the dark ocean. Right before Helen met the first wave she stopped dead, nearly yanking Orion's arm out of its socket. She danced up and down on her tiptoes. 'Nope. I can't do this!' she screamed.

The wave parted and went around her and Orion, like Moses and the Red Sea.

'Thanks,' she said, smiling at him with relief. 'I totally chickened out.' She noticed that his face was frozen and his eyes were wide.

'I didn't do this,' he said, watching the water flow back around them without touching their skin. '*You're* doing it.'

Helen stopped mentally shoving the water away and instead imagined the water touching her. The invisible envelope that held back the water collapsed and a wave rushed in, covering Helen and Orion up to their waists. She looked up at Orion with an apologetic face.

'Yeah . . . so I forgot to mention that I sort of absorbed some of your talents when the three of us became blood brothers,' she said tentatively. 'At least that's what Lucas thinks.'

'I'd say he's right,' Orion replied, giving Helen a funny look.

'The one thing he didn't figure out was *why*,' Helen said, biting her lower lip. 'Any theories?'

'About why you're crazy strong?' he asked distractedly. 'No idea. But I have a feeling the Fates are involved.'

'What?' she asked cautiously. 'Are you mad at me?'

'No. It's just that I have a talent that I wouldn't wish on anyone,' he said softly. Another wave pounded around them. 'Can you cause earthquakes, Helen?'

'I don't know. Where do you feel them?' Helen asked, knowing he would know what she meant. She felt lightning low in her belly. She felt gravity deep inside her individual cells at the smallest level and guessed that earthquakes had to be felt somewhere in the body like these other senses. Orion moved closer to her, his face serious.

'Here,' he said, brushing his hands up the inside of her bare thighs. 'Like riding a horse the size of a continent,' he added, his voice low. Helen put her hands on his shoulders, her knees suddenly weak.

The ground trembled.

Orion caught her before her legs gave out and pulled her tightly against him. 'That's a yes,' he whispered.

Helen ran her fingers across the scar on his chest, and then fanned her palm out to touch as much of him as she could at once. He lowered his head and kissed her, pulling her down with him beneath the next oncoming wave.

Helen didn't have a chance to freak out about being underwater – she was too intent on returning the kiss. She didn't even notice that she was breathing the water like it was air as she slid her hands across his shoulders and the back of his neck. The only thing that she could think was how amazing Orion felt. Amazing. But not right.

Orion pulled away suddenly. Helen opened her eyes and clearly saw the sad look on his face even though the water was dark. She knew she was making a mess of things. Her one chance to be happy with another guy – a guy who was pretty much perfect – and she was absolutely wrecking it. She reached for him again, desperately hoping to push past her ridiculous fixation on Lucas. If she was with Orion, really with him tonight, she hoped that maybe she would be able to leave Lucas behind.

Orion dodged her embrace, his jaw set. He took her hand firmly and kicked for the surface, towing her along behind him.

They had sunk deeper and drifted further out than Helen thought. She realized that she might be able to control the ocean now, but she still didn't know how to swim. It didn't matter. In a few powerful strokes Orion had them both back to shore. He didn't say a word on the way. As soon as they stood on sand, he dropped her hand and headed directly back up the beach to where they had left their clothes.

'Orion. I'm sorry, OK?' Helen called out, trailing behind him. He didn't even slow down. She scurried to keep up, but he only went faster. 'Will you just *wait*?'

'Why?' he said, spinning round. 'What about you and me is going to be different five minutes from now, or five years from now for that matter? I could wait my whole life for you, and you'd still be in love with Lucas.'

'But I love you too,' Helen stammered.

'I know you do,' he said heavily. 'But not like you love him.' Orion sat down on the sand. Helen stood over him, fretfully wringing her hands.

'Maybe it's not the same, but that doesn't mean that eventually . . .' Helen trailed off.

There was no 'eventually', and Helen knew it. Even after she'd touched the water from the River Lethe and couldn't remember her own name, she'd still remembered Lucas. She'd never get over him. Lucas was it for her.

Orion pulled her down next to him and sighed. 'My parents are like you and Lucas, you know. They love each other more than they love anyone or anything else in the world – more than they love me. My whole life I've wondered what it feels like to be loved like that. To be loved *more*.' He looked Helen in the eye, his gaze intent and hurting. 'I know you love me, Helen. But don't I deserve to be someone's first choice for a change?'

Tears burned in Helen's eyes. The look on Orion's face was exactly like the one she'd seen on Aeneas's face when his mother chose the other Helen over him. All his life, in every life he'd lived, Orion had been the runner-up to someone else.

'I can't think of anyone in the world who deserves to be loved – loved *more* – more than you,' Helen said, her voice breaking. 'I thought being with you would make me forget him. But that's just a nice way of saying I was using you.' She bent her head. 'I'm so sorry.'

Orion put his arm over her shoulder and pulled her close to him. 'Hey, I'm the one who kissed you. I put myself in this situation. And I ought to know better.'

'But I want to love you more,' she said slowly, afraid to continue. She steeled herself and pulled back to meet his eyes. 'You could *make* me love you more, couldn't you?'

'Yes,' he whispered. 'Until the next time you see Lucas. But you already know this. You didn't just fall in love with him once. You fall in love with him every time you look at him.'

'Then I'll stay away from him. Forever.'

He glanced away and bit his lower lip, debating it. 'But I'd always know,' he whispered. 'I'd always know that I forced you to love me, and that it isn't real. I think I'd rather never be loved than know that.'

Helen nodded, staring at her hands without seeing them. She wrapped her arms round his chest and let the tears come . . . for Orion, for herself, and for Lucas, but mainly because she was so sick of it all. She had power over the most magnificent forces on Earth, but she still didn't feel like she had power over the most important thing of all – her own heart.

Orion lay back on the sand and pulled her down on top of him. He banished the water soaking their skin and hair so they were immediately dry, and stared up at the stars while Helen cried a few frustrated tears. When she'd settled down, he piled their discarded clothes over them, still holding her on top of him to keep her off the cold sand. She was too tired to think straight any more.

'So are we friends?' he asked after a long silence.

'Doesn't seem enough, does it?' she said as sleep quickly set in and started to paralyse her. 'We're more than friends. We're brothers. Blood brothers.'

His chest shuddered with a little laugh under her cheek, and she felt him whisper 'brothers' to himself as he drifted off to sleep.

The last thing Helen thought before she drifted off after him was that she'd slept on a beach like this before with another boy. But this time there was no Helen-shaped dent for her to fit inside.

'Uncle?' Helen called out.

'I'm here, niece,' Hades replied kindly. Helen turned round and found him walking up the infinite beach in the Underworld – the one that never led to an ocean.

She smiled tentatively at him as he joined her. 'Thank you for coming. I have a lot of questions.' Her voice was quivering with uncertainly. 'When I'm sitting across from myself, and other people are calling me names like "Guinevere", I'm having a memory, not a dream, right?'

'Correct.'

'*How?*'

Hades's dark helmet glimmered. 'The dead have choices. They don't have to stay in the Underworld forever if they don't wish to. But in order to leave they must wash their memories away in the River Lethe, before they can be reborn.'

'And when I touched a few drops of that river water?' she asked, following up on a hunch.

'Life experiences are never annihilated. The river remembers. Your soul called to those memories in the water, and they joined you in this life. It's rare, but it happens sometimes,' he said, and then turned his cloaked head away. 'Why don't you clothe yourself?'

'Oh. Right,' she said. Embarrassed, she crossed her arms over her lacy bra. 'I don't know how.'

'Yes you do. Think, Helen.'

'I want to be wearing warm, clean clothes,' she said distinctly. Helen pictured a sturdy outfit, complete with the lined galoshes that she usually wore in the Underworld, and it instantly appeared on her body. Helen raised her eyes to the place behind the shadows where she guessed Hades's eyes would be. 'OK, first question. How can I do this? How can I control the Underworld?'

'Because you have a talent in common with me, and with Morpheus and Zeus, to name a few,' he said firmly. 'Each of us can make *one* world. I made Hades. Morpheus made the shadow lands. The Furies made the dry lands. Zeus made Olympus, and Tartarus created Tartarus aeons before any of us existed. And Tartarus left the boundaries of her land open for all who share in this power, although none of us have ever seen her.'

'But what has this got to do with me?' Helen blurted out, feeling like she was in way over her head. 'I've never made anything. I've never even made the honour roll.'

'You haven't made anything *yet*. But you will if you choose to,' he said with a small chuckle that was hauntingly familiar. 'There have been other Scions with this talent before. You call them Descenders, but that is not the correct name, really, as it only describes the allowance I made for Scions of your kind to be able to come to me for help. What help I can offer, at any rate,' he said, his voice heavy with regret. 'So far, I have failed you all.'

'My kind?' Helen's palms started to sweat. 'What *kind* am I?'

'You are a Worldbuilder, Helen. You have the power to sculpt a land for whomever you wish to enter it. A world of your own that abides entirely by your rules. Eternal youth. Fulfilment. Or eternal trials and suffering – whatever you think will serve best.'

A thin silence wreathed around them as Helen absorbed this.

'But . . . that's . . . just . . . terrible!' she stammered, the air knocked out of her lungs for a moment. 'Have you *seen* my pottery? I can't "sculpt" a new world – it'll be a disaster! Can't you find someone who can at least *draw* or something?'

'I'm sorry, Helen, but the Fates do not dole out this particular talent often.' Hades smiled before he grew serious again. 'In fact, there have only been two Scions before you who learned how to use the talent well enough to create their own lands, and even then those worlds only lasted a short while.'

'Who were they?'

'Morgan and Atlanta. One created Avalon, and the other Atlantis. Both their worlds dissolved into the mists or beneath the waves when their creators were defeated, but Scions remember those lands to this day. Especially Atlantis. They die for it still.'

'Wait. You're saying that Atlantis *doesn't* exist?'

'Not any more. Every Worldbuilder must be able to defend his or her lands against any challenger. Morgan and Atlanta both lost.'

Helen sat down on the seeping wet of the damp sand, her head in her hands. She'd shouldered a lot of responsibility because she'd had no other choice, but this was beyond her.

'No,' she said, shaking her head. 'I can't do this. I've done a lot, but this is too much.'

'And what's that?' Hades asked. 'What can't you do?'

Helen raised her head and regarded Hades with blank, desperate eyes. 'I can't go back to the rest of the Scions and tell them that all this murdering they've been doing so they could get to Atlantis has been for nothing!' Her voice took on a hysterical edge. 'What was all that crap from the Oracle about there being only one House left, and that "One House" being the key to Atlantis? They've been killing each other off for decades now, and you want me to go back to them and tell them it was all a lie, that there is no Atlantis? I can't do it!'

'It's not a lie. Just a misinterpretation of the prophecy,' Hades said calmly. She stared up at him, numb with shock.

'That's not good enough,' she replied in a surprisingly level voice. 'You need to tell me more.'

He sat down next to her on the sand, near enough that the shadows parted a bit so she could see the bright green of his eyes and a familiar beauty mark that hung like a dark tear high on the slope of one of his perfect cheekbones.

'The prophecy has been fulfilled. The Houses *are* one, Helen.' Hades took her hands between both of his, cradling them in warmth. 'You will raise Atlantis,

143

or Avalon, or Helena – whatever you wish to call it – and once your world is made you can decide who may enter, who must stay or go, and how each inhabitant experiences your land. It really is all up to you.'

'That's too much for one person,' Helen said, shaking her head like she could keep her responsibility at bay by rejecting it vehemently enough. 'It's too much power.'

Hades pushed back the cowl covering his head, removed the Helm of Darkness, and banished the shadows that clung to him. Staring back at Helen was a face she knew and loved dearly.

'There will be many Scions who will agree with that statement. Many beings, both mortal and immortal, will stop at nothing to keep you from claiming your true power.' Hades's bright green eyes were dimmed by sadness. 'If you build a world, many forces will try to rip it down. You and your Scion alliance will have to fight to defend it, and many of you may die, just as the gods want.'

'So I won't build a world.'

Hades took her hand. 'The Fates will make sure you have no choice.'

'No,' Helen said, shaking her head stubbornly. 'I refuse to believe three crones run my life. I won't build a world if the cost is that my friends and family must go to war. If I never build my own world, the gods won't challenge us, and no one has to fight.'

'You are brave and compassionate, as a Worldbuilder should be, and I am very proud of you. But a war is coming to your shores, niece,' Hades said sadly. 'You, like your namesake before you, must decide how to meet it.'

CHAPTER SEVEN

The shrill chirp of a cell phone parted Helen's reluctant eyelids. It was still dark out, and dawn was a long way off. Underneath her, Orion shook himself awake and reached for his jeans that were draped over Helen's back like a shawl. His fingers fumbling with cold and sleepiness, he finally managed to dig his cell phone out of his pocket and answer before it stopped ringing.

"Lo?' he grumbled, his voice still half asleep. 'Hey, bro. Yeah, she's safe. She's right here with me.'

Helen focused her hearing so she could listen in.

'Oh. Good,' Lucas said over the phone in a leaden tone. 'Can you both come back to my house? Cassandra is about to make a prophecy. She's been asking for you specifically, Orion. I didn't mean to interrupt anything.'

Helen's eyes met Orion's as they flared in understanding.

'We're on our way now. Luke, wait. . . .' Orion said, but it was too late. Lucas had hung up. Orion gave Helen a sheepish look. 'Sorry 'bout that.'

'Why? Maybe it's better if he thinks we slept together.

Maybe he'll . . .' She trailed off when she saw the doubtful look on Orion's face.

'He's not going to get over you, Helen. Doesn't matter how many men you spend the night with.'

Helen nodded, accepting this. Orion looked Helen over and changed the subject.

'Where'd you get the clothes?' he asked.

'I sort of called them into existence in the Underworld.'

'How long were you down there for?' he asked, starting to get concerned. 'What happened?'

Helen debated telling Orion everything that Hades told her. But after the night they'd just had, how was she supposed to tell Orion that his mother had fought in a war that drove her insane because of a misunderstood prophecy about a place that didn't even frigging exist any more? She didn't know if she would ever be able to tell him that. Instead, she just shrugged.

'Let me guess,' he said, turning away so he could shake the sand out of his jeans. 'It's another long story. You're going to have to start telling me some of these long stories of yours at some point, you know.'

'I know,' Helen said as she stood and brushed herself off. 'I just need some time to sort through it all first.'

Helen knew that Orion could see the confusion swirling around inside of her, but he didn't push her to confide in him. Instead, he dressed and then turned to her with his arms out.

'Can I get a lift?' he asked with a cheeky smile. Helen wrapped her arms round him and got them airborne, chuckling as she did so. Encouraged by her laughter, Orion kept joking. 'Captain? Are there drinks on this flight? I think I have a fake ID here somewhere.'

'A fake ID? Why would I serve you if you just admitted you were underage?'

'So there *are* drinks,' he persisted in a mock-serious tone. 'I'm not surprised. Look at all the pockets you conjured up for yourself.' He started frisking Helen, humorously cramming his hands into her cargo pants and digging around in her jacket like the nation's security depended on it. 'Of all the getups in the world you could have imagined for yourself and you pick something I'd go hunting in. Never knew you had an L.L.Bean fetish.'

'I was cold!' she said, nearly shouting with laughter.

'Cold, and apparently predisposed to pick flannel over fur.'

'I'm from New England. We like flannel.'

By this point, they were hovering over the Delos backyard, and Helen had to force herself to stop giggling so she could concentrate on landing. Serious again, she swung her feet under them.

'Ooo. Rubber boots. Very sexy,' Orion said. Helen lost it again at the last second, and they tumbled to the ground in a goofy heap.

'Are you OK?' Matt shouted in a worried voice.

'No, it's fine. We're good,' Helen shouted back to Matt,

who was standing up behind the door of his new car, the engine and headlights still on, like he had jumped out of the driver's seat a second ago.

Helen tried to untangle herself from Orion and look presentable, but he kept grabbing her by the knees and ankles so she couldn't stand.

'So *that's* what happened to the in-flight drinks,' Orion said musingly as he tipped Helen over for the third time. 'The captain drank them all. What a lush you are, Hamilton.'

Helen tried to plead her innocence, but since she couldn't catch her breath she never got a coherent sentence out in her own defence.

'Are you two finished yet?' Matt asked. 'What are you, nine?'

Helen and Orion stopped goofing around and settled down. 'Did Ariadne call you?' Helen asked Matt.

'Hector did,' he replied, helping Helen to her feet.

'Where's Claire?' she asked.

'Locked in her room. Her grandma wouldn't let her out of the house at this hour,' he replied with a chuckle. 'Any idea what Cassandra foresaw?'

'She asked for Orion. That's all we know,' Helen said. The three of them made their way to the garage and the side door that led into the kitchen.

'Huh,' Matt said, looking over at Orion with a creased forehead. 'Hector mentioned something about the Tyrant.'

Helen felt Orion stiffen and glanced over at his chest, trying to read his feelings. He was rolling them over too quickly for Helen to make any sense out of what she saw, but she could tell by the way he pinched his lips together that he was steeling himself for some kind of fight.

Helen made up her mind right then that if anyone tried to say anything negative about Orion she would walk out. His whole life he'd been treated like a bad omen, and he'd never done anything to deserve it. The words *born to bitterness* welled up in Helen's mind as she recalled some of the criteria for the Tyrant. After what she'd seen in Newfoundland, Helen knew how well that description fitted, but it still didn't make Orion the Tyrant.

Orion's only mistake had been being born to the wrong parents with the wrong talent. But apparently that was enough to make everyone shun him. And over what? Another misleading prophecy, just like the one about Atlantis? There was no way Orion was this Tyrant monster, and Helen intended to say so.

Before they even got inside, Helen could hear the haunting, multivoiced chorus of the Fates speaking through Cassandra. As she walked through the kitchen door a horrible screaming started. Three voices were tangled together into one, and Matt, Helen and Orion ran towards the source of it – the library where Castor and Pallas had their joint office. In half a second, all three of them were at the door.

'Nemesis sends her vessel to blind us! Darkness

comes!' wailed the chorus of the Fates, their voices filled with fear. 'He must be killed, or everything will be destroyed!'

Orion, Matt and Helen burst through the door to find the Delos family assembled and staring up. Cassandra hung in mid-air, glowing bright purple, green and blue with the tri-part aura of the Three Fates. She was thrashing and howling with pain as the Fates pushed their way through her and forced her to be their messenger. Cassandra, her face wrinkled with extreme age, raised a clawlike hand and pointed directly at Orion.

'Kill him!' one of the Fates shrieked through Cassandra's mouth.

'He will ruin everything!' another voice said as Cassandra's face bubbled and rearranged itself into another old woman's.

'Why does he still live? He should have been killed as a baby!' said the third Fate peevishly.

For a moment, Cassandra wrested control of her body away from her tormentors. 'No!' she said forcefully. 'Go away!'

'You are OURS!' all three of the Fates shrieked. 'You will not disobey us!'

Cassandra started tearing at herself with her nails, leaving long, bloody welts in her skin. Her face was a mask of fear, but her fingers kept digging. The Fates controlled her hands, but the rest of her was aware of the punishment her possessed hands were inflicting on her. Helen took an involuntary step back in revulsion and realized that everyone else in the room had done the same. Except for Orion.

'Enough!' he commanded, striding forward until he was under Cassandra. 'Leave her alone.'

The Fates screamed, and in a rush of strange wind and a flare of purple, green and blue, they abandoned Cassandra, leaving her to fall out of the air. Orion caught her before she could hit the ground and cradled her in his arms. She buried her face in his chest and started sobbing.

'It's all right now. Shhh,' he said soothingly. He carried her to the couch and sat down, holding her in his lap. He looked around at everyone in the room accusingly. 'You all just stand there and let those hags do that to her?' he asked, his eyes zeroing in on Castor.

'It's not like that,' Jason said, shaking his head. 'We've tried everything.'

'Every time we've tried to stop it, they just hurt her more,' Lucas said.

Orion looked over at Lucas, and his angry gaze softened. He nodded apologetically, accepting that he may have been too quick to judge.

'So why do they leave when Orion tells them to?' Pallas asked. His eyes narrowed suspiciously at Orion. 'Why are the Fates so afraid of you?'

'Maybe because I'm not afraid of them,' Orion countered defensively.

Helen tensed herself for a fight and felt Lucas and Hector go on the alert with her – all three of them ready to argue for Orion.

'The Fates fear Orion because they can't see through him. Something about their sister, a beautiful woman with a veil over her eyes. She covers their eyes when he approaches,' Cassandra said tiredly, ending the fight before it could begin. She drew a hiccupping breath and sat up in Orion's arms and looked at him. 'You're like a blank wall to them. Or a dead end.' She wiped her hand across her face. 'I don't know exactly what they think. All I get are glimpses here and there. But I do know that whenever you're part of the equation they can't see the answer.'

'Is that why you couldn't see my future?' Helen asked Cassandra. 'When I started meeting Orion in the Underworld and spending a lot of time with him, you said you couldn't see my future any more.'

Cassandra tilted her head to the side, considering this. 'I suppose that could be it. The Fates won't tell me anything about Orion. They hate it when I even think of him.'

'Good,' Orion said. 'I've never liked the Fates.' He smiled down into Cassandra's face, like he'd just put his finger on something. 'So, is this why you're always following me around the house?'

She smiled back and nodded shyly. 'I can relax when you're around because I know they won't come.'

Helen glanced at Castor, Lucas and Hector, who were all sharing troubled looks. Their hearts were filled with confused fogs, like they had no idea how they should feel about what they'd just heard. Helen wished she'd been in the room earlier. She wanted to hear this new, revised Tyrant prophecy, preferably before Orion did.

'And you're not afraid of me?' Cassandra asked Orion cautiously. He smirked.

'Ever been to Thailand?' he asked. She shook her head slowly, bemused by his out-of-the-blue statement. 'Let's just say I've eaten meals that are scarier than you. Bigger than you too.' Cassandra chuckled, but halfway through exhaustion caught up with her and she started to yawn. 'Yeah, I have that effect on a lot of people,' he said, making her laugh again through her yawn. Orion stood up with Cassandra in his arms. 'OK. I think it's bedtime for you, Kitty.'

'Will you stay with me until I fall asleep?' she asked, clutching at his arm.

'Of course.'

On his way out the door, Orion gave Helen a meaningful look. She nodded in response to let him know that she'd fill him in on anything that he missed while he tended to Cassandra. As soon as he was out of the room, several people started talking at once.

'I can't believe the Fates left like that,' Ariadne breathed to her twin.

'It looked like they were going to kill her this time,' Jason said back.

'It's worse than we thought,' Pallas said urgently to Castor, silencing all other side conversations. 'If Orion stays, we are blind. At least with the Oracle we had an edge over the gods. A small one, but better than nothing.'

'I know,' Castor replied, his face tight with tension.

'He's a good man. Anyone can see that,' Pallas persisted. 'But, good or not, he's too dangerous. He can't stay with us.'

'No. You can't send Orion away,' Lucas said in a low voice, his eyes skewering his father. All eyes flew to Lucas, surprised that he of all people would defend Orion. Lucas's face was impassive. 'He saved my life and Helen's. We're blood brothers now.'

'I agree,' Hector said evenly. 'Orion has fought alongside us. He is a part of our family,' he continued, nodding to Lucas and Helen.

'Just because someone fought alongside you does not make him a part of this family,' Pallas said to his son in a raised and frustrated voice. 'You rely too much on your honour to make your choices for you, Hector!'

Hector looked away from his father's intense stare, backing down. He was too respectful to go against his father, even if Pallas was wrong. That pissed Helen off.

'This isn't about honour or about Orion,' Helen said bitterly. She took a step toward Pallas and felt Lucas, Hector and Jason fall into position behind her. 'It's about

Cassandra. You're too scared to face the future without someone to tell you what to do. You'd rather let her suffer than have to doubt what's coming next. All this talk about Orion being dangerous is an excuse so you can keep your Oracle and not feel too guilty about what that does to your own niece.'

Pallas took a step towards Helen, his lips curling into a snarl. Undaunted, Helen took a step toward Pallas and tipped her chin up at him, taunting him to take a shot. As far as Helen was concerned, this fight was a long time coming. From the first moment Pallas had laid eyes on Helen, all he'd ever seen was Daphne. After so many years of blaming Daphne for his brother's murder, he couldn't let it go. Pallas had always looked at Helen as if any day now she was going to betray the Delos family, and she'd had enough of it.

'And do you think the same of me, Helen? That I would let my daughter go through that torture so I can . . . what? Feel better about tomorrow?' Castor said quietly as he stepped between Helen and Pallas. Helen felt Lucas put his hand on the small of her back, and she eased off.

'No,' she admitted, dropping her gaze. 'I don't think that of you, Castor.'

'Cassandra's health has always been one of my biggest concerns. But the real problem for our kind is the Tyrant. It always has been,' Castor continued, addressing the group. 'I know how you all feel about Orion, and

I think those feelings have kept you from seeing the truth.'

'Not this again!' Helen huffed. 'Orion isn't the freaking Tyrant, OK?'

'Wait, Helen,' Matt said, holding up a hand. 'We don't have all the facts yet.' He turned to Castor. 'What did the Oracle say about the Tyrant before we got here? Did anyone write it down word for word?'

'I did,' Ariadne said from behind her father's desk. In all the commotion, Helen hadn't even noticed her there, scribbling away. 'I recorded most of it on my phone too. But I don't want to hear that again. Do you?'

Matt shook his head. He held out his hand for Ariadne's pages, and she handed them over. Helen read along over Matt's shoulder while Ariadne explained.

'She repeated this first line about a hundred times, that's why I added the dots after it. I think Cassandra was trying to fight them off for as long as she could.' Ariadne dropped her eyes for a moment, collected herself and then pointed to the notes firmly. 'I made an indentation each time a new voice took over. And at the bottom there, I highlighted in blue the words they all spoke together.'

The Tyrant rises . . .

> *The Great Cycle, delayed for thirty and three hundreds of years, is nearly complete.*

> *The blood of the Four Houses has mixed and all of Olympus is contained in one.*

The time has come. The children must overthrow the parents – or be devoured by them.

The Hero

The Lover

The Shield

The Tyrant – have taken the stage.

The Warrior waits in the wings, the last to join the battle.

The Tyrant shall rise up with power unlimited. On one choice will the fate of all be decided.

Nemesis has sent her vessel to blind us! Darkness! Darkness comes! He must be killed or everything will be destroyed!

Helen and Matt stopped reading at this point and looked up at each other, brows furrowed. That last line they had both heard already – as they came into the library with Orion. 'Vessel of Nemesis' and 'Darkness comes', sounded ominous to Helen. If the Fates were talking about Orion here, their descriptions of him certainly didn't help his case much.

'Is this Nemesis an evil goddess or something?' Helen asked Matt under her breath, trusting that he had done more studying than she had, as usual.

'No, she's not evil. And she's way older than the gods,' Matt replied. 'She's a daughter of Nyx, like the Fates.'

'So, Nemesis is probably the sister with the veil that Cassandra was talking about?' Helen asked hopefully, looking around.

'It's possible,' Castor replied.

'And this is the only time all three of the Fates spoke together? This last line?' Matt asked Ariadne urgently.

'Yes. They grew very agitated,' she replied.

'That's when we walked into the kitchen,' Helen said, catching Matt's drift. 'This whole bit about Nemesis and darkness could just be because they couldn't see any more because Orion walked in.'

'Orion could have been blocking their prophecy,' Matt continued optimistically.

'So, of course, the Fates would want him dead. They've been trying to kill him since *before* he was born. Even before that, actually.' Helen stopped and restarted, trying to explain. 'The Fates have been targeting Orion ever since Troy because he made it out alive when he was Aeneas. He escaped fate. The only way Aeneas could have done that is if Nemesis was protecting him too.'

Helen saw confused and worried faces everywhere she looked. She rubbed her eyes, knowing she was making a hash of this and that she was probably hurting Orion's chances more than helping them. She looked over at Lucas pleadingly.

'Am I lying?' she asked him, calling on his Falsefinder skills.

'No,' Lucas replied immediately. 'She isn't lying.'

'Oh, of course,' Pallas said as he threw up his hands in exasperation. 'Well, it's obvious what role the Fates put you in, Lucas. You're the Lover. You'd do anything for Helen.'

'Yes I would,' Lucas admitted with brutal honesty. 'But she's still telling the truth.'

'What she knows of it,' Castor said in a detached voice. 'I'm sorry, son, but just because Helen thinks something is true doesn't make it the truth.' Castor's tone wasn't confrontational. He was just making them aware of a loophole that he'd obviously spent a long time considering.

A ghost of a thought traced across Helen's mind – a niggling doubt about something that was important, but just out of reach.

'It's not just that. Orion can't be the Tyrant because he's the Shield,' Lucas said, waving away his father's objection. 'When Cassandra made the prophecy about Helen being the Descender, she said Helen would go down into the Underworld with her Shield.'

'Granted,' Matt said equitably, like he'd already thought of this. 'But you also found a way into the Underworld, Lucas. And you went there to protect Helen – to shield her.'

'OK, but I didn't help her free the Furies,' Lucas countered, recalling the words of the prophecy.

'Yeah you did,' Helen said sheepishly, hating to go against Lucas on this. 'I was banished from the Underworld until you gave me the obol. And then you helped me figure out which river we needed.'

'Yeah, but Orion was the one who was actually there with you when you freed them.'

'Luke,' Hector interrupted gently. 'You gotta admit Matt's point raises the possibility that there is more than one interpretation of the prophecy.'

'There's always more than one interpretation,' Orion said from the doorway. Everyone turned to look at him as he came back into the library. 'Face it. The Fates speak in riddles because they don't know what the hell they're talking about. If they did, they'd say something straightforward like, "Orion is the Tyrant and he wants to eat your brains for breakfast" or whatever.'

Hector's shoulders started bouncing up and down with silent laughter. Lucas turned his head away and tried to stuff down a laugh of his own, but he made the mistake of catching Jason's eye.

'Zombie Tyrant,' Jason whispered to Lucas, his face turning red with a repressed laugh.

'Huzzah death,' Lucas whispered back, cracking up. Apparently, that was some kind of inside joke between the Delos boys because all three of them busted out laughing.

'Enough foolishness,' Pallas said, striding angrily for the door. He stopped and turned. 'What part of "reducing *all mortal cities* to rubble" don't you understand? We've been warned what's at stake here, and not just for Scions. I don't want to be the one who stood by and let a tyrant worse than Stalin or Hitler get away because he seemed like such a *nice* guy when I met him.' He looked directly at Orion, and then back at everyone else. No one was laughing any more. 'Do you?'

'Ariadne,' Matt called quietly down the upstairs hallway.

Ariadne stopped at her bedroom door and glanced back at him, holding up a finger to signal for him to wait where he was. She listened for her father, brothers and cousin, but it wasn't necessary. Matt could hear all the Delos men, he could even feel their pulses throbbing in the air, and he knew that they were occupied elsewhere. But Ariadne didn't know this, and he didn't know how to explain it to her yet. After listening for far longer than Matt needed to, Ariadne finally looked satisfied.

'Come in,' she whispered, beckoning for him to follow her into her room. He entered uncertainly, standing in the middle of her bedroom while she transferred clothes from one piece of furniture to another without even thinking about putting anything away in her dresser.

She was always a slob. I spent half the war cleaning up after her, the new part of Matt remembered. *Worst slave ever.*

Matt shook his head and tried to push aside the other consciousness that kept popping up uninvited, just as he tried to suppress the flood of familiarity and tenderness he felt towards the girl he was looking at.

Her bed was just a few feet away. Part of him had never lain beside her and another part of him had spent ten years sleeping next to her – her and no other until the day he died. His hands ached to reach out and touch her again for the first time, so he shoved them in his pockets. He turned his head and stared at the wall as she tossed something silky and lace-trimmed in her closet.

'Matt?' Ariadne asked from across the room. He looked at her as she flung a long tress of her chestnut hair behind her shoulder, desperately trying *not* to remember how soft both her hair and her round shoulder felt. 'My lingerie isn't going to strike you blind, you know.'

'I need to ask you some questions,' he said tersely, deliberately turning the conversation away from her undergarments.

'OK.' Ariadne crossed to him and sat on the edge of her bed. Matt took the chair she had just liberated from its burden of laundry and sat opposite her.

'Tell me about the different roles that the Fates mentioned tonight,' he asked.

Ariadne smiled, almost like she was expecting this. 'You know that the Greeks were in love with theatre?' Matt nodded. 'Well, the Fates were too. They always have been. It's almost like they see the world as a stage, and the Scions are merely their players. In a lot of prophecies, there is mention of certain roles that must be filled, or that the world is waiting to be filled, in order to complete the "Great Cycle" that the Fates seem fixated on. By the way, a cycle is also another name for a series of plays that are interconnected – like the plays by Aeschylus that tell the story of the beginning of the Furies. It's called the *Oresteia*.'

'Yeah,' Matt said ruefully. 'I've read that one. Now tell me about the specific roles that the Fates mentioned tonight. Have you always known about them?'

'Yes. No one really knows what those roles mean, though. Or what the Fates intend for them.'

'How can that be?'

'Because they're vague. Think about it. The roles are the Hero, the Shield, the Lover and the Warrior – and seriously? That could mean any one of the Scions who have been born, since like *ever*. We're a bunch of hero, warrior, lover, shield-the-weak-with-your-body kind of people,' she said, mildly exasperated with how predictable her kind were. 'The only role that has specific portents attached to it is the Tyrant, and all of the Houses over the aeons have been super vigilant about the signs surrounding him in order to prevent him from ever coming. But you know that prophecy already.'

'The Tyrant is born to bitterness. He bears the blood of multiple Houses and must be able to reduce all mortal cities to rubble,' Matt said seriously. He didn't like to agree with Pallas, but Matt knew he was right. He pictured someone like Hitler with Scion strength and the ability to destroy cities just by willing it.

Matt remembered Zach asking the gang a hypothetical question once: if they had a time machine and could go back and kill Hitler before he had a chance to hurt anyone, would they do it? Even if he were still an innocent child when they went back and murdered him? They had all answered *yes*.

'Matt,' Ariadne said, reaching out and putting her hand over his. 'Are you OK?'

'And the others, like the Shield and . . . the Warrior,' he continued. 'Those are set roles, roles that *must* be filled? Have these roles been there from the beginning?'

'Cassandra of Troy was the first to mention them . . . so, yeah. All of these roles have been there from the beginning.'

'And *every* role must be filled before this cycle can be completed and the Fates can move on to a new cycle?'

'I've never heard it put that way before,' Ariadne replied cautiously. Her sharp mind turned this novel idea over quickly as it shuffled through dozens of memorized bits of minutiae, until finally she nodded in acceptance. 'But I suppose that's a plausible interpretation.'

'So we're all trapped,' Matt breathed hopelessly. 'We have to play our parts or the Fates will just start over and try again with the next batch of Scions.'

Ariadne frowned in thought. 'Maybe that's why it feels like we've never really left Troy. Because something that was supposed to happen way back then didn't, and the Fates keep trying to re-create it.'

Matt smiled, sternly reminding himself not to lean over and kiss her no matter how clever she was. He waited a moment until he knew his voice would be steady before talking.

'That's what I think too,' he said. 'It's like the Scions are stuck in an endless round of auditions as the Fates shift new actors into the same roles, looking for the right cast to make their play work.'

'But they're the Fates. If they want something to happen, why can't they just *make* it happen?'

'I don't know,' Matt replied. 'There must be some other force that moves against them. Maybe their sister, Nemesis.'

'We should tell everyone about this,' Ariadne said. 'Even if they think we're wrong.'

'I agree.'

They sat for a while, each of them pondering private thoughts. The sun was starting to come up, and Matt told himself it was time to go, even though he could have sat like that with her for days.

'Good night, Ariadne,' Matt said as he stood up.

'Where are you going?' Her luminous hazel eyes were wide and troubled.

'Home. I snuck out when Hector called me,' he said, looking anywhere but at her. 'I want to be back before my parents wake up so they don't worry. The riots really freaked them out.'

'OK,' she said quietly. 'Will you come back later? The Houses are supposed to meet here tonight.'

'I don't know if I can,' he said. There was a ship out

on the water, carrying his army closer. Matt could feel it like a phantom limb – removed but still aching. 'I may have something else to take care of.'

Ariadne nodded and looked at the floor. Unable to resist, Matt leaned down and kissed the top of her head. Her hair smelt the same, like honey and summer. He let himself run his hand down the back of her bent neck, feeling how slender it was under his calloused palm – as fragile as a flower's stem.

'Will you try?' she whispered, not looking up.

'Yes. I'll try.'

'Hey. Are you mad at me?' Lucas heard Helen ask.

He turned and saw her floating towards him across the roof of the house. He shook his head, and she sat next to him on the very edge of the roof over his bedroom.

'I didn't mean to disagree with you in front of the family back there. About Orion being the Shield,' she continued.

'It's OK. You were just bringing up a good point,' he said, knowing she could hear the truth in his words. Helen's new talent as a Falsefinder made things both easier and harder between the two of them. He could never lie to her again, not even to protect her. Not that lying had ever kept her safe. Lucas briefly wondered if he'd ever protected her at all. 'I still think Orion's the Shield, though.'

'But I don't need a Shield. I never did,' she said, almost

like she was reading his mind. With all the new things she could do, Lucas wouldn't put telepathy past her.

'No. I guess not,' he agreed. Something about that troubled Lucas. Helen had always been the strongest, so what did the Shield 'shield' her from, exactly?

'Maybe Orion is the Lover. He is a son of Aphrodite,' Helen said, like she was considering it.

That made sense. And, although it killed him to think about it, Lucas was pretty sure that Orion was Helen's actual lover now. But no matter how mixed up all the signs for the different roles were, Lucas knew better.

'Orion isn't the Lover.'

'How do you know?'

'That part's taken already.'

Helen looked at him, her beautiful mismatched eyes swimming with regret and, Lucas hoped desperately, *not* pity as well. 'You know . . . all these new talents I have . . .' Her voice wavered. 'One of them is controlling hearts.'

'So you mentioned.'

'I could take your love for me away,' she offered in a small voice.

'And then what?'

Helen's brow pinched together, like she was confused by his question. 'Well, then you could move on with your life. We'd have to stay away from each other, though.'

'We tried that already, remember?' Lucas asked with a wry smile. 'It didn't work.'

Lucas had no doubt Helen could erase his love for her, but he also knew he'd only fall in love with her again the next time he laid eyes on her. There was no 'moving on' for him. No matter what else Lucas did in his life, his love for Helen would always define him. He was the Lover.

'Please, Lucas? I want to make this easier on you,' she said quietly, her head tilted down.

'Then stop talking nonsense.' He bumped her shoulder playfully with his until she dropped her pained look and smiled. 'We've been over this a dozen times. Nothing's ever going to change the way I feel about you.'

She finally met his eyes and nodded sadly, accepting what she could hear in his voice – the truth.

'So, maybe Orion's the Hero?' she asked, trying to change the subject to something more productive.

'Hector,' Lucas replied immediately, shaking his head.

'Right. That's a no-brainer,' Helen said, rolling her eyes a little. 'Unless Hector's the Warrior?'

'The Warrior joins the fight last, and Hector's never come late to a fight in his life. I'd bet just about anything Hector's the Hero and Orion's the Shield.'

Helen seemed to struggle for a moment with her next question. 'What is it?' Lucas asked coaxingly.

'Is the Tyrant really as bad as Pallas said?'

Lucas nodded slowly. He didn't want to scare her, but he also knew he couldn't lie to her. 'What little of the prophecy we have left talks about the Tyrant like he's stronger than all the gods combined. And there's supposed to be this huge battle with monsters and storms when the Tyrant rises. Even the sky is supposed to change colours, like a kaleidoscope.'

'Sounds like the apocalypse.'

'Yeah,' Lucas said, feeling Helen shiver.

They sat there for a while, dangling their feet off the side of the house. Even though the conversation had taken such a dark turn, just having Helen near him relaxed Lucas and helped him focus. He might not be able to kiss her, but if she was sitting right next to him he didn't torture himself over who else she might be with. And what they were probably doing.

He reminded himself it was better this way and swallowed the lump in his throat. He wanted Helen to be happy, and he trusted that Orion could give that to her. Lucas certainly never had. All he ever did was make Helen miserable, and as soon as he knew this whole mess was over he was going to make sure he never hurt her again.

Burying these consuming thoughts, Lucas forced his mind to drift instead. He shuffled through every image and use of a shield he could come up with.

'Shield, defence, bastion, block . . .' he mumbled. 'What does Orion shield us from? What does he block?'

'Well. He seems pretty good at blocking doorways,' Helen joked. Her smile disappeared quickly as a thought occurred to her. 'And prophecies.'

'And the futures of anyone who spends a lot of time with him,' he breathed. 'Orion shields you from the awareness of the Fates, Helen. If the Fates can't see you, they can't decide your life for you. Do you know what this means? You have free will.'

They stared at each other, so shocked they almost couldn't believe it, but both of them sensing a tingling in the air that told them they were on to something huge.

'But why me? Why am I the one who gets to choose?' Helen's eyes darted around fearfully. 'What role am I playing, Lucas?'

'You're the Descender.'

'That's not on the list.'

She was right. Lucas felt a moment of anxiety, and then relaxed as the solution came to him. 'Out of all of us, you were the last one to discover that you're a Scion – the last to join the fight. You're the Warrior, of course.'

Helen calmed down and smiled tentatively. 'Huh. Go figure.' Her nose wrinkled as she thought of something. 'The Fates know I suck at fighting, right?'

'You've got better.' He really tried to keep a straight face, but it wouldn't hold.

Helen pushed him off the roof. He floated up in front of her, holding his hands in an 'I surrender' gesture, still trying not to laugh. She crossed her arms huffily and looked away, trying not to laugh with him.

'Lover, my heinie,' she said, cracking a grin and nudging him away from her with her foot.

He caught her ankle and pulled himself between her dangling legs. Helen's eyes widened with surprise and her lips softened and fell apart.

'That's right,' he whispered. Lucas leaned in close to her, loving that in spite of everything that had happened, she couldn't help but react to him. 'Don't ever forget it.'

He grazed the curve of her cheek with his fingertips before flying away.

CHAPTER EIGHT

Helen stared off the side of the house for a while, wondering whether or not she'd done the right thing. A part of her knew she was hurting Lucas more by not setting him straight about her and Orion, but in the end she couldn't do it. Her reasons were selfish, but still valid. If Lucas thought she was with Orion, he would eventually pull away and she really needed him to do so.

She could look inside him and see he was still in love with her, but that the love had changed slightly. Regardless of what Orion said about it not making any difference to Lucas if she spent the night with another man, it *had* altered something in him – not the amount of love he felt, but how keenly he felt it. Helen figured it made sense. Even with a physical injury, there's only so much pain a person can take before they start to go numb.

Helen saw Matt leave the house and go to his car. She inhaled a breath, about to call out to him and ask him where he was going, but she remembered all the sleeping people just under the roof she was sitting on and

173

stopped herself. Matt turned and looked in her direction, anyway.

Impossible, Helen thought as he smiled and waved up at her. *There's no way he could have heard me inhale. But how else could he have known to look on the roof?* Helen waved back, and Matt got into his car and drove off.

Still mulling it over, Helen flew in Lucas's window and sat down on his bed. For a moment, she considered climbing into it, but there was a chance Lucas would come home and find her there. It wasn't fair to do that to him. Helen hauled her tired body up and walked down the hallway to Ariadne's room.

She was surprised to find Ariadne awake.

'Hey,' Ariadne said, automatically sliding over to make room for Helen in her bed.

'Hey yourself,' Helen replied with a worried frown. Ariadne's heart was a throbbing mess of emotion, and Helen knew it had to have something to do with Matt. She kicked off her shoes and got into bed. 'I just saw Matt leave. Did you two talk?'

Ariadne avoided all mention of her feelings and instead told Helen what she and Matt had discussed about the Scions being stuck in one repeating cycle. She explained how Matt thought the Fates needed all the roles to be filled and, if they weren't, the cycle would just start over again with the next generation.

'I think everyone's coming to the same conclusion,' Helen said with a nod. 'It would explain why we all look like people from Troy – we're stuck. There's something that didn't happen way back then that the Fates are still trying to bring about.'

'But what?' Ariadne asked, exasperated. 'And something else I don't understand? Why can't the Fates just make what they want to happen, happen? It doesn't make sense.'

'What did Matt say?' Helen asked, feeling a sinking sensation in her stomach.

'He said that there must be a force working against Fate in every cycle. Something that keeps ruining the play before the Scions can get all the way through it the exact way the Fates want. He said he thinks it's Nemesis, working against her sisters.'

'By blocking the Fates and giving a Scion free will,' Helen whispered. 'At least that's what Lucas thinks. Every cycle someone who's supposed to make a huge decision has free will and ruins the Fates' plan.'

Ariadne rubbed her eyes. 'Does Lucas have any idea who has free will in this cycle?'

Helen felt like the universe kept pointing an accusing finger at her.

'We aren't sure,' she lied.

Helen rolled over and opened her eyes. She expected to see Ariadne lying next to her. Instead, she saw a man's naked back, swelling and sinking with the deep breaths of sleep.

Lucas, Helen thought, recognizing his shape immediately. She wanted to run her hand between the bunched muscles of his shoulder blades and down the trench of his spine, but something was off. The room Helen had awoken to was familiar, although she had never been in it before.

The other Helen sat up slowly, watching her husband carefully to make sure she didn't disturb him. She needed to sneak out before Paris woke up, or she wouldn't be able to get away that day as she had planned.

Helen watched as Helen of Troy tied her simplest chiton over her shoulder, gathered up an old girdle, veil and worn sandals. She noticed that Helen of Troy had one brown eye and one that was turned blue by a lightning-bolt scar that ran down the centre of the iris. Helen knew that it had happened during the stoning. The beating Helen Hamilton had taken from Ares had given her the same mark.

The other Helen hurried a short way down the dark marble corridor without putting her sandals on and stopped at a door. Inside the room was a little girl, no more than three or four, still in her bed. The little girl opened her eyes with uncanny prescience.

'Mommy?' whispered the little girl, awake in an instant. 'Are we going to see Auntie Briseis today, like we promised?'

'Yes, Atlanta,' Helen said quietly, rushing into the room and closing the door behind her.

'Are we going to walk with the Lady first?' Atlanta asked. Sensitive to her mother's mood, she kept her voice down.

'Not today.' Helen dressed Atlanta in an old skirt and shawl she had borrowed from a servant.

'But the people like it when you and the Lady walk through their gardens. They hug each other and kiss your hand.'

'That's because Aphrodite brings love to the beasts and to the growing things and they multiply,' Helen said with a sad smile as she turned to finish dressing herself. 'It's why our people have lasted so long without starving inside the walls.'

'Starving – like they are outside?' Atlanta asked with a troubled frown.

'That's right. That's why we have to go see Auntie Briseis. We must bring her more food.'

Helen of Troy picked up her daughter and put her on her hip. 'Change your face, like Mommy taught you,' she said, touching half of the cestus that hung in the shape of a heart charm round Atlanta's neck. Atlanta squinted in concentration, and her face magically altered. 'Don't forget your hair,' Helen reminded her, and Atlanta's sparkling blonde locks darkened to brown. Helen then altered her own looks, adopting the plain face and stout figure of a hardworking field hand before the pair left the room.

They made their way swiftly through the palace and

down to the kitchens. An old woman who had nursed Briseis as a baby handed Helen a prepared bundle, which she tied across her back. A quick glance to make sure no one but the loyal old woman was watching, and she stole out through a back door and through the kitchen gardens. Helen ran swiftly to the wall, her daughter clinging to her tightly. Picking up speed as she reached the fortifications, she scrabbled up one side of the wall and down the other faster than the guards could see in the low predawn light.

Atlanta was not afraid, although she knew that outside the wall she and her mother were in mortal danger. Helen smiled at her brave daughter proudly, and slipped through the sleeping siege camp. They stopped at one of the largest tents and whistled softly at the entrance.

A moment later, a woman who looked just like Ariadne appeared and wrapped the disguised mother and daughter in a warm hug.

'Briseis,' Helen said softly to the woman. The sisters-in-law kissed each other warmly on both cheeks.

'There isn't much time for a visit,' Briseis said as she led Helen and Atlanta into the tent. 'Achilles will be back soon.'

'There is an easy remedy for that. One that allows us to spend as much time together as we wish,' Helen said leadingly as she allowed her real face to appear.

'Don't start,' Briseis warned. 'I won't leave him.'

'I know.' Helen put Atlanta down and gave her a small wooden figurine to play with before handing Briseis the bundle of food. 'Have you thought about what will happen when Achilles joins the battle lines again?'

'He may never join them. He detests Agamemnon and refuses to do his bidding any more.'

'He didn't cross the sea with his army for nothing, Briseis.'

'I'm aware of that.' Briseis's eyes sparkled with anger. 'But he's different now. He told me he has no quarrel with my brother.'

'It doesn't matter if he has a quarrel with Hector or not. This is war. Don't let your love for Achilles blind you.'

'I haven't.' Briseis looked away. 'But I know what side of the wall I'm on.'

'And what side of the war? What about her?' Helen pleaded quietly, gesturing to Atlanta. She saw Briseis's eyes widen with worry, and knew that the risk of bringing Atlanta was worth it for this reason alone. Helen pressed her case while she had the chance. 'Achilles came here to kill the Tyrant. That was the one argument Agamemnon made that convinced him to fight.'

'Atlanta has nothing to fear from him, I swear it,' Briseis said, glancing down at Atlanta protectively. 'He would never kill a child. You don't know him.'

The two sisters-in-law glared at each other. The only sound in the tent was Atlanta whispering to her doll.

'Do you like the pretty garden I made? The sun never burns and the bees never sting and the stones stay out of your sandals,' Atlanta cooed, completely lost in her game of make-believe.

Helen rolled her eyes comically and spoke under her breath to Briseis. 'She spends all day imagining a perfect world where no one suffers. Terrifying, isn't she?'

Briseis looked away again, her face falling into a frown as her thoughts turned dark. 'It helps that she was born a girl. No one suspects her to be the Tyrant now. Not really.'

'Then why does Achilles stay here even though his men starve?' Helen asked desperately. Briseis had no answer. 'Sister, I believe you when you say he'd never kill a child. Achilles is a man of deep principles – principles that brought him to Troy. Have you ever considered that ridding the world of the Tyrant is so important to him that he might be willing to wait for her to grow up first before he kills her?'

'You must go,' Briseis said suddenly, waving at the air like it had filled up with flies. 'He'll be back any moment.'

Helen sighed and dropped her head in defeat and then reached down to scoop up her daughter. 'I'll be back with more food in a few days.'

The two women embraced, cautiously at first as if they were still at odds, and then with true tenderness before Helen and Atlanta assumed their disguises and left the enemy camp.

*

Helen woke up with a thick tress of Ariadne's hair in her mouth. She spat it out and mentally apologized for drooling all over it before rolling over. She rolled over on to something that squeaked. It turned out to be Andy, who batted at her and made protesting sounds in her sleep. Wishing Noel would get even just one more mattress for the girls to sleep on, Helen scooted down to the end of the bed and crawled out as quietly as she could without crushing anyone.

Helen hugged herself as she left the room, trying to shake off the memory. That one had seemed closer to her than the others had, like she was more than just a spectator this time. In fact, halfway through it had started to feel like it was Helen of Nantucket, and not Helen of Troy, who was in that tent. She could still feel the warm, squirmy weight of her little girl (correction – Helen of Troy's little girl) in her arms, so of course she ran into Lucas in the hallway. She ached to hold one of them, either the little girl or the little girl's father, so desperately she actually groaned.

'I thought you'd gone home,' Lucas said after a pause.

'Haven't been there in days,' Helen said, staring at him greedily. 'I figure, why bother when everyone is here?'

'And more on the way,' he said, suddenly frowning.

Helen nodded. 'The meeting of the Houses. Did you call – '

'Orion? Yeah,' Lucas said, finishing her sentence. 'He's waiting for us in the library.'

'What time is it?' Helen asked, and peered blinkingly at the slanted light coming in a nearby window.

'Past two.' He chuckled at the shocked look on Helen's face. 'Meet us downstairs?' he said as he passed by her and made his way to the staircase. 'We need to make plans.'

'I just need a minute,' Helen said, gesturing to her rumpled clothes and ratty hair.

'Take your time,' Lucas said. As he walked by on his way down the hall, he bent close to her, running his hand up her arm. His large hand swallowed every curve of her slender muscles, cupping them one by one in the palm of his hand and leaving a trail of goose bumps behind. His skin was so hot on hers she shivered when his warmth was removed, which it was, far too quickly.

Helen peeked in on her father first. Jerry still slept deeply, but even standing over him she could hear his heart beating strong and steady. He looked like he was in another world, a peaceful one that he was reluctant to leave. Helen didn't know if it worked like this or not, but she hoped that if Jerry were merely sleeping that Morpheus was watching over him.

Helen ran to the bathroom, conniving to beat Ariadne and Andy to the shower before they got out of bed. She darted in before they'd even started scratching and shut the door behind her with a satisfied smile.

Helen turned on the tap and started pulling off her clothes, the memory of Lucas's hand on her arm still burning bright. She showered quickly. While she towelled off, another chance encounter in another dark hallway, centuries ago, billowed up in Helen's mind like the steam rising off the white tile.

Lancelot had been away from Camelot for many months.

The Barbarians – big, blond invaders from a land of ice – had kept the Knights of the Round Table busy. Guinevere's father had fought the Barbarians his entire life, as her father's father had fought before him. Now, with the marriage between Guinevere and Arthur finalized, the dragon and wolf worshippers from the world of snow were Arthur's problem and, therefore, the problem of every knight sworn to him in Britain. If Guinevere's island home was to survive, the Barbarian invasion must be stopped, or every Britain-born would be slaughtered before the year was done.

Arthur was not prepared for the Berserkers. His men were orderly soldiers, trained in the Roman fashion of warfare. They were not used to the drug-induced trances that the Barbarians employed to send their rabid hordes screaming down on men, women and children. The horrors they saw during these barbaric hit-and-run raids were taking a toll on all of Arthur's men. The knights were outnumbered, and an all-out war was brewing.

Arthur was still on campaign in the north, trying to

find a solution. Lancelot had returned to Camelot two days ago, but Guinevere had not seen him yet. He was avoiding being alone with her, and she suspected it was not just because Arthur was her husband, as they both knew far too well. There was something deeper there, hindering him. Something terrible had happened to him. Guinevere could see it in Lancelot's eyes – they burned like two freshly blown-out candles. The colour was still fierce, but all the heat was gone.

Guinevere knew she had to talk to Lancelot, set his feet right again, or he would spin away from both his duty and family. It was up to her to fix him, even if it broke her heart to be near him, to see the wounded look on his face as he imagined Arthur in her bed.

'Lancelot,' Guinevere called, touching his elbow in the dark hallway. She coaxed him gently to turn round and face her. 'Please. Talk to me.'

'Gwen,' he breathed softly, pulling her closer to him. There was a lost look in his eyes, like a little boy. He tugged on her hand, and she followed without a word or thought of protest.

Lancelot led her away from the main walkway and down a turret alcove that overlooked the dark moors surrounding Camelot. Moonlight streamed into the cross-like shape of the arrow slit, giving enough light so she could see the heavy look of lust weighing down his eyelids. Guinevere's lips parted with a dozen unsaid words as she stared into his eyes. Lancelot's hips shifted closer to hers for one tense moment, and then he pulled himself away, releasing her entirely.

'You shouldn't have come to me tonight.'

'But you brought me no word from my homeland in the Summer Country,' she replied, smiling up into his bright eyes as she closed the distance between them. 'You told me you'd sit with my father and bring back a token of his remembrance of me.'

Lancelot's face went pale, his eyes widening with pity, and Guinevere knew.

'It can't be,' she said, her voice suddenly high and girlish.

Her father was dead. That cantankerous, crafty and surprisingly hilarious giant of a man couldn't be dead. He was too stubborn to die. But Guinevere saw the truth written all over Lancelot's face. The leader of her clan, her father, was dead.

Sorrow swept over her. She lost control for a moment, and the room crackled with the white-blue light of her witch-fire.

'I married Arthur so my father and our clan would be *safe* from the Barbarians.' She sobbed disbelievingly. 'All this,' she said, gesturing with disgust to the jewels and the rich gown she wore now instead of humble homespun clothes, 'was to protect my father and my clan.'

'I know,' Lancelot said, striding forward to take Guinevere's hands. He jumped back involuntarily as her witch-fire coursed through him, but he schooled his pain and didn't let her go. 'Gwen,' he pleaded, gasping for breath. 'It's not Arthur's fault. We fought and lost. I lost. Arthur wasn't even there.'

The room went dark as Guinevere got control over herself, and the white-blue fire extinguished.

'But I married Arthur instead of you to save my clan,' she said. Her voice was shaky and reduced to a whisper. 'I gave *you* up for my clan's protection.'

'And your clan is gone now.' Lancelot's eyes darkened. 'But not because of Arthur. Because of me.'

Lancelot sat down on the floor of the turret in a heap and raked his hand through his hair. He told his story quickly and quietly, trying to keep his voice steady.

The Summer Country had flooded, as it always did in the ebb and flow of the yearly tides. The roads were impassable, and a battle unthinkable in the bog-like terrain. With the women and children safe in their flooded homeland, most of the men had all left to join Arthur's campaign against the Barbarians up north, as they always did at this time of year.

Lancelot had stayed behind to learn how the women grew all kinds of crops in the water instead of in soil, and Arthur agreed that knowledge of that technique could be useful at Camelot.

Lancelot was in the water fields with the women when he saw the dragon-crested ships sail right into the flood plains.

'I stayed with the women in the fields instead of

going to your father,' Lancelot rasped. 'When I couldn't fight any more, I stole a ship and sent as many women and children as I could gather away from the slaughter. Your father was . . . He was killed.'

Guinevere knew he had been about to say tortured. It didn't matter how Lancelot tried to soften the blow for her. The damage was done. She'd allowed herself to be offered up in marriage to a man she didn't love because she'd believed that by doing so she could save her clan. But it hadn't worked. Her father was dead, and her people scattered. She'd married a man she didn't love for nothing.

'Thank you for saving what part of my clan you could,' she whispered. 'I owe you my life for that. Again.'

Lancelot looked at her with such open need and desperation that she reached out, cupping his face in her hands. 'It's my fault,' he said, his face hot.

'No. I don't blame you for the lives lost. I bless you for the lives you saved,' she said tenderly, meaning every word and hoping he believed her enough to forgive himself.

'Gwen,' he breathed, and wound his arms round her tightly, his whole body pushing against hers in a wave of need.

He pressed his mouth against hers, startling her. For all the whispered words and longing looks, he had never dared touch her. This was their first kiss – the first time they had crossed this line. Guinevere knew that Lancelot would suffer more for betraying Arthur, his cousin, king, and closest friend, more than she would because Lancelot loved Arthur, and she didn't. Guinevere pushed against his shoulders for a moment, trying to spare him the guilt she knew he'd feel, before giving in to the swell of desperation she felt rising up in Lancelot.

His hands dug into her hair, sending her hairpins flying and her tresses tumbling down around his calloused fingers in messy locks. His lips nudged hers apart. Guinevere fell back against the flagstones and pulled Lancelot down on top of her. He slid his knee between her thighs, pushing her many-layered skirts up until his hand could reach the bare skin underneath. He ripped her under-shift off, and she cried out as the silken ties burned across her skin. Lancelot stilled and eased back.

'Am I hurting you?' he asked, his voice breaking and his eyes vulnerable.

'The only time you ever hurt me is when you leave me,' she replied, wrapping herself around him. 'Don't ever leave me again.'

Her heart still pounding away, Helen quickly dried her hair and half ran to the library to escape the borrowed memory before it got any more graphic. She stopped at the door and fanned the hot flush on her cheeks, reminding herself that in her memory Guinevere was betraying her husband, so she shouldn't have enjoyed it so much, and in this life she and Lucas were cousins so she had no business dredging up those old memories to begin with.

She could hear Lucas's deep voice through the library door, and after such a vivid flashback even that was enough to make her giddy. She recalled Lancelot taking her to his rooms, untying the laces on her dress, and . . . other things. She blushed furiously.

Stop being such a giant, throbbing hormone and get in there, she chided herself, shaking out her hands. *It's not like everyone will know what you were just thinking about.*

She pushed open the door and saw Orion immediately glance down at her chest, look back up at her, and raise an eyebrow as a knowing smile spread across his face. *Except maybe Orion*, she thought, wishing she could drop dead on the spot.

The men rose to greet Helen, but Cassandra stayed in the giant leather chair that dwarfed her fragile body. Helen bowed to the Oracle respectfully and noticed that Cassandra had her iPad on her lap.

'What's up?' Helen asked, ignoring the jolt of warmth she felt when she sat down in the only vacant spot – next to Lucas, of course.

'Another attack,' Cassandra replied gravely, handing Helen the iPad.

'A tsunami in Turkey,' Orion said. Helen scrolled through the pictures of flooded land.

'But why here?' she said, looking at the area in Turkey that had been hit. 'This isn't a major city.'

'Not any more,' Lucas said. 'But thirty-three hundred years ago, Troy was there.'

'That's some grudge,' Helen whispered, closing the iPad.

'The gods are getting bolder.' Cassandra sat back in her giant chair, her brow drawn with worry. 'The Scions can't waste any more time. We have to unite.'

'And to do that we need to figure out how we're going to deal with this meeting of the Houses,' Hector said, taking the lead. 'The three of you are all Heirs, so you'll be standing behind your House Heads. Except for Orion, of course, who is the Head of the House of Rome. I guess you'll have your second in the House standing behind you.'

'No way in hell I'm standing with Phaon at my back,' Orion said with a grimace. He saw the questioning looks on Lucas's and Hector's faces and knew he had to explain. 'Phaon and his elder brother, Corvus, disputed my succession when I was little.'

'Wait. Corvus?' Lucas asked, leaning forward. 'My father killed Corvus before any of us were born.'

'No. Castor *thought* he killed Corvus. But he survived,' Orion said. His voice dropped. 'Believe me, I wish it were otherwise.'

'Orion. You don't have to explain,' Helen said, trying to spare him.

'It's OK, Helen. I'd have to tell them about my scars eventually, anyway,' he said, giving her a sad little smile.

'My mom's cousin Corvus officially challenged me when I was eleven. I won.'

'In the Colosseum?' Hector asked. Orion nodded. 'Wow. Is it true that if members from the House of Rome kill each other in the Colosseum, they don't become Outcasts?'

'It's true. Romans have spilled so much blood into the sands of the Colosseum that the Furies lost track of the blood debts. It's a cursed place,' Orion said in a subdued voice. Hector's eyes gleamed enviously, like he would give anything to fight in the Colosseum, but the haunted look on Orion's face kept him from voicing that desire. 'When I killed Corvus, Phaon lost his only ally – the man who'd raised him like a son. Phaon'd put a knife in my back as soon as look at me. I'll never stand with him.'

'Well. That's something to consider,' Lucas said quietly, and a heavy silence followed.

Helen could see Hector's heart swell for his friend. Out of all of them, Hector could relate to Orion the most. It was strange for Helen to think about, but both of them were killers. A bright flash from Cassandra's direction caught Helen's eye. The silvery orb that hung in her chest rippled like moonlight reflecting off a dark pond.

'And you're not to go anywhere near Phaon,' Orion said suddenly, following Helen's eyes and pointing at Cassandra. His tone was uncharacteristically rough. 'If he tries to get you alone, you come straight to me. Understand?'

Cassandra nodded cautiously, puzzled by his angry look.

'Why?' Lucas asked.

Orion's lips twisted into a bitter scowl, like there was a vile taste in his mouth. He shook his head, like he was shaking off Lucas's question.

'Why?' Lucas repeated, undeterred.

'He's a monster.' Orion looked away, his volume dropping. 'He only goes for little girls.'

Cassandra looked away and frowned, the light inside her chest dimming. 'I'm not a little girl,' she said quietly, but no one responded.

'Are you sure about that?' Hector asked Orion seriously.

Orion nodded. 'My father's little sister.' He didn't elaborate. 'Trust me, Cassandra's his *type*. Some family I got, huh?'

'They're not your family,' Lucas said sharply. He tipped his chin at Helen and Hector and Cassandra, including everyone before looking back at Orion levelly. 'We're your family. You stand with us.'

'We *are* blood brothers,' Helen said, reminding him.

'If it makes you feel any better, I'll be watching for a knife in the back too,' Hector said, his face falling. 'Tantalus will be there. Who knows what he'll do when he sees me?' He looked over at Lucas, and the two of them shared a sad smile. 'Some family *we* got, huh?'

'I think the five of us have to stand together no matter what,' Helen said before Hector could get any more upset. She bit her lip, finding a snag. 'Except Cassandra is supposed to be neutral, right? She's the Oracle and she outranks us all, so she'll be the only one seated.'

'Right,' Hector said with a quick nod. 'When the Houses meet, she is considered above all bloodlines and sits alone.'

Helen looked over at Cassandra, so tiny in that big chair. She was always alone.

'Are you guys OK with this?' Helen asked sheepishly.

'It's never worked like that before,' Hector said slowly. A moment later he looked around smiling, his decision made. 'If we stand together, it'll be like we're our own House – the Scion Heirs or something. I'm willing to do it, but I think our parents will be pissed.'

'So what?' Lucas said, his eyes gleaming dangerously. 'We're not doing things the way they did them. I say we stand together.'

'I agree,' Orion said with a definite nod. 'But only if Helen's our leader.'

Helen burst out laughing. 'Are you serious?' She looked around, and saw that everyone was nodding in agreement. 'Wait. Back up. I can't be the leader.'

'Yes you can,' Hector said, nodding his head. 'In fact, you *have* to be the leader.'

'So when did all of you start eating bowls of crazy for

breakfast?' Helen asked, her patience growing thin. She didn't even like to win track races – she sure as hell didn't want to be the leader of the Scion Heirs. 'I'm the worst choice. Hector . . .'

'Hector can't be the leader, Helen. He's not an Heir,' Cassandra said, her voice low. 'And Orion has too many enemies trying to depose him already. Worse than that – too many people think he's the Tyrant. He would be challenged the moment he stepped forward as the leader of the Heirs.'

'Lucas then,' Helen said, a hint of desperation entering her tone. 'He's the smartest. He should lead us.'

'Lucas is the brother of the Oracle,' Cassandra said, shaking her head sadly. 'That would give too much power to the House of Thebes. Your own mother would fight it. It has to be you.'

'No,' Helen said simply. 'I don't want to do it.'

'Tough luck, Princess.' Hector smiled at her with infuriating smugness. 'Come on. You always knew it had to be you.'

'But I'm clueless!' she said, bolting up out of her seat anxiously. 'And the worst fighter. What if someone from another House challenges me to a duel or whatever? I'd totally lose.' Helen started pacing around, running her hands through her hair.

'If you're our leader, you'd never fight,' Lucas said, liking this new development more and more. 'Leaders choose champions to fight for them when they get challenged – usually the best fighter. It's a bad idea for our best fighter to be the leader.'

'OK, we all agree. Helen's the boss,' Orion said.

'We did *not* agree –' Helen interrupted, but Orion kept talking over her.

'Now all you need to do is choose a champion.' He stood up and bowed formally to Helen. 'I accept.'

'Like hell,' Lucas said, standing up and squaring off with Orion. 'I'm Helen's champion.'

'Can't let you do that, bro,' Orion said with an apologetic shake of his head.

'Did you just say *let* me?' Lucas asked in a disbelieving voice.

'Ladies, please,' Hector said as he nudged Orion and Lucas apart and stood between them. 'Weren't you listening? The champion is supposed to be the *best* fighter. Clearly, that's me.'

'Really? Prove it,' Lucas said coolly.

Helen could see a brawl coming. It killed her to think of any of her guys hurting each other, and although she wasn't ready to face it just yet she knew that there was only one of them that she would ever be able to send into danger.

'Hector,' she said firmly. 'If I'm the leader, I want Hector to be my champion.' Helen looked at Lucas and Orion, her face set. 'He *is* the best fighter.'

'Atta girl. Already making the right decisions. You might be a better leader than you think.' Hector grinned.

'Hold on,' Lucas objected.

'Do you accept?' Cassandra asked Hector, ignoring her brother.

'I do,' he replied immediately.

'I bear witness. Hector is Helen's champion from this day forward. If anyone challenges Helen, Hector will fight in her stead.' Cassandra looked sharply at Orion. 'Lucas will be Hector's second.'

'Wait just a damn minute,' Orion sputtered.

'And *you* will be *my* champion,' Cassandra said loudly over his protestations. 'That way Atreus leads, Thebes protects Atreus, and Athens and Rome protect Thebes. We need to show them all that the time of fighting between the Houses is over. The best way to do that is for the five of us to trust each other with our lives.'

Orion closed his mouth with a snap, thought about it for a moment and sighed reluctantly. 'That makes a lot of sense.'

'Do you accept?' Cassandra asked him, a timid note entering her tone. 'Will you be my champion?'

'Yes,' Orion answered seriously. Then he cracked a smile and gave her a little push. 'Of course I accept, Kitty.'

Cassandra smiled back, relieved.

'I'll witness,' Helen said, sensing that this needed to be voiced. 'Orion is Cassandra's champion.' She looked over at Lucas, who she could tell was barely holding his tongue. 'Do you have something you want to say?'

'I don't like being sidelined,' he said angrily. 'But I'll deal with it.'

'OK. So we're a team now,' Orion said, looking around at everyone. 'This should be an interesting meeting.'

'Matt!' Claire snapped. 'Can you focus, please?'

Matt's head turned, and he looked at Claire blankly. She had just said something about Helen, but he wasn't sure what.

He was distracted.

At that moment, a ship was landing on the beach at Great Point, right under the lighthouse. It was a small ship. Matt didn't hear it scrape across the sand all the way from his house in Siasconset – nor did he see the three Myrmidons vault lightly out of the vessel, grab hold of the sides and carry the boat up the beach at an effortless run. Matt wasn't physically present when ten more small ships followed and his soldiers took the beach, but he was aware of it happening as if he were. Even as Claire waved a hand in his face and sighed with frustration, his eyes could also see the precise steps of his thirty-three men as they tracked silently up from the waterline.

'Greetings,' Claire said with a worried grimace. 'Are you ever going to land that spaceship and join the conversation?'

An ironic laugh burst out of Matt. 'Land that ship,' he repeated as he sensed members of his landing party regarding the terrain with soldierly precision. With this new double awareness, Matt saw a Myrmidon warrior, his skin black and shiny like a carapace, kneel and lay a hand on the cold sand in one sleek, swift motion.

'*He's here. Our master's mind is with us right now,*' said Telamon.

Matt remembered that Telamon was a prince of his kind, and one of Matt's best captains.

'*Another beach, brothers,*' he said ruefully. Telamon rubbed his hands together to brush away the sand. The distasteful sneer he wore made it clear that he still detested sand after all these years away from Troy.

'*What are your orders?*' asked a soldier with faceted black eyes.

'*Make camp. We wait for our master here,*' Telamon decreed. '*When he's ready, he will join us.*'

'Are you OK?' Ariadne asked plaintively.

Matt blinked hard and was finally able to banish the image in his head.

'I'm fine,' he said, concentrating on the task at hand. 'Go on, Claire.'

'OK, so, like I said, the first time I saw something weird – well, weirder than usual – was when Lennie was reaching for a spoon. It *shook* for a second, like it was shivering, and then it just flew into her hand.'

'All three of us saw something similar to that when we were in Andy's hospital room,' Ariadne added.

'Describe it,' Matt said, turning to Andy.

'Well, first she got angry and then she lit up. Sparks started to fall out of her skin and hair like rain,' Andy said, her lovely voice filling with awe as she remembered. 'All the equipment in my room started to rattle, and I could have sworn I felt my bed move.'

For a moment, Matt's bedroom fell silent as they all thought about this.

'I felt something strange like that when Helen got angry the other day,' Jason added reluctantly.

'What happened?' Matt asked.

'She and Lucas were in checking on Jerry, and they started fighting. I guess it was pretty bad because they went down to the fight cage to settle it. I could have sworn I felt the house shake for a second.'

'That could have been an impact tremor,' Matt said. 'They're strong enough to shake the house when they hit the ground.'

'It was before they got downstairs. They were just walking, Matt,' Jason said with a shrug. Matt paused, thinking.

'Did you see any lightning?' he asked the three girls.

'Not really,' Ariadne said for them. 'What we saw was definitely electrical, but I can't figure out why that would make stuff rattle like that. The whole thing was just strange. And scary.'

'Her voice was all funny,' Claire added, rubbing her arms like she had a chill.

'Way too much reverb,' Andy said emphatically. 'I'm

a siren, I know voices, and I've never heard anything like that before.'

'She sounded like a goddess,' Ariadne said, summing it up for the three of them. 'Something's happened to her, guys.'

'You think?' Jason said, rolling his eyes. 'After everything she's been through, she's bound to have changed a bit. That doesn't mean she's changed in a bad way. Cut her some slack. She just fought a god.'

'And won,' Matt added quietly. 'She fought a god and won. How strong do you think she'd have to be to do that?'

'Stronger than any other Scion. Ever.' Ariadne's voice shook.

'She was *tortured*, you guys,' Jason countered sternly.

'Exactly,' Ariadne responded. 'And you think an experience like that is going to change her for the *better*?'

'This is ridiculous,' Jason said angrily. He spun round and stormed to the door.

'Jason,' Claire began, but he turned back and cut her off.

'I know you and Helen have been best friends since you were little, and that she's changing a lot and it's scaring you. But everyone changes. Just because you don't understand what's happening to Helen doesn't mean you have any reason to be afraid of her. I hope you all realize that before you go and do something stupid.'

Jason left them to stand around and stare at one another.

'There's one more thing,' Claire said, her voice forcing its way through her tight throat. 'I tried to talk to Helen about how she's changing. She made it pretty clear that she didn't care. She just wants to *win*.' Claire rubbed her arms again like she was cold. 'The Helen I knew didn't care about winning. She never even tried to win a track meet before.'

She was afraid. They all were. The worst part was that Matt had the sinking feeling that they *should* be.

Matt thought again about that morality question Zach asked once. Would Matt really kill someone who hadn't done anything yet, to keep that person from possibly killing millions? What was right?

'How much longer, captain?' asked one of the Myrmidons.

'Soon,' Telamon answered. *'Master is still torn.'*

'Impossible,' said another soldier. His glowing red eyes narrowed with emotion. *'It can't be him if he wavers. Achilles would never be swayed from our true mission. He died for it.'*

'Patience,' Telamon said commandingly.

'Patience,' the Myrmidons chanted back with hushed reverence, like they were reciting catechism. This was a ritual they had performed many times.

'Old loyalties from his mortal life still pull at him,' Telamon continued, momentarily putting a soothing

hand on a comrade's shoulder, like a sympathetic coun-sellor or a priest. *'But loyalties that are older still are starting to surface. Courage.'*

'Courage,' the soldiers repeated in unison as soon as Telamon fed them the word. Their soldierly version of 'amen' thundered across the dunes, and the force of their combined voices lifted up swells of sand off the undulating dunes and sent it airborne like smoke over the water.

'The end of this cycle is near,' Telamon continued knowingly. *'And in the end our master's heart will lead him back to us. Friends, remember. The blade chose this particular vessel because the blade knows that this vessel, above all others, shares our desire.'*

'Matt?' Ariadne asked.

Matt blinked hard again and focused on her. She looked worried.

'What do you think we should do?'

'First we have to find out how far she's willing to go,' he said gravely. 'And then we'll each have to decide – each of us for ourselves – how far we're willing to go to stop her.'

CHAPTER NINE

That night, Lucas dressed carefully. He knew the meeting of the Houses was a semi-formal affair, but that didn't mean that he was going to wear anything that would restrict his movement. He didn't trust any of the guests they were about to receive, and there was no way in hell he was going to put on anything that would hinder him in a fight.

Of course, fighting was strictly forbidden at these meetings. But Lucas knew that this was going to be the first time in twenty years that most of these people had seen each other. On top of that, many of them had killed someone who someone else in the room had loved dearly. It was a grudge match waiting to happen.

Lucas went downstairs and found half his family crowded around the TV in the living room, listening to the evening news. The pictures on TV showed an intense lightning storm over what looked like a blacked-out city.

'Is that Manhattan?' Lucas asked, moving closer to the screen.

'Yes,' his mother responded, her voice quiet with shock. 'The whole city is dark.'

Lucas could only imagine the chaos that would cause in New York. Subway lines would be stalled on the tracks with people inside, elevators would be shut down, stranding people at the tops of buildings – not to mention the lawlessness that was bound to break out in the dark.

'Why would Zeus do something like that?' Andy asked.

'To remind us he can,' Hector answered, his jaw set.

There was a knock at the front door, and Lucas heard everyone inhale a tense breath.

'I'll get it,' Kate offered, but Noel put her hand on Kate's shoulder to stop her.

'It has to be me,' Noel said kindly. 'It's my hearth.'

Lucas followed her to the front of the house. When Noel opened the door, Lucas felt like someone had kicked him in the gut. The man standing in the doorway had black hair, bright blue eyes and a tall, athletic build. He looked like Lucas, aged twenty years.

'Daedalus,' Noel said through a tight jaw. 'Noel,' Daedalus replied. He crossed his arms in an X over his chest and bowed respectfully, but it was clear they were not on good terms.

Lucas couldn't breathe for a moment. He'd been told many times that he looked like he was from the House of

Athens, but he had no idea that he looked so much like the man who had killed his grandfather.

'Welcome,' Noel said, barely meaning it. 'I offer you my hospitality.'

'I'm honoured,' Daedalus said, and entered. His eyes went directly to Lucas, and he smiled ruefully in recognition. Then his eyes darted past Lucas and hardened. 'Hello, son,' he said, and for a confused moment Lucas wondered if Daedalus was speaking to *him*.

'Father,' Orion said formally.

Lucas turned to see Orion standing right behind him with a closed look on his face. He'd been so stunned by Daedalus's appearance that he hadn't noticed Orion and Hector joining them.

Daedalus strode forward, his gait proud and more than a little intimidating. He offered his hand to his son, and Orion shook it without smiling.

'You look strong,' Daedalus said, his eyes measuring up Orion.

'I am,' Orion replied tersely. Their eyes locked, and Daedalus was the first to look away.

Lucas had never heard Orion speak so coldly, but after the way his father had abandoned him Lucas couldn't blame him. If Daedalus noticed that Orion was being uncharacteristically harsh, he didn't show it. He looked right past his angry son at Hector.

'Ajax,' he said under his breath. For a moment his

face looked regretful before it hardened again into a forbidding scowl.

'Come inside,' Noel said. 'Boys, make a hole.'

A knee-jerk reaction to protect his turf welled up in Lucas. He didn't want to let Daedalus through, and he could tell Hector and Orion felt the same way he did. They all stood their ground.

'Oh, will you just *move*?' Noel grumbled impatiently as she pushed past them. 'It doesn't matter that the Furies are gone – you all still act like a pack of wild dogs. Everybody's got to sniff everybody else's butt.'

Daedalus managed to crack a smile and followed Noel. Hector, Lucas and Orion finally eased up and let him through.

'Awkward,' Hector said after Daedalus had passed.

'A regular ray of sunshine, isn't he?' Orion said sarcastically, acting more like himself again. 'Oh, and that's his "happy face" by the way.'

'Why didn't you warn me I look so much like your dad?' Lucas asked, glaring at Orion.

'I thought you knew,' Orion replied, shrugging.

'I knew there was supposed to be some sort of resemblance, but this is ridiculous. How the hell am I supposed to feel about this?'

'It's no picnic for me, either. Every time I look at you I see my dad. The Fates like to mess with us, Luke. They make it so that we all look like the person it would be most ironic for us to look like.' Orion suddenly grinned.

'Take Hector. He looks like someone everyone liked, but he sucks.'

'Thanks, buddy,' Hector replied brightly, like Orion had just given him a compliment. They all chuckled, and the tension dissipated a bit.

'Don't let it rattle you,' Orion warned seriously, eyebrows lifted. 'We've got other things to deal with tonight.'

'I won't,' Lucas said firmly. 'I know what I'm here for.' He knew Orion understood that he was talking about protecting Helen.

Helen could hear lots of unfamiliar voices downstairs as more and more Scions arrived for the meeting of the Houses. She could feel the mounting tension through the floor like the deep thrumming of a subwoofer. Helen's new sensitivity to emotions left her wide open to everyone else's turmoil. She didn't know all the details of the war twenty years ago, but she was certain that there were plenty of old scores that still needed settling. One story down a toxic mixture of hatred, love, and loss threatened to explode into violence at any moment. It felt to Helen like she was standing on top of a bomb.

Helen tugged nervously at her outfit. It was a bit fancier than she was used to. She'd always been a sales-rack kind of girl, but Daphne had brought her a designer getup, insisting that it would make her feel more confident. Instead, it made her more nervous.

Helen was pretty sure the buttery-soft leather boots she wore were worth more than her entire wardrobe. She wondered where her mother had got the money to pay for all the clothes, but decided she didn't want to know. Daphne had no problem stealing priceless treasures from museums. Helen was pretty sure that department-store security systems didn't even show up on her radar.

For a moment Helen pictured her mother leaving a trail of mayhem behind her as she made her way from Newfoundland to Nantucket to get from Daedalus's house to the meeting at the Deloses' – stolen cars, robbed stores, broken hearts piling up behind her as she travelled. Her mother had been back for an hour, and all Helen could think about was how many laws Daphne had broken since they'd last seen each other.

'Stop fidgeting,' Daphne said. She pulled the chain round Helen's neck and fished out the heart necklace, laying the charm over Helen's clothes. 'The House of Atreus is descended from Zeus, so it's the highest ranking. We join the group second to last,' Daphne said, coaching Helen. 'Last, of course, is the Oracle.'

Helen pulled away from her mother, reaching for a hairbrush to hide the fact that she didn't want to be touched by her. Daphne noticed, anyway.

'It's time. Everyone's here,' Daphne said brusquely.

'How do you know?' Helen asked.

'I recognize all their voices.' Daphne laughed mirthlessly and tucked her hair behind her ear with her pinkie finger. 'Some of the people downstairs I know better than I know you.'

'And whose fault is that?'

'Not fault,' Daphne said gently. 'Choice. It was my choice, Helen, and it was the right one. You really were better off without me.'

Helen opened her mouth to argue with Daphne, but stopped. As a Falsefinder, she could hear the truth in Daphne's voice. Daphne wasn't feeding her a line or trying to excuse herself for bad parenting. She really believed that she'd done the right thing and, thinking about her father still asleep just down the hall, Helen agreed. She *had* been better off without her mother. Daphne might have abandoned her, but she'd abandoned her to a better life – a happier life – with Jerry for a dad, and Claire and Matt as best friends. It must have taken a lot of discipline for Daphne to do that. Helen started to understand how fortunate she'd been. She'd had about seventeen years of normal life that had shaped her into the person she was now. And Daphne had been the one to give that to her, by leaving.

'Thank you,' Helen whispered.

'You're welcome,' Daphne said back hollowly.

Surprised at her tone, Helen looked down at Daphne's chest and saw nothing but a dark void – a gaping hole that went on and on, like an endless well of emptiness instead of a heart. She shrank away from her mother. The gesture was not lost on Daphne.

'What, Helen? What is it?' she asked.

'Your heart's gone,' Helen answered, too overwhelmed by the unnatural hole inside Daphne to remember to conceal her new talent.

'It died the day Ajax did,' Daphne replied simply.

'But there's *nothing* there. Not even a broken heart,' Helen said, shaking her head. 'You're not sad or angry or hurt. You feel nothing. That can't be natural.' She locked eyes with Daphne and grabbed her wrist to keep her from moving away. 'What did you do, Mother?' Daphne tried to pull away from Helen, but her daughter was too strong.

'Whatever was left of my feelings I traded in order to accomplish a goal. Women do it all the time. Scion women swear it before Hecate,' Daphne said, her eyes narrowing with suspicion as a thought occurred to her. 'But how can you know what I *don't* feel?' Daphne murmured, more to herself than to Helen.

'Helen?' Andy said as she tapped on the door. 'Are you in there?'

'Yes,' Helen replied. She released her mother and quickly turned to the door. 'Come in.'

Andy pushed the door open tentatively and peeked into the room. 'Noel is getting . . . ah . . . *antsy* is the only polite word I can come up with right now. She says you and your mom need to get your butts downstairs before somebody murders somebody else and gets blood all over her clean floors.' She smiled and held up her hands. 'I'm quoting her, by the way.'

'I'll bet.' Helen chuckled. 'We're coming.'

There was still so much she and Daphne needed to talk about, but as usual, where her mother was concerned, Helen was going to have to wait until later to get any answers. She and Daphne followed Andy out of Ariadne's bedroom and down the hallway towards the stairs.

'My, my,' Daphne said quietly as she followed Andy's graceful silhouette. 'Aren't you a rare fish?'

Helen saw Andy's back stiffen at Daphne's taunt and her gait taper off to a stop.

'I'm half siren,' Andy said. She turned to look Daphne dead in the eye. 'Do you have a problem with that?'

'No,' Daphne replied. She met Andy's gaze and stood firm. 'But you obviously do, and it's time you got over it.'

Daphne brushed past Andy. Helen followed reluctantly, giving Andy an apologetic look as she passed by.

'Hector isn't Apollo,' Daphne added when she reached the stairs. 'It's time you got over that too.'

'You have no right—' Andy began angrily.

'Hector is one of the best men I've ever known, little half siren who hates herself,' Daphne interrupted, silencing Andy. Helen saw Daphne's eyes harden until they sparkled like diamonds. 'You don't deserve him.'

Helen mouthed the words *I'm sorry* to Andy as she went down the stairs, but Andy had turned on her heel and gone before Helen could finish.

Still thinking about Andy, Helen followed her mother

into the tense living room. Her eyes went immediately to a big, blond man who stood in front of Castor and Pallas in the place she knew was reserved for the Head of the House of Thebes.

He had to be Tantalus, and although she had never met him before she recognized him. She pictured his face, red, sweaty, and twisted with rage as he tried to beat her child out of her.

Tantalus stared at Daphne. It was the same way that Menelaus stared at Helen of Troy. With Helen's new talent she could see his chest crawling with need. For a moment, his eyes darted over Daphne's shoulder to land on Helen. She shivered with revulsion, remembering another life when she had been forced to be his wife after Troy fell. Then his eyes went back to Daphne, where they stayed until the Oracle entered.

As soon as Cassandra glided into the room, her bell-bracelet tinkling delicately, Lucas, Hector, Orion and Helen moved as one to join her. Cassandra sat in her giant chair. Orion stood at her left, Helen at her right. Hector and Lucas stood behind Helen, one to either side of her.

The outburst from the assembled host was immediate.

'Helen! Get back here!' Daphne scolded. Helen gladly ignored her.

'Lucas . . . *son*,' Castor said, clipping his words sharply. 'You are to stand behind your uncle Tantalus.' Lucas looked away from his father, eyes forward and face expressionless like a trained soldier, and didn't leave his chosen place behind Helen.

'You see? I told you!' hissed a slender man with full lips. He was older, about Helen's mother's age, but he was the kind of guy who just got more handsome as he aged. Definitely someone from the House of Rome, she decided. Helen didn't recognize his face, but from the way Orion and Daedalus stared daggers at him she knew he had to be Phaon.

Phaon turned his back on the group and addressed his faction. 'Orion won't even stand with us. He doesn't care about the House of Rome, but you still call him your Head? Do we need any more proof that he is unfit to lead?'

Helen glanced down at the suppurating gash that should have been his heart, and her stomach churned. Phaon's face and body might be beautiful, but this *creature* she looked at was rotten to the core. She saw Orion's heart flare with anger. She caught his eyes and pleaded with him silently, trying to calm him down.

'Enough,' Cassandra commanded in a low voice. An obedient hush descended as everyone's attention turned to the Oracle. 'The days of division are over. The Houses are one, and we have formed a coalition of our own to express that union. Each House is represented by its Heir, and we've chosen Helen as our leader.'

'Challenge,' Phaon said immediately, a smirk plastered on his face as he sized up Helen's skinny arms and soft hands. 'I challenge Helen Atreus for the right to lead the Heirs . . . and the Oracle.'

'Did Christmas come early this year?' Hector drawled as he stepped forward, grinning from ear to ear. 'I'm Helen's champion, dickhead. You challenge her, you fight me.'

Phaon's face blanched. He sputtered something about how his House didn't allow champions, that it was an archaic bylaw that should be removed. Hector glared at Phaon as he backed down, every inch of him glowing like a storybook hero in front of a cringing coward.

'And you, Orion?' Daedalus called out to his son in a demeaning tone. 'You allow Helen to lead, and Hector to be her champion. . . . What honour does the Heir to the House of Athens hold?'

'Orion is *my* champion,' Cassandra snapped. Her mouth was pinched in anger as she regarded Daedalus. 'Is that honourable enough for you, Attica?'

Daedalus bowed reverently to the Oracle, his arms crossed in an X across his chest and his torso parallel to the ground as he spoke. 'May the Pride of Athens serve you well, Sibyl, to the glory of our House.'

When he stood up straight again he regarded Cassandra strangely, his eyes darting from her to Orion and back again like he couldn't understand their connection to each other.

Helen saw the confusion inside of Daedalus, drifting aimlessly around his heart like sullen smoke. As the

House Heads conferred with their members over this new development, Helen stared at Cassandra and Orion.

Cassandra was the cold hand of Fate, and as such she was not supposed to be able to be passionate about anything. Lately, she had been pulling away from everyone, including her own family, and they had all accepted this as an unavoidable consequence of her position. But that wasn't the case with Orion. She growled like a cornered cat whenever anyone slighted him.

Chastened, Daedalus moved back to his position in front of another dark-haired, blue-eyed man from the House of Athens. Orion glanced down at Cassandra and grinned. Inside his chest, Helen saw tenderness, not attraction. He was obviously fond of his 'little Kitty', and grateful that she had defended him in front of his father, but he didn't regard her as a woman.

The silvery orb hanging in Cassandra's chest seemed barren and remote to Helen, like a dead star, but it flared with its own brand of mercurial light when Orion smiled at her. It danced. It glowed. It filled up and spilled over, just like any woman's heart would when the man she adored smiled at her.

It was exactly what Orion had told Helen he'd always wanted – to be loved *more* – and there it was, right in front of him. But he didn't seem to see it.

Helen glanced at the faction from the House of Rome, wondering if any of them saw what she saw.

Phaon was staring at Cassandra. He ogled the pure,

crystalline light inside her in a way that made Helen's skin crawl. Obviously, Phaon could see it, even though Orion couldn't.

But what Orion *did* see was Phaon staring at Cassandra.

'Don't even look at her,' Orion growled, stepping in front of Cassandra and shielding her from Phaon's view.

Daedalus and his second strode towards Phaon, their blue eyes icy with hatred. Even Castor and Pallas, usually so levelheaded, reacted to the threat to Cassandra and the whole room seemed to move towards Phaon like a menacing wave. Daphne intercepted them all with raised hands.

'Dae, I know. I do. But not here, not now,' Daphne said in an undertone to Daedalus, her eyes pleading. 'Castor. Don't break your oath of hospitality. Not again.'

Helen knew that Daphne was reminding Castor of how she had been attacked by Pandora a few short months ago while she was under Castor's protection. Daedalus, Castor and Pallas all eased back, but their faces were livid. Phaon's shrill laughter filled the room.

'Easy, mongrels,' he said as he wound down from his disturbing laugh. 'She's too old for me.'

'Disgusting,' Orion said under his breath. He made a choked sound and his hands tensed, as if he wanted to strangle his cousin. That was enough for Phaon.

Helen saw Phaon reach for the blade strapped across

his back under his clothes. It was the same kind of sheath that Orion habitually wore, except Orion wasn't wearing it then. No weapons were allowed at House meetings, and Helen knew that Orion was defenceless. She also sensed that, despite his reluctance to meet Hector in a fair fight, in a dirty fight Phaon had had more experience and would probably win. Orion could be hurt, or even killed.

Helen felt like all her insides suddenly sprouted wings and tried to fly out of her mouth. She didn't think about what she should or shouldn't do, about the sacred rules of hospitality, or about the 'cease-fire' they had all agreed upon. All she thought about was the bare blade in Phaon's hand.

She called to the metal. It was similar to how she summoned bolts, only this time instead of a bright splinter of electricity Helen took the same force and widened it into a field. It was like taking a single coin and learning the simple trick of flipping it over to discover an entirely different face. She used this field to reach out and snatch the stiletto from Phaon's grasp.

'How dare you!' she roared, her voice booming out of her like thunder.

The hilt of Phaon's weapon smacked into the palm of her hand, and she stormed forward, raising the blade high above her head to slash down and cut out Phaon's twisted little heart. The insides of her thighs burned, and Helen felt the ground rock violently underneath her. She saw Phaon tumble to the ground and grovel in front of her.

'Helen! No!' Lucas pleaded in her ear, his body convulsing against hers. 'P-Please, s-stop,' he stammered, his jaw shaking uncontrollably.

She looked around, confused, like she was waking from a dream. Lucas had her by the waist, and he was pulling her back. She glanced down and saw that her skin was glowing pearly pink and blue with ball lightning. Lucas held on to her, even though in that moment she was hotter than the surface of the sun.

She switched off the current immediately, and he fell down with a scream. Furniture was toppled over, and everyone else in the room had fallen from the earthquake she had created. The floor under her was a large disc of black charcoal that still smouldered around the edges like a ring of fire. Everyone stared up at her, terrified.

Except for Lucas. His hands, chest and cheek were black and bloody, burned down to the bone by the ball lightning she had created. He writhed on the ground in agony.

'Oh, no!' Helen cried, crouching down over Lucas. 'No-no-no,' she chanted hysterically.

Lucas moaned when she touched him. His crispy skin flaked off and drifted in the air like burnt paper. He was so terribly injured and in so much pain Helen knew that there was no place in the world she could take him that could ease his suffering.

She needed a new world.

It's not that Helen forgot Hades's promise that the Fates would bring her to this. Nor did she forget his warning that as soon as she created her own world the gods would challenge her for it. She just didn't care. She'd build a whole new universe from scratch and send all of Olympus to Tartarus if she had to – anything, anything at all, to fix Lucas.

Helen gathered Lucas up in her arms. As his heartbeat stopped and his eyes closed, she created a portal to her new world and took him there.

CHAPTER TEN

Daphne touched her hand to the spiky crust of ice that had formed over the charcoal.

Insanity was swirling over her head while she stared at the burnt-out basin that used to be a living-room floor, and the snowflake-like ice that had grown over it, smothering the fire, when her daughter disappeared with Lucas. How could she use this? Daphne wondered.

Daphne had never expected this meeting to be successful, but the bickering that had ensued as soon as Helen had made her dramatic exit was rising to a fever pitch. Before everyone started hacking each other to bits, Daphne needed to take control. She didn't plan to lose this opportunity.

'Did you make that earthquake?' she yelled up at Orion, interrupting the chaos.

'No,' he said. When he got shot several disbelieving looks, he sighed and continued reluctantly. 'Helen did it. She got the Earthshaker talent from me when we became blood brothers.'

'And how did she take the blade away from Phaon?' Daedalus asked.

'Electro*magnetism*,' Pallas replied. 'Although I've never heard of any Bolt-thrower having enough voltage to create a magnetic field like that.'

'She's too powerful,' Tantalus said quietly to Pallas. 'She could kill us all.'

Pallas nodded in agreement, as did Daedalus.

The room fell into stunned silence as they all contemplated this. Daphne couldn't let them get distracted by that detail right now.

She grabbed the Bough of Aeneas, disguised as a gold cuff on Orion's wrist as she stood. 'Did you open a portal with this and push Helen and Lucas through it?'

'No. I can only open standing portals, not create them,' he answered. 'Only Helen can make her own portals wherever she wants.'

'The ice?' Daphne asked, inviting him to explain it. She needed to get everyone thinking in the right direction.

'There's always ice when she descends. But if she went to the Underworld she'd be back almost instantly. Time stops here while you're in the Underworld,' Orion said, confused by Daphne's line of questioning.

'That's not always the case. At least not for Helen,' Daphne countered. 'I don't know why, but, in one instance I witnessed, time passed here on Earth while Helen was in the Underworld.'

Castor looked at Tantalus, who Daphne knew was a Falsefinder. Tantalus nodded. 'She's telling the truth,' he said.

'The Underworld?' Castor whispered, his voice breaking. 'Why would she take Lucas to the Underworld?'

They had all felt the terrible heat of Helen's electrical storm. Except for Daphne, who could handle the intense heat of lightning, the rest of them had raw, red burns on their exposed skin. And Lucas had held on to her while she was in that state. Marry that idea to the Underworld, and they would all come to realize that Lucas was dead or dying.

'Uncle,' Hector said gently. Castor's eyes darted around, like he didn't even hear his nephew. Hector looked across the room at Jason and Ariadne. All of them were speechless and searching each other for answers.

'Helen knows the Underworld better than anyone. Maybe she knows a place that could help Luke? Maybe that's why she took him there,' Jason said, thinking out loud. Really, he was just grasping at straws. They all looked at Orion for confirmation.

'Could that be it?' Castor asked.

Orion shrugged and shook his head as if to say that he didn't know. He didn't look very hopeful.

Daphne allowed a few seconds tick by to let it sink in. 'What if she stays down there with him, Orion?' Daphne said quietly, reminding herself not to push too hard.

She saw Orion's face crumple at the thought of losing

Helen forever. He loved her and would do anything for her, just as Daphne had planned when she shoved the two of them together in the Underworld.

It was predictable, really. Two young, beautiful teenagers, faced with incredible odds, teaming up together to fight a common cause. All Daphne had had to do was make a relationship with Lucas impossible, give Orion a chance to hope, and he would certainly fall for Helen. Now all Daphne could do was hope that he loved her *enough* . . . so that Daphne could truly control him.

'Could you go after her?' she continued, nudging him, trying to work just the right angle in this situation to get Orion to realize what, or rather *what role*, he was meant to play in the next Great Cycle. 'Could you bring her back?'

'From the *dead*?' Daedalus blurted out before he realized what he was saying. He glanced over at Castor apologetically. 'I'm sorry, Castor. But your son didn't look good.'

Castor nodded. His face was stark white, and his eyes stared blankly at the floor, like they weren't seeing anything any more.

'We don't know what happened yet. Don't give up hope,' Tantalus whispered in Castor's ear. He clasped his brother on the shoulder comfortingly while Daphne bit her tongue to keep herself from snarling at the sound of his voice. She wanted to scream at Castor not to trust him, but she knew it wouldn't do any good.

Tantalus spoke up so the rest of the room was included, easily shifting into the role of leader in the wake of disaster. He had always been the most charismatic of them all, Daphne thought bitterly. Even when they knew he was evil, they trusted him anyway. They *wanted* to trust him, just as Daphne had once trusted him.

'I say we use this meeting to discuss what we witnessed and how we should move forward,' Tantalus said as he addressed the group. His eyes moved to Phaon and hardened. 'Starting with how to punish Phaon for attempting to murder the Head of his House.'

Andy sat in the kitchen with the rest of the non-Scions – the rest of the non-Scions who didn't need to lie down, that is. Kate had taken Noel upstairs after it became clear that she wouldn't be able to stop crying. Noel was a tough lady, Andy could see that, but after what had happened to Lucas any mother would have fallen apart.

Matt and Claire waited for Kate and Noel to leave before they spoke.

'I never thought Helen would hurt Lucas. Never,' Claire whispered, her eyes blank with sadness. 'I can't believe it.'

'She's completely out of control,' Matt whispered back.

The two friends sat, their faces unmoving like pale masks. Andy didn't know Helen like they did, but she did know what malice looked like when she saw it. Having a siren for a mother had ensured that.

'But it was an accident,' Andy said, sticking up for Helen. 'She didn't mean to do it.'

'That makes it even worse,' Matt responded heatedly. 'Can you imagine what would have happened if she *did* mean it?'

Matt, Claire and Andy sat silently at the table and listened in on the rest of the meeting. The Scions fought over how they were going to carve up Phaon. Apparently, this Phaon guy was extra popular, especially with the older generation. They all wanted a piece of him, but it was Daedalus from the House of Athens who claimed the biggest grievance, and not just to avenge what had nearly happened to his son when Phaon tried to kill him just moments ago.

There was mention of a young girl named Cassiopeia, and the room grew quiet. Then it was unanimously decided that Daedalus and Phaon were to meet at dawn for a duel to the death. After that, the meeting was adjourned. Seconds later, Ariadne and Jason joined them in the kitchen. Ariadne's eyes filled up with tears as soon as she saw Matt.

'Lucas . . .' she whispered as she wrapped her arms round his chest.

Claire went to Jason and searched his face, wordlessly asking him a question. 'It's bad, Claire. We felt his heart stop,' Jason said tonelessly.

'He'll pull through, though. Won't he?' Claire said. Jason shrugged, his lip trembling. Claire pulled his head down and let it rest on her shoulder.

Jason and Ariadne were gifted Healers. They knew the true extent of Lucas's injuries. They may not have shared the details while they were in the meeting, but here in the safety of Noel's kitchen they could express what they couldn't in front of the other Houses. Neither of them thought that Lucas would make it.

Matt and Claire comforted the twins as best they could, but there wasn't much they could do apart from holding them. Matt and Claire shared a grim look over Jason's and Ariadne's shoulders. Andy knew what they were thinking.

If Helen could kill Lucas, the person she loved the most, she could kill them all.

Andy watched her new friends hug each other for a moment, and then started to feel like she was intruding. She hadn't really known Lucas, and she had no idea what it was like to have a brother or a sister – let alone what it would feel like to think he or she was going to die. She'd always wanted someone to love as much as they obviously loved Lucas.

Confused that she seemed to *want* to suffer like they were suffering, that she felt almost jealous of how deeply they all felt this, Andy made her way to the kitchen door that led out to the yard.

She was a creature of the sea, and the ocean had

always been her biggest comfort. Andy figured that maybe a quick swim would clear her head enough so that she could be there to help this family that had helped her so much. For the first time since she'd been brought to the Delos house, Andy left the property and headed to the beach.

'She walks in beauty, like the night,' said a lilting voice that was deep and dark, and bright and innocent all at once. Unmistakable.

Andy froze, although she knew it was too late. He'd already seen her, so there was no point in trying to stay still like a dumb deer in the middle of the road. Apollo was not a car – he was a wolf. Deer need to *run* from wolves.

'You didn't really think I'd forgotten about you, did you?' Apollo asked as he sauntered toward her, backlit by the long rays of the lowering sun.

The water's edge was just a few steps away. Maybe she could make it . . .

'I wouldn't if I were you,' Apollo said, tracking her intention. She felt the back of her throat close off with a sob, convinced that this was it. This was where she was going to die a horrible, drawn-out death.

'And I wouldn't if I were *you*,' said what sounded like the echo of Apollo's voice from somewhere out in the water.

Andy's head turned to see Hector rising up out of the waves. Bare-chested and dressed only in soaking-wet jeans, he strode through the tide easily, as if the water were his ally. His face, an exact copy of Apollo's, was rigid with anger.

Apollo smiled at his Scion double. 'Interesting talent you have over the water, son. Where did you get it?'

Hector didn't reply. He went straight to Andy. 'Are you OK?' he asked her gently. She nodded and cast wary eyes in Apollo's direction, as if to say 'For now.' Hector angled Andy behind him and faced Apollo.

'My, my. How brash you are,' the god admonished. 'Aren't you the least bit worried about challenging me?'

'No,' Hector said in a steady voice. Apollo burst out laughing. It was a queer-sounding cackle – not human, and a little less than sane.

'You should be.' Apollo's eyes gleamed. His skin shone with its own light, and it suddenly seemed as if the god wore full armour and carried a stout, bronze sword.

Although he was unarmed and half naked, Hector did not flinch or show the least bit of fear. After a moment, the godly nimbus of light surrounding Apollo died down and the vision of armour vanished.

'You really are him,' Apollo said, impressed. 'Hector reborn. And I should know. I rode with him in his chariot at Troy.'

Hector didn't answer. He stared at his adversary, every muscle awake under his skin. Standing just inches away from his bare back, Andy could feel a storm churning inside Hector. He *wanted* to fight this god, she realized.

Apollo's face twitched. He was afraid of Hector. For the first time in what seemed like ages, Andy felt something close to relief.

'Soon, little son,' Apollo said, speaking about the confrontation that Hector so obviously wanted. 'Soon we'll be back on the battlefield, but this time I fight for Olympus, and you for your newly made Atlantis. And if Zeus doesn't force us to resort to tricks like he did the last time we'll finally complete the Fates' cycle and prove who is superior – the parents or their Scions.'

Apollo leapt into the sky and flew away. Hector watched him go, thinking about what Apollo had just revealed. Andy knew she should be thinking about what the god had said as well, but all she could do was watch Hector. She was wondering how she could have ever mistaken him for Apollo.

Sure, their features and build were the same, but Hector's eyes were alive and full of emotion while Apollo's were missing something crucial. *Something human*, she supposed. The god's eyes had the dead-smooth quality of a marble sculpture while Hector's were quick and fierce . . . so full of feeling they seemed to burn with it.

'Thank you,' she whispered, her whole life owed to him in those two words.

He glanced at her and nodded once, then abruptly turned to leave. He walked over to his shirt and shoes, heaped in a pile a way up the beach. Andy followed his silent figure, stunned.

'That's *it*?' she said, her voice pitching up incredulously at the end. 'You aren't even going to say one word to me? Just save my life, nod and off you go like you do this every Tuesday or something?'

Hector didn't look at her. Angling his face away, he pulled his shirt over his head and reached down to grab his shoes.

'Hey!' she shouted. He ignored her. 'Hey!' She ran up to him, and pushed him as hard as she could.

'What?' he said, frustrated, as he stumbled away from her.

'What do you mean, *what*?' she yelled back at him sarcastically.

'I mean, what do you want from me, Andy? Do you want me to go, or stay, or drop dead? *What*?'

His eyes searched hers. They bounced back and forth, looking for something inside her. Andy shrugged. She had no idea what he was looking for. He sat down in the sand with his shoes in his hand, like he was giving up.

'I can't do this with you. Not tonight,' he said quietly. 'I just watched my brother get burned to a crisp right in front of me – '

He stopped and looked away from her, his shoulders swelling with a deep breath. He caught and held it before it turned into tears. Andy knelt down on the sand next to him while he struggled, feeling horrible. He was barely keeping it together, but still he'd put all his other feelings aside and risked his life to save hers. And then she'd yelled at him. Not her classiest moment.

'I'm sorry, Hector.' Andy touched his arm with the tips of her fingers. He leaned a tiny bit closer.

'The worst part is not knowing where they went or how he's doing,' he confided. 'I *hate* that I can't help them. You know?'

She did. Hector was good at saving people. She had just seen for herself that Hector was the type of guy who would rather fight a god than feel useless. Not being able to do anything was probably the worst kind of torture for him.

'Can Orion find them in the Underworld? Oh! Maybe he could even bring you with him? You could go get them,' she said, trying to be helpful.

'Orion can't find Helen. She's the one who finds *him* when they meet in the Underworld,' Hector replied, shaking his head.

'They spent all that time down there together, and they don't have a set meeting place?'

'Time and space aren't like they are here, and Helen is the Descender, not Orion. He could look for her, but unless she knew that he was looking for her, and she went to him, they'd never meet up.' Hector pushed some sand around with his hands, swirling his fingers through it in frustration. 'Helen's the one in control.'

'I've been hearing that a lot lately.' Andy looked down at the patterns he was making in the sand and frowned.

'So all we can do is wait for Helen to come back? That's pretty annoying.'

'That's why I needed a swim. There's some water nymph in my family, and I've always felt at home in the ocean,' he said, smiling and looking down at the sand. 'Helps me calm down.'

'Me too.' She stared at his profile, wondering how it was that they had so much in common already. They'd never said more than a few words to each other, but she understood him perfectly. 'And almost getting in a fight with a god isn't exactly calming. Sorry about that.'

'No. Don't say that.'

He looked up at her, and she forgot how to breathe. He was beautiful, sure. But beauty is easy. That wasn't what moved her. What moved her was all the life she saw inside him. He had such a strong spirit it seemed to reach out of his eyes and grab her.

'You showing up was the best thing that's happened to me all day,' he said, totally ruining the moment.

Andy cringed. 'Yeah, well. Thanks?' she said dubiously. 'But I'd be more impressed with that line if I didn't know what a crap day you've had.'

They both cracked up.

'That line was pretty pathetic, wasn't it?' he asked, making fun of himself.

'I've heard worse, but yeah. It was pretty bad.' She grinned at him and threw up her hands incredulously. 'What happened? I had you pegged as a total smoothie.'

'What can I say? I'm off my game,' he laughed, and looked away, growing almost shy. 'I am *so* not smooth around you.'

'Good,' she said quietly, letting the joke go. 'I like you better like this, anyway.'

When he looked at her out of the corner of his eyes and smiled, Andy knew she'd never mistake him for anyone else again. It didn't matter who he looked like. Hector was unique. Andy also knew that, like it or not, from that moment on no other man would ever quite equal him in her mind.

Matt watched Apollo leave Hector and Andy on the beach and relaxed his grip on his dagger, thankful that nothing had happened. He knew he couldn't have allowed Apollo to hurt the girl but interfering would have caused a whole mess of problems. Matt was still trying to convince himself he could live with a few misgivings as long as the greater evil was exterminated. He was just glad he didn't have to confront those misgivings yet, and he hoped the gods didn't put him in a position where he would have to.

Matt stole up the beach silently. Quiet as he was, he knew the only reason Hector hadn't heard him was that he was distracted by Andy.

He and Andromache were reunited. From what Matt saw they had the same kind of love as before. A tender, humorous companionship that could survive anything – even war, famine, and the loss of other loved ones. Their love was one of the reasons Troy had withstood the siege.

Matt wished them the best and hoped it would turn out differently this time. He really liked Hector. He always had, despite their deep political differences. Hector was the only one who really understood him.

That's the thing about walls, Matt thought. *The men on either side of them sometimes have nearly everything in common – except for the one detail that they are willing to kill each other over.*

Running up the beach to Great Point Lighthouse, Matt could vaguely make out the tents of his army's camp. Well camouflaged even during the day, they looked like nothing more than sand dunes to the casual observer, but Matt could see them for what they were. Myrmidon nests.

'Master,' Telamon said, appearing soundlessly next to Matt.

Matt smiled at him and clasped him warmly by the forearms in greeting. He was surprised to feel such a deep tie to the captain. Fond memories welled up in Matt, reminding him of the bond they once shared. Telamon peered into Matt's face.

'I look nothing like him, Telamon,' Matt said with a chuckle.

'It's not the looks that are important,' he replied sincerely. 'It's your conviction that counts.'

'I know what I believe. I would have believed it even

if the dagger never came to me. I realize that now, and I know what I have to do,' Matt said sadly, and released his old friend.

He became aware of a mass of men moving out of the dunes. They gathered around Matt like a thinking fog that bristled with arrows and swords.

'Which is precisely why the dagger chose you.' Telamon stepped back and raised his voice slightly, including the other thirty-two Myrmidons in this reunion. 'Master would never force his beliefs on another. That's why it took so long. He waited until he found a spirit that matched his own.'

The soldiers who seemingly appeared out of thin air passed in front of Matt, each of them searching his face as Telamon had. Some of the faces of his soldiers had monstrous ant-like characteristics, like antennae, shiny all-black eyes, or lobster-red skin that seemed to be made out of shell. Some appeared nearly human on the outside, but Matt knew they weren't.

Matt recognized them one by one. They must have recognized something familiar about him as well, because, as they each looked him over, satisfied looks spread across their faces.

'I know you all, and I notice that many of us have been lost along the way,' Matt said with real emotion.

They had waited for him for so long, and every single one of them had come when they were called. Matt couldn't live with himself if he wasn't honest about the doubt that he still felt. 'I'm sorry, brothers. I'm not sure this war is just. It's not our goal I question. I know what is right, and I know I need to do it no matter how hard it is for me. But I still have reservations about who we fight alongside.'

'As you did at Troy,' Telamon said with a knowing half smile, like he was reminding Matt that nothing much had changed. 'You fight for no king, and no country, Master. You fight for the right of every man to decide his own fate. As every one of us decided for ourselves when we swore on the blade.'

'*Swore on the blade,*' the mass of Myrmidons whispered.

'One man, one vote,' Telamon prompted.

'*One man, one vote,*' the Myrmidons chanted back.

Matt waited for the chorus of believers to settle down before continuing. There was something about their single-mindedness that disturbed him, especially since what they were repeating in unison was the cornerstone of *individual* thought, and the jewel of Greek philosophy.

The idea of 'one man, one vote' was the beginning of democracy. Poor or rich, god or mortal, Matt believed that every being should be counted equally. The weak had just as much right to decide for themselves as the powerful. That belief was something he would die to defend. Matt also knew that when one individual acquired too much power, those without power suffered and usually died. He couldn't live with himself if he let that happen. Not when he could stop it. But he didn't want to make the same mistakes he had at Troy.

'The god Hermes has informed me that several Scions wish to join our cause against the Tyrant, but I don't trust them. What I want each of you to consider is this: should we go it alone?' Matt asked, stepping back and raising his voice to include all his men in this decision. 'What do you say? Should we have Hermes arrange for all of us to meet the Scions? Or can we do this without making alliances with people and with gods who are not much better than the evil we fight?'

'We fight and die for one purpose, Master,' Telamon said. The word *Master* was whispered through the men in agreement, unsettling Matt again. 'Alone or with allies, it matters not. When you fight, those who seek the same goal as you will claim credit for your victories whether you want them to or not. Only one thing really matters.'

Matt nodded, his decision made, despite all he knew it would cost him. 'The Tyrant must die.'

Helen lay in the grass, staring at Lucas while he slept. In its first moments, this new world she created was nothing but that – soft grass under her, a sun in the blue sky above her and Lucas beside her. Then the world grew, because he was suffering.

She willed the sunshine to take his pain away, the air to heal his wounds, and the ground to nourish him so he didn't need food or water. In seconds, Lucas was healthy and perfect again. His eyes fluttered open and locked with hers, and Helen's whole world was in him.

'Hi,' he said, a smile spreading across his face.

'Hi,' she replied, smiling back at him.

'Am I dead?'

'Not even a little bit.'

'Oh, good.' He looked up at the bright, blank sky.

Helen hadn't had a chance to put any clouds in it yet. Clouds popped into existence as they occurred to her, hazing out the yellow sun perfectly so Lucas wasn't blinded by it.

'Are you sure I'm not dead? Cos I feel kinda dead,' he said suspiciously.

Helen chuckled and laid her hand on his chest. For a moment, the steady thumping of his heart was the only sound in Helen's world. 'You don't feel dead to me.'

'That's all that matters,' he said, turning his head to look at her. Worry darkened his eyes. 'I know this isn't possible. What did you do, Helen?'

'I made you a world.'

Lucas sat up and looked around, and she felt suddenly shy, like he was looking at an unfinished painting, and she was still sitting at her easel. Helen willed the grass to stretch out and turn into a field. She put flowers in the grass, bees in the flowers and filled the air with the scent and sounds of springtime. He watched the world grow, like a carpet unrolling in all directions, and looked back at Helen. He dropped his head, shaking it.

'It figures. If anyone was ever gifted enough to make a whole new world, it would be you, wouldn't it?'

'I'm not the only one *ever*,' she admitted, sitting up next to Lucas and regarding him seriously. 'Hades did it. Zeus did it. Morpheus did it. And . . . Atlanta did it.'

'Atlanta. As in, *Atlantis*?' he asked, frowning in thought. Helen nodded. Lucas turned to her, deadly serious. 'Helen, do you know where Atlantis is?'

Helen swallowed and nodded. Like removing a Band-Aid, she figured it would be best if she just got it over with quickly.

'It's gone. I don't know all the details, but Hades told me that it sank forever when Atlanta lost some kind of challenge.' Helen watched Lucas's face fall, like something in his body ached. 'I'm sorry, Lucas. There is no Atlantis.'

'No. But there's here,' he said, his mood lifting. Helen looked at him, puzzled.

'Yes, but no Atlantis means that there's no immortality. All those years the Houses have been killing each other to get to Atlantis and become immortal . . . and it's all a fairy tale.'

'I'll bet anything your world is better than Atlantis ever was. And I bet if Atlanta could make people immortal, so can you.'

'Well, thanks, but all I've made so far is a field of flowers. Not eternal life.'

He looked at her for a few moments. Helen knew this

look. He gave it to her when he was trying to figure out the best way to explain something complicated to her.

'Just spit it out,' she groaned, grinning at the inevitable lesson he was about to give her.

'I'm just thinking about how your world works. Everything you want to happen, happens – no matter how crazy it is, right? But there are still rules,' Lucas said, talking and thinking at the same time. 'Let me put it this way. You healed my body. And I know I was pretty close to dead.'

'Yeah, but . . .'

'When we go back to the other world. Ah, Earth,' he said, grimacing at how strange it was to say that. 'I'm assuming that my wounds won't come back, will they?'

'Of course not. You're healed.'

'So you changed my body. Whatever you did to my body here will carry over when we return to Earth. That's one of the rules.' Lucas waited for Helen to nod, which she did slowly, still trying to catch up with him. 'Then what's to say you couldn't make me immortal here and I'd stay that way, forever, no matter what world we go to?'

Helen stared at him. 'How do you *do* that? How do you figure everything out so quickly?'

'You may be all-powerful, but nothing beats plain old logic.' He smiled at her. 'Am I right? You can make anyone immortal by bringing them here and willing it?'

She nodded silently, thinking about how she'd get injured in Hades and wake up in her bed on Earth and still be injured. She knew from experience that if something happened to the body in one world it carried over into all the others. The same went for immortality. Helen knew this was right implicitly, the same way she knew her feet were there even when she wasn't thinking about them. She could make herself and Lucas immortal just by thinking it here in her world.

Just one wish made here in this world, sitting in the grass, and she and Lucas could live together, young and healthy forever.

'Don't,' Lucas said, his face immobile. He knew what Helen was considering. 'We need to really think about this before we go and do anything permanent.'

Helen thought about how Lucas had looked when she'd brought him to her world just moments ago – his charred skin, the bone showing raw and red in some of the worst spots. She knew she was tough, but she also knew that there were some things she could handle and some things that she couldn't. Losing Lucas was not something she could handle. Not now, not ever.

'Of course. We'll talk about it later.' She smiled placidly at him.

'Helen,' he began, his eyes widening at her in warning.

She stood up before Lucas had a chance to lecture her, and pulled him to his feet. 'Come on, smarty-pants. I want to go to Paris. Or Rome. Or Stockholm.'

He didn't know what she meant until a city skyline

appeared at the edge of the field of grass and wildflowers. There was no ugly transition, no garbage heaps or poorly designed public transit hubs, just flowers and then pavement. A gleaming city sprang into being, perfect and contained from the natural world right next to it, like a kingdom in a snow-globe.

They stepped on to the pavement, and the city and all of its noise and bustle and life surrounded them. The scent of roasting coffee and baking bread filled the air, and their noses led them to a murmuring, clattering café, half a block down.

'It's like New York, Vienna and Reykjavík had a baby with Scotland,' Lucas said in awe.

He looked up at the buildings, some ancient and castle-like and some gleaming and new. Right outside the tall buildings, a perfect wilderness of forests, lakes, and mountains awaited to be hiked, swam and skied.

Lucas shook his head to clear it. 'It's Everycity.'

'Yes,' Helen laughed softly. 'Every city I've never been to.'

'I promised you once that we'd travel,' he said, his face sad. 'I'm sorry, Helen. It would have only taken us a few moments, and we could have flown anywhere together. But I never took you.'

'We had other things on our minds,' she said, taking his hand. 'I didn't build this to shame you. I built it to share with you.'

Lucas raised his face to the sky, taking in the complex layers of smells and voices.

'Well, you got everything right – except for one thing.' Lucas swallowed hard and smiled, glancing at her. 'It's a lot cleaner than any city I've ever been to.'

'What can I say, I'm from Nantucket,' Helen said, shrugging. 'We don't do filthy.'

'Yeah, I've noticed. Even the dirt there is clean.' Lucas laughed and turned his whole body to face hers.

For just a moment, Helen felt like he would kiss her, and everywhere in Everycity the sun shone a little brighter. But he didn't kiss her. At the last second, he pulled back and changed the subject.

'Context clues. I know you want something to eat because you made us appear right next to a café,' he said, his voice deep and textured. He turned away and squeezed her hand, like he was trying to snap them both out of a dream. 'Come on. Let's see what you put on the menu.'

'Wait. Why?' she asked, suddenly shy.

'This world's a reflection of your desires.' He led Helen into the busy café before she had a chance to remove anything unobtrusively. He glanced left and right at the tile-top wrought-iron tables, mismatched crockery, and the open rafters above their heads, and smiled. 'This is your subconscious. I want to know what you *really* want.'

Too late to stop him, Helen followed Lucas as he walked into her subconscious. There was art on the walls – weird combinations of images that would never be on the same wall in a museum.

Ansel Adams and Toulouse-Lautrec somehow lived in perfect harmony in Helen's little world. Cancan girls showed their legs next to noble pines buried deep in winter's bleached purity.

It was everything that Helen loved about art, and everything she loved about human nature. She looked at another wall and saw a vibrant, almost violent-looking Van Gogh hanging just inches away from a soothing and orderly Mondrian.

Helen knew that Lucas saw every nuance, every dialogue between the works of art. One image informed the other as Helen went back and forth in her subconscious about what was more alluring – humanity's ability to be rational and pure, or its need to be messy and sexy.

Lucas walked right into Helen's unfinished internal argument and saw everything that was buried inside her – bare skin fresh from a hot bath, and birch trees dusted with snow. Helen felt *naked* and laid open for him to stare at. It was so embarrassing she groaned.

She pulled Lucas into a tiny booth in the corner by the window and put up her menu, like a barricade. She tried to read the menu but it was blank. Just like her mind.

'Helen?' Lucas said gently, tugging down her menu. 'You don't have to hide anything from me. You know that, right?'

'S-sure,' she stammered, shaking.

'I'm not afraid of anything inside you,' he pressed. 'Good. Bad. Creepy. I know darkness. And I'd never judge you for having a few drops of your own.'

'Oh.' Helen looked around the room. Goya's disturbing painting *Saturn Devouring His Son* captured her eye and held it. 'And what if it's more than a few drops?'

Lucas laughed. He snatched her menu away, threw it to the floor, and grabbed both her hands. 'Didn't I tell you I love you?'

'Yes.'

'I meant *all* of you. Even the weird bits.'

'Remind me to burn this place to the ground as soon as we leave,' she said, adoring him.

'Absolutely not.' He looked around at the patrons. People of every race, age and time period seemed to be hanging out together. Native Americans in feathered headdresses chatted pleasantly with pirates. Girls with eighties mall bangs flirted with guys right out of Elizabethan England. 'I like it inside your head. It's strange, but it suits me.'

Helen looked around, and it all made sense to her. How cool would it be to be able to go to a café and strike up a conversation with someone from another time and place? It was something she'd always imagined doing, and now it looked like she didn't have to imagine it any more. She could be a part of it.

Neither of them was hungry or thirsty; they were just there to taste something yummy and enjoy each other's company. It was chilly out, but pleasantly so, and when Helen looked at what they were wearing, both of them were dressed perfectly for a fall day. She hadn't remembered dressing them, but they were definitely wearing some new clothes.

'Come on,' he said, standing up and putting on his newly created coat. 'I want to take a walk before it snows.'

They left the café and started wandering down the cobblestone street, past shops and buildings that were busy with all kinds of people going about their lives. Helen had no idea where all these people came from. She guessed she'd made them up or remembered them. Whichever it was, Helen knew they were based in reality, and that was comforting to her. It would have been odd to wander around an empty city, or, worse, a city full of mannequin-like robots.

The sun was setting, and Helen smelt snow in the air, just as Lucas had predicted. Windows lit up with warm glows as people turned on their lights or lit candles. Lucas had his arm over her shoulder as they strolled down the street.

'There are no poor people. No homeless,' he said suddenly.

'No,' Helen replied. 'Everyone has what they need here.'

'But how could anyone be grateful for what they have

if they didn't know what it was like *not* to have what they need?'

Helen shook her head and looked down. 'I've always thought that was the lamest argument – that we need some people to be poor in order to remind the rest of us to be grateful. All that really means is that someone has to suffer poverty so other people can feel better about themselves. What a selfish way to look at the world.'

Lucas chuckled and squeezed her against his side. 'I agree. But you have to admit it is human nature to only really appreciate something if you've worked for it, or if you know you can lose it. How are you going make the inhabitants of your little heaven feel fulfilled if everything comes to them easily?'

'Ah. The old "heaven is boring" problem, huh? Not in this universe.' Helen looked up at Lucas, and they smiled at each other. 'We'll figure something out. We've got plenty of time.'

'Wait,' he said, narrowing his eyes at her. 'What do you mean "we've got plenty of time"?'

'Just that we're young,' Helen replied cagily.

Before Lucas could continue asking questions, Helen imagined a carnival, and it appeared in front of them. Bright, multicoloured lights flashed in the evening light, and cheerful music piped around them. The scent of spun sugar sweetened the air, and elsewhere they could smell something juicy and spicy getting grilled.

'Amazing,' Lucas breathed. 'Everything she wants she gets.'

Helen pulled on his arm, grinning mischievously. 'And what I want right now is to ride the carousel.'

Matt heard Telamon sound the alarm. No human or Scion would ever be able to discern the skritching noises that the Myrmidons made from the chorus of natural noises on a beach, but Matt could easily tell the difference between the voices of the insects and those of his soldiers.

He left his tent to watch a party of Scions coming up the beach. Matt had known most of them from Troy and had disliked most of them. Odysseus was the only one worthy of respect.

'So it's true,' said a large, blond man. Matt knew him as Menelaus. 'The Warrior has finally joined the fight.'

'Tantalus. Head of Thebes,' Telamon whispered in Matt's ear. Matt nodded.

'When Hermes told me that Myrmidons were massing on the shore, I knew the last piece of the puzzle had been found, and you were coming to fight,' Tantalus continued, although Matt hadn't asked him to. An uncomfortable silence followed as Matt stared at Tantalus, still reluctant to make an alliance with this man, although he knew it was inevitable. The Myrmidons had voted for it.

'You hired one of my soldiers. Automedon. He was one of my closest friends once,' Matt said, expressionless. 'Before he lost his way.'

'Yes,' Tantalus said warily as he sized up Matt. 'I had nothing to do with his death, though.'

'Uh-huh.' Matt looked at the two men on either side of Tantalus – Odysseus on his left and Agamemnon on his right. Pallas Delos, as Matt knew Agamemnon now.

'How'd this happen, Matt?' Pallas asked, dismayed. He gestured to the Myrmidon warriors, arrayed in precise ranks.

'He was chosen,' Telamon said defensively. 'That's all you need to know. We accept him as our Master.'

The Myrmidons whispered the word *Master* in their ghostly way, unsettling the Scions who shared a round of nervous looks. They were afraid of Matt's men, as they should be.

'And do you have all the skills of Achilles?' asked the man Matt knew as Odysseus. Matt leaned his head close to Telamon.

'Daedalus Attica, Head of Athens,' Telamon told him immediately.

'That's not your real question,' Matt said, regarding Daedalus evenly. 'You want to know if I have Achilles's weakness.'

Daedalus's mouth turned up in a half smile. 'Every mortal has at least one.'

Matt smiled back at him with closed lips, neither confirming nor denying what the crafty one was asking. They stared at each other until Daedalus looked away.

'Suit yourself,' Daedalus said. He regarded Tantalus and Pallas and raised his eyebrows. 'Well, I'm convinced.'

'Are you sure about this?' Pallas asked Tantalus.

'The gods will crush us all if we don't fulfil our end of the bargain,' Tantalus replied, eyeing Matt with open distrust. 'We bring the Warrior to the table, or all the Scions die. Zeus swore on the River Styx that if we do this our Houses will be preserved.'

It was like it always was. At Troy, the Greek kings made their own deal with Zeus and saved their skins, and the innocent children of Troy were thrown from the top of the wall. Matt learned long ago that kings cared only about preserving their own kingdoms and were more interested with what they could get out of any given situation than doing what was right. Matt was suddenly so disgusted by the hedging and the political posturing he saw in the Scions that he turned to go back to his tent. This wasn't what he'd come for.

'Hold on,' Daedalus called out, taking a step towards Matt. The Myrmidons moved as one to intercept Daedalus. He put his arms up in surrender. 'Easy. Everybody just take it easy.'

'I'll fight with or without you.' Matt stopped and turned back to face them, speaking plainly. 'I'm here to kill the Tyrant. If that's what you want, then you may join me. If not, get out of the way.'

*

Helen led Lucas into the maze of booths, tugging on his arm. He hung back playfully, acting reluctant to follow so she had to half drag him. On the way, a barker caught his attention with an outlandish dare, and Lucas just *had* to stop and throw a baseball at a stack of lead milk bottles.

It took him three tries, which he insisted had never happened to him before, but eventually he won Helen a prize. There was a fluffy elephant that caught her eye for a moment, but she finally picked a glittery wand. It had a silver star on the top and dozens of ribbons flowing out of the bottom. The wand felt right in her hand and easy to carry. She waved it a few times, willing sparks to puff off it as they paused in front of the glass-blowing booth and watched a man make a little glass dragon.

Neither of them could stop smiling. Helen heard the carousel and ran the last few steps. She hopped on to the back of a unicorn as it swung past, waving her glittery wand in air like it was a riding crop.

'Tally-ho!' she cheered to her painted ceramic mount, but it didn't go any faster. The pole down the unicorn's middle was brass, and it smelt tangy and crisp in the autumn cold.

Lucas jumped up next to her, standing by her side rather than getting a ride of his own. He stood over her, his coat opening around her when he gripped the brass pole. They stared at each other for a long time as the rest of the world spun by them. The bright fairground colours streaked and smeared in the corner of Helen's eye but Lucas was still.

'Why won't you kiss me?' she asked quietly.

'Can't you make me?' he replied, raising a teasing eyebrow at her.

'I wouldn't want to. Especially not on our first real date.'

Lucas laughed softly. 'I was thinking the same thing when we were in the café. You and I had coffee together once before school, but we never really dated, did we?'

'We never got the chance. The world was always about to end, or one of us was on fire or something equally annoying.' He chuckled. She looked up at him and tried not to blush. 'You know, we can do whatever we want here. I can make sure there are no consequences.'

She could feel his breath quicken and see his eyes gleam with more than just the cold. 'You remember, months ago, you gave me some advice about how I should go about making tough decisions?' he asked.

'Decide what you absolutely can't handle, and do the opposite,' she said, surprised that he was bringing this up when she had been thinking pretty much the same thing not too long ago.

'That's why I won't kiss you.' He raised a hand and touched her face, and quickly dropped it. 'Eventually, we'll have to go back, and I'll lose you again. I know for a fact I can't handle that.'

Nor could Helen, and she was starting to consider

other options. Like figuring out a way for Aphrodite to remove the curse that required Helen to have a daughter in the first place. Maybe instead of accepting her situation – which was ridiculously unfair – she needed to at least try to fix it.

'I'm tired of going round and round,' Helen sighed.

The carousel came to a stop. She stood up and jumped down, the lights of the carnival shutting off section by section around her as she walked off the fairgrounds. She dropped her wand, and snow began to fall. Billions of tiny stars were blotted out and seemed to fall through the night sky as unique little crystals. It looked like the air around them whirled with shimmering bits of frozen stars.

'Helen,' Lucas began, following her. She heard him bracing himself for another one of their legendary arguments.

'I'm not angry with you because you won't kiss me,' she said, turning around and stopping him. 'I get why you won't kiss me. I can't go through all that again, either.'

'So what's the matter?' he asked patiently.

'I'm sick of believing that there are these shadowy all-powerful deities who are greater than me, keeping me from what I want. Because that's a lie. I'm just as strong as any of the beings who would hold me back. And I know I can beat them.'

'Ah. Helen?' Lucas hazarded. 'You're not going to run

off and start picking fights with the gods or anything like that, are you?'

'Well, no,' she said, shifting uncertainly from foot to foot. 'I was thinking I'd start by asking a few questions and take it from there.'

'Good,' Lucas said, relieved. He reached out and took her hand, his eyes narrowing with determination. 'And if talking doesn't work, we'll bury them.'

Helen watched a dark shadow pass across his face. 'We'll think about this later,' she said, leading him to a path that wound into the woods. 'I'm not ready for our date to be over yet.'

CHAPTER ELEVEN

About half an hour after Tantalus, Daedalus and Pallas left his camp, Matt heard the alarm again. There was a commotion outside, the sound of struggling and moments later Telamon was at the entrance of Matt's tent with a report.

'A Scion was found sneaking around the beach and captured,' Telamon informed him. 'I would have sent her back to her House, only . . . it's *her*, Master.'

'It's all right,' Matt said, nodding his head. 'Bring her in.'

Ariadne was led into the tent, held on either side by a Myrmidon. Her hair was tangled, and her face was red with exertion. She'd obviously put up a fight, but she was no match for even one of Matt's soldiers, let alone a full company of them.

'Let her go. Then leave us.' The guards obeyed silently. He turned to Ariadne. 'How did you find us?'

'I followed my father. He was acting weird tonight,' she whispered. Ariadne stood as far away from Matt as she could and rubbed her arms where the guards had held her.

'Did they hurt you?' he asked quietly. She ignored his question.

'How can you be *him*? You're not a Scion.'

'Neither was Achilles.'

She dropped her face into her palms and rubbed her eyes roughly. 'No,' she said, lifting her head suddenly. 'No, I don't believe any of this. I can't.'

She ran for the exit, but Matt moved faster than she ever could and was there before her. He caught her wrist to stop her from leaving. She stared at him in shock.

'Believe it.' Her skin felt soft and warm in his hand. He let her go and turned away. He knew it was better this way, even though it didn't feel like it. 'Go home. My men won't stop you.'

She didn't leave.

Matt heard her crossing the space to him and turned, already shaking his head. 'Don't.'

She kissed him, anyway. He knew he was supposed to stop this. She might know the story word for word, but she didn't actually *remember* the ending the way he did. He was just about to pull away and send her home to her brothers when she pressed her thumb into that U-shaped hollow under his Adam's apple while she kissed him. Just like she used to a hundred lifetimes ago.

As Matt picked her up and carried her over to his bed, he marvelled at how simple a gesture it was. Really – it was a silly habit she had of touching his throat with her thumb. But, once she did that, Matt didn't care who he had to kill.

'Sing for me,' Helen pleaded. She lifted her head off Lucas's chest and stared down at him.

'Right now? With no accompaniment?' Lucas asked. Lying on his back, he looked up at the ceiling of their little cabin in the woods and blushed a bit.

'Yes. Please? I really want to listen to music, but I want it to be something from you, not from my imagination.'

She rolled off him. The stones in front of the fireplace were nice and toasty under their blanket, despite the snowstorm that swirled outside their cabin. Helen grabbed her mug of tea off the hot flagstones in front of the fire and offered it to Lucas.

'For your throat, if it's hoarse and you think you might sing badly,' she said with a challenging grin.

'My throat's fine,' he said, nudging her playfully with his foot. He sat up suddenly. 'I'll make you music. But I'm a much better guitar player than a singer.'

'Really?' Helen took his hands and held them up, looking at them. They were hardened, like a fighter's, but still sensitive, like an artist's. Just like everything else about him, his hands were the perfect blend of opposites. She ran her finger across the callouses on his finger pads, noticing them for the first time. 'Why didn't you ever play for me before?'

'Why haven't I ever taken you on a date before?' he

said through a bittersweet smile. 'There are a lot of things I've meant to do with you that I haven't.'

Helen swayed closer to him. Just to breathe his air, or feel his body heat . . . anything to get another dose of him without actually kissing him and breaking the gentle understanding they'd come to.

'How'd you learn?' she asked quietly, a little ashamed that she didn't know this already.

'My dad taught me.' Lucas paused, a serene but sad look on his face. 'He taught me classical Spanish guitar, because we lived in Spain for so long, and American finger picking. I actually haven't played at all since we left Cádiz.' Again, that slightly sad look stole over his face. 'He's better than me . . . but I'm still pretty good.'

For a long time now, Helen had taken for granted that she and Lucas were as close as skin was to bones, that there was nothing about him that she didn't know. But here she was, learning something new and important about who he was. His dad didn't just teach him how to swing a sword. Helen could imagine the hours that the two of them had spent together, discussing the art that they loved so much and had so little chance to enjoy.

'I'll bet.' Helen desperately wanted to hear him play now. She imagined him a guitar – the best guitar she think of. 'Will this work?'

Lucas took the instrument and turned it over, frowning. 'It's all right.' He laughed at the wounded look Helen gave him. 'I'm joking! It's beautiful.'

Helen slapped him on the thigh. 'Play for me!' she demanded.

Lucas cradled the guitar in his arms, preparing to play, and stopped. 'You know what I keep wondering?'

'What?' Helen asked in a mock-frustrated tone, like she thought he was stalling on purpose.

'How you can do this?' he asked seriously. 'How do you know how to make carousels and snowstorms and guitars?'

'I've had a lot of practice,' she said quietly. Helen leaned closer to Lucas and regarded him carefully. 'In the Underworld. All that time I spent wandering around, well . . . I didn't get it then, but Hades was actually teaching me to build worlds.'

'Really? And I suppose he did it out of the goodness of his heart?' Lucas asked doubtfully.

'Well, yeah. Actually, I think that has a lot to do with it,' she replied. 'He's a really compassionate guy. God. Whatever.'

'And how has Hades been teaching you, exactly?' Lucas continued, putting the guitar aside.

'The hard way,' Helen replied, rolling her eyes at the memory of all her trials in the Underworld, and all the hellscapes she'd encountered. The tree that had imprisoned her, the rusting city, the ledge of the mansion that she'd clung to – all the places that Helen thought were cleverly designed by Hades to torture her had actually come out of her own mind. She'd created her own hell, and now that she had learned how to control her fear, she knew how to create her own paradise.

'What do you mean, the hard way?' he asked as he studied her pensive expression. His eyes were narrowed in anger.

'No, no, he didn't do anything to me. I did it all to myself.' Lucas didn't look pleased with that answer, either. 'Let me start over. Descending isn't really the right name for the talent I have. I'm a Worldbuilder, Lucas.' Helen spread her hands to gesture to the room around them. 'Worldbuilding got confused with Descending because Hades has allowed *all* the Worldbuilders, not just me, to descend to his land in order to learn how to build for themselves.'

'Why would he do that?'

Helen paused, thinking about her quest to free the Furies and how much she'd learned in the process.

'I guess because he wants us to really consider what kind of world we want to live in – one based on justice and compassion for others, or one that only serves the whims of the builder. Wow. I just figured that out.' Helen looked at Lucas and smiled. 'You always help me figure things out.'

'That's what I'm here for,' he said, smiling back at her before growing serious again. 'But you could have learned those lessons without having to go through hell. Helen, I remember how sick you got. How you would come back from the Underworld covered in mud and leaves and blood sometimes. Did he have to make everything so hard?'

'Yeah, he did,' Helen said, and then stopped again, wondering if she wanted Lucas to know the next bit that had just occurred to her.

'Helen?' he said, raising an eyebrow at her. 'What *aren't* you telling me?'

She knew she couldn't hide it from him for long, and she hated keeping things from him, anyway, so she told him. 'Hades had to make it hard so I would toughen up. Because once a Worldbuilder actually builds a world, she has to be strong enough to defend it.'

Helen saw Lucas's face harden. 'Defend it from whom?' he asked, his voice low and dangerous.

'The gods, I think. "Challengers" was all Hades said, so I guess there have been more than one over the years. Look, I'm not going to lie to you. Morgan La Fey built Avalon, and it disappeared in the mists when she lost her fight. Atlantis sank into the sea when Atlanta lost hers. Those are the only two other Scions I know of who have been Worldbuilders, and they both lost. The odds are not in my favour.'

'Screw the odds,' Lucas said with a dismissive wave of his hand. 'That's not what bothers me.' His eyes skipped around as he thought. 'What I want to know is who's going to challenge you, and why is Hades taking the trouble to prepare you to fight back? What does he really want?'

Helen shrugged. 'I don't know. I could ask, but I doubt he'd tell me in a way I'd understand. Hades doesn't do easy answers.'

'I'll bet,' Lucas mumbled, still thinking.

Helen reached for the guitar and slowly nudged it into his hands. He was on to her, though.

'Is this a hint?'

'A big fat one.' Helen grinned at him.

Lucas plucked a few strings and grimaced, tightening and loosening knobs as he went. 'Figures. You're so tone-deaf even your perfectly constructed guitars are out of tune.' Helen's body crumpled as she laughed at the pained look on Lucas's face. 'And this guitar is strung for a leftie. I'm not Matt, you know.'

'Here, let me fix it.' Helen concentrated, and all the strings rearranged themselves. Lucas strummed the guitar and rolled his eyes when it made a comical twanging sound.

'It's out of tune again.'

'You did that on purpose,' she said, grabbing his toe and squeezing it. 'Just play!'

'Yes, your goddess-ness.'

Lying on her side, the warm fire at her feet, Helen's laughter died away as Lucas suddenly went from tuning to playing.

It was like an orchestra in an instrument.

He played with both hands – not one hand picking and the other holding down strings – but with *both hands* so that it sounded like more than one guitar was playing. Sometimes he hit the strings to make them hum like a harp, and sometimes he hit the body of the guitar like a drum to add bass and keep time. It was the most fascinating thing Helen had ever watched, as if Lucas had a dozen voices in his head, all singing the same song, and he'd figured out a way to make them with just ten fingers.

Helen looked at his face and could tell why he loved it. It was like thinking for him, only this was a puzzle that he could share with her as he solved it.

He'd walked into her head when he'd come to her world. And she'd walked into his when she finally heard him play.

It was heaven.

'Where have you been?' Helen scolded.

'Waiting, forlorn and heartbroken, for your return,' Morpheus answered languidly, his silver eyes melting into hers.

She laughed and squeezed his hand. Helen and Lucas had fallen asleep in front of the fire, and she'd woken up in the shadow lands, lying on her back, shoulder to shoulder with the god of dreams. Their faces were turned to each other, and their hands tightly entwined.

'Little sneak. How did you know I needed your help?' she asked.

'You brought yourself here. I can't make you come here; all I can do is leave the door open for you.'

'Is that what you did?' Helen said, thinking about the different borders that Hades had made for his world, and Morpheus had made for his. Hades left the door open for the dead, and Morpheus left the door open for dreaming minds.

Helen turned her head and looked up into the night sky of Morpheus's Dream Palace. Her head was cradled in inky silk pillows, and the strange follow-me-lights that looked like a candle-flame inside a soap bubble danced over her and her host like they wanted to play.

'Are the borders of our worlds separate from the world itself?'

'I suppose so. Minds come and go, ruffling my hair on the breeze as they let themselves into and out of my land, but they do not control my land once they are here. I make the dreams,' Morpheus replied.

'But in Hades it's the opposite,' Helen remarked, on the edge of understanding. 'The borders are hard to cross – you usually have to kill yourself to do it, but once inside his world, you make your own existence. Or at least I did when I was there.'

'I've never thought of it this way, but, yes, I'd say the borders are separate from the world. They follow a different set of rules, but they are still controlled by the maker.' Then he regarded her with narrowed eyes. 'What's troubling my Beauty so much she must come to me to talk philosophy?'

'I need your help. Who is going to challenge me, now that I've built my world, Morpheus?'

'Olympus. Zeus, mostly. In the past, the small gods challenged some of the other Worldbuilders while the Olympians were trapped by Zeus's oath.' Morpheus chuckled. 'Odysseus really was a clever one.'

'But why do we have to fight at all? Why can't Zeus keep Olympus, and I'll keep Everyland and we can call it even?'

'The Great Cycle, of course.'

'Oh yeah. The Great Cycle.' Helen rolled her eyes and looked at him again. 'What the heck is that?'

Morpheus laughed and sat up. 'The children must overthrow their parents, like the gods did to the Titans, and the Titans did to their parents, Gaea and Uranus. The Fates will make it so again. It's the Scions' turn to overthrow the gods.'

'And Zeus wants to stop me from overthrowing him.'

'Of course. If the Scions defeat Olympus, the Twelve will spend eternity in Tartarus like the Titans. Not pleasant.'

'No. Not pleasant at all.' Helen agreed. 'But why pick on me? What's the big deal about me being a Worldbuilder?'

'Because you can take the Scions to your Everyland and make all of them immortal if you wish it. And, as a Worldbuilder, you are also the only one of your kind who can open the portals to Tartarus and send the Twelve there – but be warned, Helen. Zeus is a Worldbuilder as well. He can also send you to Tartarus, like he did the Titans.'

Helen paused to think about this. If Helen made all the Scions immortal and they faced off with Olympus, it'd be an army against a handful. There's no way Olympus would win.

'So what about you and Hades? Either of you could challenge Zeus, but he's left you both alone. How did you avoid a fight?'

'I never leave my land, and it would be suicide for Zeus to try to fight me here, where I alone am god.'

'And Hades?'

'Hades rarely leaves his land, either, and when he does his Helm of Darkness makes him invisible to both humans and gods.' Helen remembered Eris walking right by her and Lucas when he had made them invisible in the hallway at school, just before the riots. Before she could think too deeply about that connection, Morpheus continued. 'More important, Zeus needs his big brother Hades. The dead must have a land of their own, and the last thing Zeus wants is to have to deal with the dead.'

'So what am I supposed to do?' Helen asked pleadingly.

'Fight. Or hide in your Everyland where Zeus cannot touch you.' Morpheus smiled at her warmly. 'I suggest the latter, even though I know you won't listen. You're not the hiding type.'

'I can't stay in Everyland. I can't leave Earth to the gods. They'd totally ruin it. But maybe there's a way to avoid a fight altogether?' Helen asked. She doubted it, but it didn't hurt to at least try to stop a horrendous war that would probably kill a lot of people.

'Can you avoid your fate? Many have tried to dodge it, like Oedipus, but has anyone ever been able to escape it in the end?' Morpheus asked in return.

'Yes. Free will exists,' Helen replied, musing as an idea occurred to her. 'All you need is a Shield.'

Morpheus looked at her questioningly, not understanding her. She shook her head and changed the subject.

'Why do you and Hades help me?' she asked softly.

'I am the god of dreams, but not even I would dream of speaking for Hades,' Morpheus replied with a mischievous look in his eyes. 'But, if I had to guess, I would say it's because he knows how destructive his little brother is. Hades, unlike most of the other gods, cares for mortals and doesn't want to see them at war. Probably because he has to tend their souls when they die. He has had to judge millions of souls and that has given him a strong sense of justice. Leaving you to fight Zeus with no training is something he would consider unjust.'

Helen frowned. She remembered asking Orion once what was more important to him than everlasting joy.

He'd said justice. It was yet another trait Orion shared with Hades.

'And what about you?' Helen asked, brushing aside this thought.

'I have much simpler, much more selfish motive. I help you because I love you and can't bear to lose you. Didn't you know that?'

'*And?*' she asked, raising a cynical eyebrow.

'*And* I don't believe I have anything to fear from you. I don't think you'd ever try to send me to Tartarus.'

'Never. I wouldn't want to live in a world without dreams. Not even my own,' Helen said, reaching out to caress his shiny, black hair. 'I've really missed you. Every time I close my eyes lately it seems like I'm too busy to dream.'

'But I've sent you dreams – mostly to inform you of the gods' actions on Earth.'

'What do you mean?' Helen asked. She figured it out fast. 'All those dreams of eagles carrying off women and dolphins and stallions attacking humans. That was awful, Morpheus.'

'I'm sorry, Beauty. I didn't mean to frighten you. I just couldn't allow that poor siren to get any more *attention* from that Apollo brat without trying to do something about it.' Morpheus fluffed a pillow, agitated. 'I am most grateful that you went to get her. I hate sending nightmares to anyone, but sometimes I just have to in order to warn people. Do you forgive me?'

'Of course,' Helen replied, sitting up.

She remembered Orion telling her once that he'd been given a dream about a field full of Scion bones. He'd interpreted it as a warning of the Scions' extinction. Apparently, he was right. A shudder ran through Helen, and Morpheus put an arm over her shoulder, concerned by her distress.

'You know, you really are a big softie,' she told him.

'I am. I should try being more terrible and garnering more respect and fear and trembling and all that. But I keep forgetting.' He pouted sweetly. Helen gave him a warm smile, then grew silent.

'What is it?' Morpheus asked.

'I need your help.' Helen looked at her friend, hoping he knew what to do. 'I need to find a way to remove Aphrodite's curse on my bloodline.'

'May I ask why?' Morpheus asked, his head tilting curiously.

Helen had a ready answer – because she wanted to be able to be with Lucas, even if he was her cousin. But before she could speak the words, she realized it was much more than that.

'I don't want to owe her or anyone else a child,' she said. 'If I ever have a baby, it will be by my choice, not someone else's.'

'Ah.' Morpheus regarded her sadly. 'There is no power I know of that can remove a goddess's curse. But if you don't want to have a child, don't. All you need to do is live forever and the Face will always exist.' Morpheus chuckled softly. 'I believe that was Aphrodite's point to begin with, wasn't it?'

Helen breathed a surprised sigh. 'You're right.' A slow grin spread across Morpheus's face, and Helen's matched it. 'Thank you.'

'You're welcome.'

'Eternity, though.' Helen frowned suddenly. 'How is it, *really*?'

'I've been enjoying it,' Morpheus said with a shrug. He gestured to his big bed, the twinkling stars and elfin people who danced and played in the outlying poppy fields. 'It helps to spend it in your own world, doing what you love and surrounded with the right people, of course. Or person.'

Morpheus changed his appearance into Lucas's and crawled across the gigantic bed toward her.

'My offer still stands, you know,' he whispered in Lucas's voice. 'Stay here with me and be my queen. Or, we can trade off if you prefer. At night we can come here, and during the day we can live in your world.'

Helen scooted away from Morpheus-as-Lucas, groaning pitifully. 'You're totally cheating.'

He caught her and rolled her under him, his face just inches above hers. 'Stay,' he pleaded. 'Here with me, or in your Everyland with the real Lucas. Or any combination you like. We can all share. But, whatever you decide, it's better if you never go back to Earth. You're going to be hurt terribly if you do.'

Helen's throat went dry at the seriousness of his look. 'I can't avoid a fight with Zeus by hiding.'

'I wasn't speaking of Zeus. I was speaking of those close to you. They are conspiring, even in their dreams, to betray you.'

Helen stiffened and pushed him back.

'What is my mother up to *this* time?' she asked, not a doubt in her mind about who in her inner circle would betray her. Morpheus shifted back to his own face, which looked confused.

'She's been drugging your father, of course,' he said. 'But that's not . . .'

'What?' Helen trilled, cutting him off as she jumped out of bed, shaking with anger. 'Daphne has been *drugging* my father?'

'Yes,' Morpheus replied in his gentle manner. 'It's not harming his body in any way. That's why the pretty Healer twins can't detect it.'

'What the hell?' Helen babbled, nearly hysterical at the thought. 'Why is she drugging my dad?'

'To keep him asleep, of course. Don't worry. I've made sure he's having nothing but wonderful dreams.'

Helen clenched her fists to keep herself from screaming, and then leaned over to give Morpheus a quick kiss goodbye. 'Thank you for taking care of my father, Morpheus. I owe you. And if you ever need anything from me, anything at all, just ask.'

'Wait, you're in danger!' Morpheus began, but Helen knew that already. She couldn't stay and listen to another one of Morpheus's well-meaning pleas to stay away from Zeus. She needed to get back because her mother had some serious explaining to do.

And then Helen was going to kick that no-hearted bitch's ass.

Helen appeared in the middle of the Delos living room, inches away from Claire who was sleeping in a chair. A gust of cold air washed over Claire, waking her.

'Helen!' Claire gasped, jumping up immediately.

'Sorry,' Helen said when she saw the terrified look on Claire's face. 'Where is everyone?'

'It's the middle of the night – where do you think everyone is?'

Helen looked around the charred remains of the living room. The chair Claire had been sleeping in was the only piece of furniture in the room that hadn't been burned, and Helen recognized it as a transplant from the study.

'What are you doing in here?' Helen asked, gesturing to the destroyed room. 'Why aren't you at your home or upstairs?'

'I'm waiting to see if either of you came back. I figured the spot you left was the best bet,' Claire answered. She looked behind Helen expectantly, and her face fell. 'No

Lucas?' she asked, her eyes widening with sadness and something else Helen couldn't place. It almost looked like distrust.

'He's fine,' Helen said quickly, ignoring the pinch of disappointment she felt. Claire was acting like she thought Helen was lying to her. 'I left him in . . . Don't worry about it. He's completely healed and totally safe.'

'How?' Claire asked. She gestured to the room around her. 'This is what you did. And Lucas was holding on to you. How could he possibly live through that?'

Helen shifted from foot to foot. She wasn't really ready to tell Claire about the fact that she'd built a new world. It was one thing discussing it with Morpheus, who shared her ability, but standing here with Claire it no longer seemed like such a normal thing to create a world.

'Long story. But, trust me, he's perfect.' She needed to change the subject. 'Do you know where my mother is?' Helen asked, listening to the breathing of all the house's inhabitants. She didn't hear her mother among them.

'No clue. Not that that's anything new. She's really good at vanishing.' Claire peered at Helen cautiously.

'Yeah. She really is,' Helen said distractedly, trying to think of where Daphne could be.

She had to admit to herself that she didn't know her mother well enough to know where she'd be at any time of the day, let alone where she went to sleep at night. Going out to look for her would probably be a waste of time. Eventually, Daphne would have to return, and then Helen would confront her.

Helen smiled cheerfully at Claire, but Claire didn't smile back. She was still looking at Helen strangely. Like she didn't recognize her any more.

'What?' Helen asked defensively.

'You look freaky. Kind of scary.' Claire quickly glanced at the floor, like she couldn't look at Helen any more.

'Jason's upstairs?' Helen asked, changing the subject again. She already knew the answer. She could hear Jason breathing in his room.

'Why do you need him?'

'Because I need a Healer. Come on,' Helen said, turning her back on Claire and mounting the stairs. 'I look freaky because I'm pissed. I just found out that my dad's being drugged.'

'No way!' Claire said loudly, and then dropped her voice. 'By who?' she whispered as they got to the top of the stairs.

'My wicked witch of a mother. Who else?' Helen replied. 'I'm hoping the twins can help him.'

'Jason will. But Ari isn't here, so he'll have to work alone,' Claire said, chewing her lower lip as the two girls got to Jason's door.

Helen could tell that Claire was also worried about Ariadne, and where she'd gone off to that night. It wasn't like Ariadne to just disappear, and Helen sensed that Claire thought something fishy was happening.

'How long has Ari been gone?' Helen asked.

'I don't know,' Claire replied, brushing off the question. 'Wait here a sec.' Helen paused outside while Claire went into Jason's room to get him.

As Claire touched Jason's shoulder to wake him, Jason responded by reaching up out of his slumber to pull Claire down into bed with him. Claire resisted gently, and Helen looked away to allow them some privacy. She could see Jason's need as a bright flash, and Claire's reciprocation was immediate, even though she repressed it quickly. Helen could read emotions so clearly now it was embarrassing for her to be around couples. It was like walking in on naked people whenever she was around her old friends. Helen wondered how Orion dealt with it. Maybe he was more understanding about emotions because he had learned how to accept how vulnerable people are in general.

We're all naked under a few millimetres of clothes, Helen reminded herself, recalling a wonderfully tense moment in her life when Lucas had stood just outside her shower door.

Helen heard Jason say, 'Luke's alive? You sure?' and then she moved down the hall. Claire joined Helen outside Jason's bedroom while he threw on some clothes. Moments later, he met them in the hallway.

'Jerry's condition has changed?' Jason asked Helen in an excited whisper.

'Well, no,' Helen said. They got to Jerry's room

and went in, closing the door behind them so they could speak more freely. 'I just found out he's being drugged.'

'Drugged?' Jason repeated in a disbelieving tone. 'If it was a drug, I'd have been able to sense the damage it would do to his body.'

'That's just it. Morpheus told me that the drug isn't hurting him. It's just keeping him asleep.'

'Morpheus. The god of dreams.' Jason stared at her blankly. 'Do you two hang out now, or something?'

'Will you please just check?' Helen asked urgently, gesturing down to her father's sleeping form.

'I'm sorry, Helen. My power doesn't work like a blood test. I can't detect chemicals, only damage to the body. I can't remove chemicals, either, unless they are the pathogen that's hurting the patient. My talent only allows me to fix what's broken.'

'So what can we do to help him?' Claire asked.

'Nothing,' Jason responded. 'All we can do is wait for the drug to wear off. And keep whoever's drugging him away so they can't administer more. Who's doing this to him, anyway?'

Helen clenched her teeth, too ticked off to even say her mother's name.

'Daphne,' Claire told him, when it became obvious that Helen couldn't. Jason sighed and nodded.

'Looking back, Daphne always did seem to show up just as Jerry was waking. She'd stay to watch him, and a few minutes later he'd go under again.' He looked at Helen contritely. 'I'm sorry, Helen. It never even crossed my mind that Daphne would do that to him.'

'It's not your fault, Jason. It's mine. I know what a nightmare she is, and I still let her be near him,' Helen said ruefully. 'Any idea how long before he wakes up again?'

Jason held a glowing hand over Jerry's head, his eyes closed in concentration.

'He's completely out,' he said, opening his eyes. 'He could be like this another twelve to sixteen hours, I'd say. That's just a rough guess, though.'

'Thanks,' Helen replied.

'So. How's Lucas?' Jason asked tentatively.

'He's totally fine,' Helen said, smiling. 'In fact, I gotta go get him.'

'Get him?' Jason asked, his relieved look fading. 'Can't he fly? Or is he still too injured to walk? We'll all come help . . . Hector!' Jason turned and started calling loudly for his brother.

'Jason – wait. It's not that at all,' Helen said, reaching out to stop him. But Hector had already come to his bedroom door. Behind him, Helen could see Orion getting out of the guest bed in Hector's room.

'What?' Hector growled peevishly at his brother, and then noticed Helen. 'Where have you been?' he asked her, coming out into the hallway.

'Helen?' Orion asked, following Hector.

'Oh, good. You're here,' she said. 'Don't go anywhere.'

'OK,' Orion said tentatively, not understanding her. 'Where's Lucas?'

Both he and Hector were looking up and down the hall for Lucas.

'Oh, for the love of Pete,' Helen mumbled to herself, running a hand over her face. 'He's fine! Would I be wandering around, *not* sobbing my brains out, if he were dead?'

By this point, Castor and Noel, Pallas, Cassandra, Kate, and Andy were all awake and looking out of their bedroom doors at Helen. She held up her hands before everyone could start talking at once.

'Lucas is absolutely one hundred per cent alive and healthy and waiting for me in a safe place,' she announced.

'Where?' Castor asked, his face both hopeful and confused.

'Ah . . . safe,' Helen said, unsure of how much she should share.

'Where did you take my son?' Noel demanded, striding angrily down the hallway toward Helen. Her face was swollen and her eyes were bright red from crying all night. Helen realized that Noel blamed her. She looked around at everyone's faces. She saw doubt, distrust and, in the best cases, confusion. She was used to Pallas looking at her like he didn't trust her any further than he could throw her, but not Castor and Noel. Or Claire.

'Lucas and I call it Everyland.' Helen threw up her hands and just said it. 'But you all know it as Atlantis.'

CHAPTER TWELVE

Helen finished explaining and a long silence followed. Looks got traded around the Delos kitchen table, where they all sat.

'How many Worldbuilders have there been?' Castor asked, finally calm.

'Not many. Hades, Morpheus, Zeus, and the Furies all have their own lands. Other Scions in history have had the talent, but I can only remember two.'

'Remember? How can you remember the other Worldbuilders if they lived long ago?' Orion asked.

'Well, you know how I touched a few drops of water from *that* river?' Helen smiled at him and Orion nodded, smiling with her at the mention of their adventure on Halloween. At least Orion was still on her side. 'When I got my memory back, I got more than just my memories. I got other women's memories too. One of them was Helen of Troy's.'

Hector muttered a colourful swear word.

'Her life sucked, by the way.' Helen looked at Castor. 'You were Priam, king of Troy. Your brother, Tantalus?

Totally Menelaus. And you were Agamemnon,' she told Pallas.

Hector and Orion looked at each other and started laughing.

'You were the great Hector, and you were Aeneas, his best friend and general,' Helen said, shrugging as she looked at them. 'But you guys already knew that.'

'Yeah, we kinda did,' Orion admitted with a grin.

'Wait,' Claire said, holding up a hand. 'Wasn't Helen of Troy the one who betrayed the city that was protecting her and let the Greeks slaughter her friends and family?'

The weak laugh Claire added on the end did not make her question funny. Helen couldn't believe the accusation in Claire's voice and glanced down at her heart. It was full of fear.

'This is terrible. You built a world,' Cassandra gasped, surfacing from her own thoughts to rejoin the conversation a few minutes late. 'Zeus will fight you. He must fight you or risk being overthrown. *That's* what the Fates have wanted all along. They want the children to overthrow the parents.'

'Yes,' Helen admitted. 'And until the Scions overthrow the gods we'll be stuck in this same cycle, repeating our ancestors' mistakes with every new generation until the Fates get what they want.'

'Apollo said something similar,' Hector said, nodding in agreement. 'And after spending a few thousand years cooped up on Olympus he looks ready for a fight.'

Several people asked Helen questions at once, but as they began debating the virtues of fighting and avoiding a fight Helen felt Lucas wake up in Everyland, and she happily turned her attention to him. He was worried about her. She made a note appear on the pillow next to him, explaining where she was and what she was telling the family.

'Wait – one thing?' he asked out loud before reading the note.

Strangely, Helen didn't hear him say it. She felt the words appear in her head attached to some sort of essence that she understood as Lucas. It was like a freaky second sense, much more subtle than actual hearing, and she knew she could tune it out if she had to. But she didn't want to. She wanted to spend as much time as could, feeling Lucas inside her world, inside her mind, like this.

'Anything,' Helen replied, placing the word gently in his thoughts so he wouldn't be frightened by some booming voice in the sky or anything too Old Testament.

'Can you make it, like, a lot warmer? What is it with you New England girls and snow, anyway? I grew up in Cádiz. I like sun.'

Helen laughed out loud and imagined a warm place for Lucas.

'Helen?' Orion asked, touching her arm to bring her thoughts back down to Earth. She looked at him and saw that her strange behaviour had startled him. He was scared of her. They all were – especially Claire. Right now, Claire was looking at Helen like she'd just run over someone's dog. Helen knew that she needed to sit down and have a chat with Claire, but she didn't want to take the time to explain herself just yet. She was too eager to get back to Lucas and their own personal paradise.

'I have to leave,' she said, shrugging apologetically. She turned to Orion and pointed at him. 'Don't go anywhere, OK?'

'I'll be right here,' Orion said.

She stood up from the table and moved away so that she didn't freeze everyone when she opened a portal. She looked at Noel. 'I'll be back with Lucas soon. Promise.'

Then she vanished.

Somewhere between Earth and Everyland Helen opened her eyes. She had been through the process of viewing the memories she'd inherited from the River Lethe enough times to know when she was doing it again. And she was doing it again.

Except, this time, when she woke with Paris's naked body tangled up with hers, she didn't watch the scene like a ghostly third person in the room. She felt as if it was happening to her. And of all the memories she'd relived this one hurt the most.

It was the night that Troy fell.

Helen joined the memory as Paris was slipping into a deep sleep shortly after they had made love for the last time. She felt his body grow heavy, his joints slacken, and watched his calloused hand curl up into a fist. She desperately wanted to stay, hold him and watch him as he watched his dreams pass behind his eyelids. But she couldn't. She had made arrangements with Odysseus and needed to sneak out as soon as possible to do his wretched bidding.

She'd already done all her crying for Paris. The only thing left now was to protect their daughter and make sure that something of Paris was left when it was over.

Odysseus had convinced her slowly. He'd explained that immortals could not fight mortals to the death. Hecate, the only Titan more powerful than Zeus, forbade it. But this technicality didn't stand in the gods' way. They were remarkably good at making it so the demigods wanted to kill each other off, anyway. Over the years she'd watched as hero after hero fell in single combat, each of them goaded on by his father-god, and she saw that Odysseus must be right.

Helen understood now that the gods were purposely perpetuating the war, and she agreed that unless one side won soon all the demigods would be exterminated. Which, as Odysseus had pointed out, was exactly what the gods wanted, and not only for the show. Aphrodite had told Helen that the gods loved to watch and place bets on whose offspring would defeat whose. But what the gods really wanted was for the greatest threat to their power to be eliminated.

The Fates had openly decreed that the gods would

fall at the hands of their children. Cassandra had made the nearly unintelligible prophecy about Houses, or bloodlines that didn't even exist yet, and of the 'children overthrowing their parents' ten years ago, at the very start of the war. They had all heard it, gods and demigods alike. But, in this case, the gods had the edge. Only the gods knew that Cassandra was telling the truth. The demigods thought Cassandra was crazy.

Helen knew she wasn't. Her sister, Aphrodite, had told her about Apollo's curse. As the war was starting, Cassandra had refused Apollo's amorous advances and he had cursed her to always prophesy correctly but never to be believed. Helen couldn't think of a more torturous curse – to always know what horrors the future held, but never to be able to steer the ones you love away from destruction.

Helen had watched over the years as Cassandra screamed at her family. She'd tried to tell them that Helen would betray them all and let the city fall, but no one believed her. The more she screamed, the crazier she'd seemed. And, as the gods laughed, more and more demigods died.

But Cassandra was right. Helen was going to betray her family. She was going to let the Greeks into Troy, and they were going to burn it to the ground.

She felt her husband's head slip off her shoulder as he tumbled from her arms into Morpheus's, and she knew this was her only chance. She edged her hips out from under his, and slid unnoticed out of bed when he rolled over on to his side.

She knew he was going to die.

She nearly woke him, desperate to tell him everything.

She thought of their daughter and knew that Paris couldn't be saved. That was the deal she'd made with Odysseus – all of Troy for her daughter's life.

It was a steep price to pay, but not an entirely selfish one. The Greeks didn't believe her when she'd tried to reason with them. They refused to end their pursuit of the little girl who might or might not be the Tyrant. Helen had tried to tell them that if Atlanta died all love in the world would die with her. They saw her pleas as a mother's desperate attempt to save her only child, but that wasn't entirely it. If Atlanta died, the Face would die with her, and Aphrodite would punish them all.

Helen's love for Paris and the rest of his family, no matter how deep, could not compare with that. She just hoped that Odysseus managed his side of it. If he didn't imprison the gods as he promised he could, then all this would be for nothing. They would simply wait a generation or two and start another war to kill off all the demigods. Strangely, Helen trusted Odysseus with this. She'd heard his plan and, as crazy as it sounded, she knew him well enough to know that if there were ever anyone who could find a way to trick the gods it would be him.

Helen leaned down over her husband and ran her

lips lightly across his bare shoulder in goodbye. Maybe, someday, she would find him by the River Styx. There, they could wash all their hateful memories away, and walk into a new life together, a life that didn't have the dirty paw prints of a dozen gods and a dozen kings marring it.

Such a beautiful thought. Helen vowed that she would live a hundred lives of hardship for one life – one *real* life – with Paris. They could be shepherds, just as they had dreamed once when they had met at the great lighthouse long ago. She'd be anything, really, a shopkeeper, or a farmer, whatever, as long as they were allowed to live their lives and love each other freely. She dressed quickly, imagining herself tending a shop somewhere by the sea, hoping that someday this dream would come true.

It was still early, an hour or two past sunset, as Helen stole out of the palace, taking her usual route down to the kitchens. As she crept through the herb garden on her way to the wall she saw Aeneas climbing the hill to the temple of the Oracle. Helen paused. No one visited the Oracle any more, unless they were summoned. What did Cassandra want with Aeneas on this night . . . *the* night? Helen wondered.

She couldn't follow him just now, but she realized it was a stroke of luck that he was distracted. Out of all of them, Aeneas did not feel the influence of the cestus. He was Aphrodite's son, and could not be swayed. This was more than luck, she realized. Again, Helen had the sinking feeling that she was just a pawn of the Fates. Aeneas was the one, the only one, who could give her trouble accomplishing her goal, and the Oracle herself had stepped in to remove him from his post on the wall. It was fated, then. Troy was doomed.

In another moment, Helen was climbing the steps up to the turret. The soldiers manning that station parted and bowed to her. Helen looked over the side of the wall, down at the large wooden horse that the Greeks had left on the beach.

'Bring it in,' she ordered.

'Princess, may I speak?' asked the commander. Helen *hated* being called that, but as this was technically her title here in Troy she had no choice but to submit to it. She nodded her assent for the soldier to continue. 'General Aeneas has ordered us to leave the horse. He thinks it's a trick.'

'How can it be a trick?' she asked innocently. 'The Greeks have gone. Sailed away. Troy has won the war.'

The men looked at each other, not knowing what to do. A young soldier, who probably didn't remember much before the war, spoke in a wavering voice, 'Excuse me, Princess. But my cousin's nurse said her husband, the fisherman, saw all the Greek ships massed just up the beach.'

'Well, I'm sure your cousin's nurse's husband the fisherman knows much more about politics and warfare than I,' Helen said jauntily, and the rest of the soldiers laughed while the young man blushed and looked at his feet. 'But I think it's safe to assume that the giant wooden horse is an offering to Poseidon. The Greeks are trying to buy safe passage across the sea. If we take the horse, then we take away their offering, and maybe Poseidon will smash a few Greek ships before they make it home. What say you to that?'

Most of the men cheered at Helen's rousing tone, but a few still looked apprehensive. Time was running short, and she knew she had no choice. As Helen used the cestus to influence the last of the soldiers, she felt true hatred for the first time. And it was for herself.

'Bring it in,' she repeated, and all the men on the wall rushed with dazed faces and blank eyes to fulfil her orders.

As the great gate was being hauled open for the first time in over a decade, Helen hurried off the wall and made her way through the city to the temple of the Oracle. If Aeneas were to return to his post now, he would ruin the whole endeavour. Helen had to make sure he stayed occupied and away from the gate, or she would have to do something drastic.

She couldn't kill him before dawn. The deal Odysseus had made with Zeus was that Odysseus could get the great gate of Troy open and the entire Greek army into the city in one night without killing a single person before the sun rose. Then, at dawn while the city still slept, the Greeks would slaughter the citizens of Troy in their beds. In exchange for such a speedy end to a war that was turning all of the gods against each other, Zeus had sworn that the gods would not return to Earth unless the Scions united and threatened his rule.

Helen had to make sure that she didn't kill anyone while she accomplished her end of the deal. That didn't mean she couldn't hamstring Aeneas and tie him up, though.

Her body trembled as she clutched her dagger. She didn't want to hurt Aeneas, who had always been a good and true man, but she would do whatever was needed. There was already so much innocent blood on her hands that adding his wouldn't make a difference, anyway. For a moment, Helen thought of Astyanax, Hector and Andromache's infant son, and her eyes filled with tears.

All the women, including Helen, were to be spared – after a fashion. They were to be divided among the Greek kings as the spoils of war. Helen was to go to Menelaus. She shuddered, repressing the memory of him trying to beat her to death, and knew that she would face that over and over in the years to come. He was impotent now, made so by Aphrodite's curse on his town, and he would be determined to take it out on Helen for as long as she managed to live through his brutality.

Helen felt like this was fair. The women were to be married off to the Greek kings, but, apart from Atlanta, all the children of Troy were going to die that night. In comparison, Helen estimated that her suffering was small.

Odysseus had refused to budge on the children, no matter how much Helen had begged for their lives. The Greeks wouldn't take the chance that the babies would grow into men who might hunt them down to avenge their fathers' deaths.

The Oracle had warned them that the Greeks could slay all the children of Troy, but blood for blood was still to be the demigod's fate. Cassandra foresaw that the Furies would not tolerate the killing of children and kin, and that they would punish all the demigods for the slaughter of innocents. But, of course, no one believed her.

Helen kept her dagger in its sheath until she needed it, and climbed the steep, rocky hill to the temple where Cassandra lived in solitude. Many times over the years, Helen had stared up at the gleaming pillars of Cassandra's plush prison and thought that her husband's little sister was like the moon. She was higher than any of them, remote and so very alone.

A few steps further, and Helen heard some unmistakable sounds. *Impossible*, Helen thought as she heard the two voices cry out in unison.

Helen darted from column to column and made her way through the forest of marble in the interior of the temple, until she was close enough to the inner sanctum to confirm with her own eyes what her ears had already told her.

Aeneas and Cassandra were lovers. And from

the surprised look on Aeneas's face as he lay next to Cassandra, still panting, Helen could see that their intimacy was a new development.

Aeneas sat up in the pile of discarded clothes and torn-down draperies that had served as their bed and ran a hand across his sweaty face like he had no idea what to do next. He looked around at the knocked-over amphorae, the ripped curtains and the general havoc that their union had wreaked on the now-defiled temple, and then down at Cassandra, completely stunned.

'Did I hurt you?' he asked her urgently.

It amazed Helen that a brutal warrior like Aeneas, who had spent the last ten years of his life shedding rivers of Greek blood, could have such tender emotions. He was more concerned for Cassandra's well-being than he was for the fact that he had just committed a crime that was punishable by death.

The Oracle was sacrosanct. Helen couldn't believe that the Fates had allowed this union at all. From what she understood, fate itself stepped in and kept Oracles from finding intimacy with men. Oracles could try, but the man they wanted would inevitably meet a fatal accident, get shipped off to a faraway land and never return or there'd be some other devastating misfortune before that love could be consummated. For whatever reason, that obviously was not the case here. The Fates either wouldn't – or couldn't – interfere with Aeneas.

Cassandra smiled and reached up to touch her lover's

pretty mouth with her fingertips. 'I hear that's to be expected the first time. It was worth it a thousand times over,' she said quietly.

He took her hand in his and turned it so he could kiss the centre of her palm. 'I'm sorry, anyway,' he whispered, placing her tiny hand over the thick muscles that hid his sensitive heart.

Cassandra gazed at him hazily, her eyes swimming. Aeneas scooped her up, pulled her on to his lap, and kissed her. Cassandra swooned for a moment in his arms, but then seemed to steel herself. She pulled away from his kiss and shook her head.

'You must go,' she slurred, drunk on him. 'Now, before anyone discovers us.'

'I'm not going anywhere,' Aeneas responded with a low laugh. 'I won't dishonour you by running off to save my own skin.'

Aeneas shifted so that Cassandra could sit comfortably astride him and still see every change of his face as he pledged himself to her.

'I am free to remarry,' he said, smiling softly. 'My wife died in childbirth years ago, and my mourning is long over. Your brother may want my life for what I've done to you, but I have every right to ask for your hand before it comes to that.'

Cassandra edged away from Aeneas, pushing him back so both of them could see more clearly.

'I am not simply my brother's sister, and this is not

a silly tryst that can be excused with a hasty marriage,' Cassandra said, like he was missing the point entirely. 'I am Cassandra of Troy and the vessel of Fate. You have defiled that vessel, Aeneas. The punishment for you is certain.' Cassandra spoke to him harshly, trying to make him understand the stakes. 'You *must* run. Tonight. Now. Or you will die.'

'I won't leave you, Cassandra. I'll take my chances, throw myself on Paris's mercy. I'll beg him to allow you to be my wife if I must. But I won't run.' A pained look crossed his face as a troubling thought occurred to him. 'Don't you want to be my wife? I thought . . . since you gave yourself to me . . . that you loved me.'

Cassandra dropped her head into her hands. Aeneas tried to soothe her. He caressed her, held her and urged her to look up at him. When she finally met his gaze again, her piercing blue eyes sank deep into his bright green ones, and she spoke with all the authority of fate itself.

'I couldn't love you more if you came to me holding the sun in your right hand and all the stars in the sky in your left,' she told him, her voice as final as a funeral dirge. 'I could live a hundred lifetimes and never wish for a more perfect man than you. I have loved you since the second I saw you and, unfortunately for me, I know for a *fact* that I will never love anyone or anything as much as I love you.'

Helen's heart jumped into her throat. She ducked

behind the column that hid her and stuffed a hand over her mouth to keep her heart, and the choked sound that followed it, from leaping out. Cassandra knew Troy was going to fall that very night. She had seduced Aeneas on purpose in order to force him to run away. It was a desperate attempt to save his life.

Cassandra had risked angering the Fates to save the man she loved, but instead, her plan had turned back round and devoured itself like a snake eating its own tail. By loving Aeneas, Cassandra hadn't made him want to flee Troy as she had planned, but, rather, she had given him an unshakable desire to stay. For all her foresight, the one thing Cassandra hadn't accounted for was that Aeneas might fall madly in love with her. But it had happened. And now she had to change his mind or watch him die at the hands of the Greeks.

'I know Paris will support our marriage,' Aeneas said, making excited plans. 'You'll have to leave your high station at the temple, of course, but that wouldn't be so bad, would it?'

'It would be paradise,' Cassandra admitted sadly. She climbed out of his lap, sought out her chiton in the heap, and put it on as she spoke. 'But you have more to fear than just my brother. We all do.'

'Are you talking about the fall of Troy again?' he asked, his face wary. He braced himself, like he was getting ready for Cassandra to start raving.

'No. I'll never speak of it again,' Cassandra said

quietly, and Aeneas relaxed. 'I'm talking of another matter that has nothing to do with prophecy.'

So he might believe her, Helen thought, trying to figure out Cassandra's strategy. *Her curse is that her prophecy is not to be believed, not other truths she might know.*

'You must leave Troy before the sun rises, or Apollo will see that you have become my lover.'

'How does this concern Apollo?' Aeneas asked cautiously.

'I refused him years ago. The only reason I'm still alive is because even he fears the Fates, and they claimed me first.' Cassandra's voice faltered when she saw the horrified look on Aeneas's face, but still she continued. 'Apollo comes with the sun. If he sees that I gave myself to you, he will curse you, your boy and your father.'

Aeneas stared at Cassandra, his face paling in the torchlight.

'I'm sorry.' She reached out to him, but Aeneas threw her hands off and pushed away from her.

'Why?' he asked her desperately. 'Why did you do this to me?'

'I'm sorry,' she repeated. He stood up, searched for his chiton and tied it angrily.

'I was ready to die for you if that was my punishment, but my son and father have nothing to do with this. You should have told me.' His voice shook with betrayal. 'You've cursed my family forever.'

'No,' Cassandra said, dashing tears off her cheek. 'If

you leave now, take your father and your son and get out of Troy before dawn, Apollo will not chase you.'

'Of course he will!' Aeneas yelled, finally raising his voice at her.

'No, he won't be able to touch you ever again, I *swear* it!' she yelled back. That made Aeneas pause. Oracles did not swear lightly. 'Shortly after dawn, Apollo will be trapped on Olympus by a vow that Zeus has made on the River Styx. Zeus thought it would be impossible for the demigods to accomplish their end of it, but by dawn it will be so. Zeus's unbreakable vow binds him and the Twelve to stay imprisoned on Olympus for many generations.'

'And what is this impossible thing the demigods will have accomplished by dawn?' Aeneas asked, like he was starting to be convinced.

'You won't believe me.' Cassandra sighed like Atlas had just rolled his burden on to her shoulders. Then she laughed, and muttered to herself. 'A giant wooden horse. Ridiculous.'

'What about the horse?' Aeneas asked, his voice dropping dangerously. 'The one outside the great gate?'

'It's already too late,' she said, shaking her head. 'Get your son. Get your father. Leave Troy. If you stay, Apollo will punish us all.'

Aeneas's shoulders shrank, and the wounded expression on his face made him look as young as he had been when Helen first met him a decade ago.

'I actually believed you when you said you loved me,' he told her quietly.

'Maybe someday you'll look back on tonight and believe it again.' Cassandra bent her head, and Aeneas left her.

Andy woke long before dawn. She was alone in Ariadne's bed for the first time since the Delos family had taken her in, and it felt too weird. She'd got used to Ariadne's snoring and Helen's thrashing about. In a few short days, it had started to feel like the three of them had grown up piled on top of each other, and now that the room was quiet it felt *too* quiet to sleep.

It also didn't help that every time she closed her eyes the only thing she could see was Hector rising up out of the water to come to her rescue, soaking wet, bare chested and not exactly sleep inducing. Giving up on getting any more rest, Andy swung her legs out of bed and rumpled her short, dark hair with her fingers until the back stood up in spikes. She decided to go downstairs to see what she could do to help Noel and Kate set up for the monumental breakfast they were going to serve before Daedalus and Phaon's dawn duel.

Noel didn't expect Andy to do chores, but Andy insisted. She'd been taking care of herself her whole life, and she wasn't comfortable sitting around while other people waited on her. If she was going to be protected by this family, she figured the least she could do was help out. Plus, there were milk and cookies in the kitchen – *Kate's* cookies, no less. Andy may not have been on Nantucket for very long, but she'd already learned that Kate baked the kind of cookies that made a person want to get out of bed.

Creeping into the kitchen, Andy saw a big, dark shape sitting at the table and gasped in surprise.

'You're not thinking of trying to go for another swim, are you?' Hector asked quietly.

'No,' Andy whispered, pulling up the strap of her nightgown. Ariadne was a bit bigger than Andy and most of the clothes she'd borrowed seemed to fall off her shoulder in an inadvertently seductive way. 'I couldn't sleep.'

'I know,' he said, watching her. 'I heard.'

'How could you . . .' Andy began, and broke off when she saw the gleam of his smile in the dark. Of course he could hear her tossing and turning in bed. He was a Scion. He could probably hear her sighing his freaking name in her sleep. The thought made her want to turn and run back upstairs, but instead she stayed rooted to the spot, staring at his shape while her eyes adjusted to the dark.

'Get a glass.' Hector gestured to the bottle of milk and plate of cookies in front of him.

'Aha. Kate's cookies. You beat me to it,' Andy chuckled. She took down a mug and slid in next to Hector on the bench. He was only wearing a pair of well-worn sweatpants that said REAL MADRID in fading letters down the side. 'Don't you ever wear a shirt?' she asked. She was attempting to joke, but her voice came out shaky and breathy, ruining the cool-girl effect she was going for.

'Not to bed.' He smiled and took her mug to fill it. Andy watched the muscles in his forearm flex and relax as he poured. His hands fascinated her. She liked the way he held things in such a solid, sure way. Andy's hands had a tendency to flutter daintily when she moved, something she blamed on her siren heritage. But when Hector's hands touched something, they took control of it.

Andy nibbled on a cookie and found herself marvelling at the difference between them. Hector was unapologetically masculine in everything he did, and just sitting next to him made Andy feel more feminine than she ever had before. Femininity was something usually equated with weakness in Andy's mind, but, now that she was near Hector, Andy realized that really feeling like a woman was just about the most empowering thing she'd ever experienced.

'Do you like soccer?' she asked, gesturing to the logo on his sweatpants.

'I like Madrid,' he replied. 'My family spent a lot of years in Spain. I'd love to go back someday.'

'I liked Spain, but I think I prefer Scandinavia. Have you ever swum in a fjord?' He shook his head. 'The ice glows milky-blue underwater. It's . . .' She broke off and smiled shyly. 'Maybe we can do that together someday.'

The silence stretched out between them as they stared at each other. She could hear her pulse pounding in her ears and knew that Hector could hear it too.

'Did you travel a lot growing up?' he finally asked.

'When I was young. Before my mother, ah . . . went her own way.' Andy looked down at her mug. 'Sirens don't raise kids like humans do. My mom stuck around a lot longer than most would have. She really tried with me.'

'When did she go her own way?' Hector asked, using Andy's phrase.

'When I was seven, she left me at boarding school.' She saw Hector wince. 'Wow. Out loud, that sounds just awful, doesn't it?'

'Yeah,' he laughed quietly. 'This must be a shock to you. Suddenly being a part of my big, crazy family.'

'No, I like it,' Andy replied immediately, conscious of the fact that he'd included her in his family. 'I love it, actually.'

It felt like a warm bubble was expanding inside her, filling up spaces she didn't even know she had, and she suddenly wanted to touch Hector very much. She leaned closer to him, hoping that if she invited him nearer he'd come the rest of the way.

'Andy. You're a guest in my house. There are rules about this,' Hector whispered pleadingly. She looked up at his face, arrested by his tone. 'You haven't spent much time around men. Have you.' It wasn't really a question, but she shook her head in answer, anyway. 'Fix your nightgown,' he said softly.

Andy caught at the fallen strap with her fingertips and slid it back over her shoulder, loving the way Hector's eyes followed every move she made, like he was trying to read something written on her skin.

'Come on,' he sighed regretfully, standing up and taking her by the hand. He led her back upstairs to his sister's room, pausing outside the door.

'I'm sorry,' she said, sensing that she'd done something wrong.

'You don't even know what you're apologizing for, do you?' Hector asked with a humorous glint in his eye.

'No idea,' she admitted, feeling a bit silly.

He leaned close to her and brushed his lips against her cheek. Andy felt a shiver radiate out from where he'd kissed her, like ripples spreading on the surface of a pond.

'I'll show you later,' he promised, his voice shaking slightly.

Hector opened the door to Ariadne's bedroom and gently pushed a very confused Andy through it.

Helen sat up in bed. The sound of lapping waves greeted her, and clear sea air, sweetened with the scent of rain-forest flowers, wrapped Helen in dewy heat.

She ran her hands over the crisp sheet under her and felt the dent next to her that still smelt like Lucas. She swung her bare legs to the side, parting the gauzy curtain of mosquito netting that hung over the wide, white bed. The teak floor was glossy and cool underfoot. A seashell wind chime announced where the entrance to the hut was, and Helen padded barefoot toward it.

Outside, sparkling blue-green water harboured teeming coral reefs. Beyond the watery expanse, impossibly steep and verdant islands jutted up out of the dazzling aqua water like the elbows of giants.

Helen walked the circumference of the wraparound deck and saw that their little hut was raised up on stilts in the middle of the water of the shallow cove. She found Lucas – out for a dawn swim.

Helen sat down on the deck next to a sceptical sea turtle and watched Lucas goof off with a lemon shark. She knew animals weren't pets here, because she had made it so.

The sea turtle wasn't about to risk getting in the water with anything that had as many teeth as a lemon shark. Helen didn't blame it. Respect for the power of other animals was something that Helen wasn't about to monkey around with, not even in paradise. Why have a shark at all if it wasn't dangerous? Where was the thrill in that?

Lucas seemed to be aware of the fact that the lemon shark was not a toy, and he met it in the water with all the respect that the creature deserved. But they darted under the waves almost like they were having a game of tag.

It reminded Helen of how Lucas moved around the

ring when he and Hector were sparring. She decided that was what Lucas was doing. He was honing his reflexes and bettering his fight skills with a creature that he'd never had the opportunity to spar with before. Maybe the lemon shark was as well.

Lucas noticed Helen watching him. He floated under the water, angling himself toward her, his arms spread out like wings. Helen's tummy hit the floor and she smiled at him, amazed that he could still do that to her after everything they'd been through. Lifetimes that she could remember – some that lasted only a few brief years, and others that lasted decades – and he still made her all tingly like a girl who had never been kissed.

He pulled himself out of the water and sat next to her, dripping wet and soaking in the newly dawning sunshine.

'I've always wanted to do that – stay under and not need a breath,' he said, so excited his voice was high and boyish. 'Hector and Jason may have envied me when I flew, but I died a little when they jumped in the water together and disappeared for hours. I couldn't follow them.'

Helen heard a sad note creep into his tone, and she realized that he must have always been slightly isolated from his cousins. He couldn't take them flying with him, and they couldn't take him under the water with them.

Helen knew it wasn't that Lucas envied Hector and Jason for what they could do. He envied that they could share their talents with each other, and he couldn't share his with anyone – until Helen had come along.

Lucas looked out at the gently folding waves, thinking. 'Am I like this from now on?' he asked. 'Will I be able to breathe underwater back on Earth?'

'Yes,' Helen replied quietly. 'In Hades, he makes it so no one has any special powers – except him, of course. That way he doesn't grant talents to individuals who weren't born with them. Hades is very smart. He avoids the whole question of giving too much power by suspending all powers when you are with him.'

'You didn't do that,' Lucas said quietly.

'I couldn't. I needed to fix you. And now I just want to please you,' Helen admitted. 'I want you to enjoy all that I have to give you. But in order to make it possible for you to breathe underwater here, I had to change your body permanently. That's why I don't know how many Scions I should bring here. I want everyone to see this, but what if I . . .'

'Inadvertently make an army of Scions who have a multitude of talents that not even the Olympians have?' Lucas finished for her. 'It is a big thing to consider.'

'Unlimited power.'

Lucas thought some more. 'Why didn't Zeus do this? Give himself and all the Olympians as many different talents he could think of?'

'I don't know. I don't think he's into sharing power,' Helen guessed. 'It could also be because, like Hades, he decided to set certain rules for his world that prohibit him from giving out powers. But I don't know what the deal is with Olympus. I've never been there.'

'I hear there's a lot of feasting,' Lucas said jokingly. 'Ambrosia, nectar of the gods, nymphs. Lots of nymphs.'

'Keep 'em fed and happy so they don't revolt,' Helen said with a nod and a grin. They chuckled with each other, their eyes locking. Lucas took her hand and looked away.

His eyes scanned the horizon, sweeping over the dazzling view like he was trying to memorize it. He turned back to her and grew serious. 'How's the family?'

'Anxious. We should go back,' she replied reluctantly. 'Time runs here just like it does on Earth, and they're waiting for me to come back with you.'

Although Helen would have loved to spend eternity in this hut over the water with Lucas, she had more than one reason to return to Earth. She had to get back to Orion, her Shield, so the Fates couldn't see her while she tried to come up with a way to stop a war with the gods. She knew she didn't have much time. Now that she'd created her own world, Zeus would be gunning for her, and she couldn't even start to plan without making sure that the Fates couldn't see her.

She itched to tell Lucas about all this, but she knew she couldn't. Even in her Everyland the Fates could still see her, and if the Fates thought she was trying to dodge them, they'd find a way to keep her from Orion. They might already know what Helen was planning, whether she'd said it out loud or not, but she figured saying it would definitely jinx it. She had to wait until she was with Orion again to tell all of them what she was planning.

'I can feel you fidgeting,' Lucas said with an indulgent smile. 'But before we go, may I ask a favour?'

'Anything.'

'Don't bring anyone else here, to this cove, OK? Let this place be ours.'

'Forever and ever,' she promised.

CHAPTER THIRTEEN

Lucas took his last look at paradise.

'Ready?' Helen asked him, holding his hand tightly in hers.

'No,' he sighed, watching her ever-changing eyes catch the light of the rising sun. 'But let's go, anyway.'

A stab of startling cold, like being plunged into ice water, and they were back at his house. It was quiet in a way that the Delos compound almost never was.

'I thought you said everyone was waiting for us,' he said, starting to worry.

'They were,' she said tentatively. 'Orion?' Helen called.

Jealousy shot through Lucas, white hot. He tried to brush it off, but couldn't. She was still holding his hand, but she was thinking about Orion. In Everyland, Helen could pamper him and treat him like he was the only person in the world, but back on Earth she had someone else to love – someone who wasn't her cousin.

'My dad,' she said, giving him a worried look.

'Come on,' he said, using the moment to pull his hand out of hers before she saw the battle in his heart.

Lucas and Helen went upstairs and found Kate watching over her father, still asleep.

'Why are you the only one here, Kate?' Helen asked angrily. 'You're not strong enough to stop Daphne if she tries to drug him again.'

'Daphne's gone down to the beach with everyone else for the duel,' Kate said, her eyes searching Lucas for injury. 'Where have you been?'

'What duel?' Lucas looked at Helen to see if she knew. When Helen shrugged, Kate quickly explained what had happened after he and Helen had vanished.

'What about Orion?' Helen asked. 'Phaon is only doing this to get to him.'

Lucas gritted his teeth and tried to remind himself that he should have expected this. She loved Orion, and Lucas couldn't blame her. It was easier to love Orion – less complicated.

'Doesn't matter.' Kate shook her head. 'Daedalus and Phaon weren't allowed to choose . . . what do you call them? Backups? Wingmen?'

'Seconds,' Lucas said, supplying the name.

'That's it – no seconds allowed for their fight.'

'Even if Phaon lives, he won't be able to go after Orion,' Lucas told Helen to set her at ease. 'Not that he would. Orion would crush him in an open duel.'

'But if Phaon wins, and kills Daedalus . . .' Helen began.

'If he wins, he wins. No one can retaliate. Not even

Orion.' Lucas watched Helen try to digest this, and he could see she was having a hard time with it. 'It's better this way. The killing has to stop somewhere.'

Helen finally nodded, accepting this even though she didn't want to. Lucas didn't blame her. He didn't want to see a murdering paedophile get away with it if Daedalus lost to Phaon, but there was no way round it. Duels had strict rules. The Titan Hecate, goddess of all portals and crossroads, made interfering with them impossible. It was said that not even Zeus could defy Hecate. She was the only Titan he couldn't send to Tartarus.

'Do you want to go? I should probably stay in case Daphne comes back,' Helen said to Kate in a weak voice. She obviously didn't want to stay, but she felt like she had to offer.

'Go? And watch a couple of sweaty dudes I don't know try to hack off each other's kibbles and bits with swords?' Kate asked with a cocked eyebrow. 'No thanks. I'll stay here with Jerry.'

'You're awesome. You know that, right?' Helen told Kate, giving her a hug.

'I do,' Kate replied. She pulled back and looked at Helen, smoothing a hand over her face for a moment and growing serious. 'And the less you vanish in a ball of fire and ice the less grey hair I grow. You know *that*, right?' Helen chuckled. Kate turned to Lucas and pointed at him. 'And no more grabbing on to Helen when she's a human torch, OK?'

'Very sound advice,' he replied as Kate hugged him.

Leaving Kate to watch over Jerry, they hurried down to the beach. As they made their way to the large group of bystanders gathered by the water, Lucas didn't try to take Helen's hand again. He could tell that she was eager to get to Orion, and he didn't want to make her feel like he was holding her back.

As soon as she caught a glimpse of Orion, she took to the air and flew to him in a rush. Lucas walked the rest of the way to give them a moment alone and to give himself a moment to cool down.

It wasn't that he thought Helen didn't love him. He knew she did. But Orion could give her what she needed, and he couldn't. All Lucas had to do to make Helen happy was get out of the way. It was simple – even if it was also killing him.

'Lucas?' his father called out, sighting him. He came running down the beach in a blur.

Castor may have had a head start, but Hector and Jason both beat him to where Lucas hung back, walking slowly up the beach.

'I can't believe it!' Hector howled, grabbing Lucas in a bear hug. 'We all thought you got toasted!'

'I did,' Lucas said, laughing as his cousin swung him around.

'Get off him, doofus,' Jason said irritably to his brother. 'Let me at least check him over before you crack his ribs.'

311

'I'm fine, Jase,' Lucas insisted as Hector put him down. 'Completely healed.'

It took him what seemed like forever to greet the rest of his family. While he tried to prove to his mother that he had all his skin still on, he caught a glimpse of Helen having an intense conversation with Orion.

When Lucas next stole a glimpse of Helen, she was glaring at her mother, and Lucas could tell that they'd had a quick exchange about Jerry. He didn't know what they had said to each other, but he was pretty sure that they'd decided to save their fight until later.

The group formed a circle round a levelled area of sand. It was a makeshift arena, probably very much like the first fighting grounds. Unfamiliar Scions – Lucas assumed they were members from the Hundred Cousins – finished their task and backed out of the ring, throwing a torch, a key and a serpent into the cleared area.

A woman appeared, and the three symbols that had conjured her vanished. She wasn't young, and her features weren't perfect, but even so she was lovely. And terrifying, Lucas decided.

'Hecate,' Hector whispered. Lucas nodded absently, momentarily transfixed on the only Titan left to wander the world, before she disappeared again.

Lucas glanced up and down the beach. It was November, not long after dawn, and bitterly cold, but there were still a few people scattered along the shore. What if someone saw?

'How are they expecting to pull off a duel without bystanders calling the police?' Hector mumbled to Lucas.

'Hecate,' Lucas mumbled back. 'Once the duel starts, nothing can stop it. She'll keep any interference away. Especially uninvited mortals.'

Lucas looked over at Orion. His eyes were on his father, who stood a few paces in front of him, his sword ready. Helen was at his side. Lucas quickly looked away when he saw Helen and Orion join hands.

He turned his attention to Phaon, who stood across the ring. His stance was slack, listless, like he wasn't really paying attention. Compared to Daedalus, who was squared off and eager to get into the fight, Phaon's mind seemed to be elsewhere.

'He's dead already,' Hector said in Lucas's ear. Lucas nodded in agreement. Phaon had given up. Although Lucas knew that Phaon deserved this death, he felt pity for him.

'I just want to say one last thing, if I may?' Phaon's thin voice barely outshouted the waves. 'I was not always a horrible person, although I've done horrible things. I understand now that what I did was wrong.'

Lucas felt his pity deepen. He took a step forward to say that this duel should be stopped, when Phaon crumpled to his knees with a shriek. He clutched at his chest, like someone had just stabbed him there.

'Try that again and I'll rip out what's left of your heart,' Orion said, his face livid. Whatever internal battle the two of them were fighting with their talents from the House of Rome, Orion won. The ground shook, and for a moment it looked like Orion was ready to tear Phaon apart with his bare hands, but Helen put her arm out and stopped him.

Lucas no longer felt pity, although Phaon had never looked more pathetic. His sympathy had strangely vanished. He realized that Phaon must have been controlling their emotions. Looking around at the rest of the group, Lucas saw that everyone was as furious with Phaon for manipulating them as he was.

'Get up,' Orion commanded, and Phaon rose to his feet. 'Pick up your sword.' Phaon took the hilt of his sword in his hand and a lascivious leer tugged his face into an ugly shape.

'Why so frustrated? I already told you, you can have the little one, Orion. You know she wants it from you.' Phaon grinned obscenely at Cassandra.

Lucas felt Hector and Jason grab his arms, and he realized that he had been moving forward to get the twisted bastard.

'Don't,' Hector growled in his ear. 'It's not your life to take.'

'I'll see you all in Hades,' Phaon said with a despotic laugh.

'No,' Helen said, her voice ringing like a goddess. 'You won't.'

She spoke with such certainty that Phaon's manic

smile melted. He stared at her, knowing that she knew better than any of them what awaited him. The look on Helen's face was sphinxlike. Merciless. It terrified him, as it should have.

'Begin,' Orion said. He moved out of the arena's circle like he knew exactly what he was doing. For a moment, Lucas wondered if Orion had duelled more than one man in the Colosseum.

'For my sister, Cassiopeia,' Daedalus said quietly, almost like he was praying.

And then he attacked Phaon with all the skill and power of a seasoned warrior.

Lucas counted four strokes before he saw Phaon gushing blood from a wound in the leg. Phaon limped around, kicking up sand to distract his opponent, but that didn't deter a veteran like Daedalus. He feinted, moved past Phaon, and reversed his thrust with the tip of his blade to pierce Phaon in the back – specifically in the kidney, a very painful wound.

Jason nudged Lucas. They glanced at each other, and realized together what Daedalus was doing. He wasn't going to go for a quick kill.

'He's going to bleed Phaon to death,' Jason whispered.

'Good,' Lucas replied. He looked to his right and saw Hector nodding in agreement.

It took almost twenty minutes. A cut here, a bone-breaking blow there, and on and on it went, until even Lucas, Jason and Hector became uncomfortable.

Daedalus was ruthless. He inflicted each injury as if he were ticking off the ultimate bucket list. This was obviously something Daedalus had thought about for a very long time.

No one spoke or moved to stop him.

Lucas looked at his father, expecting to see him growing uncomfortable as he watched the systematic torture of another human being. But instead all he saw was a removed expression on Castor's face, like his father was remembering something painful that still lingered from long ago. Glancing at all the members of the older generation, Lucas saw similar expressions, and he knew that everyone present believed that Phaon deserved the extreme punishment he suffered now.

Phaon flailed. In agony, he chattered on about how he wasn't sorry. He went on and on about how he owned innocence because he stole it, and now he was the god of innocence. He insisted that he might be a monster, but weren't they all?

The answer was a decided no. The rest of the Scions, for all their faults, were not like him. When Daedalus finally cut off Phaon's head with a straight, clean blow, they nodded as one, turning their faces to sky.

Catharsis, Lucas thought.

'Well done, my son,' said a ringing voice.

The circle turned and looked at the waterline. Striding up out of the waves was a bare-chested young man with black hair and piercing blue eyes. He carried a trident, but, because of the look on his face, to Lucas it appeared to be more like a pitchfork in the hands of a devil. A devil that looked exactly like Lucas.

He heard gasps from the group, and he felt Hector nudge him.

'There's your evil twin,' Hector said under his breath, his face enlivened by the danger he felt in the air.

Lucas knew he should have been more amazed by the appearance of a god, but he wasn't. Strangely, he could only think about his swim with the lemon shark a few minutes ago. Helen had just given him a new power over the ocean. He could breathe underwater. Not for the first time, Lucas wondered if she'd given him more powers than that.

'My Scions have always been stronger than yours, niece, and here again my Daedalus has proven the physical superiority of my offspring by killing your Phaon.'

'Like I care about a show of brute strength?' asked another voice that purred seductively.

Again, the group turned as one to see a tall woman, her blonde hair falling in clouds down to the back of her knees and her voluptuous body undulating like waves beneath it. Dressed only in a sheer white slip, she sauntered up the beach, her toes tickling the foamy crease where the waves met the sand.

'It's not the strength of the arm, but the passion

inside the hearts of those who fight that ultimately determines the winner of the war, Poseidon. We've been *through* this.' She went directly to Helen and stood in front of her as she spoke. 'Many times, in many wars, we've seen how the hearts of men and women decide the outcome of battles.' She smiled and took both of Helen's hands in hers. 'Hello again, Helen.'

'Hello, Aphrodite,' Helen replied, tears gathering in her eyes.

Helen actually remembers her, Lucas thought. For the first time he considered what that meant. Helen remembered Troy. She knew what had really happened.

'I've missed you so much,' Aphrodite said.

'And I've missed you,' Helen said, her voice catching, like she was not only surprised to find herself saying this, but surprised to be feeling it too.

'Funny, isn't it? I've known every love possible, but as the years stretched out, the love I longed for the most is the one I shared with my sister.'

The two women hugged each other tenderly, and the golden glow that grew around them was mesmerizing to see, like looking at magic. Lucas could hear the hearts of the Scions slow to beat with Helen's and Aphrodite's. It was a strong, binding synchronicity that Lucas knew they would all remember, no matter how opposed they were in the future.

Fear ballooned inside Lucas. Not because the gods were among them again, but because Helen was at the centre of it all. She inspired such love in him, in Orion, even in a goddess. There was no hate without love, and Lucas couldn't help but think that they would all soon be facing a desperate fight because of the pure love they all felt in that moment.

'A touching reunion,' said the bare-chested man with black hair. 'But your man lost, Aphrodite. And you still owe me our wager.'

Lucas pushed his way through the group and faced what looked like a wet and slightly feral version of himself. 'This is not a game for the gods to bet on. These are our lives.'

Poseidon studied Lucas, and laughed. 'The Fates *would* put my face on a moralizing sap. Let me tell you something, boy. I don't care what the Fates want. In the sea, the big fish eat the little ones. You're going to have to grow some thicker skin if you're the one who's supposed to try and replace me.'

'At least he's intelligent,' said another familiar voice. A god who looked like Hector's twin came down the other end of the beach, interrupting Lucas before he could question Poseidon's last remark. 'My would-be replacement is brave, but he's got to be the dumbest of all the Scion mongrels. He actually wanted to challenge me – still mortal as he is. It's embarrassing, really.'

Lucas automatically grabbed Hector by the arm. He could feel his cousin itching to jump Apollo, immortal or not, and that would probably get them all killed.

A burst of freezing air from the centre of the circle interrupted a fight before it could begin.

'Now, now, Apollo,' said the young, blond man who stood in the patch of newly formed ice. A gust of air passed over Lucas, but it wasn't sea air. It smelt like the mountains, laden with herbs and smelling faintly of stone. It had to be from another world. 'None of us makes wise decisions when it comes to women. Hector is no exception. He wants his Andromache for himself. Can you blame him?'

The young blond man was tall but no giant. He wasn't exceptionally muscular, either, but despite the fact that both Poseidon and Apollo were larger and more physically developed, he radiated power as he walked to Helen and Aphrodite. The goddess nodded at the god respectfully, but it was Helen whom he addressed.

'Well, daughter. You've been busy,' Zeus said in a softly scolding tone.

Lucas schooled his face so he didn't give away his emotions as he thought this through frantically. He had known for a while that the Fates assigned roles, trading out new actors in each new cycle so that everything stayed the same even as it changed. Lucas quickly looked around at the gods and their Scion doubles before his gaze settled on Orion. Orion's twin was missing.

'What do you want from us?' Helen asked, squaring off with Zeus. Lucas couldn't help but be proud of her, even though it was insane to talk to a god like that. Zeus had cursed entire generations for lesser offences, but Helen didn't show a drop of fear.

'Not *us*. It's what I want from *you*, Helen.' Zeus spoke softly but his voice still seemed to boom.

'What's that?' Helen asked cautiously, her bravado wearing thin.

Poseidon and Apollo positioned themselves behind Zeus. Aphrodite kissed Helen's cheek, released her hand and reluctantly went to stand behind her father. Hector, Lucas and Jason all reacted in kind and angled themselves behind Helen and Orion.

'I want your shiny new world,' Zeus replied.

More gods joined him. A huge woman in armour came first. Then a boy who moved so fast he seemed to buzz like a hummingbird, a hunchback carrying a hammer, a man with grapevines in his hair and finally another woman wearing a dress of peacock feathers all fell in behind Zeus.

Helen looked at Orion. Lucas bit down hard, grinding his teeth to keep himself from yelling. Didn't she just tell him a few hours ago that *he* was the one who helped her figure out everything? Lucas watched as an understanding passed between Orion and Helen. He didn't know what it was because she was withholding information. Again. Helen and Orion made a silent agreement, and she turned to face Zeus.

'You can't have it,' Helen said deliberately.

Zeus smiled like Helen had just given him keys to the world he *really* wanted. 'Challenge.'

Helen hoped like hell this worked.

'Accepted,' Hector said, barrelling forward until he was at Helen's right hand and glaring at Zeus over a few feet of sand. Voices shouted out, and several challenges were made at once as the crowd of Scions all reacted to Hector's move against the gods.

'Wait!' Helen held up an arm to stop Hector from starting a mêlée right then and there. Lucas and Jason came to keep Hector in check.

'I haven't seen such fire in a hundred generations,' Zeus said, laughing. 'You're right, Apollo. He's brave, even braver than your boy at Troy, but dumber than a block of marble.'

'Easy,' Orion said to Hector. 'Trust us.'

Zeus leaned in close to Hector, close enough for Helen to see the lightning bolts that flashed inside his amber eyes. 'If he had an ounce of sense, he would remember that no matter how skilled he is, he *cannot* kill me.'

'Exactly,' Helen said in a controlled voice. 'So it's not a true challenge. The gods aren't allowed to fight mortals in duels, which is why at Troy only demigods fought demigods. The gods can try to kill Scions with ocean waves and lightning bolts and curses. But they are not allowed to participate in one-on-one combat with us unless they're mortal as well. Like when Ares tortured me in the portal. He wasn't immortal there, so he could kill me. But away from a portal the gods need to find a way to make us fight each other instead. Like they did at Troy.'

'And like they're doing right now,' Orion continued pointedly, so more Scions could hear and understand that the gods were just trying to kill them all off.

'There are rules to these things. You're already my chosen champion,' Helen said. 'And you're mortal, so Zeus has to pick a mortal champion too.'

'How did you learn all this?' Zeus asked Helen with narrowed eyes.

'A little river told me,' she answered, inwardly sighing with relief that her Helen of Troy memories were correct.

Helen saw Hector relax and smile. Lucas and Jason eased back, finally trusting that Helen and Orion knew what they were doing.

Most of the other Scions relaxed as well. Even though the other Houses didn't know Hector personally, they had all heard of his reputation. He had killed Creon, a Shadowmaster, with his bare hands. As far as they were concerned, that was proof enough of his skill in single combat.

There really was no Scion who could match Hector, except maybe Helen herself. He was the perfect hero. The biggest physical threat was Daphne and she adored Hector. No matter what Daphne's motives were, and Helen openly admitted to herself that she had no idea what those could be, Helen sensed that her mother would never kill Hector. He reminded her too much of Ajax.

At least, that's what Orion and Helen were banking on. Neither of them could think of a Scion who could beat Hector, so they hoped that the death toll for the day would end at two – Phaon and some other poor thing, hopefully from the Hundred Cousins or from a distant offshoot of the House of Athens.

All of this last-second planning she and Orion had done should have put Helen at ease, but it didn't. When she looked back at Zeus, his smile had grown wider.

Helen noticed a disturbance around them, like the sand dunes were coming alive. A moment later, the dunes were covered in strange men, dressed in archaic armour. Helen could see that some had shiny red eyes, and others had hard, armour-like skin or pincers for hands. Myrmidons. She remembered Automedon killing Zach, and her fingertips crackled with angry lightning.

'Do you think you can take a Myrmidon?' Helen asked in an aside to Hector, realizing that she and Orion hadn't accounted for this.

'I got it,' he whispered back confidently. Helen looked past Hector to Lucas, who pursed his lips and nodded, silently confirming that he thought Hector could do it too.

'I have chosen a champion as well, Helen,' Zeus announced. Triumph gleamed in his eyes. 'Achilles to match your Hector.'

The Myrmidons parted and let a single warrior pass through their ranks to stand across from Hector. Helen knew this warrior – his walk, his haircut, even the T-shirt he was wearing, although at that moment it was mostly covered by strange armour. He'd had that shirt for two years now, and Helen knew it was his favourite. Everything about him was familiar to Helen, except for the newly developed power she could sense in him now.

'*Matt?*' Helen howled disbelievingly. 'What the hell are you doing hanging out with a bunch of Myrmidons?'

He glanced at her and quickly turned his attention to Hector.

'It's not you I want,' Matt said to Hector. 'There's only one life I want to take, and it was never yours. I came to kill the Tyrant.'

'Matt,' Lucas said calmly while Hector and Matt stared each other down. 'There is no Tyrant.'

'Oh yes there is,' Matt said harshly. He looked at Helen.

They had been friends since they were too little to stand, and she had never seen his face like this. It was like he hated her.

'She may not be doing anything to hurt you now, Lucas,' he continued. 'But absolute power corrupts absolutely, and there has never been a being with more power than Helen.'

Helen felt dizzy and slightly nauseous. Because she knew he was right.

'Helen? The Tyrant?' Orion said, guffawing with disbelief.

Tantalus, Daedalus and Pallas all moved away from Helen and positioned themselves behind Matt.

'Dad,' Orion hissed, but then quickly shut his mouth. Helen saw his eyes harden, and she could see in his heart that Orion was scolding himself for not having anticipated this.

Helen looked at Hector and saw him staring at his father, Pallas. There was genuine hurt in his eyes, but no blame. They were so different that it didn't surprise either one to find the other on the opposite side of the war.

Castor stood firmly behind Lucas, glaring at his brothers. Helen felt Daphne take a position behind her and Orion.

More Scions shuffled around on the outskirts of the group. Tense, murmured arguments flared up and then subsided as individual members broke from their Houses and decided for themselves which side they preferred – Helen's or the god's. Two distinct sides were being drawn. Matt raised his voice so everyone could hear him.

'The prophecy says that the Tyrant is *the vessel where the blood of the Four Houses has mixed*. Tell me Orion, how many powers did Helen get in the blood-brother exchange with you and Lucas?' Matt said. 'Nearly all of them, right? That's what we've figured.'

Matt gestured to Claire and Ariadne, and they moved to join his side. Helen felt her stomach slide down like she was on a roller coaster. All of a sudden, she couldn't breathe.

Losing Matt was a big enough blow, but losing Claire was unthinkable. Her Giggles. Her best friend ever, and she'd picked the other side. Helen knew that Claire had doubts about her. She should have tried to talk to Claire instead of keeping secrets, but instead she'd let the rift between them grow larger and larger. And all that fear she saw in Claire's heart had taken over.

Helen heard Jason whisper Claire's name to himself, and when she glanced over at him, it looked like he was dying inside. Helen had a brief memory flash of Troilus, whose wife, Cressida, betrayed him by choosing a Greek lover over him. Helen could see into Claire's heart, and it was obvious how torn she was. But when Helen looked at Matt's heart, there was no conflict. He believed what he was doing was right.

'Matt. How can you do this?' Helen asked, trying her hardest not to cry.

'Because you can control the earth, the sea and the sky,' Matt said as more and more Scions joined his side. 'You can call lightning, manipulate gravity and pull all the swords out of an army's hands by generating a magnetic field. You can control hearts, and now I learn that you've even created your own world. Helen, is there a force you don't command – except maybe yourself? You nearly killed *Lucas* your emotions were so out of control, and from what I've seen your behaviour is getting more erratic as time goes on, not less.' Helen looked away and made a frustrated sound, but Matt continued. 'Most important, please explain to me, if you can make your own world – a perfect world that you control utterly – what's to stop you from destroying *this* one if we don't do exactly as you say?'

Silence.

All Helen could hear were waves and seagulls. *Matt would be the first to figure that out. He'd always been so darn smart.*

'Do you remember homecoming freshman year?' Matt asked. He shifted on his feet uncertainly, his eyes sad.

'Yeah,' Helen said with a shrug. 'A bunch of us spent the whole night talking around the bonfire, like, five minutes down the beach from here.'

'Do you remember Zach asking us if we could build a time machine, would we use it to go back and murder Hitler when he was just a baby?'

'Yes,' Helen replied, her voice coming out like a croak. 'I remember. So I take it you think I'm Hitler.'

'No. I think you're the Tyrant,' Matt said. 'You have the potential to be much worse.'

'My daughter can't be the Tyrant. Listen to me!' Daphne said passionately as she waved her hands to get everyone's attention.

It was the first time Daphne had ever stood up for her, and even though Helen was still furious at her mother for what she'd done to Jerry she couldn't help but be touched.

'The Tyrant is supposed to replace Hades. He is supposed to become the Scion lord of the dead. Helen is meant to rule the sky and replace Zeus, which is exactly why he got a champion to challenge her.' Daphne pointed an accusing finger at Zeus and won over a few believers. 'Think about it. Zeus is about to get overthrown by a Scion with more powers than he has, and he's trying to turn us against her so we'll kill her for him. She's powerful, yes, but Helen can't be the Tyrant.'

'Where is it written that the Tyrant has to take Hades's place?' Matt asked, his voice frighteningly calm. 'The three major gods are supposed to be replaced by three Scions – that we know from prophecy. We've always assumed that the Tyrant would rule Hades, but the Tyrant could as easily rule the sky.'

Daphne paused. All the vigour went out of her argument, and a fearful look crossed her face. 'I'm sorry,' Daphne whispered to Helen, her cheeks pale.

'It's OK, Mom. I've suspected this for a few days now. Born to bitterness?' Helen asked, not unkindly reminding her mother of the prophecy. 'Is there anyone in the world more bitter than you?'

'No. You don't understand,' Daphne continued, and then stopped when Helen stepped forward and dared to tread on the line in the sand that had formed between the two sides.

'Matt's right. I'm the Tyrant. Or I'm supposed to be, if the Fates have their way. But you've got to trust me. I'm going to make sure that doesn't happen.'

'I know you'll try,' Matt said, and sighed heavily. 'You'll mean to do only good things with your powers, and in the beginning you'll right wrongs and defend the weak. I know you will. But it has to go sour eventually. No one person, no matter how well-intentioned, is meant to rule the world.'

Helen could see the electric change in him that she'd noticed before, that thing that made him more than just Matt. He was different, stronger and full of strange magic, but, even so, Helen knew he was making all the same choices he would have a year ago. He was still Matt – a true moral compass – and, as usual, he was right.

'You've always hated bullies. And I guess I'm the biggest bully on the block now, huh?' Helen said with a fond smile. Matt smiled with her. Neither of them wanted this to happen.

'Everybody hang on,' Claire said anxiously, rushing to stand between the factions like she could think up a bridge between the two. 'Lennie – maybe there's a way you can give some of these powers back? Is there something you can do to, I don't know, just be *you* again so we don't have to freak out?'

'Sorry, Gig,' Helen replied, knowing that she was

hurting her best friend more than she ever had before. 'This *is* me. It always has been.'

Claire's eyes filled with tears. But no matter how much she loved all the people standing on the other side of the imaginary wall that was building between the two factions, Helen knew that Claire was going to do what she thought was right.

When she took her place again behind Matt, Helen didn't blame her. In fact, she admired Claire for her strength and bravery even though it stung like crazy.

Helen wished she could shout out her plan, tell her friends and family why she was doing this, but she couldn't. The Fates might not be able to hear her while she was with Orion, but Zeus certainly could and, while the Fates might be her ultimate enemy, Zeus was the one she had to find a way to imprison. Until she did that, Helen couldn't give back an ounce of power or she knew she wouldn't be strong enough to fight him. And then Zeus would find a way to kill every last one of them.

Like Helen of Troy before her, Helen Hamilton knew that she'd happily play the bad guy and make everyone hate her, before she'd allow all the people she loved to die. She remembered Ariadne telling her once that for a Scion to name her daughter Helen was like a Christian naming her child Judas. Like all the other Helens before her, Helen Hamilton had decided that being Judas to her family was worth it – so long as they survived.

'I'm sorry, Claire,' she said, trying in vain to do a

mind-meld with her friend and get her to understand without saying anything. 'But I'm not giving up my powers.'

'And that's that,' Matt said, truly saddened. 'She won't ever be our "Lennie" again, Claire. She's made her choice – power over us.'

Matt angled his head over his shoulder and made an inhuman chittering noise. Helen recognized it. Automedon had used it to command his men when he attacked Helen, Hector and Claire in the woods outside a track meet.

The Myrmidons reacted to Matt's command by backing up and forming a semicircle on their side of the 'wall'. One of them moved forward and retrieved Phaon's body, and a second group came and swept the sand clean. They were as efficient as an army of ants, and within seconds a new battleground had been cleared inside the makeshift arena on the beach.

An offering was brought into the circle. A pumpkin.

'What's going on?' Helen said to Orion, as memories of cooking with her father, turning pumpkins into pancakes, pie and Popsicles, crowded into her mind.

'It's one of her symbols. Hecate's power covers a lot of different things,' Orion whispered in answer to her half-formed question. 'Portals, crossroads, boundaries, trades and bargains are the big ones, which is why she officiates over duels, which are a sort of bargain if you think about it. But she's also the witch goddess.

Something about *Macbeth* and bargainig your soul. The pumpkin is one of her symbols because she's the first witch.'

Helen stared at that silly pumpkin, quite certain that the Fates were laughing their heads off at her. She loved pumpkins. Of all the many life memories that Helen had recently been subjected to, the memories that she made on Nantucket were her favourites. Jerry had given her the best life she'd had in all of her many existences. Daphne had been right when she'd said Helen should thank her for making her think that Jerry was her father.

One look at that blasted pumpkin, and she knew that she'd trade all this Scion nonsense, all her wondrous powers, for one more night of baseball and ice cream with her dad. Just one night where Lucas could come over for some pasta, eat awkwardly in front of her overprotective father and then they could all watch sports and argue about politics like everyone else in Massachusetts. But that perfect night would never happen.

Helen would never be a normal high-school kid again.

A bright flash, and a strange orange fire erupted round the boundaries of the arena. Hecate didn't reappear, but her presence was manifest in the hum of power that encircled the ring. The pumpkin disappeared. The fire went out. The challenge was set.

The crowd behind Helen whispered frantically to one another. Thunderclouds rolled in off the water, and lightning flashed in the distance. Zeus and the

Olympians arranged themselves to have the best view. They were enjoying this.

Helen tried to step into the arena and found that she couldn't. Orange fire flashed. A regular person would have been burned by it, but it only threw Helen back a few paces. Matt walked easily into his spot, ten feet away from the line in the sand at the middle of the cleared oval. He unsheathed his sword, a thick, wicked-looking thing that made Helen's breathing pick up. She tried again to enter the circle, only to find an invisible barrier stopping her. Helen tried to use her talent to create a portal to get inside the ring, but nothing happened. Hecate could even bar a Worldbuilder from crossing a boundary if she wanted to. Helen paused to mull this over.

'What are you doing, dummy?' Hector asked her, half a laugh in his voice. As she had been reminiscing about pumpkin pancakes and contemplating the power of Hecate, Lucas, Jason and Orion had been busy strapping armour on to Hector piece by piece in what looked to her like a ritual.

'What do you mean, what am I doing?' Helen asked – irked as usual when Hector made fun of her. 'He doesn't want to fight you, he said he only wants me.'

Hector only laughed harder at her melodramatic tone. 'You're not about to steal my glory, Princess.'

She really hated it when he called her that.

'*Don't* call me—'

'He's your champion, Helen!' Lucas snapped, and his tone was not playful like Hector's.

Helen looked at Lucas. The fear and frustration in his eyes silenced her immediately. She knew Lucas was upset with her for not handing over Everyland when Zeus asked for it. She wanted to scream at him that she had a *plan*, damn it, but of course she didn't dare do that.

'You took an oath, and for us those aren't just words,' Lucas continued. 'You *cannot* walk into that arena. Only Hector can meet your challenger now.'

'W-wait,' Helen said stumblingly, her tongue growing heavy in her mouth with fear as the first part of her plan came undone. 'Matt said he doesn't want Hector, he only wants me. So this is my fight.'

'No it isn't,' Hector said seriously. All his lighthearted joking vanished, and Helen could hear the voice of an ancient hero in him.

For a moment she saw Hector standing on a great wall, watching Achilles half insane with grief over the death of Patroclus, beating the horses of his chariot raw while calling out Hector's name to meet him in single combat. Matt didn't look like Achilles, but he had the same presence, the same power. She didn't know how it had happened, but somehow Matt had become Achilles, the Warrior.

'This has always been my fight,' Hector said gently.

'Don't do it,' she whispered, her voice failing as she remembered what had happened the last time.

'Don't do it!' echoed another, much more strident voice.

Helen turned and saw Andy pushing her way through the disturbed crowd. Her face was shocked, like she couldn't believe what she was saying and doing, but couldn't seem to stop herself.

Andy made her way through the commotion and stood inches away from Hector, begging him with her eyes. 'Don't fight him.'

'Tempting,' he said, smiling down on her lovely and totally confused face. 'But who would I be if I didn't? Not myself, that's for sure. You know I have to do this, Andy.'

'I love you,' she blurted out, completely horrified that she was saying something so sappy in front of a huge crowd like this.

'Well, it's about time,' Hector replied sarcastically.

For a second, it looked like Andy was going to punch him, so Hector did the wise thing and kissed her. When he finally pulled away he did so reluctantly.

'Hold that thought?' he asked her, his eyes vulnerable. Andy nodded slowly and released him.

Hector turned to Lucas, Jason and Orion, holding out his hand for his sword. Lucas handed it to him, his face darkened with frustration. Embracing his brothers one by one, Hector walked into the ring alone.

Helen went to Lucas, pleading in a low voice. 'Is there anything we can do to stop this? Think, Lucas.'

'Nothing. Only one of them can leave that ring

alive,' he replied angrily. 'I hope you know what you're doing.'

She didn't. Helen had no idea if her plan would work. The only thing she knew was that she had to try to change things, and sticking close to her Shield while she thought it out was the only chance she had. Helen backed up until she was leaning against Orion to brace herself. Lucas swallowed hard and looked away.

'He's hurt,' Orion whispered in her ear. 'He thinks you're choosing me over him.'

Helen knew this. She also knew that every second she hung on Orion hurt Lucas more and more. But there was nothing she could do about it right then.

'Just help me come up with a way to save Hector,' Helen whispered back.

'I can't,' Orion replied. He wrapped his arms around Helen and squeezed, more to comfort himself than her. She stayed near him, hoping that not only was she protected from the Fates by Orion's presence, but that Hector was as well.

'It could be different this time,' she said, feeling optimistic as she watched Hector and Matt face off. She lowered her voice to the softest of whispers and pressed her lips to Orion's ear to make sure the gods didn't hear. 'With you around, the Fates can't use him.'

Orion nodded, and when he pulled back and looked at Helen there was cautious optimism in his eyes.

The first blows came so fast Helen could barely see

them. Even though Helen had fought Hector many times, and even though he'd trained her from day one, she still couldn't believe that such a big guy could move so gracefully and so swiftly.

But this new, supercharged Matt was just as fast. He parried Hector's blinding strokes, twisted, and maintained his balance even though his adversary tried to use his larger size to press in and intensify the angle. Instead of getting trapped under Hector's rain of downward strokes, Matt was able to make space between them without losing his footing on the sand.

Helen felt Lucas, Orion and Jason all inhale sharply when they saw Matt dart in and draw first blood.

'Hector!' Ariadne cried out.

Hector backed away from Matt, dropping the point of his sword and touching his ribs. His hand came back red. He looked across the arena at his sister and his father who stood with Tantalus. They had sided against him.

As soon as Hector looked at her, Ariadne ran to the edge of the circle, nearly dancing on her toes along the magically sealed rim, like she was trying to throw herself into it and stop this fight. Hector smiled at his sister.

'It's OK, Ari,' he said, forgiving her. 'I understand.'

Hector faced Matt again grimly, aware now that he had met his match. He didn't waste any time, feinting and spinning past Matt, and slashing downward at Matt's heel as he spun away. Blood flowed freely from Matt's Achilles heel, but he didn't die. He limped away from Hector and took up position on the other side of the arena.

'Wrong heel, my friend,' Matt said sympathetically as the wound closed immediately.

'It was worth a shot,' Hector replied with a shrug, and then he pressed in again with reckless abandon.

Scions healed quickly, but for Matt it only took seconds for his skin to seal back up like nothing had happened. After seeing that, Hector knew his only shot at beating Matt was to find his one weakness. Matt had to have one. He had to be at least partially mortal or Hecate wouldn't have allowed him to take part in this fight, but there were a lot of body parts to choose from. Hector tried the other heel first, but Matt only recovered faster this time.

'Cut his head off!' Daphne yelled, her eyes wide with fear for Hector now that stabbing both Achilles heels hadn't worked.

'His heart! Hit his heart!' Orion shouted after her.

As soon as these first two ideas were offered, the Scions on Helen's side began calling out suggestions in a flurry of voices. Hector fought on, stabbing at Matt's heart, liver and even trying to cut off his head, but none of these turned out to be right. Matt would feel the injury but heal immediately, and all the while Hector was getting wounded and not healing as quickly. With each furious exchange, Hector was the one who grew weaker.

The gods looked on with rapt expressions. It was clear that this was the best fight they'd seen in over three thousand years. They were soaking up every minute of Hector's and Matt's pain like they were cheering downs at a football game. It was sport for them.

Unable to bear watching the bloodthirsty gods, Helen looked over at Lucas for comfort. He wasn't even watching the fight any more. He was looking blankly at the sand, wracking his brain for the body part that Matt would choose as his one weakness. She could see him talking to himself, frantic for a way to figure it out. She thought she heard Lucas repeating the word 'heel' over and over to himself.

Lucas lifted his head and made eye contact with Helen, his face bright with hope.

He'd figured it out.

At that very moment, Helen and Lucas heard Hector shout. Their heads spun round in time to see Hector crumple to his knees. Matt's sword was buried up to the hilt in his chest.

Many voices cried at once, and bodies on both sides of the arena's circle pressed against the invisible barricade in a wave, as loving members from both factions tried to rush into the arena and come to Hector's aid. But the magic of the battleground prevented any being from interfering.

Matt stood over Hector, his lips trembling and his shoulders hunched with regret. Nearly out of her mind,

Ariadne was screaming hateful things at Matt while Claire tried to hold her back.

Hector fell on to his side, still clutching the thick blade that had run him clean through the heart. He hit the ground and his head turned upward, his eyes staring directly at the clouded sun. He pulled in one taunt breath, then another, and then no more. His mouth seemed to smile at the sky, but his eyes, which had always been so fierce and full of life, ran dry.

Hector was dead.

CHAPTER FOURTEEN

Staring at Hector's body lying on the sand, Helen couldn't help but think – *I chose him as my champion because I couldn't bear it for Lucas or Orion to be lying there. This is my fault.*

'Challenge!' Lucas shouted, his deep voice piercing through the commotion.

The gods collapsed into a tight group to confer.

'How can this be?' Poseidon asked. 'I thought you said the Face took him to her world.'

'She did,' Hermes answered defensively. 'She must not have made him . . .'

'Wait,' Zeus said, holding up a hand to silence them before Hermes could finish. 'Hecate still has to decide.'

Lucas reached the edge of the arena and strode into the ring, unhindered by the barrier that had kept everyone else out. Whatever old magic tested a challenger's fitness, it had accepted Lucas. The gods exchanged looks of confusion.

Helen followed Lucas in a daze, unconcerned with the gods' reaction. She knew why it was possible for Lucas to enter the ring. She just didn't know why he would *want* to. It didn't make any sense. Matt had killed her champion, and now he was supposed to challenge her.

'Lucas? What are you doing?' she asked, fear making her breath flutter. He didn't answer or even acknowledge that he'd heard her.

'Lucas is Hector's second, Helen. It's his right to challenge Matt before Matt can challenge you.' Jason's voice was breaking. Helen looked at him. Tears were falling freely down his face for his brother. She grabbed his hand and squeezed it.

'Can I stop them?' she whispered.

'No. This is what it means to be a champion's second.'

Helen knew it was foolish of her not to have realized that, but it honestly never occurred to her that anyone could defeat Hector in the first place. And, if they did, she figured it was up to her to do her own fighting. She looked at Orion pleadingly, and he shrugged, helpless.

Inside the circle, Lucas had crouched down over Hector's body. Matt stood back respectfully as Lucas shut his dead brother's eyes. Helen could hear Pallas and Ariadne weeping on the other side of the arena. Helen knew she was crying too, but more important to her than her own sorrow was the guilt she saw in Lucas.

'One more second,' Lucas whispered to Hector's body. A sob burst out of him unexpectedly, like it escaped without his permission. It was a rough and angry noise.

Lucas picked Hector up and carried him to Orion

and Jason who were waiting at the edge of the barrier. As he handed Hector's body over, Andy pushed her way into the tight circle that waited to claim the fallen hero.

'*Wake up!*' Andy commanded, her voice carrying that haunting note that made nerve endings strain to obey. He didn't move. Her cheeks flushed a bright red as she concentrated every ounce of power she had.

'I said, *wake up!*' she repeated, grabbing him by the shoulders and shaking him.

Her siren voice echoed across the dunes and the water. Sand and spray jumped into the air like they were trying to flee from her. But still Hector did not move. When Andy started to shout and call him all kinds of nasty names for leaving her behind, Castor was the one to finally come in and drag her away from Hector's body.

'Enough! He's gone, and not even you can wake him,' Castor said, trying to get through to her. She didn't have the strength of a Scion, but she fought him for a moment before she fell apart.

Noel was there to hold her as she cried. But even as she comforted Andy her eyes were fixed on Lucas, who had yet to fight. Lucas had his hand in his right pocket, his fingers worrying something he kept in there.

'Bow and arrow,' Lucas called to Jason.

A startled murmuring began to rise among the onlookers. Several of the gods laughed.

'This one doesn't disappoint,' Apollo said excitedly to

the goddess in armour. Helen assumed she was Athena. 'It's just like last time.'

'That's what worries me,' Athena said back to Apollo. Her shrewd eyes were trained on Lucas.

'Why didn't he pick a sword?' Helen asked Orion, ignoring the gods as they placed bets.

'I have no idea,' Orion responded.

'Well . . . how many arrows does he get?'

'Just one.'

Helen's head snapped round, and she stared at Lucas as he stood calmly in the ring. 'Why would he pick that weapon then? That doesn't make any sense,' she pressed. Orion's puzzled look deepened Helen's fear.

'Come on, Luke,' Jason said, throwing up his hands in an exasperated gesture, like he didn't know what Lucas expected of him.

'Bow and arrow,' Lucas repeated distinctly.

Flushed with anger over Lucas's seemingly suicidal choice, Jason picked a bow and a single arrow from the weapons chest that waited on the edge of the duelling ground. He pulled on the bow and stared down the shaft of the arrow to test them, and then brought them to Lucas.

'You aren't even wearing armour,' Jason said to him in harsh undertone. 'Are you trying to kill yourself?'

As soon as Helen heard Jason say this, she realized that she hadn't considered that possibility. What if Lucas was so fed up that he wanted to die?

Lucas took his weapons without answering Jason and moved away from the edge of the ring. He didn't try to communicate with his father or mother. He didn't embrace Jason or give a last-minute speech about what he was doing and why. He didn't even look at Helen or try to let her know that it was going to be OK. Lucas simply took his weapon and squared off opposite Matt, signalling that he was ready.

But Helen wasn't. 'Hang on,' she said, her voice coming out breathy and shrill with fear. 'You don't really want to die, do you?' she asked frantically. When she looked at his chest, all she saw was a dull, lifeless mass inside him that was equal parts grief and resignation. It looked to Helen like he didn't much care if he died or not. And that was the one thing that could kill him.

She ran at the invisible barrier surrounding the arena, sending orange fire coursing across the surface of the dome-like barrier. Even if she could find a way to batter it down, she knew it was too late.

Everything seemed to happen in slow motion. Lucas lifted his bow, and Matt his sword before Helen could yell. As she threw herself at the barrier and was stopped short a second time, Matt charged forward. Both his hands were wrapped round the pommel of his sword and his arms raised over one shoulder, the blade held high, to cut Lucas down with a single powerful stroke. Lucas loosed his arrow.

Matt stopped abruptly, his face shocked. The arrow stuck out of Matt's left hand.

Out of the *heel* of his left hand.

Matt dropped his sword, and Lucas lowered his bow. Staring at his hand for moment, Matt smiled and nodded.

'I shouldn't have said that,' Matt said, looking up at Lucas as his legs wobbled and weakened. 'I shouldn't have said the word *heel* to Hector. I should have known you'd figure it out.'

Lucas dropped his bow and met Matt as he toppled over to catch him and break his fall. Lucas laid his defeated foe respectfully on the sand.

'She's too powerful,' Matt whispered as his life faded away.

'I'll be there to balance her,' Lucas promised.

'Worse than Olympus,' Matt said, his voice failing. 'At least with them there were twelve.'

'We don't want to rule, Matt,' Lucas told him gently, but in vain.

Matt was already dead.

Lucas closed his eyes, just as he had Hector's a few minutes earlier. For a moment, the only sound was of Ariadne weeping. Dark shadows spun out of Lucas like a black fog, and Helen heard gasps all around her as the crowd fearfully whispered the word *Shadowmaster*. He stood and pointed a finger at Helen.

'Don't follow me,' he ordered.

Darkness billowed around him like a cloak and hid him. Before Helen could even process what he'd said, Lucas launched himself into the sky and disappeared.

Lucas soared up into the roiling thunderclouds, hidden in his cloak of shadows. He knew Helen well enough to know that by ordering her not to follow him he'd made her determined to do just that. Lucas wanted to kick himself. He would bet one of his legs that Helen had the Shadowmaster talent as well and could see through the darkness, but he was pretty sure she hadn't learned to use it yet. This was Lucas's only edge, and when he turned back and confirmed that Helen wasn't following him, he went right to her house.

From the air, he could see that it was miraculously undamaged even though no one had been home for days now. The blue tarp was still covering her bedroom window from when Helen had accidentally thrown a rock through it. Lucas ducked under it and flew into her room.

It was cold and empty and the smell of her all around made him ache.

Lucas went directly to her bed, still tussled and dirty from the time Orion and Helen had emerged from the Underworld on to it – landing on top of Lucas in the process. Throwing the bedding on the floor, he lay down on top of the bare mattress.

Reaching into the right front pocket of his jeans,

Lucas pulled out the last of the three obols he'd stolen from the Getty and tucked it under his tongue.

He shut his eyes and opened them again.

'You know, chasing a loved one to the Underworld never ends well, my friend,' Morpheus sighed.

Lucas sat up next to the god of dreams, took the obol out from under his tongue, and offered it to him.

'Please,' he begged, holding out the god's payment. 'Please let me at least speak to Hades.'

'Oh, you are so *noble*,' Morpheus huffed, punching one of his silk pillows to show just how miffed he was. 'Have you really thought this through? Do you think Helen would want you to do this?'

'Of course she wouldn't. But Helen's not making this decision and, yes, I have thought it through,' Lucas said calmly. 'There's nothing for me up there any more.'

He wasn't being self-pitying; it was the simple truth. After Lucas had refused to kiss her in Everyland, Helen had made it clear that she had chosen Orion as soon as they were back on Earth. She could barely take her hands off him, and Lucas could only blame himself. He couldn't very well expect Helen to pledge herself to him if he wouldn't even kiss her. Lucas had always known that Orion could give Helen what she needed, and now he was just making it easy for her, and making himself useful at the same time.

Andy really loved Hector. Everyone loved Hector. Lucas was an extra body now, the Lover who wasn't allowed to love. So why not do something good with his life?

'I just want to speak to him,' Lucas repeated.

'All right,' Morpheus said reluctantly, taking his coin and rising from his enormous bed. 'I'll take you to the tree.'

Morpheus led Lucas through the many rooms of his dream palace. As they passed, the impossibly long, slender elfin people who danced inside the glowing circles of mushrooms and chased the bright, iridescent bubbles that seemed to beckon 'follow me' stopped their cavorting to stare.

Lucas could hear them gasping as he passed. He thought he heard a few whisper 'Hand of Darkness', but he couldn't be sure.

Outside the palace, they walked across the plain that bordered Hades and stopped at the edge of Morpheus's land. They both stood for a moment, looking at the nightmare tree.

It was so large it seemed to take up acres along the border between the land of dreams and the land of the dead. The notched branches flared out as if they were a million fingers of bone reaching up, and trying to scratch the very black out of the night sky.

'Stand under the branches,' Morpheus began.

'And don't look up,' Lucas finished for him, remembering his last trip to the tree.

'Try not to get damned or cast into Tartarus or

anything horrid like that, OK?' Morpheus said with genuine fondness.

'Thank you, Morpheus,' Lucas said sincerely. 'I owe you.'

'You and Helen both,' Morpheus replied with a lazy wave of his hand. He turned and walked away, fading into the blur of the eye-teasing lights.

Lucas could hear the nightmares moving through the branches. He held his breath as a light feeling thrilled through him. He forced himself to walk under the branches, his legs marching forward in stiff little strides.

It was a cold fear he felt, responding to nightmares that didn't threaten him in the usual way. The tree knew he wasn't afraid of dying or pain as he had been the last time he stood under these branches. Those things were not what he truly feared any more. This time, instead of claws and teeth scraping across the bark, Lucas heard familiar voices whispering above him.

He heard Matt. He heard Hector. He heard his aunt Pandora. He heard Helen weeping, 'I'm bleeding,' over and over. The voices and the shapes of all the people who he had loved and lost hung over him in the branches of the nightmare tree.

Lucas was surprised that Matt's presence and tone of voice were so familiar to him after just a few short months of friendship. But then they had shared much more than just lunch tables and homework assignments. They had shared the last moment of Matt's life, and because Lucas was the one who took it he would carry a part of Matt with him forever.

'Hades!' Lucas called, forcing himself to shout over the sound of the nightmare-Helen's crying. 'Please, just hear me out!'

The nightmares went silent and disappeared. Lucas looked up to see Hades walking towards him. He stopped on his side of the border. It was the first time Lucas had ever seen the lord of the dead, yet when Hades pulled off the Helm of Darkness and revealed Orion's face, Lucas was not surprised. He'd already guessed at the connection between Hades and Orion.

What Lucas didn't expect was to see Hades swaddled in shadows, exactly like the shadows Lucas made. While Lucas stared, Hades tucked the helmet that made him invisible under his arm. *I can make myself invisible*, Lucas thought.

Something clicked in his head. Lucas wanted to scream it was so ironic.

'Hello, son,' Hades said softly, confirming Lucas's suspicion.

'How?' Lucas asked, although he wasn't sure he wanted to know. 'Did my mother . . . ?'

'No,' Hades said firmly. 'I had a child with a woman from the House of Thebes many hundreds of years ago.' He paused for a moment as a look of regret passed over his face, even though it had happened so long ago. 'The blood of a god does not dilute – we are immortal and so is our . . . well, our genes, I guess you could call them. You are mine and Apollo's, but I see more of myself than him in you.'

'Can you think yourself warm?'

'No. That trait you get from Apollo. You can withstand any heat, except Helen's. She can get even hotter than the sun.'

'I noticed,' Lucas said with a little rueful laugh.

'But the majority of your talents you get from me. I'm sure you find all this disturbing.'

'Not at all,' Lucas responded. 'It actually makes this easier. Like it was meant to be.'

'Go home, son,' he said kindly. 'Your absence is causing turmoil where it is least needed.'

'How can anyone know that I'm absent?' Lucas asked, confused. 'I thought time stopped in the Underworld.'

'It does, unless you are with Morpheus or with me, in which case time passes as it does on Earth. We must live *in* time in order to affect lives.'

Lucas thought it through quickly and nodded. 'Or you'd be trapped in one eternal moment – and no one would ever find either of you.'

'Very good,' Hades said musingly. 'Not even Helen noticed that, and she is very clever.' He smiled at Lucas like he was pleased with him before continuing. 'I know you grieve for your cousin, but I don't allow people to trade themselves for dead loved ones. If I did, it would lay too much guilt on those who would rather live than sacrifice themselves for the dead. This would hurt more people than it would help.'

He even sounded like Orion, except that his way of speaking was slightly more formal. They both had a compassion for others that Lucas respected.

'That makes perfect sense,' Lucas conceded. 'And I think you're absolutely right. But I didn't come here to trade myself for Hector. I came here to trade myself for you.'

'For me?' Hades repeated, surprised for the first time in what Lucas assumed to be millennia.

'I know you didn't choose to be the lord of the dead. It was forced on you. I know how that feels. I feel as if the Fates are trying to force me into Poseidon's role. But I am going to reject that fate of my own free will in favour of another.'

Lucas stepped over the border and entered Hades's land, knowing that if he succeeded he might never leave it again.

'Bring Hector back to life, and I'll take *your* place in the Underworld for the rest of eternity.'

Helen stared up at Lucas, easily seeing inside his cloud of shadows. She knew she could follow him, but if she did she would have to leave everyone else unprotected. Orion and Jason were great fighters, Daphne was a flat-out monster, and Helen knew better than to second-guess Castor's skills, but there were twenty times more fighters on the gods' side than on hers. Almost all of the House of Rome and half of the House of Athens had joined her and Orion, but it still wasn't enough to beat both the Hundred Cousins and the Myrmidons. If Helen left, she knew that her side wouldn't stand a chance.

'We wish to honour our dead,' Castor called across the arena, the sand of which was still stained with Hector's blood . . . and with Matt's.

Helen felt her eyes fill and her chest heat up with sobs. Two people she loved dearly were dead. That wasn't what she'd planned.

As the gods conferred with the generals of their mortal army, resolve solidified in Helen and froze her tears in their tracks. She knew that if she allowed herself to give in to sorrow, she wouldn't be of any use to anyone. Let Andy cry for Hector, and let Ariadne cry for Matt. Helen no longer had the luxury to mourn.

'We can't deny you the right to prepare your dead,' Tantalus shouted back at Castor, their emotions lighting up their insides like swords being sharpened on rocks. 'But the Tyrant's champion has gone missing.' Tantalus continued in a falsely innocent tone. 'How can you prove that he did not run away because he has taken a mortal injury from our champion?'

'Ridiculous!' Orion shouted. 'Matt never even touched Lucas. We all saw the duel.'

Helen spun round and looked at her mother. 'What's going on?' she asked in a whisper.

'You're in danger,' Daphne replied tersely, but she didn't have a chance to elaborate before Tantalus continued.

'The Tyrant's champion isn't here to prove that he is unharmed,' Tantalus said with a forbidding shake of his head. 'Produce your *living* champion, or hand over the Tyrant.'

'And who will enforce that?' Orion called back. 'The gods can't fight us.'

'My army will,' Tantalus replied calmly.

Orion and his entourage of loyal Athenians moved like a swarm, massing between Helen and the battalion of Hundred Cousins that seemed to materialize out of thin air around Tantalus.

'The House of Thebes goes too far!' hissed a relative of Orion's whom Helen didn't know.

'Again, Tantalus wants to wipe out every other House, starting with Atreus and Athens,' said another, even more boldly. 'And when we are dead the gods will let him plunder our Houses. Again.'

Helen felt a hand on her shoulder and glanced over to see that her mother was pulling her back in the ranks. It suddenly seemed like the beach was filled with hundreds of men. Where did they all come from? Helen wondered in a daze.

'Get behind them,' Daphne said to Helen in low voice. A flood of armoured Romans seemed to surge forward to stand with the Athenians at Orion's side. 'Back, back!'

Daphne growled in Helen's ear as she hauled her daughter away from the front lines.

In the stampede of armoured men, Helen got knocked to the ground. Daphne stood over her daughter, her hands crackling with lightning. The dry, stale smell of burnt ozone wafted all around her, and the acrid glow made the swelling wave of soldiers peel off around them as Daphne helped Helen to her feet.

'Castor!' Daphne cried desperately, searching the throngs of massing soldiers for a familiar face. 'Shelter for the Heir of Atreus!'

Helen wrapped her arms round her frantic mother and soared into the air, carrying both of them away from the danger of the trampling army.

'You can carry me?' Daphne asked, stunned. 'Ajax couldn't carry me when he flew.' Daphne smiled, thrilling in the sensation of flight, despite the desperate situation.

'My father could fly?' Helen asked, curious that no one had mentioned this to her before.

'Oh yes, he could fly.'

Daphne's voice chimed out of tune in Helen's ear.

'My *father* can fly?' Helen asked again, making them soar higher above the massing armies on the beach.

'Yes,' Daphne repeated distractedly, still laughing at the uplifting sensation of weightlessness that Helen gave her.

Helen cringed at the lie, and Daphne's smile fell.

'You're a Falsefinder now, aren't you?' Daphne asked resignedly, like she knew she'd already lost.

'Yes,' Helen whispered.

The cottony middle of a new cloud misted the cheeks of the embracing mother and daughter. Dappled sunlight made its way through the dense thunderheads that Zeus had conjured, making the dew in Helen's and Daphne's identical blonde hair fracture into tiny rainbows. Two pairs of amber eyes locked, but the blue bolt in Helen's scarred right iris sparkled when she spoke.

'Is Ajax my father?' Helen asked in a dangerous monotone, already knowing the answer – it had been right in front of her for a week now, but she'd only just put the pieces together in her mind.

Ajax looked like Hector – they were the same character in the Fate's big play, separated by a generation. And Orion had told Helen that the main characters from Troy got replaced with a new baby when they died. Hector had replaced Ajax when Ajax died. But Hector was a year older than Helen, so Ajax had to have been dead for a *year* before Helen was conceived.

'Answer me,' Helen threatened, needing to hear it from Daphne.

'No,' Daphne replied, her voice hollow. 'Jerry's your father.'

Helen wondered if she dropped her mother from this height, would she survive? Daphne looked down, as if she knew what Helen was thinking. Her breathing sped up with panic.

'Is that why you drugged him? To keep him from waking up and telling me the truth?'

'It wouldn't take you long to figure out that I lied if you talked with him. I knew it wasn't a permanent solution, but I only needed a couple more days,' Daphne answered unapologetically.

They drifted for a few moments, Daphne's words running around in Helen's head like they were too big and too awful to stop and sink in anywhere.

'Tell me why I shouldn't kill you.' Helen's voice was completely steady.

'Because I didn't kill Jerry, and I could have,' Daphne replied immediately. 'You owe me for that.'

'Why?' Helen's voice faltered, and they swooped dangerously in the sky. 'Why did you lie?'

'Helen . . . we should go down now,' Daphne said anxiously as she clutched Helen closer. 'It doesn't benefit you to kill me. Think clearly.'

'I am thinking clearly. You've never done anything but hurt me. Why should I let you live?'

'I sent you Orion.'

'And why did you do that?' Helen asked suspiciously. 'I'm sure you had a reason that served your purposes and not mine.'

Daphne opened her mouth to answer and shut it again.

'Did you just remember that you can't lie to me any more and decide to hold your tongue?' Helen scoffed.

'That's right,' Daphne replied, her eyes hard. 'And if you really want answers from me you're going to have to land. If you kill me now, you'll never know. I'm not going to say another word until you bring me back to Castor's house.'

'All right,' Helen said, her lips tight with hatred. 'But don't think you're any safer on the ground than you are up here.'

Helen flew them at an uncomfortably fast pace to the Delos house and felt Daphne squirm in her arms with fear. When they were still twenty feet up, Helen dumped Daphne and let her crash down on to the lawn. As she watched her mother do a shoulder roll to avoid breaking a leg, Helen realized that she'd landed on that same spot the first time Lucas took her flying.

Lucas. *Not* her cousin. Everything they'd gone through together, the way they'd tortured each other and pushed each other away, was based on a lie.

Helen pounded into the grass bare inches away from Daphne, knocking a great ditch into Noel's backyard and showering Daphne with dirt. Helen had only felt this kind of hatred for one other being, and she'd sent him to Tartarus. While Daphne floundered over the uneven ground, trying to get away from her livid daughter, Helen grabbed her by the back of her jacket and hauled her up like she was handling a doll, and then tossed her on to more even ground.

'Start talking,' Helen ordered as she stalked towards her mother, who was scrambling away from her on hands and knees. 'I want to know everything.'

'Helen!' Castor shouted, and a second later he was holding her arms and trying to pull her back. 'What happened?' he asked, breathless with the effort to control her.

Helen could easily overpower Castor, but even as she considered doing just that he spoke into her ear.

'It's not worth it,' Castor said in a sympathetic tone. 'Whatever she did to you, it isn't worth it. That's what they *want* us to do, Helen. They want us to kill each other off, and then all of their problems are solved. Remember that.'

She did remember. It had happened in several of the lives she could recall. The worst instances burned the brightest.

She remembered when Arthur, the champion of the gods, had fought his nephew Mordred, the champion of Avalon. Two great men mortally wounded each other, and both were killed in one fight. Avalon dissolved into the mists, and Camelot crumbled, snuffing out the two brightest lights in an age of darkness. The only winners of that fight were the gods.

Helen relaxed and nodded to let Castor know she

wasn't going to kill her mother. He released her, and she turned to see Noel had joined her husband.

'What's going on?' Noel said, looking at the torn-up yard. 'Please. Come inside and calm down.'

'She lied. I'm not Ajax's daughter. I'm Jerry's,' Helen said in a robotic voice. 'Lucas and I aren't cousins.'

'How?' Noel asked. She and Castor exchanged confused looks. 'Lucas heard her say – '

'That we were *all family*,' Helen interrupted, figuring out how Daphne had done it. 'That's what she said, word for word, in front of Lucas. And, technically, she's right. All the gods are related, so we are too – distantly.' She stopped and swallowed around the choked feeling in her throat. '*I'm* the one who told Lucas I was Ajax's daughter when he and I were alone, not her.'

Helen paused, remembering how she'd almost given in to Lucas in the greenhouse, right before she'd fed him her mother's big lie. She remembered how Lucas had kissed her as if he could breathe her in through his skin. How he'd tugged at her clothes as he'd guided her down to the ground so gently. She could still feel him, still see the shape of his big shoulders over her, and she knew that the moment when she pushed him off her was the moment that had decided her whole life.

Lucas. Her home. The mansion she'd paid for a million times over but hadn't lived in yet.

She and Lucas were meant to be together. They

should have been together that night, but instead she'd pushed away the biggest blessing of her life because of her mother. Hate hit her like a cramp, and Helen hovered somewhere between sickness and pain.

'I believed it, so Lucas heard the truth, even though it's a lie,' Helen finished in a low voice, trying to control the almost physical need to punch her mother.

'My father used to do that to me,' Castor admitted, like he understood what Helen was feeling. 'He'd make me believe a lie, then send me to tell Tantalus so all my brother would hear was the truth – the truth as I understood it. That's the only way to sidestep a Falsefinder. Turn the people who trust you the most into patsies.'

'Ajax told me that Paris used to do it to all of you to sidestep Tantalus's talent,' Daphne whispered. 'Where do you think I got the idea from?' She and Castor shared a look, recalling something that they both seemed to remember.

'Well, you're out of patsies, Mother,' Helen said bitterly. 'Get up.'

'Helen,' Castor said, trying to remind her to stay calm. Helen ignored him and kept her mounting rage focused on her mother.

'Stand up and tell me *why* you did this to me.'

Daphne looked up at her, but before Helen could get an answer they all heard a commotion coming from inside the Delos house – the sounds of gasps and shouts.

'Everyone, get in here!' Jason yelled out to them. 'He's alive! Hector's alive!'

'He can't be,' Daphne said, jumping up. They all sprinted inside.

Hector was laid out on the kitchen table, his armour and most of his clothes stripped away. Bowls of bloody water surrounded him, and a sponge lay next to him, stained red. Jason had already begun to wipe his brother down in preparation for the pyre. But Hector was certainly not dead. Not any more.

He was pale and weak from blood loss. His lips were blue, and his hands shook terribly as he sat up and clutched Jason's shoulders, trying to talk. Something clanked against his teeth and, grimacing, he spat out a gold coin. It was the obol his father had placed under his tongue to pay the Ferryman. Hector took a moment to stare at the bright disc in his hand, contemplating the Scion equivalent of his own gravestone.

'That's a first,' he mumbled. He gave the obol to Andy. 'For later,' he rasped to her, his voice weak.

'Much, much later. Don't do that again,' she scolded, her swollen, tear-streaked face beautiful with joy.

'You got it.'

Hector's whole body suddenly trembled as he tried to stay sitting up.

'He needs blood,' Jason said, worried, as he supported his brother and laid him back down on the table. Jason held up his hands, and they began to glow. He brought his hands over Hector to start healing him, but Hector stopped him.

'Wait, Jase,' Hector said, his voice barely above a whisper. 'Don't knock me out yet. Where's Helen?'

'Here,' Helen replied, stepping forward from her place behind Noel so Hector could see her. 'What is it?'

'Go to the Underworld. Now. Try to talk Hades out of it,' he said, his feeble tone turning urgent.

'Out of what?' Helen asked.

'Out of the trade. Don't let Luke stay down there for me,' he said, grabbing Helen's arm and shaking it as if to wake her. 'Luke *traded* himself.'

'Impossible!' Daphne shrieked, startling them all with her vehemence. 'Hades doesn't let anyone trade themselves for another. I tried a dozen times.'

'Luke didn't trade himself for me,' Hector gasped, his eyes rolling into his head with the effort to stay conscious.

'Shhh, don't,' Noel said, coming forward to put a soothing hand on Hector's shoulder. 'Jason. Knock him out before he kills himself again.'

'He traded himself for *Hades*,' Hector said over Noel. He pulled on Helen's arm until her face was inches away from his. 'Lucas took Hades's place as the lord of the dead.'

CHAPTER FIFTEEN

Helen knew her mother was saying something repeatedly, but it took a moment for her overwhelmed mind to actually understand it.

'It was supposed to be Orion,' Daphne kept muttering to herself. When she locked eyes with Helen, like she was trying to explain herself, it looked like she was about to crack. 'I mean – Orion *is* Hades. They look exactly the same, don't they? Orion is the only one besides you who can go to the Underworld. He's an Earthshaker and can "reduce all mortal cities to rubble" so I thought he was the Tyrant – we all did. We all thought the Tyrant was supposed to replace Hades. All the signs were there. It was always supposed to be Orion.'

As if summoned by Daphne's repetition of his name, Orion appeared at the kitchen door with Cassandra at his side.

'Castor,' Orion said, striding in hurriedly. 'The gods demand we produce Lucas, or Tantalus will send his army against us. And the Myrmidons want to kill Helen with or without Matt to lead them. I know you're in mourning – we all are – but I need you at the front lines.'

'He's alive!' Cassandra shouted before her father could answer, and ran to Hector.

'Stay back, Cass,' Jason said in warning as his hands glowed blue. 'Let me work on him.'

'How?' Orion asked, his eyes glued to Hector's chest as it swelled with obvious breaths. 'His heart was cut in two. He was dead.'

'A trade,' Noel answered. She was so torn between feeling happy that Hector was alive and destroyed by what Lucas had done that she couldn't finish.

'Lucas agreed to take Hades's place in the Underworld in order to bring Hector back,' Andy finished for her.

'Why?' Cassandra asked, her face pleading. 'Does he think we love him any less than we love Hector?'

Orion looked at Helen. 'He did it because he thinks we're together. Lucas thinks we . . .'

'I know,' Helen whispered, trying desperately to figure a way out of it. 'I have to descend and tell him it's not true.'

'Helen. I'm so sorry,' Daphne said, her eyes wide with panic. 'You have to believe me. If I knew it was going to be Lucas, I would have left you two alone. You have to explain that to Lucas – make him understand that it wasn't that I didn't like him. Please.'

'What are you talking about?' Helen asked, a sinking sensation in her stomach. 'Mother, what did you do?'

'That's why I lied,' she said quickly and quietly, like she was trying to speed past it. 'If Orion was going to become the new lord of the dead, why wouldn't he want to restore life to his one true love's father?'

'What?' Helen said, baffled.

'A dozen times now I've nearly died. Every time I've gone down to the River Styx, I've begged Hades, but why should he listen to me? My only hope was the prophecy that said a Scion would come to replace him,' she said, a desperate light in her eyes. 'Who else could it have been but Orion? Orion is Hades's twin!' She looked around at everyone pleadingly.

'And if I did replace Hades?' Orion asked, a horrified look on his face.

'You'd still have to agree to give me what I want, and even though you care for me, there was no guarantee. I had to ask myself, what would make *me* do anything? Love, obviously. If you fell in love with a girl, and that girl thought she had lost her father, why wouldn't you restore her father to life for her?'

Helen shivered, like someone had walked over her grave.

'She wasn't supposed to fall in love with Lucas,' Daphne said, turning on Helen and pointing an irrationally accusing finger at her. 'You were supposed to meet Orion first and fall in love with him. It would have been perfect. You would have Orion and I would have Ajax and no one would have got hurt. I tried to keep you away from Lucas. I tried to get you off the island as soon as I saw the connection you two had.'

Helen remembered. When the Delos family moved to Nantucket, her mother, disguised as an older woman, had tried to kidnap her repeatedly to get her away from them. Daphne had told Helen it was to protect her from the Delos family so they wouldn't kill her, but her mother had always known that Helen wore the cestus and was impervious to weapons. She also knew that Helen was stronger than all of them combined and didn't need to be rescued. Daphne's real goal had been to try to keep Helen away from Lucas.

'I meant for you to meet Orion first. I thought I had more time – you weren't even seventeen yet, and the only boy you'd ever kissed was Matt. I thought I had more time,' she repeated, like this was what she regretted the most.

Helen half collapsed, half sat down on the bench that had been pushed back from the kitchen table and stared at the floor.

'How long have you been watching me?' Helen asked, dazed.

'All your life. Always with a different face, but I never left you for long, Helen,' Daphne said, falling on her knees in front of her daughter, and taking her hands. 'One day, I was the tourist asking to take your picture, another day the customer at the News Store who chatted with you, asking questions about your day at school.

Once, I was even that exchange student that came for a month. Do you remember Ingrid? She learned all the gossip, and then disappeared? They were all me. I've never left you for long.'

Faces seemed to flash in front of Helen's eyes. Dozens of people who had struck up conversations with her over the years were all Daphne to Helen now, and she had the creepy feeling that most of her life had been staged. She glanced up at Orion and saw a matching look of disbelief on his face.

But even through the shock Helen realized that Daphne hadn't been that far off the mark. Orion was the only guy Helen had ever really considered being with apart from Lucas. And she knew that Orion would do anything for her – even raise the dead 'father' she never got a chance to know for her – if he had the power to do it.

Her mother's plan, as crazy as it seemed, might have actually worked. Except for the fact that it didn't, and in the process it had broken all their hearts.

'You're insane,' Helen whispered.

'No. Just willing to do *anything* for the man I love.'

Helen saw Andy, Noel and Cassandra all startle at this admission, like it was too close for comfort.

'So we all have something in common then,' Helen said calmly as she stood.

She looked at Orion. Lucas had traded himself, but it wasn't a fair trade because he had been tricked. Who could she go to if she wanted to object to the trade? Who would even listen to her case in the Underworld? Helen had an idea – she just hoped it would work.

'Stay close to Cassandra,' she told Orion. 'Even if the Fates will be able to see me in the Underworld, they won't be able to speak through her and maybe I can pull this off.'

He nodded once in understanding.

'Ask Lucas to give me Ajax. Please, Helen. I'm begging you!' Daphne sobbed, grabbing Helen's arm. All her plans were ruined, but she was still trying to get him back. Helen wondered if she would act any different if it were Lucas. She could only hope she would, but she doubted it.

Helen yanked her arm away from her mother and vanished in a puff of air that was so cold it left a disc of frost on Noel's kitchen floor.

The spiky crust of frost had barely started to melt when Daphne realized what she needed to do, and bolted for the kitchen door.

'Where are you going?' Orion demanded, blocking her path to stop her.

'To find out what's going on at the other camp, and to try and buy Helen some time to get Lucas back.' She dodged round him to run outside.

She heard Castor say, 'Let her go,' and continued unhindered to the beach.

As she ran to the front lines, she changed her appearance to hide herself. Remembering that there were Myrmidons on Tantalus's side, she altered her body's scent as well.

She crested a tall rise and looked down to suss out the situation. There were far too many people massing on the beach – many hundreds of men and women. As Daphne looked closer, she realized that more than just Scions were joining the line. Regular mortals were streaming in from the centre of town and from all kinds of boats gathering out on the water to swell the ranks of the gods.

Some of the gods' soldiers were even beginning to flank Orion's soldiers to the south and west. Out on the water, Daphne saw all kinds of boats coming in to shore. Yachts, fishing vessels, even little rowboats were joining Tantalus to fight for Olympus. Sure, most of the new recruits were full mortals, and scores of them could be easily mowed down by a handful of armoured Scions, but the loss of life would be staggering. Why would a full mortal even consider fighting in this war? It didn't make sense.

Daphne got closer and noticed that the mortals all moved in a stiff and unnatural way, like puppets. When she got closer still, she saw open eyes and dead looks on all their faces. Daphne cringed. It was like they were all zombies.

Or hypnotized.

'Hypnos,' Daphne mumbled to herself. Hypnos, the

god of the trancelike state in which people can be easily controlled – was obviously working with the Olympians.

It didn't surprise her that the Olympians were making the small gods like Hypnos help the Twelve. The small gods couldn't fight and kill mortals, but they could still use their talents to help Olympus win. Now that Olympus was open, the small gods would have to deal with the Olympians for the rest of eternity unless Helen managed to send them all to Tartarus. Helen had managed it with Ares, but Daphne could see that the small gods were not so certain Helen could do it with Zeus. They were hedging their bets by supporting Olympus.

The army of hypnotized humans coming by land and by sea was just the start. Daphne thought through all the different small gods and knew that bigger horrors awaited Helen's loyal defenders. There were true monsters left in the world. Daphne had seen a few of them in her lifetime, and she knew that Zeus wouldn't hesitate to unleash them.

Daphne sprinted past the hypnotized throngs, moving too fast for their dazed eyes to see even in broad daylight. She had to know if the gods were planning a war of mythical proportions, and if they were she had to find a way to either slow it down or to at least warn Helen about what was coming.

Changing her face to match one of the Hundred Cousins, Daphne strode through the rapidly growing camp, searching the tents as quickly as she could for the only people she could ask for information. Finally, she heard the familiar voice she sought and rushed towards it.

'The gods couldn't be happier about both Hector and Matt being dead,' Claire said, her tone heavy with bitterness. Daphne edged closer to the side of the tent and listened.

'They want this. They want us to kill each other until we're all gone,' Ariadne sniffled. 'This can't be right. Matt couldn't have known about this part. It's like the gods are getting off on watching people who love each other fight to the death.'

'This is all wrong. We have to go, Ari. Now,' Claire whispered fearfully. 'Matt got duped by the gods. And so did we.'

Daphne had heard enough. She hurried through the front flap of the tent, and saw the two girls looking at her, amazed. She allowed her face to shift back to her real one.

'I can get Claire out of here,' Daphne said quickly as they both gasped at her revealed identity. Daphne ignored their protests and talked over them. 'Claire is just a mortal to them and not a threat. But, Ariadne, I'm sorry. You're a Healer, which makes you far too valuable. They can't afford to let you stand with Helen, so you have to stay here.'

'Why should we trust you?' Claire said, a look of disgust on her face. 'You drugged Mr Hamilton!'

'Oh, that's right, I forgot. Because neither of you have ever betrayed the people you love.' Daphne's cold words made Claire and Ariadne shrink back.

'It's not like that,' Ariadne said in a hushed tone. Daphne ignored her, knowing that everything Ariadne said from that point on would just be an excuse for her behaviour, not a solution to the problem.

'What have you learned to help Helen's cause since you joined the wrong side?' Daphne asked impatiently.

Claire and Ariadne looked at each other, conferring with their eyes. Claire was the first one to speak.

'A lot,' Claire admitted. 'But I don't think I should tell you any of it.'

'I wouldn't expect you to confide in me, Claire. But if I brought you to Orion, would you tell him what you've learned?' Daphne held her hands out plaintively.

'Yes,' Claire said, nodding her head in a definite motion. 'What about Ariadne?'

'Don't worry about me, Claire. My father is here with me. Tell Jason . . .' Ariadne paused as her eyes dredged up another round of tears. 'I don't know. Make something up for me.'

'OK,' Claire responded with a defeated shrug. 'But I doubt he'll listen to me ever again.'

The two girls embraced, whispering encouragement to each other, and then Claire turned and looked at Daphne with a level gaze, as determined as Daphne remembered her to be when she was a baby girl.

'Do you need me to do anything to sell this?' she asked.

'Just look like a prisoner,' Daphne replied as she grabbed Claire by the neck and shoved her roughly out of the tent.

Daphne instantly changed her face to look like one of the girls from the House of Rome – one of the few from the House who had turned against Orion, Daphne recalled – and made a bit of a show about how she had taken Claire hostage as she dragged her through the camp.

The Myrmidons noticed immediately, as they always did.

'Why do you abuse her?' asked the one they called Telamon. 'She was loyal to my master all the way to the end.'

'Up to the end and no further, it appears. Since your master's death, her heart shows signs of doubt,' Daphne answered, staring at Claire's chest like she had the Roman talent to read emotions. 'Ask anyone else from the House of Rome. This girl has doubt. She is not committed to killing the Tyrant any more.'

'Then she must die,' Telamon answered with a sad nod of his head. Claire trembled under Daphne's hands, but she didn't try to run away.

Daphne had often wished that she had had a daughter who didn't remind her so much of herself. Claire was everything a girl should be. Smart, strong, brave and she didn't have the damned Face.

'That's not necessary,' Daphne replied nonchalantly, pulling Claire close to her so the Myrmidon didn't get any ideas about taking her away. 'She's still useful. I'll just bring her to Hypnos and have him change her mind.'

Telamon glanced down at Claire sceptically. All he saw was a skinny mortal girl who could be snapped in two by even a half-rate Scion.

'She was the Tyrant's best friend for all their lives,' Daphne said enticingly. 'She may know the enemy's plan.'

Telamon's face changed, and he nodded his assent. 'Bring her to Hypnos then,' he said. 'He's at the ferry's landing in the centre of town, recruiting the mortals from the mainland as they arrive.'

Daphne and Claire hurried through the camp. It had swelled at an exponential rate. Claire looked around, overwhelmed by the population explosion. Tents had sprung up all down the shore. The sounds of clanking armour and the smell of campfires hung in the foggy sea air. Zeus's storm clouds darkened the afternoon sky, and Poseidon made the ocean churn, sending angry waves crashing into the sand.

'But it's only been a few hours,' Claire mumbled, amazed.

'They're gods, Claire. They get things done quickly.'

Claire craned her head around and watched one of the hypnotized 'recruits' pass them, his eyes blank. 'I know him,' she whispered frantically, practically pointing at the boy with the leather fetish. 'He's a senior at my high school.'

'Well, if he lives, I doubt he'll remember any of this.' Daphne forced Claire to keep walking like she would a real prisoner.

'My parents,' Claire said, her voice thin.

'The best way to protect them now is to help Helen,' Daphne said.

'I wanted to stop *this*,' Claire said, gesturing to the growing army.

'I know,' Daphne replied, hushing her with a little shake.

Hermes darted by, his eyes and ears open for information that he could bring to Zeus. For a moment his gaze rested on Claire, but he looked away and sped past. Daphne and Claire reached the no-man's-land between the two camps and began sprinting for Orion's tent.

Halfway there, the sky darkened like a shadow passing over the sun. Daphne looked up to see the storm of Myrmidon arrows arcing high to hit a target in the sky.

'Move, move, move!' Daphne barked at Claire, urging her forward. The arrows reached their apex – and began a deadly fall back to Earth.

When she descended, Helen expected to find herself in one of the many landscapes of the Underworld that had become familiar to her. She was expecting to appear on the infinite beach that never led to an ocean, or in the boneyard of the Ice Giants where Cerberus had chased her and Orion, or even in the ever-creepy Fields of Asphodel where the hungry ghosts fed on the white blooms of the asphodel flower. But instead she found herself inside a great hall she'd never seen before.

Black marble floors studded with Doric columns stretched out like a dark, petrified forest reaching up and back on to a seemingly infinite space. Giant brass braziers, twice her height, flickered with the golden fire of clean-burning oil scented with jasmine and amber. The air was desert dry. Jewels, embedded in every column's decorative seams, took up the light. They refracted it around Helen so that everywhere she looked there were tiny rainbows – night rainbows that were created with neither sun nor rain.

There had been one other time that Helen had seen the air sparkle like this all around her. It was when Lucas had made her invisible.

'Lucas?' Helen cried, her voice splintering down the many avenues of columns in what she could only assume was Hades's palace.

'I'm here,' Lucas answered.

Helen ran towards his voice, the sound of her shoes pounding against the ground, ringing out in all directions through the petrified forest of columns. She reached the head of the hall and skidded to a stop in front a giant, white marble throne on top of a raised dais. It was carved to look like hundreds of skeletons, contorted in agony to support the man who had claimed it. She stopped.

Lucas sat on the throne of death, black shadows seeping out of him like oozing tar. Helen looked for his heart and saw only darkness.

'Oh, Lucas,' she said, her voice high and breathy with disbelief. 'What did you do?'

'The only useful thing left for me to do.'

'You're usually right,' she said, clenching her fists in frustration. 'But this time you are *so* wrong.'

'Hector's the one everyone needs in their lives. Not me.'

'I need you.'

'You have Orion.'

'I don't *have* Orion. We're just friends.'

'Helen.' He sighed tiredly like he didn't want to hear it.

'I know that the lord of the dead has to be able to judge hearts. So judge mine,' she said, striding forward and mounting the steps that led to his throne. 'Look at me, Lucas. Am I lying?'

He studied her as she came closer, and doubt began to creep into his eyes.

'I'm not with Orion,' Helen continued, climbing the steps slowly towards his throne. 'I never really have been, and I'm certain now that I never will be, and you know why? Because it's impossible for me to love anyone like I love you – and I *really* tried with Orion.'

'I'm sure you did,' Lucas said, trying to sound forbidding, but there was the hint of a laugh in his voice.

'It didn't work. It's like I have a built-in heckler in my head. I can't even make out with another guy without hearing this stupid voice, telling me I'm an idiot and I'm screwing everything up.' Helen climbed a few more steps, and all the joking left her tone. 'You're the only one I'll ever love. The only one I'm capable of loving completely. You're it for me.'

He looked away and swallowed. 'So we love each other. So what? That doesn't change the fact that we can't be together.'

His voice sounded convincing but, even as he spoke, the doubtful look on his face began to deepen, like he didn't really believe what he was saying any more. Like he didn't fully understand why they couldn't be together.

Helen trudged up the last few steps, the weight of what she was about to tell him suddenly pressing down on her, slowing her pace.

She knew what it felt like to have her heart broken. Lucas had done that to her once. This wasn't simple and straightforward like that – like a single stab that was so painful you wished it just frigging killed you. What she felt now had so many barbs attached to it that no matter which way she turned the situation around in her head she found a new way to get wounded by it.

She crossed the dais to where Lucas sat in his throne and climbed into his lap. He stiffened with surprise as she sank against him, but was so overwhelmed by her sadness that he instinctively held her close. She couldn't make herself say it out loud, so she put her arms round his neck, placed her lips close to his ear and whispered the whole truth to him.

Helen could feel his skin heat up with emotion as she told him about Daphne's desperate plan to raise Ajax from the dead. Helen wasn't exactly sure what she said. She just let the whole ugly mess tumble out of her mouth and into his ear. A few times she felt him cringe and the breath rush out of him in disbelief as a new revelation sank in. Finally, when she started talking about her behaviour towards Orion on the beach and said the word 'Shield', Lucas pulled back and held a finger to her lips.

'Don't tell me any more,' he whispered. He understood that when she left Orion's presence, any hope of salvaging her plan to defeat the gods was endangered. 'Don't even think it here. You need to get back to Orion immediately.'

'I'm not going anywhere without you.'

'You have to go back, Helen,' he said firmly, but instead of pushing her away, he only held her tighter. 'I have to stay here. I made a vow.' He choked on the word, realizing the enormity of his mistake.

'But, Lucas, the gods are using your absence to say you're dead and you didn't really win the duel. This isn't just about you and me. You have to come and show yourself to the gods, or they'll send Tantalus's army against us.'

'My little brother will send his army against you regardless of what you do, niece. If Lucas returns to the battlefield and proves he's alive, Zeus will just find another reason to attack,' said Hades's sad voice. Helen eased off Lucas's lap and the two of them stood side by side, holding hands, while Hades approached from the stairs.

'Did you know?' Helen asked Hades. 'About Daphne? Did you know what she was doing?'

'I see a lot, but I don't see everything,' Hades said, shaking his head. 'No being is omniscient. Even the Fates have Nemesis to block them.'

'I need him,' she whispered, squeezing Lucas's hand.

'And I told him that, several times, but he wouldn't listen to me,' Hades replied, looking away. 'No matter how much I feel for you both, I cannot release him. He made a vow, one that binds me too.'

'It wasn't his vow to make. He's not fit to be your successor.' Helen separated herself from Lucas and raised her voice. 'I call the Eumenides to bear witness to my claim. Lucas is not fit to rule the dead.'

'Clever girl,' Hades said under his breath in a musing tone, like Helen's tactic hadn't occurred to him.

As the three girls who used to be the Furies came gliding out of the darkness behind the throne, Hades smiled at Helen almost like he was proud of her. The three ex-Furies, now known as the Eumenides or the

Kindly Ones, were like supernatural defence lawyers for the Underworld, and they owed Helen *big*.

The Eumenides arranged themselves to the right of Lucas's throne while Hades stood to the left. The littlest one smiled briefly at Helen, and Helen smiled back, resisting the urge to wave at her like a pal.

The littlest one stilled her face completely and turned her eyes away. The Eumenides might owe Helen their freedom from the suffering they endured as the Furies, but Helen could see now that they would do what was right, no matter what Helen needed.

'Let the dead enter and judge,' the Eumenides said as one.

There were ghostly sighs on the air as invisible presences pressed up against Helen and Lucas, tipping them this way and that as they passed. In moments, the hall filled with hundreds, then thousands, then billions of dead souls stacked up to the impenetrable dark of the ceiling and tucked into the furthest corner.

'Let the qualities of the candidate be known,' the leader of the Eumenides said, striding out and waving a pale arm in Lucas's direction. 'First and foremost, he is intelligent. Proof of this – he is the only supplicant to ever offer the lord of the dead the one prize he seeks by offering himself as Hades's replacement. In terms of intelligence, the candidate is the best we've ever seen.'

Helen bit her lip and frowned. Of course, Lucas was the smartest person Helen had ever met. Smart enough to handle being the lord of a confusing place like the Underworld.

'He commands the shadows and can make himself invisible at will. He can walk among the living unseen, like Hades does,' said the one Helen always thought of as the whiny one. Again, Helen had no rebuttal.

The air crackled quietly, like the sound of burning leaves, as the dead conferred.

'He is a Falsefinder and can judge hearts, as the lord of the dead must,' said the littlest of the Eumenides, almost like she was sorry to add her voice to the case against Lucas. 'And he is immortal.'

'No he isn't,' Helen objected immediately.

'Fact. He cannot fall ill, age, be killed by any of the natural elements, or by any weapon,' the leader reminded the jury of the dead, like a moderator at a debate. 'He carries the light of an immortal in him. The dead can see it.'

Helen heard Lucas gasp and felt him turn to her, about to ask a million questions. She held out a hand to stop Lucas from saying anything and continued.

'I understand. And you're right. He cannot be killed by an outside source,' Helen replied with a nod. 'But Lucas can still die. Proof of that was given when Hecate let him into the ring of fire to fight Matt. He couldn't have fought Matt in it if he was an immortal.'

'Helen speaks the truth,' Hades said, impressing Helen with his fairness even though she knew that justice was one of his largest concerns. 'Hecate would never allow an immortal to fight a mortal to the death. There must be something that can kill Lucas.'

The Eumenides spoke quietly among themselves. Finally, the whiny one raised her voice. 'If this is a trick, and he can only be killed by something that is impossible, like a blade made out of a make-believe metal that doesn't exist, then we will *consider* him immortal.'

'We demand to know what it is that can kill him,' said the leader.

'His own will,' Helen said. 'If he doesn't want to live any more, he'll die. It's his choice. I'd never take that away from him.' Helen turned to Lucas to make sure he was OK with this, but the look on his face was unreadable. She turned back to the throngs of the dead and continued. 'If he wants to die, he will, and if you make him lord of the dead what's to say that someday he won't get sick of it all and just let himself die, leaving you with no one to lead?'

The dead moved around them in agitation, making the air boil. Helen saw the littlest Eumenides tilt her head, like she was listening to a voice in her ear.

'The dead judge him to be too honourable to break his word, now or ever,' she said. 'Hades can see that his heart has the commitment they require, and they trust that the candidate will not let himself die and leave them to Chaos.'

'But how can you be sure? He doesn't want this,' Helen pleaded.

'Neither did Hades. But the candidate chose this, which is more than Hades did,' said the leader of the Eumenides. She looked at Helen apologetically for a moment, and then continued stoically. 'The candidate was not coerced or bribed in any way. Hades tried his best to dissuade him to go back to the light, but he wouldn't. He willingly and knowingly chose to be the Hand of Darkness. Does the candidate deny this?'

'No,' Lucas said, dropping his head. 'I don't deny it.'

Helen knew Lucas would not say he was misled, even though he had been, because he was too honourable to shirk his responsibility. Helen was reminded of the time Lucas had caught her drifting up to the edge of space and pulled her back to Earth. They'd resolved their horrible fight on her widow's walk, and she'd asked him if Castor had been the one to make him push her away, but Lucas wouldn't put the blame on his father. He'd only say that it had been his choice.

She loved him all the more for his sense of responsibility. Which only strengthened her resolve to say the worst about him – whether she believed it or not. She just hoped her hunch about what Persephone had said on Halloween was correct.

'He is intelligent, and loyal, and he has a strong sense of justice. He has all of Hades's talents. But he's missing the most important quality,' Helen said in a loud voice so every last soul could hear her. 'Orion and I were the ones who passed the test of the Furies. We freed them with compassion, and the dead found us worthy to rule. Lucas has never passed that kind of test.'

Helen paused and took a deep breath, because she knew what she was about to say would hurt Lucas, and probably change the way he saw her. Regardless, she knew she had run out of options and had to do it.

'Lucas is not fit to be the lord of the dead because he hasn't proven to anyone that he is a compassionate man,' Helen said loudly.

Lucas's head snapped round to look at Helen in surprise. She did not look back, even though she felt him staring at her. The Eumenides paused to speak to one another quietly. The whole time Lucas kept staring at Helen, but she wouldn't look back at him.

'He traded himself for his cousin,' the leader of the Eumenides said in rebuttal. 'That takes compassion.'

'That was guilt,' Helen said, deliberately turning to Hades so he could read the truth in her. 'When Hector died I saw guilt, sorrow and resignation in Lucas's heart. Those were the emotions that made him willing to trade himself. Not compassion. If it's compassion that the dead value above all other qualities, then Lucas is not fit to rule here.'

The dead conferred, the rustling and creaking of their voices reminding Helen of the sound of the wind in a field of tall marsh grass. Helen couldn't bear to look at Lucas. She just hoped that he'd forgive her for this someday. Instead, she looked over at Hades, who was watching her with a small smile on his face. She wanted to tell him that she was sorry for working against him like this, but she knew she didn't have to. He could read the regret in her heart.

The leader of the Eumenides tilted her head to the side, listening to the verdict of the dead.

'The candidate has been found unworthy,' she said, and Helen nearly collapsed with relief. But the Eumenides weren't finished. 'However. He must still fulfil his vow.'

'What does that mean?' Helen asked the spirits on the air, even though she couldn't understand their whispery speech.

'It means that someday the Hand of Darkness must replace Hades,' replied the littlest of the Eumenides. 'He cannot rule until he is found worthy, but *someday* he must offer himself up to be tested by the dead, and if he passes he must take Hades's place in the Underworld.'

Helen couldn't speak. She wracked her brain for a reason to object, something that would trump Lucas's vow, but she came up with nothing.

'Helen,' Lucas whispered in her ear. 'Let it go. It's OK.'

'No it isn't!' Helen hissed back at him. 'It means that at any time you can be called down here. We won't know when, or how, but *someday* the dead will call your number and you'll have to go to Hades.'

Lucas laughed softly and shook his head. 'That's *life*, Helen. That's what everyone faces. It just means I'll have to live every day like it could be my last day on Earth. I can do that.' He looked over at Hades, his eyes shining with that inner light that Helen hadn't seen in him in weeks. 'Thank you.'

'You must go. Now,' Hades replied gravely. 'The two of you are needed back on Earth. And, Helen? Don't let Zeus win. No matter what you have to do to stop him – do it.'

Helen sighed and nodded, knowing what Hades meant, but not sure if she was strong enough to go through with it now that she knew Lucas had to serve in Hades *someday*. Could she face the long future, knowing that if she wanted to be with Lucas she would have to do it in Hades? Would she end up like Persephone?

'Thank you again, Uncle,' she said. 'Give your queen my love.'

Chapter Sixteen

Helen and Lucas appeared on the beach. Hoping to end up close to Orion, Helen figured that the best place to appear was near the spot of the makeshift arena where the duels had taken place. She was expecting to find that the battle lines being drawn on the beach wouldn't be that much bigger than when she had left, so that she would instantly know which way to go to find Orion. She couldn't have been more wrong.

When Helen and Lucas stepped out of the ring of frost, they found themselves in the middle of a gigantic camp crawling with thousands of fighters. Scions, Myrmidons and mortals were all preparing themselves for battle.

'Son of a biscuit,' Helen said, gaping like a hick at the bustling tent city that had sprung up along the beach. Helen saw Mr Tanis from the hardware store sharpening a sword on a large, round stone. His eyes looked blank and strange. Helen was just about to call out to him and check if he was OK, when she felt Lucas yank roughly on her arm.

'Up!' he growled fearfully, and threw her into the air.

As she disengaged gravity, he flew past her and took her hand to pull her along. 'Wrong side!' he shouted back at her, steering them inland.

From the air, Helen could see the two camps, but she still couldn't believe the scale of it all. She and Lucas floated for a few moments, studying the new map that had been drawn over the beach on the westernmost side of Nantucket Island. From Siasconset all the way up to Sesachacha Pond, the shore was lined with the tents of Tantalus's army. Orion and his soldiers had been backed up on to the dunes, where they huddled on the high ground, ridiculously outnumbered. Helen could hear Lucas whispering to himself, like he was memorizing a list of things for later.

'Didn't we just leave?' Helen gasped, incredulous. There were too many people down there, too many tents. 'How did this happen so fast?'

'Hephaestus has enough arms stored under Mount Olympus to put a sword in the hands of every man, woman and child in the world,' Lucas replied distractedly. Helen watched his eyes skip around, and his lips move as he counted tents under his breath and marked supply lines.

Arrows started whizzing past them. A few of them bounced off Helen, and Lucas instinctively jerked her out of their path. They had been spotted by a phalanx of Myrmidons, and more arrows followed until the air was thick with them.

'I'm fine,' she said, knocking a shower of arrows away from her face. She touched the gold heart she wore round her neck to remind Lucas that she wore the half of the cestus that protected her from weapons. 'It stings, but arrows can't kill me. Or you, either.'

Lucas watched as arrows bounced off him, his expression blank. Helen looked at his heart and saw a dozen different emotions swirling around inside him.

'Are you angry with me? ' she asked pleadingly, placing her hand on his chest. Lucas looked up at Helen, but his eyes were so wild she had no idea what was going through his head. 'I know I made you mostly immortal without even asking you first. But it's still up to you. If you want to die, you still can whenever you want. Not that you'd want to die right now. But say someday in the future – you know, you still can.'

Lucas's face crumpled with confusion.

A flaming ball catapulted past, barely missing them, but neither Helen nor Lucas paid it any mind. Another hail of arrows darkened the sky around them, but it was all background noise, easily ignored now that she had this chance to tell Lucas everything.

'And then there's all that stuff I said about you not being compassionate,' Helen continued, her eyes suddenly filling with tears. 'You have to know I don't really think that about you. I just said it because you hadn't been tested like Orion and I were. It was the only thing I could come up with to use at the trial – the only reason the dead would vote you down.'

Lucas's expression was still blank. Helen took that to mean that what she had said about him during the trial had made him see her differently, just as she had feared. In order to save him, she'd made him stop loving her. Tears spilled down Helen's face.

'You hate me now, don't you? But I had to point out your one big flaw, even if it did change the way you feel about me. I did it to get you back, even if it means I've lost you.'

'You couldn't lose me, Helen. Not even if you tried,' he said, pulling on her arm to bring her closer to him. 'And for the record, I agree with you. I should be more compassionate. I never expected you to think I was perfect. I know I'm not.'

'You are to me.'

'That's all I care about,' Lucas said quietly. '*Not*-my-cousin Helen.'

For just a moment, Helen was scared he wouldn't do it. She'd got her hopes up so many times now and been disappointed that she doubted it would ever actually happen again. But it did happen. He buried his hands in her hair, pulled her to him and kissed her.

The sky filled with flaming arrows and giant projectiles that smelt like melted asphalt. Everything starting exploding around them, but Helen couldn't care less. She was home, and she never wanted to leave it again.

Helen tightened her arms round him desperately, and the kiss grew frantic. Arrows flew this way and that as Orion's soldiers retaliated against the Myrmidons. Noticing that they were caught in the crossfire, Lucas ended the kiss, but still held her close.

'We'll finish this later,' he promised breathlessly, pressing his forehead to hers for a moment to calm down. Then he turned and led her back to earth.

They flew swiftly, avoiding the stinging onslaught of weaponry as best as they could, and landed on their side of the battle line. Archers bristled with arrows. Armour clanked and leather creaked. An army of Scions, small though it was, faced the first wave of Tantalus's army – thirty-three Myrmidons that stood opposite them over a wide strip of sand, with Tantalus standing at the rear as their leader. Helen listened to Tantalus shout orders to the standing army and decided that she had to hand it him. He'd been her personal boogeyman for several months now, but he was no coward.

As soon as Helen and Lucas touched down, Orion and Castor ran forward to meet them.

'How did you . . . ?' Orion asked Helen as they watched Castor hug his son tightly.

'Tell you later,' Helen replied.

'Where's Hector?' Lucas asked.

'In my tent,' Orion responded, leading Helen

and Lucas to it. 'He actually thinks he's going to fight.'

'I don't *think* I'm going to fight, I *am* going to fight,' Hector said in his grouchiest voice from inside the tent.

'Hector, if you get yourself killed again, when I take over from Hades I'll give you a really long time-out in Tartarus,' Lucas said jokingly as they entered.

Helen and Lucas went inside, and the first thing that Helen noticed was six sets of armour, hanging from their racks like hollow soldiers standing guard over the room.

Bronze for Hector, white for Orion, silver for Castor, red for Jason and black for Lucas, Helen thought. Apart from the rest, there was a set of golden armour – the size and shape indicated that it was made for a woman. *That's mine.*

Beneath the sets of armour, Jason was wrapping gauze around Hector's chest. Jason looked pale and shaky from healing his brother.

'Lucas!' Cassandra said, and launched herself at her brother. He caught his little sister and hugged her. His cousins swarmed him, hugging him and thumping his back, but despite their happiness at seeing him everyone was distracted by what he'd said.

'What do you mean, "when you take over from Hades"?' Cassandra asked, releasing Lucas.

'What happened?' Castor asked Helen accusingly, like she'd only done half her job.

'Dad, look, there's no way out of the vow I made. But, thanks to Helen, I don't have to take over right now. Let's focus on the battle at hand.' Lucas squeezed his father's shoulder, then turned to Hector. 'Helen and I saw behind the enemy lines from the air. Where's the map?' He sounded like he'd planned a battle a million times.

Cassandra led the men to a table in the corner, and Lucas immediately began breaking down the set-up of the enemy camp. Helen was about to join them when she heard a familiar voice. It was distant and weak, calling out from the no-man's-land between the two sides.

'Somebody help!' Claire was screaming.

She was in pain.

'Gig?' Helen called, and ran outside the tent, blindly heading for the edge of the line. The burning balls of pitch that the Myrmidons had launched at Helen and Lucas blotted out everything with huge clouds of black smoke.

'Here!' Claire shouted back hoarsely, somewhere behind the smoke screen.

'Helen, don't!' Orion yelled, but Helen didn't listen.

It didn't matter to Helen if Claire had chosen Matt over her. The sound of her best friend in pain wiped everything else away. Helen charged into no-man's-land.

A new wave of arrows was unleashed as soon as Helen set foot on the line – warning shots from the Myrmidons.

'Lennie!' Claire howled, her voice jagged with pain.

Claire was somewhere out there in the dunes, but

397

Helen couldn't see her. Too many arrows were falling, and fires were raging in the rose-hip bushes and in the marsh grass.

Helen felt a giant swell of power surge up and out of her, as a desperate need to find Claire overtook her. Several things happened at once. The fires on the ground extinguished in a hiss of frost and steam. A great wind blew and whipped all the smoke back, revealing Claire and Daphne crouched on the sand. And a hundred arrows paused in mid-air, their bronze tips balancing on the edge of Helen's magnetic field. Everything was still for a moment.

Her heart in her throat, Helen saw that even though Daphne was shielding Claire from the fires with her body, they had both been shot several times with arrows.

Claire was bleeding badly.

Helen ran to her, her hands tingling with panic. She was belatedly aware of the fact that by running into no-man's-land she had taken the field. Inadvertently, Helen had made it OK for the Myrmidons on the other side to do the same.

Helen heard Lucas, Orion and Hector sound their battle cries behind her to summon their soldiers. As one, they charged headlong into the fray that Helen had unwittingly started. All she could see was Giggles, crying and clutching at the arrow in her chest.

'Get out of her!' Helen screamed nonsensically to the arrows sticking out of Claire. They all obeyed and jumped out of Claire's skin, making matters much worse. Rivers of blood began to flow from Claire's body.

Helen got to Claire and Daphne before the charging armies met. She pulled them both close and rocketed into the air as the Scions and the Myrmidons met in a clash of swords and shields beneath her.

As she rushed Claire and Daphne to Jason, she glanced down and saw Castor, Hector, Orion and Lucas ploughing into the Myrmidon phalanx without their armour. Lucas took the lead, blocking furiously. The sight of Lucas knocking blades out of the way with his bare hands sent a shiver through Helen, and even though she knew a sword or an arrow couldn't kill him, she was relieved that she had to focus on flying and couldn't watch. In a moment she had Claire and Daphne in the tent.

'I'm fine,' Daphne insisted, limping off towards the table and chairs. Helen laid Claire down in front of Jason and Cassandra. Jason reacted immediately, his hands glowing blue to stop Claire's bleeding even as his heart crawled with hurt over what she'd done.

'Jason, wait!' Claire pleaded.

'Claire, for once in your life, could you please just shut up?' Jason said angrily. Helen looked in his heart, yellow and bruised, and she could see he was so wounded by Claire's betrayal that he couldn't even look her in the eye.

'Pallas won't fight you and Hector,' she gasped, stubbornly continuing. 'Daedalus refuses to fight Orion, and the gods have lost the support of most of the Scions on their side because they're hypnotizing mortals.' Blood began to pour out of her mouth.

The one frigging power Helen didn't have, and it was the one that she most wished for – the ability to heal her loved ones when they were suffering.

'Do something!' Helen yelled at Jason.

'Her lung is punctured,' he said as Claire struggled under his hands. 'I have to put her under.'

'Claire, please, calm down,' Cassandra said soothingly. 'Let Jason work.'

'No!' Claire replied, knocking Jason's glowing hands away. She tried to sit up, but more blood poured out of her mouth. Still, she fought to deliver her message. 'Tantalus, a handful of the Hundred Cousins, and the Myrmidons are all that's left,' she said, choking on her own blood. 'Tantalus leads them all. He's the brains, and he's heavily guarded by the Myrmidons.'

'Try to keep still,' Cassandra said, easing Claire back down.

'I'm so sorry,' Claire coughed. 'Ari and I thought we were doing the right thing.'

'I know,' Jason replied, and the mustard-coloured bitterness that Helen saw in his heart morphed into a gorgeous red-gold cloud. 'Now, seriously, shut the hell up,' he whispered tenderly.

He passed a glowing hand over Claire's head, and she blacked out. Helen watched for a moment as Claire's

JOSEPHINE ANGELINI

wounds began to close, and Jason's face grew paler with the effort to heal her, before she turned to Daphne.

'Thank you,' Helen said grudgingly. 'For getting her.'

Daphne nodded and looked down at a wound in her thigh. 'I'm in no position to request anything in return. But I'm asking you to leave Tantalus to me.'

'He's all yours,' Helen said unfeelingly, before leaving the tent to fly over the battle and find her men.

She spotted Lucas first. He was fighting alongside his father. She knew that Lucas would be fine, and that he would protect Castor. She looked around for Orion. Arrows whistled around her as the Myrmidons behind the front lines emptied their quivers. Seeing the arrows bounce off her, they quickly put up their bows, pointing and crying out at the impossible sight.

From the air, Helen found Orion and Hector fighting back to back. A circle of six Myrmidons had them pinned down. Helen flew to them, and once she was in range she called the swords out of the Myrmidons' hands. Six swords jumped into the sky and hovered there as Helen landed with an earthshaking thud next to Hector and Orion.

Her arrival did not have the effect she expected. Instead of running away, the Myrmidons began to close in.

'The Tyrant,' they chanted in unison as they moved towards her like a congealing mass of hate. 'Kill the Tyrant.'

'Not your best move, Princess,' Hector scolded. He pointed a frantic finger at Orion. 'Get her off the battlefield!'

Before Helen could figure out why Hector was so bent out of shape, Orion threw her over his shoulder and started running to the tent. As she bounced uncomfortably against Orion's back, she managed to prop herself up enough to see the entire phalanx of thirty-plus Myrmidons zeroing in on her, and she figured it out.

The queen may be the most versatile piece on the chessboard, but if she gets taken out the game doesn't end. It's only over when the king gets cornered and someone calls checkmate. Belatedly, Helen realized that she was the king in this game, not the queen.

As she thought this, Helen noticed someone running through the battlefield dressed in golden armour – *her* golden armour.

'Wait!' Helen screamed, reaching out for the girl in gold who was foolishly impersonating her. 'That's suicide!'

But the girl disappeared in the smoke, fog and the surging throngs of fighters without pause.

As Scions from the House of Athens closed ranks behind Orion and faced the pursuing Myrmidons, Helen realized that the girl in gold could only be one person. Her mother.

*

Daphne waited until Jason had nearly knocked himself out to heal Claire, and Cassandra had gone to fetch him some food and water to revive him, before she brought the gold armour down off its rack. She donned it quickly and, wearing Helen's face, charged into the battlefield.

She knew she'd never make it out alive, but she had never cared about her own life. Ajax was lost to her. Finally, after all these years, she'd accepted that. There was only one thing left to accomplish. One promise left that she had to keep.

All she had to do was get across the lines while the majority of Tantalus's fighters were occupied with the battle. Then she would be close enough to kill him.

She'd traded her heart for this months ago – her heart for Hecate's help in taking one man's life. It didn't matter what precautions Tantalus took. Hecate, the guardian of all crossroads and thresholds, had promised that she would open any door for Daphne.

As she ran across no-man's-land, part of Daphne hoped that Helen believed that she was doing this to help her. An even bigger part of Daphne wished that it were true. But she knew better. She was doing this mainly for revenge. The fact that it helped Helen was just a bonus.

The Myrmidons were distracted, chasing the real Helen, who was thrown over Orion's shoulder and being carried back behind the lines. Embarrassing, but Daphne knew her daughter's removal from the battlefield was for the best. For all her awe-inspiring power, Helen was not a born fighter, and Daphne was glad that Orion had the good sense to get her out of the way.

Unlike her big-hearted and easily bewildered daughter, Daphne had been in many battles and she knew how to use a sword. Ignoring the rapidly healing wounds in her thigh and shoulder, she cut down a few members of the Hundred Cousins where they stood and began clearing a path to the enemy line.

Daphne spun round in a circle to engage as many of them as she could to distract the enemy from Hector, Lucas and Castor. None of Helen's men was wearing armour and they needed to regroup. The only way for that to happen would be if Daphne could win the field and push the enemy back. As long as the Myrmidons were chasing the real Helen, Daphne might just have a chance to get across the lines and on to her real goal.

She killed three men and electrocuted another before her lightning caught Castor's attention.

'Helen!' he shouted. Seeing Daphne surrounded by more and more soldiers, he began to charge to her rescue.

'Get back, Caz!' Daphne yelled, purposely using his old nickname. He was a smart man and quickly realized that the girl in the golden armour wasn't Helen, even if she looked exactly like her.

Castor held out an arm to stop Lucas from flying to her and quickly explained things to his son. The two of them turned their attention back to fighting the Hundred

Cousins, and Daphne killed the last of the men who had surrounded her.

Breaking across enemy lines, Daphne kicked a few hypnotized mortals out of her way. All the Scions and Myrmidons were on the battlefield, and the mortal reserves had yet to be deployed. Daphne didn't want to use her sword on full mortals and sheathed it in favour of nonlethal hand-to-hand combat.

Even bare-handed, she tore through the reserves in seconds and headed for a cluster of big tents, calling out her challenge.

'Tantalus! Let's decide this right now!' Daphne-as-Helen yelled. 'One life instead of one thousand!' The crowd started whispering the word *Tyrant* all around Daphne. They were buying it. 'Your life or mine. We'll end this war before it starts.'

Tantalus flipped back the front flap of his tent and stepped out in full armour. Daphne dropped her face visor and wrung the pommel of her sword between her hands.

'But I have no lightning. I can't summon earthquakes. I can't fly,' Tantalus said, holding his hands out as he walked towards her, like he had nothing to hide.

'Sword against sword,' Daphne-as-Helen retorted. 'No other talents allowed. Just your blade against mine.'

The crowd murmured their assent, except for one.

'Helen, don't!' Ariadne yelled. Her father prevented her from running to Daphne's side. 'He's too good.'

'No other talents and no tricks?' Tantalus asked Daphne uncertainly. He didn't want to face her unless he was certain he could win.

'None,' Daphne said without pause, knowing she had already paid for this lie with her whole heart.

'Let Hecate decide,' Tantalus said, warming up to the idea of being the big hero by winning the war in one duel. 'Offering!'

Pallas stepped forward and threw a handful of saffron into the air between Tantalus and Daphne. Orange fire erupted out of the sand to form an oval. Tantalus and Daphne stepped into the arena unhindered. Tantalus unsheathed his sword slowly and smiled at her.

'Pallas tells me you're a *terrible* swordswoman,' he whispered with a cold smile.

Daphne let her own face show through for just a moment so Tantalus knew whom he was facing. When she saw recognition paralyse his expression, she quickly shifted back to Helen's youthful version of the Face and smiled back at him.

'I think you'll find me much improved,' she said.

The gods converged on the duel eagerly, each of them taking a prized position at the edge of the sealed arena. Tantalus turned round, about to protest that it was Daphne and not Helen he was fighting, but was met with a wall of orange fire. Seeing that it was impossible to back out now, Tantalus smiled sadly to himself and nodded at the sand.

'Every evil thing I ever did, I did because I love you,' Tantalus said just loud enough for Daphne to hear. 'You, of all people, should understand that by now.'

'I do,' she replied quietly. 'And I hate you for teaching it to me.'

He stood at one end of the oval, and Daphne at the other. By putting as much distance as possible between them, they had opted for a one-strike duel. This was not going to be a long fight, filled with fancy footwork and genteel fencing. Like medieval jousters or Wild West gunslingers, they were both going for the single, killing blow.

They broke into a run at the same time and charged each other. It was over in a moment.

Daphne ignored the hot sting that traced across her neck, and cut off Tantalus's head with one strike. Just as he had done to Ajax. She saw Tantalus's head roll past her and hit the barrier of orange fire, his dead eyes staring back at her.

It was finally finished. Daphne fell to her knees as she listened to his headless body fall to the ground in stages behind her. Silence followed – then a ringing in her ears. Daphne felt a familiar, seeping cold. Looking down, she saw blood pooling in the sand around her. She tried to inhale, and sucked in salty liquid instead of air, like breathing tears. Her body collapsed, and she toppled into the sand as her almost completely severed neck bled out in an instant.

One line from 'The Scottish Play' ran through her head: *The sleeping and the dead are but as pictures.*

Ajax used to love to draw her while she slept. He was such an amazing artist . . .

Orion threw Helen down next to Jason, who was sleeping – or passed out – on the floor next to Claire. He was so angry Helen didn't know if she should even try to get him to calm down. She decided to hazard an apology.

'Orion, I'm sor—' she began.

'Shush!' Orion said, holding up a hand to silence her. He took a few deep breaths to calm himself before starting again. 'What the hell were you thinking?'

'That this is *my* fight, not yours. Not Lucas's. Not Hector's. *Mine*,' Helen said, standing up and facing Orion. 'I was trying to fight for myself.'

'You realize that's not how these things are done, don't you? We choose champions for a reason – because if you die, we lose. I thought you understood that.'

'Yes, I do. Helen of Troy had no choice but to sit back and let other people fight for her, and we all know how well that worked out for Troy,' she said pointedly. Orion shut his mouth and turned to the armoury.

'You're really pissing me off, Helen,' he said, undoing his belt and yanking off his clothes, stripping down so he could get into his armour. Helen moved quickly to help him.

'I know I am,' she replied, pulling down Orion's

white breastplate. 'Because I'm too chicken to do what I really have to do.'

'And what's that?' he asked, holding out his arms for Helen to tie his breastplate at the sides. Cassandra appeared at Helen's elbow, the bracelet Orion made her tinkling prettily. 'Kitty, what are you still doing here?' Orion asked her impatiently as if he'd just noticed her presence.

'I—' she started.

'Go home to Noel and Kate. This place is too dangerous for you,' he scolded. Cassandra wavered, about to put down the gauntlets she carried, but Helen grabbed her hand and stopped her.

'Cassandra is here to be close to you so she doesn't prophesy,' Helen reminded him. She fumbled with the ties on Orion's armour for a moment and quickly threw up her hands. 'And she's here to dress you. I have no idea how these dratted things are put on.'

Helen backed off and let Cassandra do what she so obviously wanted to do. Touch Orion. He didn't even look at her.

'So, keep going. I'm dying to hear what it is you're "too chicken" to do,' Orion said with a doubtful look, like he didn't really believe Helen could be chicken about anything.

'Make myself immortal,' Helen replied, her voice breaking. 'And not mostly immortal – not immortal except for one tiny clause where I can let myself off the hook in a jillion years if I get sick of it all – but really, honestly, till-the-stars-wink-out immortal so I can fight Zeus one-on-one. I don't want to be immortal.' Helen felt tears sting the backs of her eyes. 'I'm terrified of forever.'

Orion broke away from Cassandra like she wasn't there and hugged Helen.

'OK, yeah. That would terrify me too,' Orion said, holding her gently so he didn't crush her against his armour.

Helen opened her eyes as Orion held her and saw Cassandra staring at them, her blue eyes wide and glassy with hurt. Helen pulled away from Orion and put some distance between them. How could Orion be so insensitive to Cassandra?

Did he simply not like her? Helen knew that wasn't true. He was genuinely fond of his 'little Kitty' – he just didn't see her as a woman. Yes, she was a bit young for him at the moment, but there was still something weird about how he couldn't seem to *see* inside her the way he could with other people. *Like the Fates can't see through him,* she thought. Aeneas was a son of Aphrodite, but he never suspected Cassandra of Troy loved him, either.

Helen realized that the Fates must hide Cassandra from Orion in much the same way that Nemesis hid Orion from the Fates.

'Why do you have to become immortal in the first

place?' he asked, interrupting Helen's train of thought and bringing her back to the more pressing situation.

'To make it my fight. Like it should have been right from the start,' Helen mumbled, rubbing the palms of her hands against her jeans nervously.

They heard noises outside the tent – the sound of their army returning. Helen heard Scions from the House of Rome saying, 'He's dead! Tantalus is dead! The gods have no champions left!'

But Helen knew the gods would not be beaten so easily. They would unleash every storm, every earthquake and every tidal wave at their disposal before they allowed Helen to walk away with a win.

'Who killed him?' Orion shouted happily, striding to the entrance of the tent.

'My mother,' Helen answered behind him. She ran and grabbed him by the shoulders before he could join his men in celebration. 'Orion. Don't let Poseidon destroy this island. Fight his earthquakes, and fight the tidal waves. Are you strong enough to take him on like that?'

'I'll try,' Orion said, his face blanching. 'Is that where this war is going?'

'Yes,' Cassandra intoned. Helen shivered at the sound, like someone had poured ice water down her back.

Orion and Helen turned to look at the Oracle. The air around her flashed with colour, and her body rebounded like she was being punched from the inside, but her face and voice remained her own as she fought the Fates.

'The Twelve immortals cannot meet mortals in open combat. Tyrant, they will unleash their darkest weapons to fight you until you meet Zeus in battle as an equal. Do not delay. One of you must go to Tartarus and complete the cycle.'

'We'll see about that,' Helen said defiantly.

Cassandra's frail body shook like she was being electrocuted. Her face shrivelled and her eyes filmed over with cataracts as the most terrifying of the three Fates, Atropos – she who cuts off the thread of life – pushed her way through and possessed Cassandra.

'The veil of Nemesis does not always work on the one already blinded,' Atropos said, poking her finger into Cassandra's eye.

'Orion!' Helen screamed, and he ran to Cassandra to stop the violent prophecy that was trying to shatter her from the inside out. But the old woman danced away from him in Cassandra's body.

'You'll not steal our vessel again, pretty one,' Atropos cackled. She made Cassandra's hips sway suggestively, taunting Orion. 'Poseidon is raising his darkest pets from the bottom of the ocean. The Kraken comes to kill you this time!'

Orion wrapped his arms round Cassandra, and she swooned as the Fates were finally driven away. He picked her up as easily as he would a doll and carried her to a chair so he could sit down and hold her in his lap.

'Kitty?' he said gently, touching her face. She didn't respond. 'C'mon, now, wake up.' He shook her, fear making him angry. 'Cassandra!' he commanded, but she didn't even flinch.

Helen saw something flare inside Orion, and before he could snatch the emotion away, she recognized it. It was a bright flash of love.

Shouts and screams of panic began to sound from the soldiers on the battlefield. Lucas, Hector and Castor entered the tent in a rush, their faces stark white and staring.

'What's going on?' Helen asked, fearing the worst, but the men were still too stunned to speak.

From outside the back part of the tent, on the inland side, Helen heard Andy's siren voice commanding soldiers to hold the line. A moment later, Andy ducked in under the flap at the back and did a grossed-out dance like her skin was crawling.

'There are *things* coming out of the water!' Andy squealed, just shy of hysterical. 'Freaky fish men, and crab women, and –' She broke off and wiggled her fingers, a horrified look on her face. 'They're all *gooey*! I'm half siren. I've seen most of the creepy crawlies on the ocean bed, but these things are disgusting!'

Andy's freak-out woke Jason and he stumbled to the

group, his face so drawn it was nearly skeletal. He pointed to Cassandra sprawled across Orion's lap.

'What happened?' he croaked.

'Prophecy,' Orion answered. 'She won't wake up.'

'What did she say?' Lucas asked.

'That I have to go do something because if I don't the gods will – and I can't believe I'm saying this – unleash the Kraken.' Helen still couldn't grasp it. 'Is the Kraken even *Greek*?' she gibbered.

Castor pulled himself together first, and he rushed to take all their armour down. 'Boys!' he said roughly. 'Help each other with your armour. Quickly!'

Helen stood stock-still while they all stripped and then began strapping each other into their armour. She could hear her heart beating in her ears. How could she watch all these people she loved die?

'How would you all like to see Everyland?' she shouted, her voice shaking. Everyone paused, stunned by Helen's seemingly insane offer.

'Helen?' Lucas said, his voice deadly serious. 'Are you thinking of making everyone immortal?'

'No,' she replied. 'If I make everyone immortal, and I lose to Zeus, he'll have no choice but to put you all in Tartarus for eternity. There's no other way to get rid of a full immortal. I can't do that to you.' Helen was panting. She couldn't seem to catch a breath. When next she spoke, her voice was so high it squeaked. 'But how would you all like to be *mostly* immortal, like Lucas?'

414

A deafening sound rumbled through the sky and shook the ground. Collapsing to her knees, Helen felt Lucas throw himself over her, covering her ears. Panicked screams were drowned out by the single unearthly bellow that Helen knew could only mean one thing.

The Kraken was rising.

CHAPTER SEVENTEEN

Helen felt Lucas pulling her to her feet, and then they ran to the front of the tent with Orion and Hector to look out at the apocalyptic scene that was unfolding in front of them.

The sun and sky were blotted out by a huge dome rising up out of the water. A long, ropelike shape, as wide as a city block, soared up in the air and then came crashing down across the beach, crushing mortals, Scions and Myrmidons indiscriminately. The Kraken was so enormous that the tip of its tentacle reached all the way from the deep ocean offshore where the head of the giant squid breached the surface, crossed leagues of water, and ended inside Helen's camp. It was an angry red colour, striated with veins as thick as tree trunks, and covered in suckers.

Soldiers hacked at the Kraken's tentacle as it slid past them, trying to cut it off. In retaliation, the tentacle grabbed one of its assailants, wrapped round him like a snake and squeezed. Lucas pulled Helen back into the tent as the soldier died a gruesome death. Even though she didn't have to watch, she could still hear him screaming.

Helen turned to see stunned and horrified looks on every face. They had no idea how to tackle something this enormous. She glanced at Claire's and Cassandra's unconscious forms. Turning back to everyone else, she saw consensus building.

'Who's with me?' Helen asked.

Hector looked at Andy, his emotions naked in a way they never were with anyone else. 'Only if you come too,' he said.

'OK,' she whispered, and reached for his hand. He took it and pulled her against his side, nodding at Helen to let her know they were in.

'What about Claire?' Jason asked anxiously.

'Take her,' Helen said. 'Orion. Take Cassandra.' Orion narrowed his eyes in question. He glanced down to Helen's heart, reading it, and a troubled look creased his brow. 'Trust me,' she told him.

'Castor?' Helen asked, turning to him.

'I'm sorry, Helen. I've dreamed of Atlantis my whole life. But I can't go with you,' Castor said sadly. 'Not without Noel.'

'Dad,' Lucas began to argue, but Castor held up a hand to stop him.

'I've lived long enough to know I don't want to live much past the time allotted to me, anyway,' he said shaking his head firmly. 'That doesn't mean I'm out of the fight. I'm still on your side, Helen.'

'If you're not coming with us you can't fight,' Lucas insisted. 'It's too dangerous.'

'No it isn't.' Helen said as a thought occurred to her. She unclasped the heart necklace she'd worn since she was a baby, and gave it to Castor. 'I don't know if you're capable of using this or not.'

Castor nodded and drew his dagger. 'It may be a relic only daughters of the House of Atreus can use,' he said knowingly. He handed his dagger to Helen and bared his forearm for her, meeting her eyes without a hint of fear. With no time to waste, Helen drew the blade swiftly across his skin. It didn't cut him.

'Just don't let the Kraken get hold of you,' Helen said, relieved she hadn't injured him. 'The cestus will only protect you from weapons, not forces of nature.'

'I'll remember that,' Castor said, fastening the clasp behind his neck. Once Castor was wearing it, the heart shape altered, but he quickly tucked it under his armour before anyone could see what form it took.

'Thank you,' Castor said, hugging Helen tightly before letting her go. 'Now hurry.'

'Everyone join hands,' Helen said. Orion picked up Cassandra as Jason lifted Claire.

All the people they *weren't* bringing with them flashed through Helen's head – her dad, Kate, Ariadne, and, yes, even Matt. There were so many people she had to leave behind in order to do this that she could barely bring herself to go. But she knew she had to, or all of them would die this day.

'Back in a sec,' she promised.

Helen heard the Kraken make that terrible sound again, and then it was gone.

The only sound was of the wind in the wildflowers. The sun was high and warm, and the mountains that rimmed the valley to the north-west were capped with snow. To the east, the eclectic skyline of Everycity gleamed, part glass-and-steel modern, and part ancient stone citadel. To the south, the smell of the ocean beckoned.

'Beautiful,' Andy breathed in awe as an iridescent butterfly tumbled past, just inches from her face.

'Definitely,' Hector mumbled, staring at Andy and not the butterfly.

Cassandra's eyes opened sleepily, and she cuddled like a kitten in Orion's arms, smiling up at him. Orion watched Cassandra, and that same troubled look crossed his face again. Helen could see his heart vacillating between tenderness and fear.

'Do you remember that conversation we had about *more* on the beach that night?' Helen said to Orion. He nodded. Helen gestured to Cassandra with her chin. 'Trust me, she does,' she told him.

As Orion puzzled over this, Claire inhaled sharply as she gained consciousness, flailed and accidentally smacked Jason across the face.

'Thanks,' Jason said sarcastically as he put her down.

'Sorry!' Claire sheepishly patted the spot on his jaw where she'd clocked him. Her tone dropped, but she kept her hand on his cheek. 'Do you forgive me?' she whispered, her meaning broadening past the accidental slap. Jason nodded and pulled her into a hug.

'Where are we?' Cassandra asked groggily as Orion placed her on her feet.

'Everyland,' Lucas replied, smiling at Helen in a way that made her tingle. 'Helen's world.'

Lucas bent down and picked a single, white wildflower from the field, pulled his wallet from his back pocket, and folded it safely inside. He looked up at Helen and smiled, melting her.

Their injuries were healed, and they were all refreshed. All their senses were heightened, like a dull film had been washed away, making the world around them brighter. Every sensation, from the cool wind on their cheeks to the warm sun on their arms, was like a flood of pleasure. While her family soaked it all in, Helen took the moment of silence to make the toughest choice of her life.

'Helen?' Lucas said in that knowing way of his, like he could sense mischief in her. 'What are you up to?'

'It's done.' Helen smiled and shook her head, refusing to tell him. 'Time doesn't stop here. We have to get back to the fight.'

'What's done?' Claire whispered to Jason.

'Ah . . .' he began, and looked at Helen pleadingly.

'I made you pretty much immortal, Gig,' Helen said. 'All of you. You can only die when you decide that you don't want to live any more.'

Claire stared at Helen, still not fully believing it.

'So don't worry about getting killed in the battle – just keep your head down and stay out of the way. Everybody join hands,' Helen said urgently. As they joined hands, she looked at her circle, the circle she would take with her as far into the future as they could stand, and was grateful for the company even if they found that they couldn't stay with her forever.

She looked into Lucas's eyes last, his bright blue eyes that held a pool of strength deeper than any ocean, and thought about his vow to take Hades's place someday. Helen knew that when that time came she would go down with him. Hell was wherever Lucas wasn't. They would never be parted again, no matter how long forever turned out to be.

Unless, of course, Zeus won and sent her to Tartarus. *That* eternity, Helen knew, she would have to suffer alone.

The air was thick with acrid, black smoke. As soon as Helen and her group appeared, bodies seemed to rush at them from all sides. A Myrmidon with red skin and flat, black eyes charged Helen, his sword swinging over his head. As the blade came down, Helen caught it in her bare hand, and wrenched the sword out of his grip.

She spun round, back-fisting him, and watched him drop.

She looked at the sword in her hand, and had no idea what to do with it, so she handed it to Jason. When next she looked up, she saw that Lucas, Orion, Hector and Jason had formed their own line of defence with Andy, Claire and Cassandra behind them. They might be mostly immortal, but Claire, Cassandra and Andy were not Scion strong, and they were even worse fighters than Helen was.

Helen heard Cassandra's bloodcurdling scream and saw Orion step in front of her to cut the head off one of Poseidon's sea monsters. The creature kept charging at Cassandra, anyway, as if it didn't need its head, which it probably didn't.

'Prophet!' the creature hissed out of one of its many holes. Orion swung his sword again and cut its carapace in two – cleaving the lobsterlike creature in half and killing it, but too late.

Alerted to her presence, a wave of misshapen creatures began to ooze towards Cassandra. Like limping nightmares, they were not made for land, and their too-soft or too-hard body parts flopped hideously as they dragged themselves towards the precious Oracle.

'Zeus needs her! Apollo lusts for her! Poseidon demands we capture her for Olympus!' they gurgled, reaching their fish-stinking limbs towards Cassandra. She screamed in terror as the largest of the creatures clamped on to her arm with one of its claws, and in a flash dragged her under its shell.

'No!' Orion bellowed, jumping on top of the horseshoe crab-like creature that had imprisoned Cassandra, hammering away at its armoured shell with his bare hands.

The Kraken sounded again, shaking Helen from the inside out. The intolerable noise made her and everyone around her clutch their ears and drop to their knees. A shadow darkened the sky above her. Helen craned her head to see one of the Kraken's tentacles descending directly over her.

'Enough!' Helen shouted.

The Kraken's tentacle landed on top of her and she caught it, just as she had done with the Myrmidon's blade seconds earlier. Every muscle in her body strained under the impossible weight of the Kraken's blow, but Helen did not break. Instead, she threw the rubbery, sucker-covered limb aside and launched herself into the air.

Helen called storm clouds and lightning to her presence. She made the wind howl around her. She stopped the waves and turned the Atlantic into a watery mirror. She twisted the Earth's magnetic field until the aurora borealis bent and glimmered around her like the footprints of angels.

'I challenge Zeus!' she cried, her voice echoing across her island home and the vast expanse of ocean beyond it. 'Face me or forfeit Olympus!'

Nothing happened. Helen belatedly realized that she had no offering to give Hecate in order to make the duel official.

The number three popped up in Helen's head, and for some reason she thought of wishes. She had no idea if immortals worked on a barter system or not, but at that moment, Helen had nothing to give but her word and nothing to lose but the whole world.

'Titan Hecate, I offer you three favours in return for your guardianship over the boundaries.' Helen bit her lip and tried not to think anything too incriminating, in case the Fates were listening. 'As long as you guard *all* the boundaries. Do this for me, I beg you, and I will do your bidding three times in the future.'

Orange fire sprang up in a giant ball around Helen, making an airborne arena. A young, bare-chested man passed through the flames and floated in front of her. Zeus was gorgeous and ruthless and so much like Helen that she could hardly stand to look at him.

They were alone here. No one was watching but the Titan Hecate. This battle was not for spectacle or for the amusement of the Olympians. The whole Earth, Everyland and Olympus hung in the balance, but it was so private Helen felt like she'd walked into his bedroom.

'Hello, daughter,' Zeus purred.

She felt his pull. Even though she knew she needed to defeat him, Helen was not immune to the half-animal, half-divine presence that surrounded him. And it was mesmerizing.

'How powerful you are,' he said, moving closer to her. 'The clouds twist with colour at your command, but they still pale in comparison to your beauty. They'd cry with jealousy if you'd only let it rain.'

'I'm not your daughter,' she replied quietly. 'My father is a shopkeeper. He's a single dad who had to raise me all by himself. He worked twelve hours a day, six days a week his whole life in order to keep a roof over our heads. My father's worth ten of you, and probably ten of me too. You don't get to say you're my father. You didn't earn it like Jerry did.'

'He's awake, you know,' Zeus said in an offhand way. 'Give me Everyland, and I'll leave Jerry and his woman, Kate, alone. After I send you to Tartarus, of course.'

Helen narrowed her eyes at him. 'You'll leave them in peace if I give you Everyland?'

'I swear it by the River Styx,' he said, and the sky rolled around them like a sheet on a clothesline, undulating in the wind. 'I have no interest in punishing mortals who haven't offended me. I never have.'

Helen knew this to be true. Zeus never held grudges against mortals. It was his wife, Hera, who did that.

'And what about my nearly immortal family?' Helen asked. 'Lucas, Hector, Orion, Cassandra, Jason, Claire, Andy . . . will you leave them alone too?'

'Yes, yes. Them too,' Zeus said with a bored wave of

his hand. 'Why not? They won't want to face eternity without you, anyway. A few centuries and they'll opt for a peaceful death.'

'Yes,' Helen said demurely. She looked up at him through her lashes. 'But you won't curse any of them, or Ariadne, in any way, as long as I give you Everyland?'

'By the River Styx,' he swore, and reached out to touch her cheek with his hand. 'So caring about those you love. But you do understand that you face an eternity in Tartarus, don't you?'

'Been there,' Helen said unflinchingly. 'I figure spending eternity trapped in any one place, even paradise, is the same as hell after long enough. In a thousand years, I bet even a field of wildflowers begins to feel like a festering bog.'

'How right you are,' Zeus murmured darkly. His eyes shifted strangely, wildly, almost like he'd lost his grip on the here and now. 'And so much time left to go.'

'And what about the rest of Olympus? Will they retaliate against my friends and family with curses if I go for this trade?' Helen asked innocently.

'I swear by the River Styx that the Olympians will not curse your little group,' Zeus said.

Helen pretended to think about it. She bit her lip and wrung her hands. Finally, she nodded quickly in assent, as if to get it out of the way.

'Hecate will not allow you to back out of this trade once you agree to it,' Zeus reminded her tentatively, gesturing to the sacred space around them, carved out of mid-air in orange fire.

'I know,' Helen said, truly saddened for a moment that she had to give up her world. She could feel it inside her. Every lake, every tree and every pane of glass in her sweeping city was a part of her – a part of her that she had to abandon forever to her enemy to save her family. Her voice broke with real pain when she spoke. 'I'll give you Everyland.'

'Swear it before Hecate.'

'I swear before Hecate to give you Everyland in exchange for the safety of my friends and family.'

Zeus smiled at her, lightning flashing across his face. 'Aphrodite told me you'd do anything to protect the people you love. She said it was the quality she adored most in you. It certainly will save a lot of lives. For now.'

Helen dropped her gaze, so he wouldn't see eagerness and regret warring with each other in her eyes. 'So how does this work? Do we go to Everyland first?'

'Yes. When we get there, you simply make a new rule that Everyland answers to me alone,' Zeus said, tucking her hair behind her ear, almost like he cared about her. 'And then I'll take you to Tartarus.'

Lucas saw Helen throw the Kraken's tentacle to the side and launch herself into the air. He was about to follow her out of sheer habit, but he saw Orion on top of a giant horseshoe crab monster, screaming Cassandra's name.

Lucas's little sister was nearly immortal, but that didn't mean she couldn't be captured by the Olympians and used as their Oracle until she willed herself to death.

After seeing how she'd handled the Kraken, Lucas trusted that Helen could take care of herself and ran to help Orion get his little sister back. The monster was huge, and it had spikes sticking out of its sides and a long, swordlike appendage for a tail that it used to slash at anyone that came near. Avoiding the razor-sharp tail, Lucas ran to the front, crouched down and tried to flip it over, only to find about a dozen hairy legs that all ended in pincers under the dome of its top shell, clawing at him. He heard his sister screaming somewhere in there with all those legs.

'Luke, hold it so it can't get to the water!' Orion yelled, and slid down the side of the carapace.

Lucas held the monster in place while Orion began hacking his way through the forest of appendages. They could both hear Cassandra crying Orion's name frantically, and finally they saw her white face and tiny hand reaching up out of the suffocating bristles and grasping claws. Orion pulled Cassandra free while Lucas tipped the monster over on to its back.

'How do you kill it?' Lucas asked, climbing on top and hacking away at the underbelly with no idea where to aim.

'I don't know,' Orion replied, dumbfounded.

'You're the sea-god guy!' Lucas yelled.

'It doesn't have a central heart or a brain!' Orion yelled back. 'Maybe try boiling it?'

'Son of a . . .' Lucas swore, and jumped off the struggling creature. Lucas wanted to end its misery, but he didn't know how. He scrambled away, and turned his attention to his little sister.

'Orion!' Cassandra sobbed against his chest.

'It's all right, Kitty,' Orion said soothingly, running his hands over her to make sure nothing was broken or bleeding.

Cassandra quieted down, and he checked every limb and every joint on her body. Then she reached up to put her fingers in his thick hair and turned her mouth up to his like a shy flower opening for the first time. In a daze, Orion lowered his lips and kissed her.

Lucas's foot connected with the side of Orion's head before Lucas was even aware that he was angry.

'She's just a child!' Lucas growled, jumping on top of Orion's sprawled body and hitting him as hard and as fast as he could.

'I am *not*!' Cassandra screamed.

Lucas was vaguely aware that Cassandra was scratching his face and trying to claw him off Orion. She kept repeating that she loved him, but it didn't matter much to Lucas. His little sister really was like a kitten. Her claws stung, but they didn't have the strength to injure.

'I know!' Orion hollered. 'I shouldn't have – I'm sorry!'

Orion was holding up his arms to shield himself, and Lucas noticed he wasn't even trying to fight back.

'You better kill me now, Lucas, because I'm not going to stay away from her. I *can't*.' Orion's voice was breaking with emotion.

'What the hell are you two morons doing?' Hector bellowed, pulling Lucas off Orion.

Before Lucas had a chance to tell Hector what Orion had done, Helen's voice boomed out across the island issuing a challenge to Zeus. Lucas realized that as a full immortal she could meet him in single combat, and none of her partially mortal champions could step in to stop it, not even him. *Clever girl*, Lucas thought. *I could strangle her right about now.*

They all looked up and saw the clouds flash with lightning. The waves stilled like time had stopped and the aurora borealis appeared, sending eerie neon colours dancing across the sky.

The chaotic battle on the beach paused for a moment as man and beast craned their heads to watch the impossible spectacle.

Thunder rolled. Orange fire erupted in mid-air as Hecate set the battleground in the sky. Lucas thought about flying to Helen.

'She can handle it, Luke,' Hector said urgently. 'I need you here.'

The Myrmidons took that particular moment to regroup into their precise phalanx, shields front and top, spears sticking out like a porcupine. A full unit again, they surged forward like an ancient war machine.

'Form the line!' Hector commanded, holding his bloody sword aloft.

Lucas, Orion and Jason jumped up like a chip in their heads made them automatically respond to their general. They spread out across the front line, each of them taking a battalion to lead, and their infantry fell into ranks behind them.

The Myrmidons charged.

Helen and Zeus appeared in the middle of the field of wildflowers. Zeus looked around, taking in the purple mountains, and the half-modern, half-ancient metropolis that worked like a counterbalance in the distance across from the alpine range. He stared at every flower, every bug, every gust of wind, measuring them all.

'Well done,' he said approvingly. 'Alive in every detail. Hades taught you a lot about life by making you slog through that barren hellscape of his, didn't he?'

'He did. As hard as it was, I love him for the training he gave me. I can see more clearly because of it.'

Zeus breathed in the air, letting his head drop to the side in pleasure, appreciating every nuance of Helen's world, like a foodie would a fine wine. 'You learned well. You are truly gifted, sweet girl. Pity you can't do more with Everyland. It's still unfinished.'

'No it isn't. It served its purpose,' Helen said quietly.

'And I give it to you without reservation. You are the sole ruler of Everyland.'

Zeus tested Helen's commandment by turning a white flower red and then white again with a thought.

'Thank you,' he said, smiling at her. He held out a hand gallantly. 'Shall we to Tartarus?'

Helen looked at his offered hand and shook her head slowly. 'That wasn't actually the deal, as you'll recall,' she said. 'I agreed to give you Everyland in exchange for my family's safety. I never agreed to go to Tartarus.'

Zeus sighed like he regretted Helen's decision. 'I really wanted to avoid a fight. You know I'll have to destroy you if you do this,' he said reluctantly.

'How?' Helen asked, backing away from him. 'I gave you Everyland – my gift to you – but I didn't give you its borders. Those I keep for myself.'

Zeus looked around in a panic. Helen knew he was trying to open a portal and leave. She could feel it, but he couldn't do it. And as long as Helen existed and held ownership of the borders, he never would be able to leave.

'Welcome to my Trojan horse,' she said with a tight smile. 'Enjoy. You're going to be stuck inside it for eternity.'

Helen saw Zeus's face freeze with horror, and then she left him, locked in her heavenly prison forever.

Helen appeared on the battlefield and looked around frantically. A part of her expected to find Zeus standing right behind her, laughing at her insane attempt to imprison him, but he wasn't. She concentrated and could feel him in Everyland, screaming at the beautiful blue sky. He really was trapped. Helen allowed herself one half-crazed laugh before she started running.

Helen negotiated the uneven ground, trying to peer through the confusion of smoke, shouts and combatants running this way and that. The Kraken was still pounding the beach with its tentacles, killing indiscriminately. Combatants from both sides scrambled over the dunes in their desperate attempt to flee from it.

She stumbled forward, her feet catching on something and sending her sprawling. When she looked back, she saw that she'd tripped over a dead Myrmidon. Something moved under her, and she realized she'd landed on another Myrmidon. This one was barely alive, but he still recognized her.

'Tyrant,' he hissed, clamping on to her wrists.

Helen broke free and clambered off him. She looked around and saw dozens of bodies – Scions, Myrmidons and strange sea monsters – all entangled in death after what must have been a huge skirmish. She climbed to her feet and ran to the tent. Luckily, she found her family there as she'd hoped.

There were several dozen soldiers left, standing at the map table, which they had pulled out in front of the tent so they had room to gather around it.

Lucas spotted Helen first and ran to her.

'What happened?' he asked, holding her tightly to his chest. 'We heard you challenge Zeus.'

Helen pulled back and looked Lucas in the eye. 'I beat him,' she said, still not wholly believing it herself. The other Scions grouped around her, making shocked sounds. 'I tricked him and trapped him in Everyland. As long as I exist, he's never getting out. What about the Myrmidons?' she asked.

'We think there are only three left,' Castor said darkly. 'Telamon had them retreat. They're done – for today, anyway.'

'We still have that Kraken to deal with,' Hector reminded her, his face grim.

Helen nodded and turned to Orion. 'Does Poseidon control the Kraken?' she asked.

'Sort of,' Orion replied. 'He can set it loose and call it back again, but once it's free it mostly does its own thing.' He gestured to the slapdash carnage around them.

'All right,' Helen said with a sharp nod. 'I guess Poseidon's next.'

'Helen? Are you sure that's the wisest—' Jason began, but Helen didn't let him finish.

'Challenge! I challenge Poseidon!' she shouted, somewhere in the direction of the ocean. Nothing happened. 'Damn it!' Helen swore, turning to face the group. 'Does anyone have a pumpkin?'

Cassandra went to one of the campfires and pulled a pot off the flame. She dumped the liquid out quickly and came back to Helen, placing the pot on the sand in front of her. Helen looked at the pot sceptically.

'Cauldron,' Cassandra said with a shrug, like it was self-explanatory. The pot disappeared, and orange fire erupted in a circle as Hecate accepted the offering.

Poseidon came up the beach, flanked on all sides by his fellow Olympians. He stopped just outside the ring of fire but wouldn't enter it. Hermes was at his side, speaking to him urgently.

'She did what?' Poseidon remarked, his surprise making him loud enough for Helen to hear. He glanced back at Athena, and she nodded once to confirm what Hades had told her.

'She defeated Zeus,' Athena announced. Helen could have sworn she saw a small smile tilt up the edges of Aphrodite's lovely mouth before she schooled it straight again.

'Poseidon. I'm calling you out. Get in the ring,' Helen commanded, trying hard to ignore the fact that he looked exactly like Lucas.

'And why would I do that?' Poseidon answered with a sneer. 'So you can send me straight to Tartarus? I'm no Worldbuilder. I can't control the portals like you can.'

'That's right. I can control the portals, and none of you can. You'd better remember that,' Helen yelled back, her anger rising until her cheeks were hot and her fingers dropped sparks from the tips, like her hands were spilling stars on the sand. 'And if one of you even *breathes* on a mortal the wrong way I swear I'll hunt you down and send you to Tartarus. Now, get in the ring, Poseidon. Or forfeit this fight, take all your smelly monsters and get the hell away from my family.'

Poseidon took a step forward and glared at Helen from across the ring as Athena whispered frantically in his ear. Finally, he settled down, but Helen saw a grudge growing in his eyes.

'I forfeit!' Poseidon snarled. Helen felt her knees quiver with relief, but she couldn't back down just yet.

'Anyone else?' she said, looking each Olympian in the face. 'Does anyone else want to fight me?' They all dropped their gazes. 'Good! Now shut that giant, rotten squid *up* or I'll send it – and one of you – to Tartarus on principle.'

Helen stared extra long at Apollo, just so he knew who would be joining the Kraken in Tartarus if it came to that.

Poseidon's eyes drilled into hers from across the ring. His bare chest swelled with incensed breaths. Helen met his stare and didn't flinch. She held all the cards. He couldn't even curse her and, somehow, he seemed to know it. After a few tense moments, he raised a hand, concentrated and the Kraken began to retreat. Strange trumpets sounded, and the rest of his sea-creature army pulled back, slithering or scurrying to the water.

'Forever is a long time, Helen,' Poseidon warned as

his army retreated. He narrowed his eyes at her. 'We'll be seeing you.'

'And we'll be watching you,' Helen warned, gesturing to her group of Scions. Unless Helen put all the gods in Tartarus, she couldn't stop them from wandering the earth. All she and her family could do was make sure the Olympians didn't hurt anyone. She shared a look with Hector and saw her worry mirrored there. The Scions may have won the war, but that didn't mean the threat was gone.

Poseidon turned and walked down to the waves, disappearing beneath them. As the rest of the Olympians dispersed, some with looks of bitterness, others with respect, Aphrodite came forward and took both of Helen's hands in hers.

'Sister,' she said, kissing Helen on the cheek as if they had just met up for lunch. Helen laughed, shaking her head. Aphrodite had always hated wars and tended to ignore that they were happening altogether. 'Come visit me soon. You and Lucas. I'll let you know where I settle, but I'm thinking Cyprus for the winter.'

'We'll see you soon,' Helen promised, chuckling and shaking her head.

Even though Aphrodite had caused Helen as much trouble as Zeus, there was no way she could ever stay upset with her for long. Like Claire, no matter what Aphrodite did, Helen knew she would end up forgiving her in about five seconds. Sisters were annoying that way.

Aphrodite pulled back and stroked Helen's cheek. 'That beautiful face,' she murmured, before flying away in a nimbus of golden light.

Helen turned to look at the crowd gathered behind her and saw her father first. Jerry was propped up between Kate and Noel. He looked pale and thin, but he managed to stand up mostly by himself.

'Dad!' Helen said, surprised.

'Hey, Len,' he said. He gave her a lame wave, looking awkward and uncertain – and a little scared of her.

'Are you going to be all weird with me now?' she asked, dreading it.

'No,' he answered a little too quickly.

'You better not,' she said, giving him a hug. It took a second before he relaxed into it and hugged her back, but when he did she knew that things would figure themselves out between the two of them, given some time.

After she and her father separated, there was a blur of congratulations and hugs from everyone – except for Lucas. She scanned the scene around her, looking for him.

Helen saw Hector ordering people to get busy, directing them to dismantle the camp and lead the dazed mortals away from the multitude of strange bodies on the beach before they woke up from Hypnos's influence. She saw Pallas and Daedalus trying to explain themselves to Castor, who listened to them in stony silence. She saw

Jason and Ariadne rushing to aid as many of the most seriously injured as they could. She even saw Orion and Cassandra. They had broken away from the group and were speaking softy to each other. But no Lucas.

Helen spun round, her heart sinking as she searched for him. She found him a few paces behind her, waiting patiently for her to discover him there.

'My turn?' he asked with a small smile. Helen nodded, thinking how strange it was that he and Poseidon looked exactly alike, but Poseidon made her skin crawl, while Lucas made it tingle.

'I think it's *our* turn,' she said, walking into his arms.

'Finally,' he breathed, and kissed her without guilt or shame or any worry about what it meant for the future. He kissed her out in the open, in front of everyone, and for once there was nothing to hide and no reason for either one of them to stop.

It was like they were kissing for the first time.

EPILOGUE

The Patriots won, so Helen's dad was in a great mood all night. Kate made Lucas and Helen eat way too much at dinner, insisting that since Christmas was three days away there was no point in trying to eat healthy until after New Year's, anyway. Kate hadn't officially moved in yet, but she was there nearly every day. Jerry and Kate were waiting until after the wedding in May to officially live together. For Helen, it was the perfect Sunday night 'dinner with the boyfriend' she thought she'd never have. They even argued a bit about politics.

They stayed up late, just hanging out. Helen and Lucas didn't have school the next morning – not because the high school was still going through major reconstruction (which it was) but because they were on winter break. Despite the fact that the high school had been half knocked over, the students had been taking their regular classes, dodging rubble and wearing their jackets in the freezing-cold classrooms without missing too many days because Whalers are stubborn like that. The drama club had even started rehearsing *A Midsummer*

Night's Dream again even though they had to do it out in the subzero cold and not-at-all-summery parking lot because the auditorium didn't exist any more. The show must go on. Hergie would have been proud.

There was still a lot of confusion over what had happened. For the past month and a half, everyone on Nantucket had gone around scratching their heads about the 'tidal wave' that had ripped up the beach, killed twelve unfortunate people and injured many more so soon after the Halloween riots. It was the only topic of conversation at the News Store and at Kate's Cakes. Every time a customer asked Helen what she remembered about that day, she'd say she was too far inland to actually see the wave, and she was glad for it. Then she'd hustle off to get them more coffee.

Some people remembered the Kraken, but they were slowly being talked out of the so-called hallucinations. When someone got belligerent about what they'd seen, the Delos family would make sure that Andy got together with them for a little 'talk'. Her powers as a siren came in handy when it came to making sure no one panicked and gave a story to the reporters who had started hanging around Nantucket. Helen had tasked Hypnos with rehabilitating the worst cases – hypnotizing them into re-remembering the whole thing as something else. It worked for the most part, but there would always be stories about the giant squid that had attacked Nantucket Island. A new myth had been born, and Helen wondered if this was how most of them had got their start.

Like Hypnos, the other small gods were eager to get on Helen's good side. They'd bet on the wrong side when they'd stood with Olympus and now they were doing whatever she asked to make it up to her – starting by cleaning up the mess that the battle had left behind and helping to sell the tidal-wave cover story. Helen couldn't give those twelve people their lives back; she was just happy that the mortal casualties had been so low.

The Scions hadn't been so lucky. Every House had suffered severe losses, but mostly the House of Thebes. Castor was now Head, and there were many supporters who whispered that he always should have been, regardless of which Delos brother was born first. Daedalus had somehow talked his way out of being overthrown. He'd given a great speech, agreed to share leadership with Orion and his House had forgiven him. All the Houses would rebuild, as would the army of Poseidon's creatures, unfortunately. Helen knew that someday the Scions would have to deal with that threat again. Poseidon and the other Olympians couldn't curse her friends and family, but they could still find ways to work against them. The Scions would always have to be ready for that.

Just like Helen would have to be ready to repay those three tasks she'd promised Hecate. Helen hoped that the Titan didn't ask her do anything immoral. But, even if she did, someday Hecate would call in the debt, and

Helen would have to pay no matter what was asked of her. Her debt didn't worry Helen as much as Lucas's did.

They were both painfully aware of the fact that Lucas could still be called to serve in the Underworld at any moment. He'd insisted that Helen stay on Earth while he went to Hades, which she thought was a ridiculous idea. It was an argument in process, but Helen was pretty sure she'd win. There was no way she was ever going to live without him again, and she knew that he couldn't live without her, either. She figured in another century or two he'd give up.

Unlike the Myrmidons. There were only three of them left, for which Helen was grateful. She knew they would hunt her forever, always seeking a way to get rid of her. Hector watched the family like a hawk and kept on the alert for Myrmidons. Helen had the sneaking suspicion that he liked it that way. Hector was always happiest when there was someone close to him who needed protecting.

The one person Hector couldn't save was Ariadne. She was devastated about Matt and starting to pull away from the family. Helen checked in on her every day, but she knew there was no solution. Ariadne would miss him always. At least she and Helen had that in common.

Things were still a bit shaky between Lucas and Orion, despite the fact that Orion did little more than hold Cassandra's hand. Helen knew from experience that Orion would wait as long as he had to for Cassandra to be ready for something more, but Lucas was still keeping his eye on the situation. Helen supposed a big brother was a big brother, especially when the guy that's following his little sister around like a puppy was an actual Adonis, like Orion. Eventually, Lucas would come around. Cassandra and Orion were opposites in a lot of way, but they obviously adored each other more and more with every passing day. Helen couldn't think of two people who deserved happiness more than they did.

Except maybe Daphne.

Helen knew her mother had done some terrible things; most of them to Helen herself, but Helen didn't feel anger when she thought about Daphne. She felt sadness. She truly hoped that Hades gave Daphne her wish and reunited her with Ajax in the Elysian Fields. She'd earned it, after all. In the end, Helen's wicked witch of a mother turned out to be quite the hero.

Last on Helen's list of never-ending worries was Zeus. She could still feel him in Everyland when she turned her concentration to it, which she did several times a day, just to make sure.

Everyland. The loss of it still hurt like crazy, but even setting foot there would be impossible for Helen now. She'd taken Zeus by surprise when she'd tricked him, but she had no illusions about what would happen if she tried to go back to Everyland. Zeus would be ready for her, and he'd send her to Tartarus before she took three steps. That didn't stop Helen from dreaming of it every night. When she closed her eyes, Helen could smell the wildflowers and hear the wind.

'Helen,' Lucas whispered, waking her. Her head was in his lap, and his hand was stroking her hair. 'I have to go.'

Helen sat up on the couch and nodded, rubbing her forehead and trying to shake off the dream. Lucas narrowed his eyes, studying her.

'Are you OK?' he asked gently. 'Was it Everyland again?'

'Always,' she admitted, looking down at her hands.

'Helen! Come upstairs, now,' her father called down impatiently. 'It's time for Lucas to go home.'

Helen and Lucas grinned at each other and stood. They both thought it was adorable when Jerry got overprotective.

'I'll be right back,' Lucas whispered in her ear, brushing his lips across the sensitive skin on her jaw before pulling quickly away.

'Tease,' Helen whispered as he went to the door.

'Good night, Mr Hamilton,' Lucas called upstairs as he left.

'*Good night*, Lucas,' Jerry replied testily.

About an hour later, Helen heard a tap on the window that Mr Tanis had finally fixed about week earlier, and she rushed to open it. Lucas soared into her bedroom silently, dusted with snow. Helen started kissing him before he even had a chance to land, guiding his weightless body to her bed and pulling him down over her.

'Hold on a sec,' he said with a warm smile. Lucas held up a wrapped present and gave it to Helen. 'I couldn't wait for Christmas.'

She peeled the wrapper off as quietly as possible, both of them listening for the sound of her dad waking, and found a framed picture of a single white flower. When Helen looked closer, she saw it was actually a dried wildflower, pressed and mounted behind glass.

Tears filled her eyes instantly. It was the only thing from her world that existed in this one – the only souvenir she had of Everyland.

'Thank you,' Helen whispered, clutching the frame to her chest.

Lucas nodded, wiping her tears away. He took the picture out of her hands and placed it on the table next to her bed before standing.

'Where's your swimsuit?' he asked, rubbing his hands together excitedly.

'W-why?' Helen replied, confused. It was minus ten degrees out. And snowing. Helen was immortal, not crazy.

'Because you're going to need it when we get to Puerto Rico. It'll still be dark for a few more hours, but we can swim, watch the sunrise and be back before your dad wakes up.'

Helen jumped off the bed and rushed to her dresser. She pulled out a little red polka-dot bikini and waved it in the air like a flag before grabbing her coat and stuffing it in the pocket.

'Live every day like it's our last day on earth together,' she said, beginning their new motto as she jumped out the window.

'For forever if we can get away with it,' Lucas finished, joyfully following her.

Acknowledgements

This is hard. It takes a small miracle to get a trilogy out into the world, and there are a lot of people that have worked very hard to make that miracle happen for me. I'm just about to forget half of them. The two people I can't forget, mostly because they call/text/email me about every ten minutes, are my amazing agent, Mollie Glick, and my fearless manager, Rachel Miller. They have been my guides, my cheerleaders and my champions every step of the way, and I am blessed to have them in my life. Stephanie Abou, Rachel Hetch and Kathleen Hamblin have been my go-to team for all things foreign and confusing, and I can't thank them enough for their expertise and support. Heather Toth, the Chancellor, has proven her infinite patience by answering all of my dumb questions and keeping track of my crazy life. My ever-understanding editor, Barbara Lalicki, and her ninja of an assistant, Alyssa Miele, have helped both shape my story and shepherd it through the vagaries of the publishing world. Many thanks to them both. I want to give lots of love to my beta readers and fellow 'Elevensies' authors,

GODDESS

Amy Plum and Tara Hudson, for their encouragement
and support. The past two years have been quite a trip,
and it's been a joy to share it with them. My friends and
family know the drill at this point, but, just in case, I
want to send them my love. And, lastly, I want to thank
my husband, Albert. Quite simply, there would be no
Starcrossed trilogy without him.

STARCROSSED

JOSEPHINE ANGELINI

DESTINY BROUGHT THEM TOGETHER.
THE GODS WILL KEEP THEM APART.

WHEN shy, awkward
Helen Hamilton
meets Lucas Delos
for the first time,
she thinks two things:
the first, that he
is the most ridiculously
beautiful boy she
has seen in her life;
the second, that she
wants to kill him
with her bare hands.

AN ancient curse
means Lucas and
Helen are destined to
loathe one another.
But sometimes love is
stronger than hate,
and not even the
gods themselves can
prevent what will
happen next . . .

DREAMLESS

JOSEPHINE ANGELINI

THEIR LOVE COULD LAST FOREVER.
IF IT DOESN'T DESTROY THEM FIRST.

HEARTBROKEN and forbidden from being with Lucas, Helen has been tasked with breaking the curse that keeps them apart by killing the Furies. She spends her nights wandering the Underworld in search of them and, tormented by her worst nightmares made real, she's beginning to suffer from extreme exhaustion on top of her heartbreak.

ONE night, Helen meets another person down in the shadowy Underworld: Orion, descended from Adonis and with the power to control desire. Still in love with Lucas but drawn to this destructive stranger, Helen must make a choice that could save her life but break her heart . . .

My Kinda Book
your kinda book club!

Join up and discover great new books like these . . .

FORETOLD
THE DEMON TRAPPERS
JANA OLIVER
Devilishly clever and totally unique P. C. Cast

SHE MUST RISE
GODDESS
OR THEY WILL FALL
JOSEPHINE ANGELINI
'A gorgeous and haunting start . . . OMGods, I can't wait to read more!'
Lauren Kate, author of Fallen

Alyson Noël
EVER LASTING
THE IMMORTALS
Will their love pass its greatest test?

Log on to **MyKindaBook.com** to read extracts, chat to authors and win **FREE** stuff!